COZY
MYSTERY
Collection

Leighann Dobbs

This is a work of fiction.

None of it is real. All names, places, and events are products of the author's imagination. Any resemblance to real names, places, or events are purely coincidental, and should not be construed as being real.

Cozy Mystery Collection
Copyright © 2015
Leighann Dobbs
http://www.leighanndobbs.com
All Rights Reserved.

No part of this work may be used or reproduced in any manner, except as allowable under "fair use," without the express written permission of the author.

Cover Art: Tina Adams
http://www.tina-adams.com/design

COZY MYSTERY Collection

GHOSTLY PAWS

Of course they didn't.

I looked in the direction of the library anyway. That's when I noticed the beam of light spilling onto the granite steps from the half-open library door.

Which was odd, since it was only ten past seven.

My stomach started to feel queasy. Lavinia never opened up this early. Should I venture in to check it out? Maybe Lavinia had come in early to catch up on restocking the bookshelves before the library opened. But she never left the door open like that. She was as strict as a nun about keeping that door closed.

I stood on the sidewalk, staring at the medieval-looking stone library building, my pre-caffeine fog making it difficult for me to decide what to do.

Pandora had no such trouble deciding. She raced up the steps past me. With a flick of her gray tail, she darted toward the massive oak door, shooting a reproachful look at me over her shoulder before disappearing into the building.

I took a deep breath and followed her inside.

"Lavinia? You in here?" My words echoed inside the library as I pushed the heavy oak door open, its hinges groaning eerily. The library was as still as a morgue with only the sound of the grandfather clock marking time in the corner breaking the silence.

"Lavinia? You okay?"

No one answered.

I crept past the old oak desk, stacked with books ready to return to the library shelves. The bronze bust of Franklin Pierce, fourteenth president of the United States, glared at me from the end of the hall. I didn't have a good feeling about this.

"Meow." The sound came from the back corner where the stone steps lead to the lower level. Dammit! I'd warned Lavinia about those steps. They were steep and she wasn't that steady on her feet anymore.

I headed toward the back, my heart sinking as I noticed Lavinia's cane lying at the top of the stairs.

"Lavinia?" Rounding the corner, my stomach dropped when I saw a crumpled heap at the bottom of the stairs ...

Chapter One

In over thirty years as head librarian for the Mystic Notch Library, Lavinia Babbage had never once opened the doors before eight a.m.

I knew this because my bookstore sat across the street and three doors down from the library. Every day, I passed its darkened windows on my way to work. I watched Lavinia turn on the lights and open the doors every single morning at precisely eight a.m. from inside my shop.

Most days I didn't pay much attention to the library, though. It was really the last thing on my mind as I walked past, my mind set on sorting through a large box of books I'd purchased at an estate sale earlier in the week. The edges of my lips curled in a smile as I thought about the gold placard I'd had installed on the oak door of the old bookshop just the day before. *Wilhelmina Chance, Proprietor*. That made things official—the shop was mine and I was back in my hometown, Mystic Notch, to stay.

I hurried down the street, deep in my own thoughts. The early morning mist, which wrapped itself around our sleepy town in the White Mountains of New Hampshire, had caused the pain to flare in my leg, and I forced myself not to limp. I continued along, my head down and engrossed in my thoughts when I nearly tripped over something gray and furry. My cat, Pandora, had stopped short in front of me causing me to do a painful sidestep to avoid squashing her.

"Hey, what the heck?"

Pandora blinked her golden-green eyes at me and jerked her head toward the library ... or at least it seemed like she did. Cats didn't actually jerk their heads toward things, though, did they?

Lavinia.

I raced down the steps two at a time, my heart pounding as I took in the scene. Blood on the steps. Lavinia lying there, blood in her gray hair. She'd fallen and taken it hard on the way down. But she could still be alive.

I bent down beside her, taking her wrist between my fingers and checking for a pulse.

Lavinia's head was tilted at a strange angle. Her glassy eyes stared toward the room where she kept new book arrivals before cataloguing them. I dropped her wrist, ending my search for a pulse.

Lavinia Babbage had stamped her last library book.

***

I called my sister Augusta, or Gus as I called her, who also happened to be the sheriff, and sat on the steps to wait. I might have drifted off, still sleepy from the lack of caffeine, because the next thing I heard was Augusta's voice in my ear.

"Willa, are you okay?"

I opened one eye to the welcome sight of the steaming Styrofoam coffee cup that Gus was holding out to me.

"I'm fine," I said, reaching for the cup.

"What happened?" I studied Gus who stood on the steps in front of me. No one would have guessed we were sisters. She was petite, her long, straight blonde hair tied back in a ponytail, which, I assume, she thought made her look more sheriff-like. Even in the un-flattering sheriff's uniform, you could tell she had an almost perfect hourglass figure. I was tall with thick wavy red hair, my figure more rounded—voluptuous, as some described me. The only thing we had in common was our amber colored eyes—same as our mom's.

"I was on my way to open the bookstore when I noticed the lights on in the library." I glanced down the street toward the municipal parking lot.

Now that the spring warm-up was here, I was trying to work in some extra exercise by parking in the lot two blocks away instead of on the street near the bookstore.

"Was that unusual?" Gus asked.

"Yep." I looked over my shoulder at the front door of the library. "It sure was. Lavinia never opens the library before eight. Plus the front door was cracked open, and she never leaves it open."

Gus started up the steps toward the library. "Did you touch anything?"

I stood up, wincing at the pain in my left leg—a reminder of the near fatal accident over a year ago that was one of the catalysts for my move back to Mystic Notch. The accident had left me with a slight limp, a bunch of scars and a few odd side effects I didn't like to dwell on.

"Nope, other than Lavinia. I didn't know if she was alive and needed aid," I said as I followed Gus into the library.

Gus stopped just inside the door and looked around. The metallic smell of blood tinged the air, making me lose interest in my coffee.

"It doesn't seem like anything is out of place ... no sign of struggle," she said.

"Nope, I think she just fell down the stairs." I started toward the back. "You know she was getting on in years and not that steady on her feet."

We turned the corner and my stomach clenched at the sight of Lavinia at the bottom of the steps.

"That's her cane?" Gus pointed to the purple metal cane, which was still lying as I'd found it.

"Yep. Looks like she lost her balance, dropped the cane, and fell."

Gus descended the stairs, her eyes carefully taking in every detail. She knelt beside Lavinia, studying her head. "She's pretty banged up."

"I know. These stairs are hard stone. I guess they can do a number on you." I winced as I looked at the bloody edges of the steps.

"So, you think this was an accident?"

"Sure. I mean, what else could have happened?"

"Yeah, you're probably right. No reason to suspect foul play." Gus stood and looked back up the stairs, down the hall and then back at Lavinia.

Her lips were pressed in a thin line and I wondered what she was thinking. I knew she was a good cop, but the truth was I didn't really know her all that well. Eight years separated us and she was just a teenager when I'd moved down south. Now, twenty-five years later, we were just becoming acquainted as adults.

"Mew." Pandora sat on the empty table in the storage room where Lavinia temporarily stored new books or returns before she catalogued them. I'd forgotten she was here. She wasn't really my cat ... well, not until recently. I'd inherited her along with the bookstore and my grandmother's house. I still wasn't used to being followed around by a feline.

"Isn't that Pandora?" Gus asked. Gus had been close to grandma—closer than I had, and it was somewhat of a mystery that Grandma had left me the shop, her house and the cat. In her will, she'd said she'd wanted me to come back home and have a house and business, which was odd because the timing had been perfect. She'd left a tidy sum of money for Gus, so at least there were no hard feelings.

"Yeah, she rides to work with me."

Gus raised a brow at me, but didn't say anything. Pandora stared at us—her intelligent, greenish-gold eyes contrasting eerily with her sleek gray fur.

"So, if it was unusual for Lavinia to be here at this time of the morning, why do you think she was here and what do you think she was doing?" Gus asked.

"I'm not sure."

Gus reached out to pet Pandora, who still sat on the table staring at us. "Are there any mice in here, Pandora? Maybe Lavinia heard something down here and wanted to investigate."

"Maybe." I looked around the floor for evidence of mice. Lavinia ran a pretty tight ship so I doubted there would be any mice in the library. And, since the room was empty of books, she hadn't come in early to catalogue new arrivals.

Which begged the question ... why *was* Lavinia in the library this early in the first place?

Chapter Two

The EMTs and Gus's deputy arrived and got busy with their crime scene investigation. After Gus asked me the standard questions and had the nerve to tell me not to leave town, I headed down the street to open the bookstore.

The crowd of four 'regulars' were already waiting outside, their necks craning to see what was going on at the library.

You wouldn't think a bookstore would have regulars, but mine did. Apparently, I'd inherited them, along with the store and the cat. They'd been gathering there in the mornings with their coffee and tea for decades. I guess the coffee shop down the street didn't have the same ambiance.

"What's going on down there?" Cordelia Deering looked at me with bright sparkling blue eyes. Her twin sister Hattie, stood beside her and, dressed almost identically, gave me the exact same look of expectant excitement. The women were in their mid-eighties, but had more energy than people who were decades younger. They were always up for hearing a tidbit of juicy gossip and liked to keep up on town happenings. This particular happening, though, I hoped wouldn't be too much of a shock.

"I'm afraid I have some bad news," I said as I dug the key out of my pocket and put it in the shiny brass lock of the antique oak door of the bookshop.

"Oh?" Bingham Thorndike, another of the regulars, raised a bushy white brow.

I pushed the door open and gestured for them to go inside. Cordelia and Hattie went first, then Josiah Barrows, the retired Postmaster, then Bingham, or Bing as we all called him.

They all looked at me expectantly as I turned the sign in the door to 'Open' and switched on the inside lights. I took a deep breath of the comforting musky-vanilla scent of leather and old paper.

"So, what's going on down at the library?" Josiah broke the silence. I was surprised he didn't already know since he seemed to know everything that went on in town, sometimes even before it actually happened.

"I'm afraid Lavinia took a fall." I bit my lower lip and tried to figure out a gentle way to break the news. After a few seconds, I hadn't come up with anything so I just blurted it out. "She's dead."

Hattie and Cordelia gasped. Bing sipped his coffee. Josiah rubbed his chin. Pandora jumped up on the counter next to my nickel-plated old-fashioned cash register and let out a mournful wail.

"Mercy sakes," Hattie said as she maneuvered her way past the chair toward the sofa.

"Poor Lavinia," Cordelia whispered.

I'd recently added a set of purple micro-suede chairs and a sofa to the front of the shop for customers who wanted to sit and read a book while browsing. The four of them settled somberly into the plush seating.

I watched them sip from their Styrofoam cups, their faces in thoughtful repose. They looked comfortable on the sofa. At home. I started to wonder if maybe I had made it *too* comfortable for them.

"You sure she fell?" Josiah wrinkled his brow at me.

I nodded. "She was getting up in years and not so steady anymore. I found her at the bottom of the stairs—the ones in the back."

"You found her? What were you doing in the library?" Bing asked.

I explained how I'd seen the light on, gone in to investigate and found her lying at the bottom of the steps. I left out the part about all the blood.

"Oh dear, that must have been terrible for you," Cordelia clucked.

"That must have happened early on." Josiah scrunched

up his weathered old face. "In all my years as postmaster, I don't recall Lavinia ever gettin' to the library before eight o'clock."

"That's true," Hattie and Cordelia said at the same time, then looked at each other and giggled.

"Seems odd she fell. She got along pretty good every time I saw her around town," Josiah added.

"But it must have been a fall," Bing said. "No one would want Lavinia dead."

I half-listened as the four of them rambled on about the subject, distracted by the swirling gray mist that was forming over by the mystery section. A prickly feeling of uneasiness settled over me—I knew what that gray mist was.

Pandora hopped off the counter and trotted over to the mist, batting at it playfully.

"Right, Willa?" Bing's question tore my attention away from the swirly mist.

"Huh?"

"Lavinia came in early sometimes when she had a backlog of returns or books to catalogue."

I thought about the question as I watched Bing weave a large gold coin in between his fingers. A retired magician, he was always fiddling with coins and doing impromptu tricks with various objects. I'd known Bing since I was a little girl, and he taught me a few of his tricks. Some of them I still practiced, but there were quite a few more of them, the ones he wouldn't teach me, that had me baffled. I couldn't figure out how he did them. It was almost as if he really was using magic.

The effect of the coin was mesmerizing. I watched it weave in front of his index finger, then behind his middle finger, then in front of the Magicians Guild ring he wore on his ring finger then behind the pinkie and around, making its way all the way back to his index finger. As I watched, I contemplated his question. Had Lavinia come in early sometimes? I was having a hard time remembering.

"I'm not sure, Bing. I can't remember." I looked at Josiah. "Do you remember, Josiah?"

Josiah looked like he was about to nod off. He tilted his head and looked up at the ceiling. I was about to prompt him again when he finally spoke.

"I can't say for sure. I think one time she did come in early but that was before a big book sale," he said. "Was she fixing to have a book sale?"

We all looked at each other and shrugged.

"I have no idea," Hattie said.

"We could look in the Gazette," Cordelia said, referring to the town paper. "There would be an announcement if she was planning one this week."

Out of the corner of my eye, the mist was getting thicker. It swirled around the edge of the bookcase, beckoning to me. Pandora sat next to it, her eyes drilling into mine.

Bing drained his coffee and pushed up off the couch. "Well, I gotta be on my way. Lots to do today."

"Me, too," Josiah said.

"I guess the party's over." Cordelia stood. "We'll let you get to work, Willa. Let us know if you find out anything more about Lavinia."

"Will do," I said as I watched them file out the door.

As soon as they were gone, I turned my attention to the misty swirl. The swirl was one of the side effects of my accident—the one I didn't like to dwell on. But, I'd found out the hard way that if I ignored it, things only got worse.

So, I straightened my shoulders and walked toward it.

I marched past the rows of books to the end of the aisle. Rounding the corner, my breath caught in my throat as I came face to face with ... Lavinia Babbage.

***

"Eeek!" Lavinia screeched, her ghost turning to static like an off-air channel on an old television set.

"Lavinia!" I squawked, my heart thumping in my chest. I knew the swirl meant a ghost was around the corner, but I wasn't expecting it to be *Lavinia's* ghost.

Ever since my accident, I'd been seeing ghosts. It started off as just random sightings of misty swirls. Then the swirls started to form into human shapes. Then they started talking to me. It wasn't something I wanted, it just happened ... and it was impossible to ignore them. Each one of them seemed to want something and would pester me until they got it. I wondered what Lavinia wanted.

"Sorry, Willa," she said, her form materializing into a semi-solid shape. "I wasn't expecting you to come barreling around the corner like that. And I'm sorry you had to find me ... you know ... at the library."

"Oh. Right. Sorry you ... umm ... died."

"Thanks." She held her hand up toward the window and we both watched the sunlight filter through it. Lavinia waffled her hand back and forth, apparently fascinated with the effect.

"So, did you want something?" I prompted as I glanced over my shoulder into the shop, praying no customers would come in and find me talking to thin air.

She put her hand down. "Yes, sorry, I'm still getting used to being dead. It's not easy, you know."

"I'm sure it's not."

"Anyway, I didn't fall down the steps."

I was afraid she was going to say something like that. "What do you mean?"

"I mean I didn't trip and fall. I got whacked on the back of the head and was pushed!"

"Pushed? Are you sure?"

"Sure as shinola," Lavinia said, then leaned forward and lowered her voice. "I was on my way to church to ... umm ... light a candle for my Harry. I often did that before opening the library. Anyway, I was on my way when I saw the lights on in the library. I knew I didn't leave them on, so I went in to investigate. I thought I heard something downstairs, but as I approached the steps, I heard something behind me. I turned to see what it was and then ... whack! Lights out!"

"You didn't see who it was? Did you get any sense of whether it was a man or woman?"

"Nope. All I saw was a big shadow ... like the person was wearing a cape." Lavinia pressed her lips together and looked out the window. "Oh, and they wore a big ring."

"Ring? What kind of ring?"

She looked back at me, her ghostly form rippling like

water disturbed by a pebble. "I'm not sure. It was chunky, like a class ring. I remember hearing the noise, seeing the shadow, feeling pain and getting pushed. I saw the ring in a blur as I went down. Next thing I know, I'm waking up on a steel table inside Stilton's funeral home. Scared me half to death. Of course, I didn't realize I actually *was* dead at first. Anyway, once I figured it all out, I knew I had to come here and get your help."

"You did? How did you know to come to me?" I felt a little disturbed by this. Was there some sort of sign in the afterlife telling these ghosts to seek me out? I certainly hoped not.

Lavinia tilted her head. "You know, I'm not rightly sure about that. Might be because I know you were a crime journalist down south. Anyway, I just got this feeling and it must have been right because you're the only person that's been able to see and talk to me since I ... err... died."

"Okay. Well, I'm not sure what you think I can do for you. I didn't see any evidence of anyone being there in the library. Maybe you're confused about what happened, you know—with being so newly dead and all?" I asked hopefully.

"No, I don't think so. I'm sure someone did me in."

"But, *who* would break into the library and why would they want to kill you?"

"I have no idea," Lavinia said. "That's for *you* to find out. All I know is that I need your help to find the killer and neither one of us is going to be able to rest until you do.

Chapter Three

Lavinia's ghost started to fade, her final words barely above a whisper. "Only *you* can help me, Willa."

Pandora batted at the last trailing wisp of ghost mist, then looked up at me and meowed something that sounded like, "*You have to help.*"

I frowned down at the cat. "Did you just say—?"

My words were cut off by the sound of the bells over the door. I looked between the bookcases in time to see Pepper St. Onge bustle in carrying a silver tray complete with teapot and two porcelain teacups on dainty saucers. She wore a cute vintage skirt set in violet, which complemented the mass of auburn hair piled on top of her head. Pepper usually wore her hair up like that. She'd been growing it since kindergarten, where we'd met and become best friends. Last I knew it fell below her waist. My heart warmed thinking of our close friendship that had lasted for forty-three years, even though I'd spent almost half of those years "down south" in Massachusetts.

"I heard what happened at the library, so I figured you could use a nice calming cup of tea." Pepper peered down the aisle at me as she put the tray down on the coffee table.

She settled her tall, slim frame onto the couch, then patted the seat beside her as an invitation for me to sit.

"Thanks."

I sat beside her and she poured the tea, then added a splash of cream from the tiny silver creamer she'd brought.

"I put something a little special in there to calm your nerves," she said as she handed me a pink chintz cup perched atop its matching saucer.

I looked into the cup dubiously. Pepper had fallen in love

with herbal teas when we were in high school. It was no surprise to me when she opened a tea room in our small hometown. People came from all over New England to drink tea and eat finger sandwiches and cakes in her cozy shop. Pepper claimed that her teas had healing powers.

At first, I had thought she was just being fanciful, but after witnessing several examples of her healing teas in action, I believed they *did* have some sort of powers. The problem was that they usually backfired and had the opposite effect than was intended.

I sipped the tea politely, wondering if it would have the opposite effect and make me more anxious.

Pepper watched me from over the rim of her teacup. My heart warmed at the concern in her emerald green eyes.

"How did you find out about Lavinia already?" I asked.

"The twins stopped by for a bag of peppermint tea," she said, referring to Hattie and Cordelia.

"Ahh..." I nodded sagely. The grapevine in our small town worked quickly, so I wasn't surprised that word had gotten out already.

"So, what happened?"

She clucked with sympathy as I told her how I'd seen the library door open and light on and then found Lavinia at the bottom of the stairs.

"And that's not even the worst part," I said.

"Oh?" Her brows crept up her forehead.

"Lavinia's ghost claims she was pushed."

"Ohhh." Pepper's eyes grew wide. She was the only one I'd told about my strange new ability and she was fascinated with it. "What did she tell you?"

"Just that someone hit her on the head and then pushed her, and she won't rest until I find whoever did it," I said.

"And you're going to find whoever did it?"

"I don't have much of a choice, because I know that when she says she won't rest, it really means that *I* won't rest because she'll keep pestering me."

"So what's your plan? Did she give you any clues?"

"Two clues. The person was wearing a cape and had a big ring."

Pepper frowned. "A cape? Like a super hero?"

I laughed. "More like a super villain. I'm not sure if her account is reliable ... she only saw a shadow of the killer and their hand, so I think it could have been just a loose coat they were wearing. I mean, who wears a cape?"

Pepper sipped her tea. "So what are you going to do?"

I sighed, leaning back on the couch. I was starting to feel more relaxed—maybe Pepper's tea had worked its healing magic as intended this time.

"Well, I guess first I'll have to ask the other shop owners if they saw anyone around the library early this morning," I said. "Not too many people are here at that time."

"I know Myrna comes in to the coffee shop early," Pepper said. "Maybe she saw something?"

I glanced out the window toward the coffee shop. "I'll pop down and ask her later. Lavinia said she was lighting a candle at church and that's why she was here early. Maybe Pastor Foley saw someone."

"What about the police?" Pepper started to stack the teacups back on the tray. "Surely they'll investigate?"

"Yeah, that's the problem," I said. "It *looks* like Lavinia fell. I thought that's what happened and I'm sure Augusta thought so, too. So, unless something comes to light, I don't think there'll be an investigation."

"But, Lavinia told you—"

"Not Lavinia," I said, cutting her off. "Lavinia's *ghost*. And who's going to believe I found out about the murder from her ghost? Nobody. In fact, it's probably better if I don't say anything to the police. I have a funny feeling that if I did, it would only point the finger of suspicion at *me*."

***

I woke up to Pandora digging her razor sharp claws into me. In my dream, I swore she was talking. *Get up now. Now. Now.*

"Meow. Meow. Meow."

"Ouch!" Pandora was crouched on my chest. I swatted her away before her claw ripped a hole in my black knit turtleneck.

I glanced at my watch. Noon! Had I really fallen asleep in

my bookstore?

I sat up and wiped the drool off my cheek. Good thing no customers had come in. Or maybe they had come and found me sleeping.

Pandora trotted over to the large front window, hopped up onto the wide ledge where one of her overstuffed cat beds sat and stared pointedly down the street.

My eyes followed her gaze straight to the coffee shop—*The Mystic Cafe*. Come to think of it, I *was* getting a little hungry. The cafe had a great selection of sandwiches. I could close up for lunch, get something to eat and drink ... and ask Myrna if she saw anyone this morning.

I pushed up from the couch and wiped the cat hair off my sweater, then grabbed my wallet, locked the bookstore and headed down the street. I was halfway to the cafe before I realized my leg wasn't even hurting anymore. I felt thankful that the pain was slowly lessening with time.

The Mystic Cafe was abuzz with activity. Almost all the local merchants came here for lunch. It was off-season now—too late for the crowds that came for skiing and too early for summer tourists, so the cafe wasn't quite as crowded.

I made my way to the counter, nodding at the locals I knew, which was most everyone in there, seeing as I'd grown up here and most people didn't leave Mystic Notch. Ever.

I was the exception, going "down south" as they called it, to become a journalist. I felt a pinch in my chest at the thought of my former life. Best not to think about that now. Fate had stepped in and I was happy to be home again and starting a new life at the age of forty-eight.

As I walked through the cafe, I caught myself sneaking a peek at people's hands to see if anyone was wearing a large ring. What was I doing? These were my friends and neighbors. A shiver went up my spine as I realized that anyone could be the killer—even someone I trusted and had known my whole life.

Myrna Littleton stood behind the counter, her gray hair piled in a bun, her vintage red cherries apron barely covering her plump figure.

"What can I get'cha, Willa?" Myrna pulled a pencil out of her bun and poised it over the long pad of paper she held.

"I'll have a tuna on rye ... and if you have a second, I've got a few questions."

Myrna wrote down the order, ripped the paper off the pad and clipped it onto a round metal holder, then twirled it so the order was facing Bud, the guy who made the sandwiches in the back.

Her steely gaze assessed the crowd, then she nodded at me and shouted to one of her employees, "Alice, can you watch the front?"

Myrna pulled me to the side, out of earshot of the workers and customers. "What's up?"

"Well, you probably heard Lavinia was found dead this morning," I said tentatively. There was no love lost between Myrna and Lavinia and I wasn't sure what her reaction would be.

"Darned old fool fell down the steps, I hear."

"Maybe..."

She looked over her blue framed cats-eye glasses at me, her brow wrinkling in confusion. "What are you saying—she didn't fall?"

"It's possible she had some help."

Myrna snorted. "Well, I know a few people that would have liked to help, but I thought the police were ruling it an accident."

"They are. It probably was. But I was just wondering if you saw anyone around this morning. I know you open up early, and it looks like Lavinia went in early for some reason, so I was wondering if someone else was in there."

Myrna crossed her arms over her ample breasts, scrunched up her face and tapped the pencil on her lips. "Let me think ... I came in to set things up early—you know we get an early morning coffee crowd—so I spent most of my time out back."

"Oh, so you didn't see anyone or anything out of the ordinary?"

"Well, now come to think of it, I did. I took the trash out to the dumpster in the alley. The church is right at the end of the alley and I happened to glance down and saw that woman that runs the new real estate business."

"Ophelia Withington?" I asked. Ophelia had come to town about ten years ago and opened a real estate business. She was hardly 'new', but these Yankee old-timers considered anyone not born here to be 'new'. Ophelia had married auctioneer Pete Withington, who had passed away a couple of years ago.

"Yeah, that's her. I thought it was strange that she'd be out that early in the morning and even stranger what she was wearing," Myrna said.

"Why? What was she wearing?"

Myrna looked at me with a funny look on her face. "She was wearing one of them big old raincoats ... a trench coat, I think they're called. I can't imagine why she'd want to traipse around in that thing. Heck, they weren't even forecasting rain."

Chapter Four

I couldn't wait to interrogate Ophelia, so I grabbed my sandwich and raced to my old Jeep Cherokee in the parking lot. The bookstore wouldn't suffer too much if I kept it closed for a few hours over lunch.

The day had warmed to an invigorating seventy degrees. The fresh mountain air gave me a burst of energy as I pulled out onto Main Street. I drove past the early 1900s storefronts. Some were brick, some clapboard, but all had been recently renovated so as to keep the nostalgia of the town's past while looking neat as a pin.

Withington Real Estate wasn't much more than a mile's drive. I munched on my sandwich as I drove, enjoying the mountain vista view revealed by the steep drop to the left. On the right, the stark granite face of the mountain jutted up into the sky.

I pulled up in front of my destination just as I swallowed the last of my sandwich. The building was an old colonial Ophelia had purchased and retrofitted into office space. I recognized her Beamer in the parking lot.

Brushing the crumbs off my lap, I trotted up to the door and opened it, revealing the wide pine flooring of the reception area that used to be the living room of the house.

An antique oak desk sat at one end of the room. Comfortable looking upholstered chairs and a sofa sat along the walls. It almost looked like a regular living room, except for the receptionist sitting behind the desk.

I approached the young girl. She couldn't have been more than twenty, but the way she caked on the makeup made her look older.

"Can I help you?" she asked through bright red lips.

"I was hoping to talk to Ophelia."

The girl looked at me uncertainly and I got the impression she was about to give me the brush-off, so I said, "Tell her it's Wilhelmina Chance. I know she'll want to talk to me."

I knew Ophelia would want to talk to me because she'd been pestering me to sell my grandmother's thirty-five-hundred square foot Victorian on twenty acres since I'd inherited it. If she got the impression that's why I was here, it certainly wasn't my fault.

The receptionist picked up the phone, told Ophelia I was there and replaced the receiver, then stood up. "This way, please."

She scooted out from behind the desk and I followed her down the hall. I couldn't help but notice her skirt was a bit too short, but if I still had legs like hers I'd probably wear one that short, too. Not that my legs were *that* bad, especially for pushing fifty. I exercised a lot and was still slim, but they were scarred up from the accident and I didn't like to show them off anymore.

Ophelia met us at the door of a bright blue and yellow room that boasted a tasteful, marble-mantled fireplace. Her frosted blonde hair was perfectly coiffed and a strand of creamy white pearls hung around her neck, the only accent to her tasteful beige and black dress.

I pushed my frizzy red curls into place self-consciously.

"Wilhelmina; how nice to see you." Ophelia held out her hand and I got a whiff of Chanel No. 5. Although her voice sounded pleasant, her dark eyes bore into me with a predatory glare. It was clear to me that Ophelia was interested in only one thing—getting big commissions from selling houses.

"Same here," I lied as I shook her hand.

She gestured toward a chair and I sank down into the tufted leather while she went back around to the other side of her desk.

"So, what brings you here?" Her brows raised in hopeful arcs. "Did you finally decide to sell? That property is so much for a single woman to manage."

"It is, but that's not why I'm here," I said, ignoring her obvious disappointment. "I'm sure you've heard that

Lavinia was found dead at the library this morning."

"Yes, such sad news." Ophelia's face showed no emotion.

"Well, I heard you were there this morning and I wondered if you saw anything."

Ophelia's back stiffened. "Me? I wasn't at the library. And why are you asking about it? I heard she slipped and fell."

"Oh, she did," I said to soothe her and put her off guard, afraid she might clam up if she thought I was accusing her. "It's just that Lavinia was in there earlier than usual and I was wondering if someone else was there, too. Someone said they saw you near the church right down the street. I was wondering if you noticed anything unusual or saw anyone."

Ophelia's eyes darted around the room, her mouth set in a firm line. "Who told you they saw me?"

"I'd rather not say. What were you doing there that early anyway?"

"Well, I'd say that's none of your business," she huffed. "But if you must know I was ... err ... lighting a candle in memory of Pete."

She placed her palms on the desk and pushed up from her chair. I noticed she still wore her wedding rings—a large diamond and wide gold band that blinked in the sunlight.

"So you didn't see anything strange or notice anyone at the library? Did you see Lavinia?"

"No. No. And no." She came around the desk and opened the door, inviting me to leave.

I can take a hint, so I stood. "Okay, let me know if you remember anything. Sorry to bother you."

I felt her eyes drill into my back as I walked down the hall, through the reception area and out the door.

A niggle of doubt tickled my stomach as I got into my car. I was almost certain Ophelia was being evasive. Lavinia had said she was lighting a candle at almost the same time—wouldn't Ophelia have seen her? It *was* possible they had missed each other. I wasn't sure of the exact timing.

I doubted Ophelia had pushed Lavinia—what would be

her motive? But if she wasn't being evasive because she knew something about Lavinia's murder, then what, exactly, was she hiding?

***

"Ophelia Withington?" Pepper scrunched up her nose. "I don't think she's the killer."

"Why not?" I asked. "Maybe she had some kind of grudge against Lavinia. She does seem to be mean, selfish and spiteful."

"She wasn't always that way, you know." Pepper sat down on the sofa while she waited for me to organize my sales receipts for the day.

"Really?" I cocked my head at her.

"She was actually very nice and kind when she first came here. Pete's lengthy illness and death made her bitter." Pepper looked at the canister of tea leaves she'd brought from her store. "Come to think of it, she might benefit from one of my teas."

My brows shot up. Pepper's special tea's sometimes backfired—I shuddered to think of Ophelia Withington being even meaner than she was now.

I took a sip from the tall glass of iced tea Pepper had brought. She usually closed up the tea room earlier than I closed the bookstore. Sometimes she'd bring a snack or tea over, which we'd enjoy before we walked down to our cars together. Today she'd brought iced tea to celebrate the beginning of spring—it was only sixty outside, but after a long winter in the White Mountains, sixty felt like summer.

I finished my record keeping and pushed the drawer of my antique cash register shut.

"All finished?" Pepper asked. "Looks like you made some sales today."

"I had a pretty good day. Sold a mint condition, first edition of Nancy Drew and made a few sales from the used book section." The Nancy Drew made me a couple thousand richer—the used books would buy me coffee for the week.

"That's great," Pepper said. "I had a visit from Derek Bates. He wanted some Wolfsbane tea. He's such a nice guy."

"He is. He came here, too. He was looking for an old family scrapbook. I guess his mother sold it at a yard sale by mistake."

Pepper burst out laughing. The Bates family came from old money. Actually more like old-old money. So old that no one remembered how they originally made the money.

"Idris let her have a yard sale? I can't imagine that."

"Me, either." I smiled as I pictured the look of delight on the faces of local antique dealers when they saw yard sale tables loaded up with antiques spread all over the lawn of the gigantic stone mansion just outside town.

"Felicity must have snuck in a sale while Idris was away."

"I hear the old guy is pretty tight-fisted with the money."

"Yep, he sure is." Pepper nodded. "He controls the money Felicity inherited from Derek and Carson's father with an iron fist. He lets her and the boys live in the mansion like they did when his son was alive, but doesn't give her much else to live on. Rumor has it she's been selling stuff off secretly for years."

"I feel sorry Derek and Carson ... dependent on Idris for money. Of course, they could just go out and get jobs and gain their own independence." I grabbed my key and started for the door. "You ready?"

Pepper stood up. "So, what are you going to do about Ophelia?"

I pressed my lips together as we walked toward the door. "I'm not sure. I guess I need to do more checking. Myrna saw her near the library this morning and she was wearing a bulky coat. It might have looked like a cape in the shadow Lavinia described." I remembered the sunlight glinting off Ophelia's ring. "And she wears a wide ring. Not exactly the kind Lavinia thought she saw, but maybe she wasn't accurate on that. I mean, she only saw it as she was being pushed down the stairs."

"But *why* would she want to kill Lavinia?"

Pandora let out a wail and we both turned to look at the cat, who was sitting by the very spot I'd last seen Lavinia's ghost.

"I guess that's what I need to find out."

Chapter Five

I pulled my Jeep into the long driveway that led to the one-hundred-and-fifty-year-old Victorian I'd inherited from my grandmother. My heart warmed at the sight of the house that held so many wonderful childhood memories.

It was a large house, painted white with black shutters, and consisted of three stories with two living rooms and four or five bedrooms, depending on how you looked at it. The front boasted turrets on either side. Those turret rooms with their rounded walls were my favorite. The house was too big for one person, but I loved it and couldn't imagine ever selling.

I parked at the end of the driveway on the side of the house, just short of the red with white-trim barn. The barn was almost as big as the house and had been home to five horses at one time. The inside still smelled of old leather saddles, hay and manure. The stalls bore teeth marks where the horses had chewed the wood. I loved going in there. Sometimes I could almost hear the horses whinny. I fancied I might get one myself someday.

I opened the car door and Pandora shot across my lap and ran onto the porch on the side of the house. Looking back at me, she meowed impatiently as I limped up the porch steps—it had been a long day and my leg was starting to hurt.

The porch led straight to the kitchen and Pandora didn't waste any time getting over to her food bowl.

"Meow!" She paced back and forth, rubbing her face on the whitewashed country cabinets.

I pressed the button on my answering machine, then opened the cabinet and pulled out a bag of cat food. I had a cell phone like most people, but still preferred people to leave messages on my home phone. I guess I was kind of old-fashioned and didn't really like being all that accessible or being interrupted at all hours of the day on my cell.

"Willa, it's Barry. Just wanted to let you know I picked up a box of books in my travels for you. Let me know when we can get together—*Beep*."

Barry was one of the local antique dealers. Most of the antique dealers in the area had a good working relationship. If one of us was at an auction or yard sale and saw something that we thought another dealer would be interested in selling for a ridiculously low price, we'd pick it up for them. Last summer, I'd purchased a set of sterling silver Tiffany nut dishes at a yard sale for Barry for only a dollar. He'd made a bundle on them and I'd gotten a steak dinner as a 'thank you'.

"I wonder if there will be a treasure in that box of books," I said to Pandora as I bent down to fill her dish.

Something in the living room caught my eye. A greenish glow. I realized it was the round crystal paperweight my elderly neighbor, Elspeth Whipple, had given me as a 'moving-in' gift. From my bent-over position, I must have been looking at the paperweight at just the right angle to catch the reflection of light.

The paperweight was beautiful—a large, clear orb that reflected prisms of light almost magically. Elspeth had presented it to me the day I'd moved in and said I should keep it handy as I might find it very useful. I guess she didn't realize everything was done digitally now and I wouldn't have much paper that I needed to weigh down. Still, I kept it displayed prominently on my coffee table just for its beauty and sentiment.

Which reminded me—I should go over and check on Elspeth before supper. She was as old as the hills and had been Gram's neighbor forever. They'd been close and Gram had even put a note with her will asking me to check on Elspeth frequently.

I pulled my jean jacket off the peg by the kitchen door and shoved my feet into black rubber boots. The

My stomach tightened. Funny she should ask. I certainly wasn't going to tell her that I talked to ghosts, so I simply said, "We don't think so."

"Is Augusta investigating it, or did she simply rule it as an accident?"

"I'm not sure if she's made a final decision on it yet." I made a mental note to call Augusta and find out if they'd gotten autopsy results and made a ruling.

"Oh, dear." Elspeth turned back to the pies. "That *is* disturbing."

"Sorry to bring bad news. I hope you're not too upset."

"Oh, no. I'm fine." Elspeth handed me the pie, nicely packed in a Tupperware carrier and inside a cloth bag with a carrying strap.

"Thanks. I guess I'd better get home, then."

Elspeth followed me down the hall and opened the door for me.

I stepped out onto the porch, then turned back to her. "Don't forget, if you need anything, just give me a call—I'm only across the woods, just a hop, skip and a jump away."

"Yes, dear," she said. As I made my way down the steps, she added, "Oh, and Willa?"

I half turned and looked at her over my shoulder.

"Yes ...?"

"You be careful now ... there may be danger about."

Chapter Six

Pandora's whiskers twitched as she watched Willa and Elspeth disappear into the kitchen before following the orange tomcat, Tigger, out the cat door to the small barn where the cats usually gathered.

Pandora trotted into the barn behind Tigger. Nine sets of eyes blinked at them in the dark.

"I figured you'd show up eventually," Otis, the fat calico's sarcastic voice rang down from atop a tall bale of hay.

Pandora felt the hairs on her back prickle. She got along well with all the others of her kind, but Otis had been a thorn in her side since the beginning. He was one of the old ones ... an ancient feline that had served many humans. Pandora was a newer soul, with new ideas. For some reason, Otis felt threatened by these ideas.

Pandora arched her back and hissed at the calico.

"Now stop it, you two." Kelley, the Maine Coon swiped her paw in the air between them.

"So, you heard about the trouble brewing from the other side," Snowball, the fluffy white Persian, purred as she licked her paw.

"Lavinia came to the bookstore and verified her death was no accident," Pandora started, then paused for attention. She was one of the few cats that could talk to the other side. All eyes were on her and she savored the moment before continuing. "She didn't see who did it, though."

The others heaved a collective sigh.

"So, the evil ones have spilled first blood." The deep baritone of Inkspot, the twenty-two pound black cat rang out from the back of the barn.

"Do you always have to be so dramatic?" Snowball hissed at him.

Inkspot trotted toward the other cats that had formed a small circle in the middle of the barn and stood in front of Pandora.

"Is it not true?" he asked.

Pandora wrinkled her pink nose, remembering the noxious metallic smell of blood in the library. Her senses, many times more sensitive than humans, could smell it even out on the street that morning.

"Well, there was a lot of blood ..." she said.

"I think he was talking metaphorically, you know, trying to show off," Snowball said.

Sasha, the sleek Siamese jumped into the middle of the circle. "Let's not argue. We need to help our humans any way we can."

Pandora sat on her haunches and licked her paw. They were an elite species of cats sworn to help humans since ancient times—a task made more difficult by the fact that humans simply didn't have the feline's superior methods of communication. Some of them could learn, but others never did.

Pandora flicked her paw behind her ear as she thought about Willa, her human. She'd been with Willa's grandmother, Anna, since the beginning.

Anna had understood her.

Willa, on the other hand, obviously had no idea what Pandora was trying to tell her. Pandora missed Anna terribly, but she was starting to develop a small liking to her new human—even though Willa was rather skinny and her lap not nearly as comfortable as Anna's.

She didn't yet have the rapport with Willa that she'd developed with Anna, but it had taken years to get to that point with the grandmother, so there was still hope. Though that didn't help her much now ... and it seemed that right now, communicating with her human was critical.

Pandora narrowed her eyes. "How can we help them?"

"We must make sure the evil ones do not gain ground," Inkspot said in his usual vague manner.

"Anyone got an idea on how to do that?" Sasha's luminous blue eyes scanned the crowd.

"Only true magic can stop them for good," Otis spoke from his perch on top of the hay. "But it's not time for that. The best we can do is to guide the humans to slow down the evil ones."

"And how do we do that?" Pandora asked.

"By helping them find the killer before he gets what he wants," Otis replied.

"But how can we help them if we don't even know who the killer is?" Sasha asked.

A small cat padded into the middle of the circle. Her name was Truffles and she was a Tortoiseshell, predominantly black with orange mottling. Her large, greenish-yellow eyes glowed with excitement. "I think I know how."

"You?" Inkspot turned his green eyes on the small cat. "Have you been talking to the wild ones again?"

The wild ones were the feral cats of Mystic Notch. They served no humans and lived on the streets of town and in the forests, surviving on scraps and taking shelter as they could. They had eyes everywhere and knew much about what was going on in Mystic Notch.

"The wild ones found something." Truffles turned with a flick of her tail and headed toward the door. "Follow me, and I'll take you to it. I think it might help reveal the killer."

Chapter Seven

I traipsed back through the woods toward my house, feeling the absence of Pandora at my side. She hadn't been in Elspeth's house when I left and I didn't see her outside.

Where was she? I glanced back over my shoulder as I pulled my cell phone out to call Augusta.

"Pandora!" I yelled. Was I expecting her to come bounding through the woods? She'd never come when I called before.

I felt a stab of worry for the cat—I had to admit, I was getting kind of attached to the fur ball even though she did act strangely at times.

I waited a few seconds, then turned with a shrug. It would be dark soon and I didn't want to be in the woods after sunset. Pandora would find her way home—she always did.

I pulled Augusta up on my contacts list and pressed the button. She answered on the first ring.

"Hey, Willa. What's up?" Her voice was muffled like she had a jelly donut stuffed in her mouth.

"Are you eating?" I asked.

"Yep. Chocolate cruller." Not a jelly donut, but I was close. I wondered how she could eat so many donuts and still not gain an ounce.

"I was just calling to see if there was anything new about Lavinia. Do you have any idea why she was in the library that early?" I asked.

Augusta paused. I could hear her swallow the cruller. "You know I'm not supposed to talk about ongoing cases."

"Oh, so it is still open?" My house came into view in the distance and I picked up the pace.

Augusta laughed. "I guess I can tell you that I have some

doubts. I can't just write it off if I have a doubt, so I sent the body from Stilton's to the medical examiner."

"Ahh ... so you *do* suspect foul play." I said it as more of a statement than a question.

"Not necessarily. But I have a funny feeling and my duty is to err on the side of caution."

Augusta often had 'funny feelings' about cases and they usually turned out to be quite accurate. She was a natural cop, with good intuition.

"Okay. Well, let me know what you find out," I said as I jogged up the farmers porch steps and opened my back door.

"Will do." Augusta said. "Hey, wait a minute. Why are you so interested?"

"Oh, no reason, really." I stepped into the back entry, the back stairs were in front of me, the kitchen to my right and a small area for boots and coats to the left. I turned to the left, placed the bag with the pie on the floor and slid my left boot off with my right toe. "It's just that I found her, so I kind of feel like I want closure or something."

"I hope that's all it is, Willa," Augusta warned. "I don't want you going off on some wild investigation."

"Who, me?" I asked as I slid my right boot off. "Never."

Augusta laughed. "Okay, just be careful, then."

"I will." I snapped the phone shut and shrugged out of my coat, hanging it on the hook.

"So you didn't find my killer yet?"

I whirled around, my heart seizing in my chest. The cell phone slipped from my hand and clattered to the floor.

Lavinia's ghost sat at the oak claw-foot kitchen table, her hands folded in front of her as if she were waiting for me to serve tea.

"Lavinia! You scared the crap out of me."

"Sorry, dear. I just wanted to catch up and see if you'd made any progress."

I blew out a puff of air, picked the bag with the pie up and headed toward the fridge. On the way, I grabbed a tube of *Iced Fire* out of the basket I kept handy on the kitchen island. My leg was starting to hurt and I needed something to ease the pain.

"Myrna saw Ophelia Withington in town that morning." I put the pie in the fridge, then sat across from Lavinia, pulling the chair next to me closer so I could rest my leg on it.

Lavinia pressed her ghostly lips together. "That woman! I wouldn't put it past her to push me down the stairs."

I raised my brow at her as I eased up the leg of my jeans. "You didn't get along?"

"Not one bit. Oh, she was fine when she first came to town, but after Pete died she turned into a miserable witch trying to make everyone else around her just as bitter as she was."

"So you think she did it? But why? Why would she be in the library?" I opened the tube of *Iced Fire* and rolled some of it onto my leg, the medicinal peppermint smell tickling my nose.

"I'm not sure ... unless ..." Lavinia's voice trailed off.

"Unless, what?" I massaged my leg, the ache starting to disappear as the sensation of cold and hot from the *Iced Fire* worked its way into the muscle.

"No, I can't say." Lavinia shook her head. "Anyway she wouldn't have any reason to be in the library. She'd already scoured it."

"Scoured it? For what?"

"Oh, that's not important. It has nothing to do with my murder," Lavinia said, pushing herself up from the table. "You keep looking, and please do be careful. There may be danger about."

And with that, Lavinia disappeared, leaving me staring at the empty chair across the table from me.

Her parting words caused a chill to run up my spine ... Elspeth had said almost the same exact thing to me.

Shaking my head, I stood up. I was getting creeped out for nothing. A good, hot bath would fix that and make my leg almost as good as new. I tossed the *Iced Fire* into the basket and walked through the living room to the front stairs.

A sound made me pause at the foot of the stairs. Was that the flap of the cat door? Peeking back over my shoulder into the living room, I strained my ears, listening for the sound of Pandora's paws or her subtle meow. My heart hitched as I realized it had only been my imagination—Pandora was still outside.

I turned back to the stairs with a sigh. Pandora had been taking care of herself long before I came along and she certainly could take care of herself without me worrying about her, I thought, as I ascended the stairs.

Below me in the living room, the paperweight lit with an eerie glow. If I'd noticed, and cared to investigate further, I would have seen Pandora running through the streets of downtown Mystic Notch deep inside the globe.

But I didn't notice, so I went ahead with my bath and climbed into bed with a good book, never knowing that my furry feline friend was running around in the night, miles from home.

Chapter Eight

Pandora must have returned sometime during the night because I woke up with her tail flicking me in the face as she sat on my chest, kneading my bladder. She really knew how to wake a girl up.

I pushed her off, but not too hard. Truth be told, I was relieved she was safe. I sat up and pulled her onto my lap, scratching her behind the ears. She rewarded me with a few seconds of purring before wriggling out of my arms and running downstairs.

I used the bathroom, took a quick shower and threw on jeans and a sweatshirt before trotting downstairs where I fed Pandora and myself a quick breakfast. Fancy Feast for her—Corn Flakes for me.

We got to the bookstore late again and I was just turning the sign to 'Open' when Hattie, Cordelia, Bing and Josiah filed in through the door.

Bing handed me a Styrofoam cup filled with coffee just as my cell phone made a noise.

"Damn, I thought I shut this thing off." I pulled it out of my pocket. The display showed a text from another antique dealer friend, Maggie.

Picked up a box of old books for you.

"More books?" I said to myself as I shut off the phone.

"What's that about books?" Bing looked at me curiously.

"Oh, nothing. Maggie picked up a box of old books for me."

"Where?" he asked. Maggie had grown up in Mystic Notch and Bing had known her since she was a kid, just like he'd known me since I was a kid.

I frowned at him. What was he so interested in that for? "Umm... I have no idea. We do that for each other sometimes—you know—if we see something cheap enough that the other might be interested in. Barry has a box for me, too. Remember last summer when I gave him those nut dishes from the yard sale?"

"Oh, right. Of course." He shrugged, and then took a pack of cards out of his shirt pocket and joined the others who were already lounging on the couch. "So, did you find out any more about why Lavinia was in the library?"

"Not really," I muttered. It didn't seem fair to mention Myrna had seen Ophelia that morning until I knew exactly what she was up to and I sure as heck couldn't tell them that Lavinia's ghost had told me her death was no accident.

Bing raised a bushy eyebrow at me as he made a card disappear in thin air, then made a show of retrieving it from his sock.

"We checked in the Gazette and there was no notice of a book sale at the library," Hattie said as she sipped her tea.

"But she could have come in early for another reason," Josiah said.

"Right," I offered. "There are probably lots of reasons she could have come in early."

Cordelia bit her lower lip. "I never knew her to come in early, Josiah."

"Well, something brought her there," Bing said.

Hattie shrugged. "I guess it really doesn't matter. It was an accident, right?"

Everyone looked at me and I felt like a deer trapped in the headlights. Thankfully, I was saved by Pandora, who let out an ungodly wail from the other end of the bookstore just before something landed on the floor with a loud crash.

"What the heck?" I sprinted toward the source of the noise and found Pandora sitting in the mystery aisle amidst a pile of books.

"Did you knock these down?"

"Mew."

"That's not nice." I stooped and picked up the books, putting them back on the shelf while she watched with her golden green eyes.

I stood and pointed my finger at her. "Don't do that again."

She gave me a bored look and started washing her face.

"Is everything okay?" Cordelia yelled.

"Yep. Pandora just knocked some books down." I walked back to the front, picking my coffee up from the counter where I'd left it.

"So, anyway, we were saying that Lavinia's unfortunate accident was just that." Bing slid his eyes over to me. "That's what Augusta says, right?"

"That's what she thought when we were in the library, but you know how she is ... she won't say a word about an ongoing case to me." I crossed my fingers behind my back. It wasn't exactly a lie. She really didn't like to talk about cases. I was sure she wouldn't want me repeating her doubts to everyone in town.

"All this talk is making me depressed," Hattie said. "I think I need to visit the chocolate store."

"Me, too!" Cordelia jumped up from her seat.

Josiah drained his coffee cup. "Yep, guess I better get going and let you do your work."

The four of them made their way out the door. Bing was last and he held back for a second, half-closing the door, then turning to look at me.

I'd busied myself with some work behind the counter, but sensed him looking and glanced over at him, my brows creeping up my forehead.

"Willa ... it might be best if you didn't dig into this whole thing with Lavinia. It could be dangerous," Bing said, ducking out the door before I had a chance to answer him.

I stared at the door. Was that a warning ... or a threat? I couldn't tell by his tone or the look on his face and I didn't have much time to think about it because just then I heard another crash and Pandora's wail.

I ran to the back of the store. Pandora sat amidst a pile of books ... again. The same darn books.

"Really?" I bent down to put the books back. "What is wrong with you?"

Nothing. I'm trying to give you a clue. Her meows almost sounded like words as I put the books back in their place.

"Now, no messing with these books again." I tapped my finger on her pink nose.

She looked at me defiantly, reached out her paw and pulled a book off the shelf.

I rolled my eyes. "Cut that out!" I picked up the book and shoved it back into its spot.

"Mew!" She pulled it out again.

I felt my temper starting to rise. What was up with her? I glanced at the title as I picked up the book to put it back, yet again. *Murder Weapon Mayhem*. How appropriate, given what was going on with Lavinia.

I slid the book back in place.

"Wait a minute ... murder ... weapon." I looked at Pandora, who stared at me expectantly.

"Of course!" I snapped my fingers and stood up. "Why didn't I think of that before? Lavinia said she was whacked on the back of the head, which means that somewhere out there is a murder weapon that might have a clue to the murderer ... all we have to do is find it."

***

The rest of the day was uneventful. I spent most of it trying to decide where to search for the murder weapon. As the day drew on, doubt bloomed in my gut. The warnings I'd had from three people—well, two people and a ghost—echoed in my head.

It could be dangerous to look for the murder weapon on my own, but I couldn't very well tell Augusta I knew someone had clonked Lavinia on the back of the head.

It was up to me to find the murder weapon. I wasn't sure how I'd explain finding it to Augusta, but I was sure I would come up with something.

Of course, if I knew what I was looking for, it would make it a lot easier to find. Something heavy that one could easily use to whack someone else on the back of the head with.

I figured the best place to start was the library, so I closed up shop at five and headed down the street with Pandora following me ... well, I should say in front of me.

The cat had the strangest way of following me by walking ahead of me. I had no idea how she knew where I was going, but somehow she did.

I thought back to the morning I'd found Lavinia. Impossible to believe it was just yesterday, but it was. She hadn't been dead long when I'd found her, so that meant the killer had to make his—or her—escape through town in the morning hours. If I were a killer, I'd want to ditch that murder weapon as fast as I could, which is why I figured it would be somewhere near the library.

As I stared at the gothic stone building, I realized the killer wouldn't have come back out the front. There were too many people around on Maine Street.

"Meow." Pandora peeked out from the side of the library, then turned, her tail flicking like a finger beckoning me to follow her.

"Good idea, Pandora." The killer would have gone out the only other door, which was in the back. I followed her around the corner of the library. I'd never been behind the building before and was surprised that the area behind it was so small. It was paved, and there was a dumpster that I hoped I wouldn't have to jump inside of to find what I was looking for.

I chose to look everywhere else first. I walked around the edge of the pavement and looked in the corners of the building. I was squatting down, the side of my head almost on the ground so that I could peer under the dumpster, when I heard a low, guttural animal sound coming from behind me.

The hairs on the back of my neck stood up and I jerked my head around to see Pandora, her back arched, having a stare down with another cat. The other cat was a raggedy looking ginger-colored thing with wild yellow eyes. Three other cats stood about five feet away behind it.

I'd heard there was a feral cat colony around here and I guessed these cats were part of it. I noticed a small black and white kitten that couldn't have been more than six months old with a torn-up ear and my heart tugged. They looked well-fed, though, and I wondered briefly how they found shelter and what they ate.

I stood motionless, not knowing exactly what to do. Pandora and the other cat must have come to some sort of agreement, because they stopped making their noises and the other cat and his minions backed up.

Pandora trotted off after them and I could just barely make out a trail into the woods. The train tracks were back there somewhere—it would be a perfect get-away route for the killer! The tracks wandered behind several buildings then crossed Main Street at the other end of town. The killer could have run down them, then popped back out onto the street as if he had never been near the library.

I rushed in after Pandora, scanning the ground for something that could be the murder weapon.

She stopped in front of me and that's when I saw it.

It had been thrown off to the side and was half-buried in the leaves, but I recognized the part of it that was sticking up ... it was the heavy metal embosser Lavinia used to emboss the pages of the books with the library insignia. The library had three of them and, apparently, no one had noticed one was missing.

I stepped off the trail toward the embosser, bending down to get a better look. Yep, that was definitely the library's embosser. A thread of navy blue fabric caught on one of the screws flapped in the wind ... and was that blood on the side?

My heart thudded in my chest as I reached out to pick it up ...

"Stop right there! Put your hands in the air, stand up slowly and turn around!"

Chapter Nine

A steely gray glare coming from the broad shouldered behemoth who was holding the gun on me rooted me to the spot. Adrenalin shot through my body as my mind registered a chiseled jaw, trim waist and sheriff's uniform.

Sheriff's uniform?

Augusta was the sheriff here, and this guy sure as heck wasn't Augusta.

"Who the hell are you?" I probably should have asked more nicely, but I was mad ... and a little scared.

His left eyebrow quirked up and I thought I saw a smile tease the corners of his lips.

"I might ask you the same," he said, his eyes shifting to the embosser still lying on the ground. "What are you doing here and what is that you were bending over?"

Panic lapped at my stomach as I considered how to explain exactly what I was doing there. I certainly couldn't tell him I was looking for the murder weapon since I wasn't supposed to know there even *was* a murder.

"Meow!"

I shot the cat a grateful look. "My cat ... I was here looking for my cat."

As if on cue, Pandora trotted over to my side and rubbed her face against my leg.

Relief washed away the panic as a familiar figure came around the corner—Augusta.

"Willa? What's going on here?" Augusta looked from the behemoth to me, her brow wrinkled in confusion.

"You know her?" Behemoth asked.

Augusta sighed and holstered her gun. "You can put your gun away, Striker. It's my sister."

"Who the hell is *he*?" I asked Augusta, gesturing toward

Striker with my chin. I still had my hands up because the behemoth was still pointing his gun at me.

"This is Eddie Striker." Augusta nodded toward Striker. "He's the sheriff over in Dixford Pass. I asked him to help out since I don't have much experience with homicides."

"Homicide? So Lavinia *was* murdered." I tried to sound surprised.

Augusta shifted on her feet. "Yes, I suppose I can tell you since it's going to come out sooner or later. The medical examiner determined she was hit on the head with something. That probably didn't kill her, but it stunned her and the push down the stairs finished her off."

"Poor Lavinia," I said.

Augusta narrowed her eyes at me. "So, just what are *you* doing here behind the library?"

"What are *you* doing here?" I asked, wondering if they'd come to the same conclusion I had and were also looking for the murder weapon.

"I asked first," Augusta replied.

Striker was sliding his eyes back and forth between us, an amused expression on his face. I was not so amused that he still had his gun aimed at me.

"Pandora ran back here and I was trying to get her," I lied. Was I in store for some bad karma for lying to my sister? Probably.

"Are you sure that's all it is?" Augusta looked at me suspiciously. "I know how you have a habit of sticking your nose into investigations."

"Can I put my hands down?" My arms were starting to hurt, plus I wanted to avoid addressing Augusta's comment. It was true, I *did* have a habit of investigating on my own from my years of training as a crime journalist.

"Yes," Augusta sighed.

"No!" Striker shot Augusta a look.

I held my hands halfway up, my eyes wavering between the two of them.

"She could be a suspect. I caught her bending over that." Striker nodded toward the embosser.

"What is that?" Augusta walked over and bent down to inspect it.

"It's the embosser from the library. I saw it when I came back here after Pandora. I was going to pick it up and return it to the library when King Kong over here tried to shoot me down." Another lie ... bad karma was coming my way for sure.

Augusta took a plastic bag out of her pocket and deftly bagged the embosser without ever touching it with her fingers.

"Did you touch this?" She held the bag up in front of my face.

"No." At least I wasn't lying that time.

"Okay, I think we can let her go," Augusta held her hand up to squelch Striker's protest. "Striker, she's my sister. She found Lavinia and called it in."

"She found the body and now I catch her bending over the murder weapon? In Dixford Pass, she'd be my number one suspect," Striker said incredulously.

"I'll vouch for her. Let's take this to the lab. I think I see blood on the corner." Augusta turned to walk away and Striker reluctantly lowered his gun and followed. When they got to the corner of the building, Augusta half turned back toward me.

"Willa, you can put your hands down now," she shot over her shoulder. "Oh ... and don't leave town."

***

I walked to the parking lot, Pandora trotting at my side with a satisfied look on her face.

"Well, looks like we found the murder weapon," I said to her as I started the Jeep.

She ignored me, curled up in the passenger seat and went to sleep.

I thought about the murder weapon as I drove home. I couldn't really picture the perfectly-coiffed Ophelia smashing Lavinia on the back of the head with the embosser, but she was the only lead I had.

The embosser had blood on it. There was no doubt in my mind it was the murder weapon. I remembered the thread of navy blue fabric that was caught on one of the screws.

Was the fabric already on there or could it have come from the murderer?

Who else would have been in the library that morning and why? Did Lavinia have any enemies? Or was the intruder after something in the library, anyway? What would someone want in a library? All that was in there were books, and as far as I knew, none of them were valuable. Could there be something else of value in the library?

I pulled into my driveway and walked into the house like a zombie, exhausted from thinking.

As usual, Pandora sped ahead of me, making a beeline for her dish.

"Are you hungry?" I asked the obvious as I searched in the cupboard for her favorite food. "You deserve a special treat, since you led me to the murder weapon."

I studied the cat as she ate. She *had* led me to the murder weapon, which was rather odd. But who was I to talk about odd? I talked to ghosts and that wasn't exactly normal.

I wished Lavinia's ghost would appear now. I had some questions for her. Maybe if I called her out?

"Lavinia?" I ventured.

No one appeared.

"Lavinia, I have some questions that might help solve your murder."

Still nothing. Darn ghosts, appear when you don't want them to and then they aren't around when you need them.

I opened the fridge to rummage for something to eat and spied Elspeth's apple pie—the perfect supper for a crazy day like today.

I cut an extra-large piece and topped it off with vanilla ice cream. Sitting at the table, I stretched my leg out on the chair and dug into the pie. The apples practically melted in my mouth, the sugar and cinnamon tantalizing my taste buds. The crust was perfectly crunchy and Elspeth had sprinkled it with large sugar crystals for an extra boost. The slightly melted ice cream added the perfect creamy complement.

I finished the pie and brought the plate to the sink,

suddenly feeling exhausted. Limping up the stairs, I threw on pajamas and slid into bed with a good book about a pirate in 1820s England.

Pandora positioned herself at the foot of the bed. Her greenish-golden eyes glowed in the dark, watching me as I fell into a deep sleep.

In my dream, I was taken aboard a pirate ship against my will. Not that I minded, though ... the pirate looked kind of like Striker and I vaguely remember half-hoping he would ravish me like the pirate in my book had ravished the heroine. It was incredibly real and I slept deeply without moving a muscle.

So deeply, in fact, that I would never have noticed if someone snuck in and did a thorough search of my house and barn.

Chapter Ten

I got to the bookstore early the next day. Pandora settled into her cat bed in the window and I started sorting and putting away the books that had accumulated, which included a boxful from an internet auction I'd won and a pile of old books I'd picked up in my travels.

Inside the box was a wonderful set of five poetry books bound in rich brown leather with gold leaf on the edges of the pages. I carefully carried them to the poetry section and made room for them on the shelf at eye level.

"I shall tell you with a sigh, the poetry section needs some bulking up."

I gasped, momentarily startled at the voice in my ear, then turned to see the ghostly figure of Robert Frost at my side. The poet's ghost often hung around here in the poetry section where I had quite a collection of his books—he'd lived in New Hampshire while writing many of his poems, and his books were quite popular here.

I scanned the shelf critically. "You know what, Robert? You're right. These shelves are practically bare."

"Oh, and you could use some more historical books, too," a voice piped up several aisles down in the history section. I recognized the ghost as that of Franklin Pierce, the only US President from New Hampshire. He hung around here, too.

I had no idea why they choose to hang around in the bookstore, but they seemed like nice guys. At first, it was a little off-putting, but once I got used to them, I realized they could actually be good company ... except when they were arguing or being mischievous. You wouldn't expect it from such proper gentlemen, but I'd seen them run off giggling after knocking a book off a shelf in front of a customer, just to startle them.

Anyway, they were both right. I *did* need to get some fresh stock.

I remembered that both Barry and Maggie had called about books they'd picked up for me. I'd been so busy trying to find Lavinia's killer, I hadn't had time to go pick up the books. Well, I'd just have to make time.

"Did someone call me?" Lavinia materialized in the middle of the aisle.

"Sure, now you show up ... where were you when I was calling you at my house?"

Lavinia straightened, eyeing Robert and Franklin. "Well, now, we ghosts can't be at your beck and call, you know. There's lots to do on the other side."

"Are you going to introduce us?" Franklin raised a brow as he glided toward me.

"Where are your manners?" Robert asked.

I introduced them all and they swirled misty greetings to each other. I guess ghosts didn't just shake hands.

"Anyway, did you need something?" Lavinia asked.

"I was wondering if there was anyone who had a grudge against you. You know ... who might have wanted you ... dead."

"No one. I don't think it had anything to do with me," Lavinia said. "They were in the library before me. It must have been something in the library."

"You mean you were murdered?" Franklin's eyes widened. "My dear, how ... exciting."

"Yes, do tell us all about it." Robert drifted toward the end of the aisle and Lavinia followed, the three of them fading away as they chatted about Lavinia's murder.

"At least she won't be bugging me today," I said to Pandora as I unlocked the door and turned the shop sign to 'Open'.

Slipping back behind the counter, I set about examining the rest of the books. I was almost done when the bells over the door jingled. I looked up in time to see Hattie, Cordelia, Josiah and Bing come in, carrying the usual Styrofoam cups. Josiah had gotten mine this time and he pushed it across the counter toward me.

I flipped the plastic tab and took a sip, the bitter coffee warming my veins.

"Are you going to Lavinia's service tomorrow?" Hattie asked.

Lavinia materialized, peeking around the edge of one of the bookshelves, her ear cocked to hear the conversation.

"Yessuh," Josiah said. "I hear there's no viewing."

"Nope, the family didn't want it." Cordelia said. "Said they were being hounded enough by the press now that it's been deemed a murder."

"Did you know that, Willa?" Bing turned to me.

"I just found out," I said, watching Lavinia make motions of her nose growing like Pinocchio telling a lie.

"Is something wrong over there?" Hattie leaned forward in her seat, looking toward the spot where Lavinia was. Of course, she couldn't see her.

"No, I just noticed the books are out of order. I'll have to straighten them later," I said.

"Well, anyway, it's all over town about the murder," Hattie continued. "Who do you think did it?"

"Yeah, Willa. You're the crime journalist," Josiah cocked his head at me. "Who do *you* think did it?"

I shrugged. "I'm at a loss. You guys know the townspeople better than I. Do you have any idea who would want to hurt Lavinia?"

The four of them shook their heads.

"I don't."

"Can't think of a soul."

"Everyone liked Lavinia."

"Maybe it wasn't about Lavinia," Cordelia said. "Maybe she just got in the way."

Hattie frowned at her sister. "In the way of what?"

"Someone who wanted to take something from the library," Josiah said.

"But there's nothing, 'cept old books in there." Cordelia wrinkled up her face and turned to me. "None of those books have any value, do they?"

I shook my head. "Not that I know of."

"Not the books," Josiah said. "There are some valuable bronzes in there."

"Oh, you mean that bust of Franklin Pierce?" Cordelia asked.

"That one's not worth much. The real treasures are the ones by Frederick Remington."

"You mean the horse ones?" Hattie asked.

Josiah nodded. "Most people think they are replicas, but I'm pretty sure a few of those are originals. I remember back in sixty-five when Idris Bates donated them to the library. It was quite a to-do back then. 'Course, as the years have gone by, people have forgotten about them."

I looked at Josiah, open-mouthed. Although my area of expertise was antique books, I'd picked up enough information on general antiques to know that an original Remington bronze bust could be worth hundreds of thousands. Heck, even the good replicas are worth thousands.

"I don't remember ever noticing the busts in there," I said.

"Most people don't. Over the years they got shuffled around." Josiah turned to Bing. "Bing, you remember those don't you. I seem to recall even back then you had an interest in bronzes."

Bing nodded. "Now that you mention it, I do remember. I did have quite a collection of bronzes in my younger days, but I don't collect them anymore. Never had a Remington, though."

I remembered that Bing had an extensive collection of antiques, many of which he'd acquired from various parts of the world where he'd performed as a magician. He'd been collecting since he was a boy. When I was young, I used to love to go to his house and look at all the old stuff. He had a treasure trove of items stuffed in the attic, basement and barns. It was no surprise he'd collected a bronze or two in his day.

Josiah looked back at me. "You younger people wouldn't remember. They weren't worth nearly as much at the time they were donated, so no one paid much mind to what happened to them and they got moved downstairs."

Downstairs ... where Lavinia's body was found.

"Gosh, I had forgotten all about those," Cordelia said.

Hattie looked at the group solemnly. "Maybe someone else remembered about them and broke in to steal them."

"... And Lavinia stumbled across them and they killed her!" Cordelia added.

"Were any of the statues missing from the library?" Josiah asked me.

"I'm not sure, but you can bet I'm going to find out," I said.

"Well, then, I think I'll be on my way." Josiah pushed himself up from the couch. "I'll ask around about the bronzes and let you know if I come up with anything."

"Us, too," Cordelia and Hattie chorused, then gave each other a knuckle tap as they rose from the couch.

Bing got up with the others. I noticed he'd been unusually quiet.

"I wish you'd be careful if you are going to look into this, Willa," he said as he followed the others out the door. "There's a killer on the loose and now that the police are on it, it might be best to leave it to them."

"I'll be careful," I promised.

Bing looked like he was going to say something else, then he must have decided better of it as he turned and disappeared out the door.

Chapter Eleven

I finished sorting through the rest of the box, then left a message for Barry letting him know I'd be out to his place tomorrow to pick up the books he was holding for me. Maggie was in New York on a buying trip, so I'd have to wait until she got back to pick up the books from her.

It was a slow day, but between inventorying the new stock and putting the books on the shelf, I'd made a few sales, one of which was a book on US Presidents. I wondered how the buyer would feel if he knew Franklin Pierce was standing behind him nodding his approval as I rang up the sale.

I was taking a break in one of the purple chairs when the bells over the door jangled and Pepper came in, holding a tray of tea and finger sandwiches.

"It's slow over at the tea shop, so I left Camilla in charge and brought you some lunch." She set the tray on the table and sat beside me.

My stomach growled at the sight of the tiny sandwiches—thin white bread, cut into triangles with the crusts removed.

"Is that ham salad?" I asked as I reached for a sandwich.

"Yes, with pickles."

I loaded my plate with three of them, and poured some tea into the dainty china cup. Pepper had a collection of antique teacups that she used in her shop and this one had a thick gold lining inside and big yellow roses on the outside.

I poured some cream into the cup, glancing at her out of the corner of my eye. "You didn't put anything special in here, did you?"

Pepper laughed. "Nope. No special herbs in there, don't

worry."

I bit into the sandwich, reveling in the burst of sweet ham and tangy pickle. "Nummy," I mumbled with my mouth full.

"So, did you find out any more about Lavinia's killer? I heard it's an official murder investigation now." Pepper settled back on the sofa, taking a teensy nibble from one of the molasses cookies stacked up on the tray.

I told her about the incident behind the library.

"Augusta must think this is serious if she called in Eddie Striker," Pepper said.

"You know him?"

"Of course." Pepper looked at me quizzically. "He grew up here. Don't you remember him from grade school?"

"Grade school?" I dug around in my memory, which to tell the truth wasn't that great anymore. I didn't remember any extra-large second grader named Eddie. "I don't remember."

"Anyway, he moved away to Dixford Pass when were about ten, I think. He went on to work for the CIA—super secret spy stuff, from what I hear. Then something happened and he came back to Dixford Pass to be the sheriff."

I pressed my lips together. "Well, I didn't like him very much ... he seemed like he wanted to shoot me."

"Was that because you acted less than hospitable to him?"

"Maybe," I laughed. I had been pretty hostile to him. "Anyway, I'm pretty sure that embosser is the murder weapon and I found something on it that might be a clue."

"What?'

"One of the screws that attached the seal to the handle was sticking out. There was a thread of navy blue fabric stuck on it. Like a thread that would have ripped off a coat ... or a cape."

"And you think that could have come from the murderer." Pepper said it as more of a statement than a question.

I nodded.

"So, now we need to find out who has a navy blue coat."

"Yes, I'd especially like to know if Ophelia has one. And there's something else..."

A movement at the shop door caught my eye and I glanced over to see something large blocking most of the light. I noticed a brown shirt and the ham salad spoiled in my stomach. "Please tell me that isn't—"

The door opened and in stepped Eddie Striker.

***

Striker paused just inside the doorway, his light gray eyes scanning the shop before he noticed us on the couch. Did I see his lips twitch upwards in a smile? I stared at the stone-faced look he was wearing and decided that must have been my imagination. Probably he just had indigestion or some kind of a strange twitch.

"Sheriff Striker, what a pleasant surprise," I said sarcastically. "What can I do for you?"

"Ms. Chance," he said, then frowned at Pepper.

"Hi, Eddie," Pepper cut in. "It's Pepper St. Onge ... from second grade."

"I thought you looked familiar." Striker shifted his weight from one foot to the other. "How are you?"

"Oh, great. Hey, would you like a sandwich?" Pepper gestured toward the tea tray and I almost laughed out loud picturing the tiny sandwich and teacup in Striker's large hands.

He frowned down at the tray and I figured he was probably thinking the same thing I was. I couldn't help but notice how his frown made the dimple on his cheek more prominent.

His face was slightly tanned, making his eyes look even lighter. His short-cropped dark hair had just a peppering of gray. I touched my own hair self-consciously, wondering why a little bit of gray always makes guys look more handsome, but just makes women look old. Not that I was noticing, but Sheriff Striker did look a lot more appealing now that he wasn't pointing a gun at me.

Striker looked up at me and our eyes met, sending a jolt through my heart. I was probably just scared he was going to arrest me. I ripped my eyes away from his in time to notice the bemused look on Pepper's face as she flicked her eyes from me to Striker and back again.

Striker cleared his throat. "Thanks, but I already ate lunch. I have some questions about what you found in the library the other day."

"Okay, fire away." I remained seated and rudely didn't invite him to join us.

Striker glanced at Pepper uncertainly.

"You can ask me in front of Pepper. She knows all about me finding Lavinia."

Pandora jumped down from her bed on the window and started sniffing around Striker's feet. He looked down at her, but didn't shoo her away.

"Where was the body when you found it?" he asked.

"Same place it was when Augusta came. I didn't touch it other than feeling for a pulse on her wrist."

"And you didn't notice anything out of the ordinary or see or hear anything?"

"No."

Pandora looked at me and cocked her head back toward Striker as if to tell me she approved. I glared at her in response. *Don't get used to him, he won't be around much ... I hope.*

"And just what were you doing at the library?"

I blew out a puff of air, disturbing a red curl that was dangling down across my forehead. Hadn't Augusta told him all this? "I was on my way to work, here, when I saw the lights on and the door open. I went in to investigate."

"Mew Mew," Pandora meowed. I wrinkled my brow at her—had her mew sounded like 'me, too'?

Striker continued as if he hadn't even heard the meow. "But you usually don't come to work that early, do you?"

I started to feel uneasy. Had he been asking around about me like he would ask around about a suspect? "I do usually try to get in earlier, but things don't always work out that way. That day I was a little late."

He narrowed his eyes. "I see. And what were you doing behind the library yesterday?"

"I told you yesterday. I was getting my cat." I pointed at

Pandora who was now rubbing her face all over his ankles. To my surprise, he bent down to pet her.

Striker looked up at me from his crouched position. "Really? Are you sure that's all it was? Because I heard you like to get involved in cases and I don't need an amateur messing things up with this one."

Amateur?

"I was a pretty good crime journalist down south. In fact, there's more than one case that probably wouldn't have been solved without my help," I said indignantly, even as my traitorous cat purred loudly at his hands.

Striker stood up, causing Pandora to mewl with disappointment. "I know. I heard all about you. But I don't like anyone else looking into my cases. Besides, there's a killer on the loose and it could be dangerous. Best to leave this one to the pros."

And with that, he turned and walked out the door, robbing me of the chance to spear him with a nasty reply.

***

"Have you ever heard anyone be so rude and condescending?" I asked Pepper who was still staring at the door.

"He sure did grow up nice," she replied.

"What? He's a condescending jerk."

"Oh, I don't think you *really* think that."

I scrunched up my face. "What is wrong with you? Did you hear the way he talked to me?"

"I saw the way he *looked* at you ... and the way you looked at him," she said smugly. "I think there's a spark there. I could feel the heat myself—don't try to deny it."

The truth was I felt the heat, too, but at my age I just figured it was another hot flash.

"Pffttt..." I flapped my hand at her. I didn't like the way she was looking at me. Pepper loved playing matchmaker. "Now, don't go getting any ideas about fixing a special tea for me or Sheriff Meanie."

"I won't," she said innocently. Too innocently. I put my teacup down and made a mental note not to drink anything she served me any time in the near future.

"So anyway, what was this other thing you were starting to tell me before Eddie came in?" Pepper picked up her teacup and sipped.

I scrunched up my face. Sheriff Meanie had gotten me so worked up I'd forgotten what we'd been talking about.

"You told me about the fabric on the embosser and said there was something else..." Pepper prompted.

"Oh yes, the bronzes," I said, then told her what Josiah had told me about the old bronzes that had been donated to the library.

"Why would Ophelia be after bronze statues?" Pepper asked. "She already has enough money."

I shrugged. "Who knows? She seems money-hungry to me. Plus, with her background being married to an antique auctioneer, she'd know the value of them."

"But how would she even know they were there? Bates donated them long before she came to town and, as you said, everyone has pretty much forgotten about them. They aren't on display in there or anything, are they?"

"No. I remember noticing them once downstairs in the paperback section, but they aren't in the main section upstairs." Something niggled at the back of my mind. "Lavinia said that Ophelia had scoured the library, so she would have seen them."

"Did Lavinia say Ophelia was looking for the bronzes?"

"No, in fact she was kind of cagey about the whole thing." I picked up a molasses cookie and took a big bite, relishing the combination of sugar and spice. "But if we could match one of Ophelia's coats to that navy blue fabric, then we'd have something concrete."

Pepper wrinkled her nose. "I'm still not convinced Ophelia is the killer, but I do have a special tea for her. Maybe we could pay her a visit."

"You're not trying to make her nice with one of your teas are you?" I could only picture what would happen if that backfired like some of Pepper's other attempts. I shuddered to think of a meaner Ophelia Withington.

Pepper smiled. "Not trying to *make her nice*. Just restoring her faith and her natural personality."

I rolled my eyes.

"I know she always leaves the office at three p.m. and goes home to sort through her client list and match the new properties to potential clients," Pepper said. "We could stop by and catch her off-guard. I'll bring some tea and cookies and distract her and you can pretend you need to use the bathroom and look through her closet."

"That sounds perfect."

"So, I take it you're not going to heed Eddie's warning and step out of the investigation?"

"Heck, no." I gave Pepper my, 'you-know-me-better-than-that' look. "I'm going to do just what Lavinia asked and find her killer, even if it's the last thing I do."

Chapter Twelve

Ophelia Withington lived in a big, old barn converted into a house just outside of town. We stood on the granite slab doorstep—Pepper in her prim sweater set and plaid skirt and me in my plain old maroon turtleneck and faded jeans.

Pepper held a warming bag made from a bright paisley print at her side. She'd had the bags specially made so she could prepare tea at her shop and keep it warm for travel.

I wiped my sweaty palms on my jeans and rang the bell.

We heard some noises inside, and then the door opened to reveal a surprised-looking Ophelia Withington.

"Hi, Pepper." She started to half-smile until she saw me standing next to Pepper, then her face turned to an ugly frown. "Wilhelmina ... I hope you're not here to harass me again. If so, I'm calling the cops."

I held my hands up. "We come in peace."

She looked from me to Pepper skeptically, ready to slam the door in our faces.

Pepper held out the bag. "I made you some tea and cookies. I know the anniversary of Pete's passing is coming up and I thought it might help comfort you."

I shot a look at Pepper. She was really laying it on, but it seemed to work.

Ophelia's face softened. "Well, I *was* working ..."

"Oh, it will only be a few minutes." Pepper pushed her way inside. "I have the tea already hot right here in the bag."

"Err ... well, okay, but just for a short visit."

We both followed Pepper into the living room and watched her produce a tea towel, tray, teapot, creamer and bowl with tiny sugar cubes, cups, saucers and shortbread cookies from the bag.

"Shortbread cookies are my favorite." Ophelia looked at Pepper. "How did you know?"

"Oh, just a lucky guess." Pepper poured hot water from the tea kettle into a light blue cup, then took out a small tea bag and placed it inside. She repeated the process for two other cups, laid the cookies out on the tray, then sat back with her hands folded in her lap. "The tea needs to steep for a few minutes."

Ophelia looked as fidgety as I felt. Pepper produced some napkins stamped with her Tea Shoppe logo in gold and passed them out while we listened to the clock tick. Finally, when the silence was just about to become unbearable, Pepper picked up the blue cup and handed it to Ophelia.

"This should be perfect now." Pepper lifted a miniature silver creamer from the tray and lifted her brow to Ophelia, who nodded and pushed her cup toward Pepper so she could pour in the cream.

Pepper rummaged in the bag again and pulled out silver tongs, the ends in the shape of bird claws. She put the tongs in the sugar bowl and pushed it toward Ophelia who shook her head. Apparently, she didn't take sugar. I bit my tongue so I wouldn't urge her to take some, as it might make her less bitter.

Ophelia settled back in her seat, eyeing Pepper suspiciously. "So, what brings you by, really?"

"Well, truthfully, I know how down you've been since Pete died and I have a new line of herbal teas to soothe the soul. I thought it might help and, well, if it does, I know word of mouth is the best advertisement."

Ophelia screwed up her face. "I don't believe in that stuff."

"What? You mean herbs?" Pepper asked. "There are many medical studies about their effectiveness."

"Anyway, it's been a few years since Pete died." Ophelia sipped the tea and her voice softened. "I don't get nearly as upset as I used to."

I almost felt sorry for her until I saw Pepper looking at me pointedly and I remembered the real reason we'd come.

"I'd known Pete since I was a young girl," Pepper said. "My parents used to take me to his auctions. What are some of your fondest memories of him?"

Ophelia relaxed into her chair and smiled ... yes, she actually smiled. She opened her mouth to say something.

"Excuse me," I said as nicely as I could. "Could I use your bathroom?"

Ophelia barely looked in my direction as she waved a hand toward the hall. "Help yourself. It's down the hall on the left."

I got up, taking care not to knock over the tea tray in my excitement. I had to admit, whatever Pepper had put in that tea did seem to be mellowing Ophelia. As I started down the hall, I heard Ophelia telling Pepper about the day she and Pete met.

The hallway had three doors. One led to a study, one to the bathroom and the third to the hall closet. I opened the bathroom door and made a lot of noise shutting it, then crept over to the closet and opened it quietly.

I thumbed through the coats one at a time, my stomach sinking as I got closer to the end. Tan trench coat, black rain poncho, white wool jacket, a faux fur—or was it real? I had no idea how to tell. There were also several blazers and a tweed wool coat.

There was nothing in navy blue wool.

I eyed the stairway leading upstairs. A woman didn't keep all her coats in the hall closet, did she?

I could hear snatches of conversation from the living room. Ophelia was engrossed in her stories of Pete. She sounded almost pleasant. I felt a stab of guilt, but not enough to stop me from tiptoeing down the hall and creeping up the stairs.

Ophelia's bedroom was at the top of the stairs, and to the right was what looked like a spare bedroom. At my own house, I kept my overflow coats in the closet of the spare bedroom, so I turned right.

Trying to walk lightly so they wouldn't hear me downstairs, I slowly opened the closet door. I didn't have to look far...right in front of me was a big old wool cape ...

in dark navy blue.

***

I had to stop myself from racing down the stairs—I didn't want Ophelia to hear me and know I'd been up there. I crept down them, keeping close to the sides so as to avoid any give-away squeaks. Then, once in the hall, I rushed down to the bathroom and flushed the toilet.

Back in the living room, Ophelia was still reminiscing about Pete, her back to me. Pepper looked over at me and I gestured wildly with a thumbs up, jerking my head toward the door to indicate we should going.

Ophelia turned around and I quickly composed myself.

"Oh, Wilhelmina, I was just telling Pepper the funniest story—"

"That's great, Ophelia, but we really should be going." I looked at my wrist where a watch would have been if I wore one.

"Oh, so soon?" Ophelia looked crushed and I narrowed my eyes at Pepper. What the heck had she given her?

Pepper started to gather everything up and put it in the bag. "Yes, sorry. We do have to get back to our shops."

"Oh, of course." Ophelia stood and extended her hand to Pepper. "Thank you so much for stopping by. I feel much better now ... though I didn't even realize that I didn't feel good before."

"You're welcome. See, my teas really do work wonders." Pepper shook her hand then started toward the door.

"Oh, and Wilhelmina, I do hope you will excuse my nasty behavior at my office. It's just that ... well ... I wasn't in the library that morning and I guess I felt like you were accusing me."

"I was just checking on what I heard. I didn't mean to accuse you." Like heck I didn't, I thought, as I pictured the navy blue cape hanging in her closet.

I opened the door and pulled Pepper outside. Ophelia stood just inside the threshold, her hand on the door, about to close it.

"You know, there is one thing I remember from that

morning that was strange." Ophelia said as we were walking away.

I turned back, wrinkling my brow at her. "What's that?"

"I *was* in town ... but not at the library." A pained look crossed her face and she shook her head. "Anyway, as I was leaving after doing my banking, a long black car went speeding past me up the mountain road. They were going very fast, driving recklessly, as if they wanted to get away from something fast. Nearly ran me off the road."

Chapter Thirteen

"See now, Ophelia isn't so bad, is she?" Pepper asked as she drove back to town in her yellow Fiat.

"Not so bad? I found a navy blue cape in her closet—she's probably the killer!"

Pepper glanced sideways at me. "Oh, come on. Didn't Myrna say she was wearing a raincoat?"

I pressed my lips together. "Yeah, but maybe Myrna was mistaken. I'm pretty sure that cape was the same color blue as the thread, and Lavinia said whoever pushed her was wearing a cape."

"Are you sure you aren't just so focused on the possibility that it could be Ophelia that you are blinded to anything else?" Pepper asked. "I mean, you saw how nice she was today."

"Yeah, what did you give her, anyway?"

"Oh just a special tea," Pepper said smugly.

"Well, nice or not she could be a killer." I pulled out my cell phone. "I should call Augusta and let her know Ophelia has a cape that matches the fibers on the murder weapon."

"Augusta ... or Eddie?" Pepper smirked.

"Very funny." I stared at my phone.

"What's wrong?" Pepper asked as she pulled into the municipal parking lot.

"I'm not really sure what to say. I can't very well tell Augusta I was in Ophelia's house rummaging through her closet and happened to discover a blue cape. And how would I explain that I know the killer wore a cape? Sheriff Meanie would probably arrest me if I came out with that."

Pepper parked the car, then reached in the back for her bag of tea items. "Sounds like you need something more solid ... something that will cause the police to search Ophelia's house and find the cape themselves."

"That's right. I need solid evidence." I opened my door and hopped out of the car. "I need to find a motive or place her at the scene of the crime."

Pepper fell in step beside me as I walked down the sidewalk toward our stores. The birds were chirping, the sun beaming down and buds starting to form on the trees, but I didn't notice any of it. I was too focused on figuring out what to do next.

"How are you going to do that?" Pepper asked.

"Her motive could have been the bronzes. Of course, they are valuable, but I wonder if Bates bought them from Pete? Maybe they have special meaning to her. I suppose I could talk to Bates about that."

I glanced sideways as we passed the library. Across the street, a side street opened up to the front of the church, the church that Ophelia had said she was lighting a candle at that morning. "I can't really do too much about her motive right now, but I can check out her alibi."

Pepper's eyes followed my gaze. "At the church?"

"Yep. She said she was lighting a candle. Maybe Pastor Foley saw her there and can verify the time and how long she stayed. Maybe he saw where she went afterward."

Pepper shrugged. "I guess it's worth a try. I think you're wasting your time, though, because I'm sure she didn't do it. Maybe you should be checking out that black car Ophelia said she saw instead."

"Maybe, but if I learned one thing as a crime journalist, it's that you've got to cover all your bases and check out *all* the leads thoroughly." I turned down the side street.

"You want some company?" Pepper called after me.

"No, thanks. This will only take a few minutes, then I'm going to grab Pandora from the shop and head home."

"Okay, see you tomorrow." Her words echoed down the street as I walked toward the church.

The First Hope church was one of the oldest buildings in Mystic Notch. I'd only been inside a handful of times. My family wasn't active in organized religion and I realized as I approached the large cathedral style doors that I didn't even know what kind of religion they practiced there.

Inside, the church was dimly lit. Rows of pews in dark oak lined the sides. The church was rather plain, painted in white. A large round stained glass window sat high in the gable end wall, casting shards of muted red and yellow light on the altar. Rows of large frosted glass rectangular windows with rounded tops lined the sides, but, surprisingly, didn't let in a lot of light. It was as quiet as a library and smelled like exotic spices.

I walked toward the front, the sound of my footsteps on the shiny marble floor echoing hollowly. Was Pastor Foley here somewhere?

As I approached the altar, a rustling sound to the left caught my attention and I noticed a hallway led out of the chapel to the side stairs. I followed it to a small room. Inside, a tiny gray-haired lady rummaged in a box exploding with wadded paper. She pulled something out and straightened.

I cleared my throat.

She whirled around, startled, keeping the item she'd taken from the box behind her back.

I recognized her as Emma Potts.

"Sorry. I hope I didn't startle you," I said. "I'm looking for Pastor Foley."

"He's not here. I'm the church secretary, though. Can I help you?" She peered at me through the thick lenses of her eyeglasses. "I don't believe I know you ... are you a church member?"

I took a step into the room. "It's me, Wilhelmina Chance."

Her brows dipped in a V as she studied me. "Oh, that's right. Anna's granddaughter who went down south quite a few years ago."

"That's right. I inherited my grandmother's bookstore, so I'm back to stay now."

Emma pushed her glasses up on her nose with her free hand, keeping the hand with the object she'd retrieved from the box behind her back. "What can I do for you? Any relative of Anna's is a friend of mine."

"Well, I'm sure you heard about Lavinia Babbage..."

"Yes, that's so sad. She was part of our flock, you know. Dedicated to helping others and always donated to our causes ... which we are in dire need of money for." Her face crumbled with sadness and she shook her head. I heard a jingling noise come from behind her. What the heck did she have back there and why was she hiding it?

I leaned to the left trying to see what was behind her and she leaned in the same direction to block me.

"So, what can I help you with?" she prompted.

I straightened back up. "Well, it's just that I found her and I'd like to follow up on a few things. I feel a bit responsible for helping to bring her killer to justice."

"Oh, well, that seems reasonable, but how can *I* help with that?"

"I was looking into who was in town that morning and someone saw Ophelia Withington here at the church."

Emma's back stiffened at the mention of Ophelia's name, and her face took on a sour look.

I continued, "She said she was here and I was wondering if you saw her."

"Here? At the church? Certainly not. Why, she's done everything she can to..." Emma let her voice trail off and looked around as if to make sure no one had heard her.

"To what?" I prompted.

"Well, let's just say she was no friend of the church," Emma said primly. "Just what did she say she was doing here?"

"She said she was lighting a candle for Pete."

Emma huffed. "Well, that right there proves she was lying."

"Why's that?"

"This church doesn't have candles."

Chapter Fourteen

Pandora was waiting for me in the bookshop window. I unlocked the door, cashed out the register and then locked up again. We trotted to the Jeep together.

I glanced back toward the church as I drove out of the parking lot.

"So, Ophelia lied about lighting a candle at the church ... which makes me wonder what else she lied about," I said out loud.

"Meow." Pandora blinked at me, her luminescent eyes taking on more of a green tint in the afternoon light.

"But, then again, that also means that Lavinia lied about lighting a candle."

Pandora licked her front paw, running it behind her ear a few times.

"Why would they both lie? Did the two of them share a secret? And, if so, did that have anything to do with Lavinia's death?"

"Meoow!" A gray paw snaked out and tapped my arm.

"What?" I looked at Pandora who simply withdrew her paw, but not before snagging her claw on the fabric of my turtleneck.

"Ahh, geez." I twisted my arm, looking at the pinprick-sized hole in my shirt. "Thanks a lot."

"Mew." She curled into a ball and purred noisily all the way home.

I pulled into the driveway, and instead of racing me to the back door, Pandora trotted off toward the path that led to Elspeth's house.

"Hey, where are you going? Don't you want supper?" I yelled after her.

She responded by flicking her tail at me and breaking

into a run.

"Sheesh, I must be lonelier than I thought. Now I'm talking to the cat," I said out loud to no one. Thoughts of Sheriff Striker invaded my head. He *was* kind of cute, but I wasn't really sure I wanted to get involved with anyone right now. My marriage had ended badly only a few years ago and the thought of going through anything like that again didn't appeal to me.

Of course, no one said I had to marry the guy, I thought as I looked at the empty cat bowl. It sure did feel like the house was missing something without Pandora. My eye went to the pie plate and carrier I'd washed that morning. Might as well follow in Pandora's paw steps and return it to Elspeth.

I shrugged on a sweater and boots, then headed out through the woods carrying the pie plate and carrier inside the bag Elspeth had sent them over in. It was less than a ten-minute walk to Elspeth's and I could see her sitting on her porch as I approached the house. She was wrapped in a green crocheted shawl, her right arm held straight out and resting on the porch railing, a pile of birdseed in her open palm.

I watched in wonder as a gray tufted titmouse landed on her hand and pecked at the seeds. A brown chickadee bobbed his head up and down on the rose vine, twittering loudly as he waited for his turn at the buffet of seeds and nuts Elspeth offered.

The birds flew off as I approached the porch. "Sorry, didn't mean to scare away your friends."

"Oh, that's okay. I've been feeding them by hand for years now. They'll be back tomorrow." Elspeth stood and leaned over the railing, wiping her hands together and letting the seeds fall into the garden.

"I brought your pie plate back. The pie was delicious." I set the bag down on the porch as Elspeth settled back into her wicker chair.

"Meow." Pandora peeked out from behind Elspeth and I noticed the orange tiger cat sitting next to her. A Siamese lay at the foot of Elspeth's chair, and a big jet-black tomcat sat off to the side.

"I figured you had run over here," I said to Pandora who came over and rubbed herself against my ankles.

"Have a seat." Elspeth gestured to a green wooden rocking chair. I sat and Pandora jumped into my lap.

"I was wondering what you know of Ophelia Withington." Pandora dug her claws into my leg and the orange cat hissed.

"Shush, Tigger," Elspeth said to the cat. "Ophelia isn't a bad person ... she just got a little lost when Pete died."

"Someone saw her around the library at the time Lavinia was killed." I looked at Elspeth. "Do you think she could have done it? Did Ophelia and Lavinia have some sort of grudge or secret?"

"Secret?" Why do you ask that?"

I chose my words carefully. I couldn't tell Elspeth that Lavinia's ghost had lied to me about lighting a candle. "Oh ... just something I found out when I was asking around."

"So, you *are* looking into Lavinia's murder?" Elspeth nodded. "I figured you would."

I didn't have a good comeback for that so I just shrugged.

"I don't think anyone killed Lavinia on purpose, especially not Ophelia. She does have her demons, but she's no killer." Elspeth glanced out into the woods and her eyes took on a faraway look. "Do you remember living in Mystic Notch as a little girl?"

I felt my lips curl in a smile. I had happy childhood memories. "Yes."

"Didn't it seem like a magical place?"

"Of course. I loved pretending there were magic fairies in the woods and time spent with my grandmother was always special. Those were happy times." I remembered that time spent with my grandmother always involved lots of reading. We shared a love of books, which was probably why she'd left me the bookstore.

As a child, I'd read voraciously. Maybe I'd been a bit too much of a bookworm. I'd gotten so involved in some of the books I'd read that I could almost remember some of them coming true. It was probably just my memory fooling with me, but I swore that some of the objects from the books I'd read had appeared in my room.

Like that worn stuffed rabbit I'd had as a child and that favorite locket I had later on as a teen. It seemed like those had been identical to the ones in books I'd read, but I'd probably bought them in the store because they reminded me of the book—my selective memory just didn't remember actually buying them.

"I bet you never felt that way down south." Elspeth's words pulled me away from my thoughts.

I shrugged, wondering what this had to do with Lavinia's death. "Once you grow up, you lose that carefree, magical feeling you have when you're a kid."

"But, maybe you felt some of that magic when you came back here ... or shortly before you made your decision to come back."

My breath caught in my throat. Was Elspeth referring to my strange ability to see ghosts? Certainly, some might think that was magical although I thought it was just a pain in the butt. No, she was probably just referring to that 'coming home' feeling that I did experience when I finally made the decision to move back.

As if reading my thoughts, Elspeth said, "Well, it always feels like magic coming home. But Mystic Notch is special. Don't you feel it?"

She stuck out her hand, waving it back and forth. To my astonishment, a bright yellow and black butterfly drifted over, landed on her pinkie finger and flexed its wings back and forth in the air. Wasn't it too early in the season for butterflies?

I nodded and stroked Pandora's silky fur, mesmerized by the slow flexing of the butterfly's wings.

"Magic can be good," Elspeth said, turning her keen blue eyes on me. "But just remember, it isn't *always* good. There's always been an age-old battle between good and evil. One must be careful not to let evil get the upper hand."

She lifted her hand high in the air and the butterfly flew away. My head felt a little foggy and I took a deep breath. That was some strange stuff she was talking about.

My heart pinched with concern ... I hoped Elspeth wasn't getting dementia. She was quite old. I wrinkled my brow in thought—just how old was she? I realized I had no idea. She'd always been my grandmother's neighbor, since I was little. She seemed old even then, but that was from the perspective of a child.

The wind chimes tinkled softly in the corner of the porch and I glanced over at them, watching their bronze tubes rub together in the breeze. Elspeth would remember the bronzes being donated to the library, so maybe she would know who might want to steal them?

"Do you remember anything about Idris Bates giving bronzes to the library back in the sixties?" I asked.

Elspeth shivered and I realized it was getting colder out. "I don't remember anything about bronzes, but Idris Bates is one you should steer clear of."

Elspeth pulled her shawl tighter and stood up. "I'm getting a bit chilled. Would you like to go inside?"

"No, I'd better get home and rustle up some dinner. I just wanted to return your pie plate and carrier." I stood, dumping Pandora from my lap. She landed on the porch floor with a soft thud, then let out a muted "mew", shook herself and trotted over to the stairs.

Elspeth opened the door while I started down the steps after Pandora.

I turned around, walking backwards for a few steps. "Thanks for the pie, it was delicious."

"You're welcome. Be careful on the way home."

I turned around, waving to her over my shoulder, and followed Pandora into the woods.

"What was she talking about, Pandora?" I asked, glancing backwards over my shoulder at Elspeth's house. "All that magic talk didn't make much sense."

Pandora glanced up at me but kept trotting along beside me.

"Was she trying to warn me?"

"Meow!"

"Don't tell me magic has anything to do with Lavinia's murder ... I don't believe in that stuff."

"Oh, you don't?" Lavinia's ghost appeared beside me and I practically fainted. You'd think I'd be getting used to ghosts appearing out of nowhere by now, but it still startled me.

"Jeepers. Will you stop doing that?" I pleaded.

"What? Appearing? That's what ghosts do," Lavinia said, gliding along beside me. "Anyway, you were just telling your cat you don't believe in magic."

I frowned at Pandora. Had I become one of those crazy cat ladies who talk to their cats?

"Of course I don't believe in magic."

"Then I suppose you don't believe in ghosts, either."

I chewed on my bottom lip. Two years ago, I probably would have said I didn't believe in ghosts, but now with Lavinia's ghost gliding along happily beside me I could hardly say that anymore. Maybe just because I hadn't experienced magic didn't mean that it didn't exist. Maybe I should give more consideration to what Elspeth had said.

Did magic have something to do with Lavinia's murder?

As if reading my mind, Lavinia said, "So, are you making progress finding my murderer? I heard you telling Pepper about the embosser you found behind the library."

I glanced over at her. "You were eavesdropping?"

"Not really. I was just floating around in the back of the store and heard you."

I had no idea the ghosts floated around when I couldn't see them and it kind of creeped me out. "Then you heard about the navy blue fabric?"

"Yeeees."

"I found a navy blue cape in Ophelia Withington's closet."

Lavinia gasped. "You don't say? A cape? I remember it seemed like the killer was wearing a cape, but I only saw a shadow. So, why didn't you tell the police and have her arrested?"

Pandora let out a yowl beside me and Lavinia reached down to pet her, all the while gliding along perfectly beside me without even slowing down.

"Well, that's the problem. I can't really tell them I know about the cape, because I'm pretty sure they won't believe I talk to ghosts, and if I tell them I just went through her closet they might get mad. I need more proof." I thought about my visit to the church and how they didn't have any candles. Lavinia had said she'd been in town early to light a candle ... that's how she saw someone in the library in the first place.

"Lavinia, you said you were at the church lighting a candle that morning, but I stopped by today and there's no ca—"

"Ooops, gotta go." Lavinia cut me off and then promptly vanished.

I stared at the empty space where Lavinia's ghost was just seconds ago. Pandora looked up at me, and I swear she shrugged. Something fishy was going on at the church—why was Lavinia acting so secretive about it? Did it have something to do with her death?

My house came into view and I noticed clouds had rolled in, turning the sky as ominous as my thoughts. There were too many unanswered questions.

Why had Lavinia *and* Ophelia lied about the church? Had Lavinia really been murdered because she just happened across someone stealing the bronzes? And what was all this magic talk Elspeth was spouting?

I didn't know the answers to any of these questions, so I turned my thoughts to the one thing I could do—figure out a way to tip Augusta off to the navy blue cape hanging in Ophelia's closet.

Chapter Fifteen

The next morning, I wasn't any closer to figuring out how to tip Augusta off about the blue cape. Maybe the best course was to tell her I'd seen the fiber on the embosser and then let her know that Ophelia had a blue cape. I didn't have to mention that Lavinia had told me about a cape or that I'd searched Ophelia's closets. I could just pretend I'd seen Ophelia wearing it.

Of course, it would be better if I knew Ophelia's motive. I made a mental note to check in the library for the bronzes. If one was missing, then all I would need to do would be to find out who had it and I'd have the killer. Hopefully, I would see it in Ophelia's house. I didn't recall seeing one on my visit, but I guess if I killed a librarian and stole a valuable bronze, I'd hide it somewhere, too.

But first, I had to head out to Barry's and pick up those books. Lavinia's funeral was in the afternoon and I planned to catalogue some of the books at the store before that, so I threw on my jeans and a pink sweater, then tossed my black wrinkle-free polyester dress, black sheer nylons and pumps into a bag to change into later.

I usually didn't bother too much with my hair, but I tried to force the curls into waves that framed my face instead of the unruly red mop it usually arranged itself into. It was, after all, Lavinia's funeral and I wanted to look halfway decent.

Pandora and I did our usual morning routine of cat food and corn flakes, then got into the Jeep and headed out to Barry's.

The air was crisp, the light blue sky dotted with clouds. The heavy clouds had rolled out after the overnight rain, but at the edge of the horizon it looked like a new storm was coming. As I drove the mountain roads, I noticed the birds and squirrels actively foraging in the woods for nuts and seeds as they usually did before a storm. I kept watch on the sides of the roads for moose or deer. They often crossed the road at this time of morning and an accident with one of them could be fatal for either one of us, so it paid to keep one's eyes open.

There weren't many other cars out this early. I passed Myrna on her way into town, then turned on the road that led higher up into the mountains toward Barry's. The road was narrow and I noticed a familiar black pick-up truck coming down the other way.

Whose car was that? I squinted toward it and recognized the head of white hair. Bing Thorndike.

I raised my hand in a greeting, but he didn't seem to see me, his eyes focused on the road, which he was traveling down rather fast.

"I wonder where he's going?"

Pandora sneezed and hopped into the back, running to the hatch to stand up and look out the back window.

A few seconds later, I pulled down the lonely road that led to Barry's, then drove my Jeep up the gravel driveway and parked in front of his 1800s farm house. Next to the house was a big barn he used as his antique shop. The shop wasn't open yet, so he'd told me to come right to the house where he was holding the box of books for me.

I cut the engine, then turned to Pandora, who had hopped back into the passenger seat. "You stay here."

She narrowed her eyes at me. Then, as I opened my door, she shot out and ran onto Barry's front porch.

I slipped out of the Jeep, wincing in surprise as I landed on my bad leg. The pain had been getting much better and I'd almost even forgotten about it, but I must have twisted it or something, because it was throbbing now.

I rested for a few seconds, stretching my leg and wishing I had some *Iced Fire* to rub on it, then started toward the porch. A cloud passed over the sun, sending a chill into the air, as I stepped onto the old wooden boards. A light wind kicked up some of fall's leftover leaves and I watched them swirl around the steps in a circle.

Barry had put his screen door on already—or still had it on from last summer—I wasn't sure which. I wrapped my hand around the iron handle, thick with layers of green paint, and pulled it open with a squeak. Raising my fist, I tapped on the wooden door, my heart leaping in my throat when it swung open under the light pressure of my tap.

"Barry?" I peeked through the crack of the open door, not sure if he meant for me to just walk in.

He didn't answer, and I felt the roots of doubt spreading in my stomach.

"Hello. It's me, Willa," I said even louder.

"Mew!" Pandora looked up at me impatiently then pushed her way through the door, causing it to swing open. She trotted into the living room, sniffed the air, then headed toward the kitchen.

I stepped inside, my heartbeat drumming in my veins, uncertain of what I would find. The old, wide pine floorboards creaked eerily as I made my way through the living room.

"Barry, I'm here!" I tried one more time.

"Meeoww!" Pandora's howl quickened my pace and I rounded the corner to the kitchen at breakneck speed, my heart leaping in my chest as I skidded to a stop, right before stepping on Barry's body.

***

"Barry!" I squealed. He didn't move, and my first thought was how suspicious Striker was going to be when he discovered I'd found another body.

Then Barry groaned, which scared the crap out of me. Then I realized he wasn't dead and relief flooded through me. I knelt down beside him on the yellow linoleum floor.

"Barry, what happened? Are you okay?"

"Wha?" Barry tried to push himself up then fell back. He rose up on his elbows and shook his head, looking at me with unfocused eyes.

I took his hand. "I'm going to call nine-one-one."

"No, wait a sec." His voice was thick, but his eyes seemed to be focusing better. He sat up and rubbed his face with his hands. "What happened?"

Pandora sniffed his pant legs, then rubbed her face against his hip. He scratched her behind the ears.

"I have no idea. I came over to get those books and found you here on the floor." I looked around the old country kitchen. There was a box on the floor with various silver items in it. A silver candlestick, pie server and pitcher sat on the table next to a laptop. Nothing seemed out of place and it didn't look like there had been a struggle. "Did you pass out?"

He tilted his head, his eyes narrowed to slits. "You know, I'm not sure. I guess I must have."

He struggled to his feet and I helped him into a chair, then sat at the old pine trestle table across from him. Pandora took the opportunity to sniff around the room.

"Have you ever passed out like that before?" I asked.

He shook his head. "Never."

"Does your head hurt? Did you hit it on something?" *Or did someone hit him*, I wondered.

Barry touched the back of his head, then the sides. "Nope, doesn't hurt at all."

"We should call nine-one-one and have you checked out."

"No. I feel fine now. I'd rather call my doctor and make an appointment."

I narrowed my eyes at him. Folks up here could be stubborn and I hoped he wasn't just putting me off. "Well, if you promise you'll call ..."

"I will." He looked around the kitchen. "It's funny—I don't remember passing out, though."

"What *do* you remember?"

"I was in here, cataloguing the silver I bought at Dodd's auction." Barry gestured to the items in front of them on the table, then a shadow crossed his face. "Wait a minute. Someone came to the door ..."

The hairs on the back of my neck started to tingle and my leg throbbed. I remembered how easily the door had swung open when I arrived. It wasn't unusual for people to leave their doors unlocked in Mystic Notch, but Barry's door hadn't even been shut all the way—almost as if someone had left in a hurry and only loosely closed the door behind them.

"Who came to the door?"

"I'm not sure." Barry's forehead creased in concentration. "One of the Bates brothers, I think. No, everything is so fuzzy, I might be imagining that."

I remembered the way Bing was driving down the road, as if he was in a hurry. "Was it Bing Thorndike?"

"I don't think so. Now that I'm thinking about it, I'm not really sure anyone was here at all. I saw Carson Bates at the auction last night and my memory is getting confused."

"What was Carson doing at an auction? Surely they already have enough antiques at home." My mind drifted to the bronzes in the library. The Bates family had so many antiques they could afford to donate them.

"Apparently, Felicity sold off some stuff at a yard sale and he was looking to get some of it back. Old family heirlooms and such. He was going on about some books, quite insistent. Wanted to know if I'd come across them."

"Oh, right. I remember Derek came by the shop wanting to know if I had some old family scrap-books."

Barry laughed. "I guess Felicity needs to find clever ways to get at the Bates money. She always was kind of strange. Come to think of it Carson's kind of strange, too."

I nodded in agreement, looking around the room. "You're not missing anything?"

Barry glanced around, looked at the silver on the table and in the box. "Nope, everything is here. Now that I think about it, I'm sure no one came ... my memory's just a little screwed up. Anyway, I have that box of books for you over here." Barry retrieved a cardboard banana box from the pantry.

I noticed he was steady on his feet and my worry for him started to subside as I peeked into the box, eager to check out the books. An old leather-bound was on the top and my stomach flitted with excitement as I pulled it out.

Barry frowned at the book, then looked into the box. "That's strange. I'm sure I put the leather-bound on the bottom. I wanted to surprise you with the best book last."

"Oh?" I frowned, only half-hearing him, my attention riveted on the beautifully preserved book. My fingers caressed the soft leather as I carefully opened the front to look at the publishing information. The musty smell of old paper hit my nose and I closed my eyes to breathe it in. I loved that smell.

Barry pressed his lips together as he thumbed through the books. "Maybe I don't remember, though. I might have switched them around. I'm not remembering correctly because of passing out."

I set the book aside and looked into the box, pulling out some of the books and stacking them on the table.

"Is there anything good in there?" Barry asked.

I tapped the leather-bound. "This one is pretty good. It's not a first edition, but I could probably get a couple hundred for it."

"Good. I want to repay you for those silver nut dishes, so I hope there's something else good in there."

I picked some more books out of the box. "There are some great children's books here and a few classics that are always popular. I'll have to do some research to see if there are any rare editions, but I'd say I'll make a pretty penny. What do I owe you?"

Barry waved his hand in the air. "Forget about it. I only paid a couple of bucks at a yard sale."

"You sure? I took the buck from you for the silver dishes."

Barry laughed. "You can buy me a coffee next time we see each other at an auction."

"Deal." I pushed up from the table and grabbed the box, hefting it onto my hip. "I hope you're really feeling okay."

"Don't worry, I'm feeling fine." Barry wrestled the box away from me. "Let me take this to your car for you."

I followed Barry to the front door. Pandora was fervently sniffing the threshold and she looked up at me. "Meow."

"Yes, we're going now," I said.

I could have sworn she made a face. "Meeeooow."

"What is with your cat?" Barry asked.

"I have no idea. She's probably cranky because she misses her soft cat bed." We crossed the threshold and

Pandora gave me what seemed like an exasperated look before following us to the Jeep.

I took the box and loaded it in the back. Pandora hopped up on the tailgate and made her way to the passenger seat. "Well, thanks for picking these up. If you see any more, feel free to grab them. I'm woefully low on stock."

"Will do. You do the same for me. Anything silver at a reasonable price."

"Okay." I hopped into the Jeep and started it up while Barry made his way back into the house.

I drove toward town, feeling uneasy. Finding Barry lying on the floor had unnerved me. Pandora put a comforting paw on my thigh and I felt my heart surge. Could it be I was really getting attached to the fur ball?

"Doesn't it seem odd that a healthy young guy like Barry would pass out for no reason?" I said out loud, then realized no one was in the car except me and Pandora.

"Mew." Pandora nodded her head.

"But, if someone was there, surely Barry would remember. And if they hit him to knock him out, surely he'd feel the lump on his head, wouldn't he?"

I snuck a look at Pandora, but she merely gave me a blank stare

"And why would someone knock him out? It didn't seem like anything was taken. All his silver was there and the books were all in the box, although he did think the leather book had been moved."

"Mew."

"But, who would do that?" My mind drifted back to the truck I'd seen racing down the hill. Bing's truck.

"Probably just coincidence, right?" I turned to Pandora.

"Meow."

"I guess it's a mystery," I said to Pandora. "Probably has nothing to do with Lavinia's murder, though, and that's what I need to focus on today."

Pandora let out a string of meow's and, for a second, I thought it sounded like "*you never know.*"

I shut my mouth and focused on the road. Not only was I getting into the bad habit of talking to my cat, but now I thought she was actually answering me. I really did need to get a social life.

Chapter Sixteen

I parked in the small parking lot behind my store since I had the box of books to lug inside. I went in through the back and dropped off the books. When I finally got to the front, I could see Cordelia, Hattie and Josiah waiting outside with coffee mugs in their hands. I rushed to open the door for them.

"I was wondering if you were going to make it today." Josiah handed me a Styrofoam cup and I practically swooned with gratitude. The happenings out at Barry's had made me late for my morning caffeine fix.

"Sorry," I said between sips. "I had to pick up a box of books this morning and it took me longer than I expected."

"Oh, that's no problem," Cordelia twittered. I noticed she and Hattie were dressed in matching polyester pantsuits—Hattie's in lemon yellow and Cordelia's in lime green. They wore the same exact lemon and lime colored blouses underneath the jackets.

"Well, don't you ladies look nice," I said.

"Thanks," Cordelia answered for both of them. "Lavinia's funeral is today, you know."

"Yes, I'm going," I said, my attention captured by a light, misty swirl coming from the end of the biography row. Was it Lavinia listening in again?

"I imagine most of the town will turn out," Josiah said. "Everyone knew her from the library."

"Where's Bing?" I asked, suddenly realizing he was missing.

"Oh, he called this morning," Josiah answered. "Said he didn't feel good this morning and not to worry about him if he didn't show up."

I frowned at my coffee. He sure looked okay when I saw him rushing down the road. Then again, maybe he was rushing to the doctor's office.

"Did you find out any more about those bronzes?" Hattie asked.

"No. You?"

She shook her head. "Some of the old-timers remember them being donated, but no one knew they were valuable."

I caught a glimpse of Pandora trotting over to the biography row and watched her swat at the mist out of the corner of my eye.

"I was going to close up early today and check them out at the library before I headed out to Lavinia's funeral," I said.

"Good idea." Hattie nodded. "I'm sure the police must be looking at them by now."

"We don't even know if the police know about them." Cordelia turned to me. "Did you mention them to Augusta?"

I shook my head.

"Not yet." I'd been too busy snooping around in Ophelia's house.

"Well, you probably have work to do seeing as it's a short day, and I have to get home and start getting spiffed up for the funeral." Josiah started toward the door.

"Come on, sister. We need to get some tea over at Pepper's and then take a little nap before we go to Lavinia's service." Cordelia grabbed Hattie's elbow and they followed Josiah to the door.

Josiah opened it and gestured for the ladies to precede him. They stepped through, then turned back to me. "See you there, Willa."

I nodded and waved, then the three of them spilled out onto the street and the door shut, leaving me alone in the store. Well, alone as far as earthly inhabitants go, that is.

The swirling mist at the end of the biography row glided toward me, slowly forming into the shape of Lavinia. "So, you're going to my funeral?"

"Of course. The killer might be there. Maybe I can pick her out."

"Her?"

"My money is on Ophelia, although I have to admit I still can't figure out her motive."

"Oh yes, you found that blue cape. I remember that cape, now that you mention it. She used to wear that out a lot with Pete." Lavinia leaned in toward me. "Haven't seen her wear it since he died."

"So? You're not trying to tell me she wouldn't have been wearing it, are you?"

Lavinia shrugged. "I just think you might have blinders on here. Maybe you should consider some other suspects."

"I don't *have* any other suspects."

"Because you haven't been looking. It's never good to focus on one thing. Besides, my feeling is there may be more to this than meets the eye."

"What do you mean by that?"

"Maybe there are other forces at work."

"Other forces?" I scrunched up my face at her. Now she was starting to sound like Elspeth.

"Oh bother," Lavinia waved her hand in the air, making a swirly trail of misty goo that hung suspended for a few seconds before falling to the ground and evaporating. "What other clues do you have?"

"Well, Ophelia did say she saw a long, dark car speeding away from town that morning." My leg was starting to throb, so I turned back toward the front of the store where I kept a tube of *Iced Fire*. Lavinia floated along beside me, Pandora at her heels.

"See? Now, that's a clue you should be looking into." Lavinia suggested. "And what about the bronzes?"

"You know about those?"

"I overheard you talking about them yesterday. I had forgotten all about them until you mentioned them. They're downstairs, just like you said."

"How many are there?"

"Four. At first we had them on display upstairs, but then people's tastes changed and Western stuff wasn't as popular. We moved them downstairs decades ago," Lavinia said. "Do you think I stumbled across someone trying to steal them and they did me in?"

"Maybe." I plopped onto the sofa, then pulled up the leg of my jeans and rubbed some *Iced Fire* on my leg. Pandora came over to investigate, sniffed at my leg, yowled and ran to the back of the store.

Lavinia laughed. "That *is* a rather potent smell."

"Yeah, but it works wonders."

Two misty figures materialized before us—Franklin Pierce and Robert Frost—and they were both holding their noses.

"Iced fire? Will the world end in fire or ice? I know not, but either way I hope it doesn't smell like *that*," Frost said, pointing down at the tube.

Pierce and Lavinia burst out laughing at the poetry reference. I didn't think it was so funny. Did I really smell that bad?

"I heard you talking about bronzes, and I do say some are quite valuable." Franklin Pierce looked at us importantly. "In fact, I could boast that there were a few bronze busts made of me in my day."

"That's right," Lavinia said. "We have one in the library."

"I've had one or two made of me as well," Frost said, not to be outdone. "In fact, mine was so valuable it was stolen from its spot at Wichita State University some years back."

Pierce narrowed his ghostly eyes at Frost. "I heard that was a drunken prank."

Frost shrugged. "Whatever. Anyway, I dare say the scoundrel that killed Lavinia might have been after those bronzes. Money makes people do strange things."

Pierce nodded. "On that, I concur."

"Your theory on the bronzes could be a good one," Lavinia said. "But I don't think Ophelia would be breaking into the library to steal them. It's just not her style."

I had to admit, Lavinia was right about that. But I *wanted* to continue thinking it was Ophelia. Mostly because I didn't like her and if the killer turned out to be her then I wouldn't feel bad. Plus I had some good clues pointing to her and I knew there was a secret between her and Lavinia ... that secret might be the true motive.

On the other hand, maybe I *had* been ignoring other clues because I'd been so focused on Ophelia. Bing had been acting strangely ... did his odd behavior have anything to do with Lavinia's death? I certainly hoped not. Bing had been almost like a grandfather to me for as long as I could remember. I'd much rather the killer ended up being Ophelia.

And what about the weird thing with Barry this morning? It had looked like Bing was driving away from his house. Barry thought someone had been looking in the box of books ... but what would books have to do with anything?

I looked up and realized all three ghosts were staring at me expectantly.

"I plan to go to the library and see if the bronzes are there before I go to your funeral," I said to Lavinia.

"That sounds like a good idea," she replied. "But don't be so focused on one path that you are blind to the others."

"That's right." Robert winked at me. "Sometimes it's best to take the path less traveled."

"Well, I think we should be off." Lavinia linked her arms through the two men's elbows. "Shall we?"

They both nodded and the three of them disappeared, leaving me sitting on the sofa, blinking at nothing.

"Wait." The word tripped off my lips and fell into the silent room. I had wanted to ask Lavinia about the candles in the church, but she'd disappeared too fast.

I waved my hands at the empty space in frustration. I had been so sure the killer was Ophelia, but Lavinia had sprinkled my thoughts with doubt, and now I had to take some of the other clues more seriously.

That didn't mean I was going to drop Ophelia off the suspect list, though. I was still going to tell Augusta about that blue cape just as soon as I could. In the meantime, I'd just have to broaden my investigation to include some of the other clues ... even if it meant investigating an old friend.

Chapter Seventeen

More clouds had rolled in while I was in the bookstore and the somber atmosphere in the library echoed the weather outside. Lavinia's assistant, Myrtle, who, I supposed, was the new head librarian, sat mournful and lonely behind the big rounded desk.

I found myself thinking that if Myrtle *did* get the head librarian position, then she had benefitted from Lavinia's death. Standing in the doorway, I studied the short, bespectacled octogenarian. She must have weighed all of eighty pounds and I doubted she had enough strength to push Lavinia, never mind smash her on the head with the embosser. She was too short. And anyway, who would kill someone over a librarian job?

I walked into the library, nodding at Myrtle as I passed by. I'd changed into my wrinkle-free black dress and it swirled just above my knees while my heels made clickity-clack noises on the marble floor as I walked toward the back. I noticed the flag was at half-mast and Pierce's bust was draped with a black band. Apparently, they were taking Lavinia's death hard here.

I turned the corner to the back steps and a chill ran up my spine as I remembered finding Lavinia crumpled at the bottom of them. I hesitated a second, picturing the scene.

"Go on down," a voice whispered, startling me and almost sent me falling down the stairs. It was Lavinia swirling beside me. Why hadn't I just sent her over to look for the bronzes and saved myself a trip? She nodded pointedly at the stairs and I started down.

Stepping gingerly down the stone stairs, I turned right at the landing and walked into the main library area, my footsteps growing silent as the hard stone floor changed to carpeting.

The bottom floor of the library was like a maze. Tightly packed rows of ten-foot high bookshelves were laid out with barely three feet of aisle space between them. There were various sections and rooms off the main room that one could wander into. It seemed always to be void of other humans and entombed in silence—the massive amount of books and carpeted flooring absorbed most of the noise. I'd gotten lost down there more than once.

"Where are they?" I whispered to Lavinia. My question was met with silence.

I looked beside me, then turned to look behind me, scanning for any sign of a ghost. Nothing ... not a faint swirl of mist ... not even a drop of condensation. Figures she'd disappear when I needed her most.

I decided to do the search methodically, row by row. The most likely place to display the bronzes was at the end of the rows or in one of the many alcoves, so moving along the perimeter would be my best choice.

I turned left, then walked to the end of the row where I was met with another row of books.

"Okay, maybe the bronzes are at the other end," I said softly, just in case Lavinia was listening and might offer her help.

I started down the row, then noticed a little alcove off to the left. "Is it here?" I whispered.

I took the sharp corner and almost jumped out of my shiny black pumps. Standing in front of me was Sheriff Eddie Striker ... and he didn't look happy.

***

"Were you talking to someone?" Striker's gray eyes drilled into mine, then shifted to look behind me.

"Me? No." He was standing in front of a two-foot square alcove indented in the wall. I tried to peer around his wide chest to see what was in the alcove and caught sight of a mahogany pedestal ... was a bronze on top of it?

"What are you doing here?" he asked.

"What are *you*?" My hands fisted on my hips and my

brows dipped in an angry V. I felt like we'd been through this routine before. At least he wasn't pointing a gun at me this time.

His lips curled in that annoying half-smile and butterflies flittered in my stomach. I suddenly felt glad I'd made an attempt to tame my hair, and then immediately admonished myself for feeling that way. What did I care about looking good?

"Don't tell me you were coming here to borrow a book dressed like that." His gaze wandered from my face, down my body to my shoes and back up, lingering in some places longer than others.

I crossed my arms over my chest, feeling self-conscious about my clingy dress and scarred leg. At least the leg wasn't one of the parts where his gaze had lingered. It started to ache as if it knew I was thinking about it and I shifted my weight onto my right leg.

"What's wrong with what I'm wearing?"

"Nothing," he shrugged. "But I don't think you got all dressed up to borrow a book. You're up to something and my detective skills tell me you're here for the same reason I am."

"Oh? And what's that?"

Striker stepped aside to reveal what was on top of the pedestal ... a bronze statue of a cowboy on a bucking bronco in amazing detail. It was a deep chocolate color and I knew if I touched it, it would feel silky, but hard and cold. Which was exactly the same way Striker was looking at me right now.

"There are four of them," I blurted out.

"I know. They're all here."

"Are they really that valuable?" I asked.

"I just had an expert here and he said only one is original, but even the recasts are worth thousands." Striker glanced back at the bronze. "The library is moving them out today and putting them somewhere more secure."

"How did you find out about them?"

"Probably the same way you did. I'm investigating the case and got a lead. But see, there's a difference between me investigating and you investigating." He paused and fixed me with a serious look. "I'm a cop and you're not. So *you* shouldn't be following up on leads."

"I'm just curious by nature," I said weakly. "So you think someone was trying to steal the bronzes and Lavinia stumbled onto them?"

Striker shrugged. "That's one possible motive. But seeing as the bronzes are still here, it's not likely."

I frowned at the statue. "Why not?"

"Don't you think the thief would have grabbed at least one of them after going to all the trouble of clobbering Lavinia?"

"But what if he got scared off? Maybe he didn't have time." Maybe I had scared him off when I came into the library. An icy chill ran up my spine when I realized I might have suffered the same fate as Lavinia.

"Maybe." Striker sniffed the air. "Do you smell peppermint?"

I thought of the *Iced Fire* I'd doused my leg in at the bookstore and felt my cheeks grow warm. I shook my head and he frowned at the air.

"So, what other motives are you looking at?" I asked innocently.

Striker disarmed me with a full smile this time. It was the first time I'd seen him smile and I realized it was quite charming.

"Oh, no ... you can't get information out of me *that* easily." He shook his head at me. "Besides I don't want you running around investigating the other motives."

"I don't need *you* to give me leads." I tilted my chin up. "I have some of my own."

"I was afraid you were going to say that. I hope I don't have to arrest you to keep you out of trouble."

I narrowed my eyes at him, not knowing if he was joking or serious. He couldn't actually arrest me, could he?

"I don't think Augusta would keep me in jail." The truth was I *wasn't* sure that she wouldn't keep me in jail—she'd warned me many times about investigating.

Striker laughed, and I was annoyed to discover his laugh was actually pleasant. "I think your sister would agree. She doesn't want you getting caught up in anything that might get you hurt. It's funny—your last name suits you to a tee."

"How's that?"

"You take a lot of chances ... unfortunately those chances could end up getting you hurt."

I almost melted a little at the concern in Striker's eyes, but I really hated it when people tried to tell me what to do and I was more than a little annoyed that it was probably true that my own sister would let me sit in jail.

"Well, maybe if you and Augusta could find the real killer, I wouldn't feel the need to take those chances," I said haughtily then swung around and started to walk away.

"Hey, Chance," he called after me, and I half-turned looking over my shoulder at him.

"What?"

"You look nice."

I spun back away from him, my heart fluttering at the compliment. Okay, maybe he was being sarcastic, but he'd actually seemed sincere.

It wasn't like me to get all flustered when someone complimented me, and that made me mad. Should I say something? I couldn't think of a snappy comeback, so I focused on keeping my eyes straight ahead while I walked away.

Chapter Eighteen

Outside the library, the weather had turned downright gloomy. Dark clouds hung overhead and the air had turned chilly. The street was dry, but it smelled like rain.

I had a few minutes to kill before Lavinia's service, so I decided to pop in and visit Pepper at *The Tea Shoppe*.

The smell of herbal tea and cookies hit me as soon as I opened the door to Pepper's shop. The color scheme of light greens, pink and turquoise brightened the room, making me forget about the dismal weather outside. The scroll designs of the white cafe tables and chairs added whimsy to the old-fashioned setting. Petite chandeliers glittered from the ceiling, dazzling the room with soft light. The tables boasted crisp white tablecloths and napkins made from vintage fabric.

Pepper stood behind the counter at the far end of the shop. Behind her, a wide, tall shelf was stacked with various jars and bags, adorned with ribbons and filled with herbal tea.

Pepper greeted me with a smile and I started toward her, doing a double take when the person she'd been waiting on turned around.

Ophelia Withington.

I hesitated. Did I really want to talk to Ophelia? Pepper and Ophelia both stared at me expectantly and I realized I didn't have much choice. I slowed my pace, not so eager to get to the counter anymore.

"Hi, Willa," Pepper greeted me cheerfully.

Ophelia smiled at me. "Willa, so nice to see you again."

I raised a brow at her. It was?

The two other ladies turned their attention back to the purchase Ophelia was making. My gut twinged as I noticed they were laughing it up like old friends. Pepper put the purchase, which looked like a bunch of dried up leaves, twigs and sticks, into a crisp white paper bag stamped with the gold logo of *The Tea Shoppe* and handed it across the counter to Ophelia, who grabbed the two sturdy twine handles and turned to leave.

"You girls take care, now." Ophelia waved at us graciously as she sashayed out of the shop.

"What's up with her?" I frowned at Pepper.

"She wanted to buy some of the tea we brought to her the other day."

"She did?" I turned and looked at the door through which Ophelia had disappeared.

"Yes, did you notice how pleasant she was? She's such a dear, really." Pepper leaned across the counter and whispered. "I think my tea really helped her."

"Maybe." I was still suspicious of Ophelia, and to tell the truth, not too confident in Pepper's teas either. Pepper was beaming like a lighthouse, though, and I didn't want to crush her, so I plastered a smile on my face and tried to act enthusiastic. "That's great."

Pepper turned around and plucked various herbs out of jars she had sitting open on the counter behind her. She took a pinch of this and a twig of that, placing them all into a silver ball infuser.

"Sorry I can't go to Lavinia's service with you. Camilla can't come in today and I have no one to watch the shop," she said in between pinching and plucking.

"Oh, that's okay; I need to talk to Augusta anyway about you-know-who." I jerked my head toward the door Ophelia had just exited. "So I couldn't hang around with you anyway."

Pepper poured water into a teacup and then dunked the infuser in. "Oh, you still don't think Ophelia did it, do you?"

"Well, the evidence does point to her ..."

Pepper's lips were pressed in a thin line as she bobbed the infuser up and down, turning the water in the teacup from clear to a rich mahogany. "What about the other clues?"

I tapped my finger on the counter as I thought about the other clues. The bronzes hadn't been stolen, but that didn't mean someone hadn't been trying to steal them that morning. Ophelia mentioned she'd seen a big black car, but she could be trying to cast suspicion away from her. The blue fabric on the embosser might help provide physical evidence, but I knew from my crime reporting days I'd need something else to make that stick.

"I'm trying to figure out the best way to follow up on those," I said.

Pepper slid the tea across the counter to me and I picked it up, sipping it absently, my mind on the clues. Maybe Lavinia was right and I *had* been too focused on Ophelia. The truth was, I couldn't come up with a motive for her to be in the library or to want Lavinia dead ... unless it had something to do with the lies they had both told about the church.

My mind went back to my conversation with Emma at the church—she'd seemed secretive, too ... and what had she been holding behind her back? I made a mental note to investigate the church further.

"Don't you have to get going?" Pepper nodded at the green 1930s kitchen clock on the wall and I realized Lavinia's service was going to start in ten minutes.

"Yeah, I guess I'd better."

"I bet you'll run into Eddie Striker," Pepper teased in a singsong voice.

My stomach did a flip-flop and the teacup clattered in the saucer as I put it down. I felt my cheeks burn. What was up with that? Had it been so long since I'd had a date that even the mention of a cute guy made me act like a teenager?

And come to think of it, the abrasive, annoying Sheriff Striker wasn't even all that cute.

I faux smiled at Pepper. "Funny."

My stomach felt a little queasy as I turned and started toward the door, pushing thoughts of Eddie Striker out of my mind and replacing them with ideas on how to find Lavinia's killer.

By the time I got outside, I'd forgotten all about Striker.

My mind so focused on how to investigate the few clues I had, that I didn't even realize I'd sucked down the entire cup of tea.

***

The air had grown heavy with moisture and I wished I'd been smart enough to bring a raincoat. I realized ruefully that the time I'd spent that morning taming my hair had been in vain—the rain would make it go wild and it would re-arrange itself however it wanted.

I wrapped my arms around myself as I walked down the side street that led to the church. Lavinia's family had decided on a short graveside ceremony, so I skirted the perimeter of the church to get to the graveyard behind it.

The cemetery was on a hill with the older graves at the bottom and newer ones at the top. I could already see people starting to gather about three quarters of the way up and I picked up the pace, passing the old-fashioned gravestones with their strange etchings on the way.

A mist had formed on the hill and it hung low to the ground, creating a ghostly effect that I thought was quite appropriate for Lavinia's funeral. My leg started to ache halfway up the hill and I was limping by the time I reach the site where several mourners were already gathered.

Lavinia didn't have any children or husband left living, just two sisters, their frail bodies huddled around the hole in the ground that would eventually become the final resting place of Lavinia's earthly remains. Her sisters seemed genuinely upset and I had already decided they were too frail to be considered as suspects. Was there someone else here who could be the killer?

I scanned the crowd, recognizing most of the people. It had started to drizzle and I noticed most everyone wore a raincoat or trench coat. I automatically started checking to see if any of them were navy blue.

The hearse pulled up and the dark-suited pallbearers from Stilton's Funeral parlor slid out the casket and carried it to the grave. I half expected to see Lavinia's ghost sitting on top of it, but apparently she had better things to do than attend her own funeral.

Pastor Foley appeared at the head of the grave and started talking about Lavinia. I stood off to the side, trying to gauge people's reactions. If the killer were here, would they do something that gave them away?

Most everyone had his or her head bent in prayer. I caught the eye of Bing, standing off to the side next to Cordelia, Hattie and Josiah. Apparently, Bing had recovered enough to attend the service. He nodded and bent his head, staring at his hands that were clasped in front of him. I took note of the large trench coat he wore—in tan, not navy blue.

Movement further up the hill caught my attention. The hairs on the back of my neck prickled as I saw something scurry between gravestones.

A small, furry animal ran out from the woods, making a beeline for one of the large monuments.

I watched in fascination as more furry figures came out of the woods, darting behind gravestones and making their way closer. About fifty feet away they stopped, and I saw the head of a cat peek over the top of one of the stones. I recognized it as the large feral cat Pandora had the run-in with behind the library. Beside it, a tiny face peered around the edge of the stone—the small kitten with the torn-up ear.

The cats were playing in the graveyard, watching us warily, almost as if they were attendees at the funeral.

Pastor Foley rambled on and I noticed Augusta and Striker had pulled up in Augusta's black pickup. They got out quietly and stood on the other side of the street.

Striker's eyes scanned the crowd, much like I had been doing and probably for the same reason. My heart jerked when his eyes met mine and then narrowed in suspicion before he nodded slightly and continued scanning.

I tried to keep my attention on the crowd, looking for anything suspicious, but my eyes kept sliding over to Striker, who I almost didn't recognize in his dark suit. He towered over Augusta, who looked like a midget standing beside him in her black pantsuit. I guess they didn't want to scare off the crowd by wearing police garb.

Foley finished his eulogy and the crowd started to disperse. Bing turned and made a beeline for his truck. The cats scampered into the woods. I raced over to tell Augusta about Ophelia's cape and find out why both sheriffs were here before they drove off.

On my way over, I noticed that Ophelia had been conspicuously absent from the service.

"Hey, Gus, what brings you here dressed like that?" I nodded at Augusta's outfit, sliding a sideways glance at Striker.

"Oh, just, paying our respects, same as you," Striker cut in. His suit looked like it was tailor-made. Of course, it would have to be in order to fit his broad shoulders. The dark blue color highlighted his gray eyes, making them look like slate. He looked good ... almost as good as the chocolate donut hole Augusta had slipped out of her pocket and popped into her mouth.

"So, did you guys notice anything out of place?" I asked.

Striker was right about one thing. They were here for the same reason I was, but it had more to do with detecting than paying our respects.

Striker smirked at me and my stomach started to feel queasy. "Well, you know they say the killer usually shows up at the funeral."

"So you think someone who was here did it?" I asked.

"There is one person here who keeps suspiciously popping up in the investigation," he answered.

"Really? Who?"

"You."

I tilted my head and fisted my hands on my hips. "Surely you don't think—"

Striker raised a brow at me and smiled that damned dimpled smile. "You sure do seem to know a lot about it."

I felt fury race through my veins, took a deep breath and was about to ream him out when Augusta interrupted.

"Willa, he's joking." She looked up at Striker and popped a jelly donut hole in her mouth. "Aren't you?"

"Yeah. Mostly. But she does keep showing up everywhere ... almost getting in the way. I warned her we might have to arrest her for her own safety." He looked down at

Augusta. "Isn't that right?"

Augusta pursed her lips at me. "Yes, that *is* right. I've warned you before, Willa. Investigating on your own can be dangerous."

I shifted my weight to my right leg to ease the throbbing in my left and looked around at the dispersing crowd. Time to change the subject.

"Did you hurt your leg?" Striker asked, surprising me with the gentle tone of concern in his voice.

"Just remnants of an old accident," I said vaguely, hoping he got the hint that I didn't want to talk about it. Something flashed in his eyes—was that sympathy? I certainly didn't need his sympathy and I felt my stomach turn queasy again. I sure hoped I wasn't catching some kind of stomach bug.

"Anyway, we have to get back to work." Augusta opened the driver's door of the truck and Striker started around the back to the passenger side.

"Before you go, I have a lead I wanted to share." They both stopped and looked at me.

"What is it?" Augusta asked.

I bit my bottom lip. This might really get me in trouble with them, but I *had* to get them to investigate Ophelia's closet. "I couldn't help but notice the embosser we found in back of the library had a blue thread on it."

Augusta crossed her arms over her chest. "And?"

"Well, I happen to know that Ophelia Withington has a blue cape that looks like a color match ... and Myrna at the coffee shop said she saw Ophelia there that morning."

Augusta and Striker exchanged a look and I felt a spark of hope. Did they know something about Ophelia already?

"Also, I noticed Ophelia wasn't at the service today," I added triumphantly. Surely, her absence was a sign of guilt?

"Willa, that doesn't really mean anything," Augusta said.

"Yeah, but shouldn't you get a search warrant or something and match the fibers of the cape to that on the embosser?"

"We could, but even if they matched it wouldn't prove anything. That fiber could have been on the embosser before Lavinia was killed," Augusta said.

"And besides," Striker added, "we've already investigated Ophelia, and she has an alibi."

"She does?" My brows mashed together and I looked from Augusta to Striker.

"Yep," Augusta nodded. "An air-tight alibi. She was at the bank making a deposit and their security cameras have her time-stamped picture to prove it. According to the M.E., she was there at the exact time Lavinia died—Ophelia couldn't have killed her."

I stared at her incredulously, disappointment weighing my stomach down. I'd wasted a lot of time and energy chasing down the clues that pointed to Ophelia.

So, if Ophelia wasn't the killer ... then who was?

Chapter Nineteen

"I can't believe Ophelia has an alibi," I muttered to myself as I rolled my damp dress into a ball and threw it down on the floor in the tiny bathroom of my shop.

"Mew." Pandora pushed a paw under the door in agreement.

"I still think she's up to something." I slid on my jeans, then slipped the pink sweater over my head. A quick look in the mirror confirmed that the combination of humidity from the weather and static electricity from the sweater had made my hair frizz. I rummaged through the medicine cabinet and found an elastic band that I used to corral my shoulder-length curls into a ponytail.

Leaning closer to the mirror, I plucked out a white hair—darn things had been making an appearance in one spot at my temple and I was doing my best to avoid having a thick white stripe in my red hair.

I made my way out into the shop, turned the sign to 'Open' and brought the box of books I'd gotten from Barry to the counter so I could enter them in my computer program before I put them in their new temporary home on one of the bookshelves in the store.

Pandora slunk over and got busy sniffing and rubbing the side of her face on the box, stopping to stare up at me with round eyes every few seconds.

My mind wandered as I worked on the tedious data-entry.

"I wonder if Barry's strange fainting spell has anything to do with Lavinia's murder?" I asked out loud, squinting out into the store, hoping to see the swirly mist of Lavinia's ghost. I had questions for her.

"Meow." Pandora rubbed her cheek vigorously on the

now empty box.

"You're right, that's too farfetched. There's no way they could possibly be related."

Pandora let out a low "mew" swatting in the air at something only visible to her.

"Right, I thought so. But what about Bing? Why was he driving down the road so fast?"

Pandora made a sneezing noise and shook her head.

I pictured Bing in his truck, so intent on driving that he didn't even notice me coming the other way.

"He was driving away from Barry's ... or was he driving *to* some place?" I'd seen him driving on the road that went past the turnoff to Barry's, but that didn't mean he'd been at Barry's. He could have been coming from further up the mountain. And where had he been driving *to*?

I finished cataloguing the books and hit the button to print the price tags for each book. The printer hummed to life, startling Pandora and causing her to jump sideways and hiss at it. I couldn't help but laugh ... that printer got her every time.

I grabbed the stickers and shoved them in my back pocket, then lifted a stack of half the books and headed out toward the row of bookcases where I kept the children's books, Pandora trotting obediently at my heels.

"There's still that strange secret at the church that Lavinia and Ophelia both seemed to share. Even though Ophelia has an alibi, I think that's worth checking into."

I hoped Lavinia would show up and clue me in herself, but ghosts hardly ever appeared when you wanted them to. They liked to show up when they were least expected and scare the bejesus out of you, instead.

I slapped the price tags on the children's books and slid them into their slots, then headed to the section where I kept the classics.

"So, the only real clues I have are the black car Ophelia saw and the bronzes," I said, still talking to Pandora, who I'd like to think was hanging onto my every word.

"Meow," she said as if to encourage me.

"I have no idea how to start investigating the big black car." I put the prices on the three books I had left in my arms and found a place for each of them on the bookshelf. "As for the bronzes, I know exactly where to start."

***

I closed up the shop promptly at five, locking Pandora inside despite her belligerent howls. Guilt ate away at me as I headed out of town and up the mountain, but it was for her own good. She never stayed put in the car and I just couldn't bring her with me this time. I was going to start my inquiries about the bronzes at the source and I didn't need to be chasing my cat around the Bates estate if she decided to take off and run wild.

The humid fog had turned to drizzle. Dark clouds rolled in along the valley as I drove the winding mountain road to the Bates mansion. I passed the cutoff to Barry's and wondered if I should check in on him in case he had had another fainting spell, but thought better of it. He was a grown man and didn't need me looking after him.

The Bates mansion cut into the side of the mountain—an immense old estate. The granite house boasted four stories, complete with million-dollar views from every window. An imposing black iron gate surrounded the main buildings. Thankfully, it was open and I drove my Jeep up the crushed gravel driveway, which circled around a giant fountain in front of the house.

I couldn't say the house was friendly. The gray stone was cold and the oak door with black, cast-iron hinges looked like something you'd see in a medieval castle. A black iron fence ran along the roofline, its posts stabbing angrily up into the sky.

I slid out of the Jeep, my stomach twisting and my leg burning as I approached the gothic wood door. I pushed the doorbell and felt a twinge of panic.

Maybe I should have planned what to say first?

The door glided open and a man in what looked like butler garb stood in front of me.

"Yes?" He quirked an eyebrow at my frizzy hair and faded jeans.

"I'd like to talk to Idris Bates, please."

He stiffly stepped aside and gestured for me to enter.

"I'll see if Mr. Bates is available," he said, then glided off down the hall.

Did the Batesesreally have an honest to goodness butler? As I looked around the foyer, the word 'opulent' came to mind. The shiny, travertine marble floor reflected light from the giant crystal chandelier that hung in the center of the round entryway. To the right, a carved mahogany staircase wound its way upstairs. To the left, French doors led into another room. In front of me was a round table with a whopper of a flower arrangement on it.

Were those flowers real? I reached out to touch one...

"Can I help you?"

I jerked my hand back and spun around to see Derek Bates standing behind me.

"Hi, Derek," I smiled. "I was actually coming to talk to your grandfather."

"Grandfather is napping. He's rather old, you know. Needs his sleep." Derek's words were clipped, not like his usual friendly self. Maybe the Bates family didn't like it so much when people came to see them unannounced.

He stood in the same spot, making no move to invite me in further. I tilted my head to the side to see the room behind him. It seemed to be some sort of library. He raised a brow and looked at me expectantly.

I cleared my throat. "I ... umm ... I was coming to ask your grandfather about some bronzes he donated to the library many years ago."

Derek narrowed his eyes. "Bronzes ... oh, yes. We have a big collection. I don't remember him donating any to the library, though."

"It was in the sixties, before our time," I said, remembering that even though the family trait of a thick streak of premature gray in Derek's hair made him *seem* a lot older, he was really only a few years my senior. He would have been a kid when the bronzes were donated.

Derek chuckled, relaxing a bit. "Ahh ... what did you want to know?"

"I was wondering if your grandfather would remember who was around at the ceremony when he donated them."

"Why would you want to know that?"

"We think someone might have broken into the library to steal them and I was trying to figure out who might have known they were there. They were moved downstairs years ago and I think most everyone has forgotten about them."

"We?" Derek's smile faltered and he looked at me funny. "Are you working with the police or something?"

I shifted uneasily. "Well, no, it's just—"

Crash!

We both swiveled toward the sound that had come from the room on the left.

Derek's face took on a look of panic and we started toward the room, only to be met by Felicity Bates, Derek's mother, who swept out of the room in a long black dress, wide sleeves flowing around her wrists.

She stopped short at the sight of us, a look of surprise on her face.

"Mother, what's going on?" Derek's voice was tinged with panic.

"Oh, dear, I was just practicing ..." Felicity let her voice trail off as she noticed me standing there. "What is she doing here?"

My brows shot up. She didn't sound very friendly. "I just came to ask—"

"She was just leaving," Derek interrupted me, grabbing my elbow roughly and jerking me toward the door.

"Was that a crash?" Derek's brother Carson came running down the stairs, taking them two at a time. "Mother, are you okay?"

"Yes, but there's a mess in there." Felicity pointed toward the french doors and Carson looked in that direction, catching sight of me on the way.

"Oh. Hi, Willa." His eyes went to Derek's hand on my elbow and he shot me a confused and apologetic look.

"Hi, Carson—" Derek cut off my words by tugging me forcefully in the direction of the door. I turned, looking back over my shoulder at Carson, then craning to see what was going on in the room beyond the French doors. I couldn't see a thing, though, and the movement was making my leg hurt.

Derek pulled the front door open with one hand, and shoved me through the threshold backwards. Inside the house, I could see Felicity gesturing wildly to Carson about something. Carson was making soothing motions, I assumed to calm her down. I looked at Derek.

"Hey, wait. I—"

Derek slammed the door in my face and I stumbled backward. I could feel my bad leg starting to give out on me and I braced for the impact of the cold, granite steps, screwing my face up into a grimace and flapping my arms.

But, instead of feeling the sharp edge of the hard rock steps, I found myself in a pair of strong arms. I twisted around, my heart thudding against my rib cage and looked straight into the steely gray eyes of ... Eddie Striker.

Chapter Twenty

"What are *you* doing here?" I asked through pain-clenched teeth.

"I should be asking the same of you." He looked up at the imposing oak door. "What did you do to him to make him slam the door on you like that?"

"Nothing," I said, although not with as much indignation as I'd intended, because I was distracted by his woodsy, leathery smell. I probably smelled like medicinal peppermint.

"So, what *are* you doing here?" He gently eased me back up onto my feet.

Instead of answering, I gingerly tested my left leg, wincing in pain as I increased the pressure.

Striker's face turned hard. "Did he hurt you?"

"No, the weather makes it act up." Of course, Derek's forceful exit didn't help any, but I didn't need Striker getting all macho and defending me.

"Where does it hurt?"

I pointed to where it hurt, an area on the side, running mid-thigh to mid-calf. He knelt down, poking and prodding at the area, causing me to yip and groan at various decibels, depending on how much it hurt. He was surprisingly gentle, but even the slightest pressure was painful.

After a few minutes, he stood up. I shook my leg out, surprised to find it actually felt a little better.

"The muscle is knotted up. Probably from previous damage ... you mentioned you were in a car accident ..."

"Yes, a little over a year ago."

"You should be getting massages, maybe even acupuncture." He looked down at my leg. "That would help it heal quicker and give you less pain."

"Oh, thanks." I wasn't sure what to say. Why was he suddenly being so nice, and how did he know so much about muscle pain?

His head was tilted, still looking down at my leg. The drizzle had stopped and the late afternoon sun made an appearance from behind the clouds. I noticed how the angle of the light accentuated his chiseled features, making him look dangerously handsome. My stomach started to flip-flop uncomfortably and I took a step away.

"You didn't answer my question." Striker's eyes followed me as I slowly backed toward my car. "What were you doing here, and why was Derek throwing you out?"

"He wasn't actually throwing me out." I pressed my lips together, puzzled as to why he did throw me out. "There was a crash in one of the rooms and I guess they needed to clean it up."

Striker looked at me like he didn't believe me.

I half-shrugged and spread my arms. "I know it sounds weird, but it's true. Why are you here?"

"Police business."

No kidding. I wondered if he was following the same trail that I was. "About the bronzes?"

Striker narrowed his eyes at me. "Maybe."

We stood there staring at each other for a few electrically charged seconds while I decided whether to keep badgering him for information or just leave.

He must have been thinking the same thing, because he said, "I get the impression you're not going to stop looking into this. Maybe it would be best if we compared notes. How about we meet back at the *The Mystic Cafe* in say ... fifteen minutes?"

Compare notes? Since when did the police want to let me in on their investigation? He must have thought I had some information he could use ... but maybe he had some *I* could use.

My pulse kicked into high gear and I heard myself say, "Sounds good. I have to go back to town before I go home anyway."

"Okay, I'll only be a few minutes here. Order me a small

coffee. Black." Striker turned to the door and I hobbled to my Jeep, wondering if I'd just accepted an invitation that was finally going to give me a break in the case ... or that would lead to our first date.

***

I found a parking spot on Main Street between my shop and the Mystic Cafe. Glancing over to the bookstore, I could see Pandora glaring at me from her cat bed in the window. Her displeasure was obvious in her slitted golden-green orbs and I wondered if she'd demonstrate it to me by leaving a hairball on my purple sofa ... or worse.

It was just a little after five and the cafe was fairly empty. I chose a booth near the back and sat facing the door. I ordered Striker his coffee and one for myself, along with a roast beef and melted Swiss cheese on an onion roll. I was hungry.

Striker strolled in just as the sandwich appeared on the table.

"Roast beef and Swiss?" He eyed the sandwich before taking a sip of the coffee I'd shoved over to his side of the table.

"You want half?" I raised my brow at him and slid the sandwich toward him.

"No, thanks." He watched me smear some horseradish from the condiment dish on the sandwich and take a bite. I suddenly felt self-conscious, my face flushing—probably from the horseradish. I swallowed and the food sat like a leaden lump in my stomach.

"So, what have you got?" I asked.

"You go first."

I shrugged. "I don't really have anything. My best guess is that it has something to do with the bronzes."

"How did you find out about the bronzes, anyway?"

"Josiah Barrows, the old postmaster mentioned it. He remembered when they were donated." No way was I going to tell him Lavinia had verified that.

"So that's why you were at the Bates'?"

I shrugged.

"And how did you happen to be behind the library, conveniently finding the murder weapon?"

"Aha! So that *was* the murder weapon."

Striker nodded. "We found Lavinia's blood on it. But how did you even know to look there?"

I narrowed my eyes. I didn't like how this was going. It was starting to feel more like an interrogation than sharing information. So far, it was all take and no give.

"I actually wasn't there because I thought I would find a murder weapon. At that time, I didn't even know Lavinia had been murdered. I was looking for my cat," I said, then tried to turn the tide so I was the one getting information instead of giving it. "So, you were at the Bates mansion because of the bronzes, too? That must mean you think the same thing I do."

"Not necessarily. But I have to follow every lead."

I took another bite of my sandwich. A string of cheese dribbled down my chin, causing the corners of Striker's mouth to curl up in an alarmingly charming grin. I swiped at the cheese with as much dignity as I could. "Have you and Augusta come up with any other clues, besides the embosser and the bronzes?"

Striker studied me, probably deciding if he could trust me. I stared back with my most earnest look. It must have worked, because he said, "We did find some gray hairs clutched in Lavinia's hand."

My brows shot up. "Gray hairs? You mean like from an old person?"

Striker shrugged. "Or a young person with gray hair."

My eyes immediately looked up at my hairline where those pesky white hairs were starting to appear. I noticed Striker looking, too.

"Mine are white," I said.

Striker laughed. "You hardly have any—this was a clump."

"So you think she grabbed onto the killer's hair?" I made a mental note to ask Lavinia about that.

"It's possible."

"Maybe it was her own hair. She did have gray hair." Like half the town, I thought, as I looked around the half-empty cafe noticing most of the patrons were senior citizens.

"It's not a match with her hair." Striker rubbed his chin. "Unfortunately, the forensics lab here doesn't have all the latest equipment, so we couldn't tell much more about it. Augusta sent it out for more analysis, but that's going to take a while."

Striker watched patiently while I polished off my sandwich. He'd given me a clue and now I supposed I should reciprocate.

I wiped my mouth with the brown paper napkin. "Ophelia said she saw a long, black car speeding away from town that morning."

Striker's left brow lifted a fraction of an inch and I realized with satisfaction the he hadn't known about that.

"You talked to her?" he asked.

"Yep. She said she saw the car after she did her banking." I paused. "Didn't you say she was at the bank at Lavinia's time of death?"

Striker nodded. "I suppose that could have been the killer making a hasty get-away. Did she see who was driving?"

I shook my head.

He pressed his lips together. "Hmm ... well that's something to keep in mind, anyway."

"It doesn't seem like there's much to go on." My words were weighted down with disappointment. How were we ever going to find Lavinia's killer with these skimpy clues? "I mean, there are so many people that each of these clues could point to."

"I know it seems that way." Striker finished his coffee and made 'getting ready to leave' motions. "But the trick is to find the one person that all the clues fall into place for. So, if you come up with any others, let me know ... it could mean the difference between narrowing things down to the real killer or not."

He pushed up from the table and I followed suit, all the while thinking about the big ring Lavinia had said the killer was wearing. Glancing around the shop, I picked out several people who had big rings on. Like the other clues, it wasn't much to go on and I couldn't tell Striker about it anyway ... not unless I wanted to tell him I talked to ghosts. Which I didn't.

Striker swiped up my sandwich wrappings and paper cup and tossed them in the trash, then opened the door for me and we stepped out onto the street. It was dusk, but the clouds had dispersed and a setting slice of sun glittered cheerfully on the street.

"I'm parked down there." Striker pointed down the street, and I could see the police car a few spots past my shop.

"I have to go that way, too," I said, starting in that direction. "Gotta stop in the shop and pick up my cat."

Striker fell in beside me and I was suddenly awkwardly aware of his presence. He was walking kind of close, which, I noticed with annoyance, made my pulse skitter.

I tried to stick to business. "So, what made you share the clues with me?"

Striker snorted. "It was obvious you weren't going to stop looking into this, so I figured it was better to join forces so I could keep an eye on you."

"Are you sure it's not because you thought I had some clues you couldn't figure out?" I teased.

Striker laughed, and his wide smile made my stomach flip. We'd reached my shop and he stopped beside me on the sidewalk as I dug around in my pocket for the key.

"Well, thanks for sharing." I turned toward the door and he touched my arm, turning me back to him.

I looked up at him. His face had turned serious. "Willa, I want you to be very careful on this. Don't go off on any investigations without talking to me first. We still don't know the motive for this killing and ... well ... it could be dangerous."

His gray eyes turned dark with feeling and my mouth dried up.

"Okay," I croaked.

His grip on my arm tightened and he pulled me a little closer. I held my breath, my stomach tossing the roast beef sandwich around like the *Andrea Gail* in *The Perfect Storm*.

Was he going to kiss me?

He dipped his head toward mine.
And that's when I threw up on his shoes.

Chapter Twenty-One

"You threw up on his shoes?" Pepper stared at me, her emerald eyes as big as saucers.

"Yeah, I think I might be coming down with something, although I feel fine now." I pressed my fingertips against my temple in a futile attempt to make the painful pounding stop. "Other than this headache."

"What happened?" She busied herself behind the counter of her shop, getting things ready for the morning crowd, glancing up at me every so often as I told her how I'd run into Striker at the Bates mansion. Her lips quirked up in a smug smile when I told her about how we'd had coffee and exchanged clues.

"His car was parked up here, so we were standing in front of my shop while I dug out my key." I leaned across the counter, lowering my voice even though no one was in the shop to hear me. "It almost seemed like he was about to kiss me."

I had Pepper's full attention. "Really? What happened?"

"I felt sick and threw up. Lucky thing he was wearing police issue shoes—they should clean off pretty easily."

"That sounds awful ... what did he do?"

"He was a complete gentleman," I said, grimacing at the memory. "He acted like it was nothing. But I noticed he didn't seem like he wanted to kiss me anymore after that. It was humiliating ... took me three Appletini's to recover.

"Maybe that explains the headache I have this morning. Funny thing though, I didn't feel sick when I was drinking those."

"Oh, dear," Pepper wrung her hands together, her eyes darting around the store as if she was trying to avoid eye contact with me.

"Pepper, do you have something to tell me?" I didn't like the way she was *not* looking at me.

"Well ..." she wrinkled her face. "I was only trying to help ..."

"You didn't!" My heart dropped—had she given me one of her crazy herbal teas thinking she could fix me up with Striker?

Pepper nodded. "I guess maybe I shouldn't have made it a love-*sick* potion."

"Pepper! I asked you not to." I gave her a 'how-could-you' look, but the stricken look on her face made it impossible for me to be too mad at her. "So now I'm going to get sick whenever I see Striker? Did you give him a tea, too?"

"No, he didn't need one." Pepper tucked a long strand of hair back into the swirly bun on top of her head. "But don't worry, I'll make this right."

I felt a moment of panic as she turned around and started throwing herbs into an infuser. Her previous tea had made me throw up, who knew what this one would do to me?

I held my hands up in front of me. "Oh, no. I'm not drinking another tea from you. Not with the way those things backfire. Besides, it's probably for the best if I throw up every time I see Striker. The last thing I need is to get involved with him."

Pepper stopped what she was doing and turned to me, her hands on her hips. "Actually, Willa, I think you do need to get involved. How long since you and Jake split up?"

My heart twisted at the thought of my ex-husband. Our break-up hadn't been pretty. "Two years."

"Right, so it's about time you got interested in someone else. I'm not saying you have to marry the guy, but go out and have some fun, at least. You don't want to end up a shriveled up old maid, do you?"

Did I? The thought didn't seem all that unappealing if it meant I could avoid another heartbreak.

"I'll think about it," I said, mostly to get her to stop talking about it. "I did find out a new clue, though."

"When you were at the Bates mansion?"

"No, but come to think of it something strange happened there."

"What?"

"I was talking to Derek and there was a big crash. Felicity came out of a side room and then everyone got all weird and Derek rushed me out of there."

Pepper's brow creased. "Did Felicity drop something?"

"I'm not sure." I chewed my lower lip trying to remember what she'd said. "She said something strange ... that she was practicing something. Maybe she does karate or something."

"Or maybe she was practicing her spells and they went haywire." Pepper looked at me out of the corner of her eye as she dunked the infuser in the hot water she'd poured into a teacup.

"Spells?" I wrinkled my face up at her.

"Some people say she's some kind of witch." Pepper slid the teacup across the counter at me and I eyed it suspiciously, wondering what might happen to me if I drank it. Would it cure me of throwing up on Striker, or simply cause me some other embarrassing malady?

"That's silly." I lifted the cup to my lips and sniffed. It smelled like mushrooms and dirt. "There's no such thing as witches."

Pepper simply shrugged and I thought back to my conversation with Elspeth about magic. I'd never been one to believe in magic or paranormal activity ... but that was *before* I started talking to ghosts.

"So what was the clue?" Pepper prompted.

"Oh, right." I took a tentative sip of tea. It was actually pretty good. "Striker said they found some gray hairs clutched in Lavinia's hand."

"From the killer?"

"Presumably. Although, we don't know for sure. I plan to ask Lavinia if she remembers pulling her killer's hair."

Pepper's lips curled in a triumphant smile. "So the killer couldn't have been Ophelia."

"No, you were right. It's not her. She has an airtight alibi." I told her about the time-stamped photo of Ophelia at the bank.

"I knew it!" Pepper snapped her fingers. "So now you can narrow your list down to just people with gray hair."

"We don't know that hair was from the killer, and anyway, that still leaves quite a long list of people."

"Yeah, but I have a good idea where you can start." Pepper thrust her chin in the direction of the window.

Outside, Cordelia, Hattie, Bing and Josiah were strolling by, Styrofoam coffee cups in hand, on their way to my bookstore. My stomach dropped as I realized they all had gray hair.

***

I jogged the short distance from Pepper's shop to my bookstore where Bing, Cordelia, Hattie and Josiah were huddled together in conversation outside my door. Could one of them be the killer?

Of course not … I hoped. These people were my friends. I'd practically grown up with them. It just wasn't possible one of them had killed Lavinia.

"Hey, Willa," Bing said as they parted to let me open the door.

We filed inside and Hattie handed me a coffee. I leaned against my front counter, watching them settle on the purple sofa as I sipped the coffee slowly. The tea that Pepper gave me had already given me a boost and I didn't need the caffeine as much as usual.

"That was a lovely service for Lavinia yesterday," Cordelia said.

"Did you go, Willa?" Hattie raised a white brow at me.

"I did," I answered. "I saw you over on the side, but you guys left and I had to talk to Augusta about something."

"Oh?" Bing glanced up from his coffee. "About the murder?"

"Sort of." I didn't want to get into the whole thing about how I'd suspected Ophelia now that she'd been cleared.

"Seems to me that anyone who would be so bold as to try to steal those bronzes must have some big money problems," Hattie said.

Cordelia nodded. "I imagine the police are looking into that."

"Well, I hope they're making some progress," Hattie said. "It's disturbing to know there is a killer in our midst."

"*Are* they making progress?" Josiah asked, his eyes boring into mine.

"I'm not sure. You know how little Augusta tells me." I chewed on my bottom lip. Josiah had been the postmaster his whole life. Surely, he didn't make a ton of money in his retirement. And he was one of the few people that remembered about the bronzes and knew their value.

My stomach clenched. Surely, I wasn't suspecting Josiah ... was I? I caught myself looking at his hands to see if he wore a big ring. He didn't ... at least he wasn't wearing one *today*.

Bing closed the plastic tab on the lid of his coffee and stood up. I noticed that he *was* wearing a big ring. His Magician's Guild ring—he always wore it. I reminded myself that lots of people wore big rings, especially class rings and rings from organizations.

"What if it wasn't the bronzes? What if they were after something else?" Bing said. His eyes held mine and I got the impression he was trying to tell me something. Or warn me.

Cordelia, Hattie and Josiah swiveled their faces toward Bing.

Cordelia's forehead took on another layer of wrinkles. "What else would they be looking for? The only other thing in there is books."

"That's right," Hattie said, pushing herself up from the couch. "Unless there is something else of value that the killer knows about and we don't."

Josiah tilted his head. "That could be. Seems like this is getting to be more and more of a mystery."

"It sure is," I said.

Cordelia and Josiah stood up and the four of them made their way to the door.

"See you tomorrow, Willa," Cordelia said.

"Bye," Hattie turned and waved.

"See ya," Bing nodded.

"Later," Josiah said as he shut the door behind him, leaving me alone in the bookstore.

Well, almost alone ... Lavinia's ghost swirled into view as soon as the door was firmly shut.

"So, how was my funeral?"

"It was nice. I'm surprised you weren't there." I got to the bottom of my coffee and tossed the cup in the trash.

"Oh, it's kind of tacky to show up at your own funeral." Lavinia looked at me as if she was surprised I wasn't up on the latest ghost etiquette. "So how does it look on finding my killer?"

"Well, it wasn't Ophelia," I said.

"Oh, that's too bad." Lavinia made a face. "I mean, I figured it wasn't, but still, I would have liked it to have been her. We didn't get along."

"But I did find a new clue that I need your help with."

"Oh?" Lavinia's ghostly brows swirled upwards.

"The police found some gray hairs clutched in your hand. They think you might have pulled them from the killer," I said. "Do you remember pulling out the hair of the person that pushed you?"

"Let me think ... I was walking toward the back of the stairs. I saw a shadow, then felt the pain in the back of my head. Then someone pushed me, right at the top of my back ... I flailed my arms, grabbing out for anything to keep from falling." Lavinia looked up at the ceiling, screwing her face up in thought. "Yes! I remember reaching out and grabbing on as I was falling. I heard a grunt. A few hairs ripped out. And then I fell."

A prickle of excitement rippled through my stomach. "You heard a grunt? Did you recognize who it sounded like?"

Lavinia shook her head, her shoulders drooping. "No, sorry. It was just an odd grunt. It sounded like a man, though ... most definitely a man."

"Well, I guess that narrows it down some." My head was starting to throb and my leg was aching. I glanced at the clock, my stomach sinking when I realized the day was just beginning. I made a mental note not to drink so many Appletini's on a work night.

"Willa?" Lavinia pulled me out of my thoughts.

"Yes?"

"I don't want to rush you, but I feel it's urgent that you step up the investigation."

I felt a tinge of annoyance. Who was *she* to be so pushy? "Oh, sorry I'm not investigating fast enough. I do have a business to run, you know."

"There's no need to get snippy. I'm simply telling you this for your own good."

"My own good? What does *your* murder have to do with my good?"

Lavinia looked confused. "I'm not sure, but ever since I died, I get these feelings and that's what I feel. Besides if you want to get rid of me, you need to find the killer."

I pressed my lips together and stared at her. I sure *did* want to get rid of her. Having ghosts pop up when you least expected them was annoying. It was enough just to have Frost and Pierce lurking in the store. They didn't seem like they were ever going to leave, and I didn't want to add any more perpetual ghosts to the mix.

"You have all these clues now and you *were* a top notch crime journalist," Lavinia pointed out. "How hard can it be to figure out who it is?"

"Right. Should be child's play," I said, feeling a sinking sensation in my stomach. "All I have to do is find a gray-haired man wearing a big ring and a blue cape that has financial trouble *and* doesn't have an alibi for the time you were killed."

Chapter Twenty-Two

The day went by quickly and I pulled into my driveway that night, exhausted from my Appletini hangover.

As usual, Pandora raced me to the farmer's porch, stopping short at a large box that blocked the path to the door.

"Mew!" She looked up at me as if it was the most important box in the world.

"What is that?" I bent down to read the note on top of the box.

Willa, here are the books I picked up for you - Enjoy! Maggie.

With everything that was going on, I'd forgotten that Maggie had the books for me. She must have returned from her buying trip and dropped them off. I made a mental note to call her and thank her as I opened the door and pushed the box inside.

Glaring at the bottle of vodka on the counter, I rummaged in the fridge for supper. I didn't have much, but managed to dig up a jar of jalapeños, shredded cheese and spaghetti sauce. I piled them on top of a toasted English muffin and then set it under the broiler to melt the cheese while I filled Pandora's bowl.

I pulled the muffin out from under the broiler before I caught the house on fire and settled at the kitchen table to eat it. My leg had started aching again. I grabbed some *Iced Fire* and rubbed it in while I waited for the muffin to cool.

Pandora sniffed in my direction, made a sour face, then trotted over to the box of books where the smell must have been more to her liking, judging by the way her nose was getting familiar with it.

I took a bite of the muffin, savoring the contrast of the creamy melted cheese and the spicy hot jalapeño. The muffin was toasted perfectly to add just the right amount of crunch.

I thought about my clues and suspects as I ate, my spirits sinking as I realized I didn't really have much of a list.

The killer had worn a cape or loose coat and had a big ring and gray hair.

A long, black car had been seen racing out of town that morning.

Valuable bronzes were in the library, so the motive could have been financial.

Who needed financial help? Maybe that was the best place to start. But the killer also had to have had means, motive and opportunity.

I hated to suspect my old friends, but Bing and Josiah both knew the value of those bronzes. Bing had said he didn't remember they were in the library, but he had been acting suspicious and it was weird that I'd seen him driving so strangely when I was going to Barry's. Once again, I wondered if Barry's passing out had anything to do with this case.

Both Bing and Josiah had gray hair. Bing wore a large ring. I didn't know if Josiah or Bing had a navy blue cape, but Bing certainly had lots of capes he used for his magician act.

I knew they were both in the area that morning because I'd seen them at my shop. Could one of them have killed Lavinia and then been so cold as to join the rest of us for coffee only an hour later?

I sighed in frustration. I hated the thought it could be one of them, but I had to explore all the angles.

"Mew." Pandora must have really liked that box because she had hopped inside and was pawing around at the books.

"Hey, don't mess those up." I pulled the box closer to me and peeked inside. The books looked interesting and I needed something to take my mind off the murder investigation.

I reached in and pulled out a book, turning it to look at

the cover. *Gone With the Wind*. I opened it eagerly looking for the publication information. Most copies of the book weren't worth much, but if it was a first edition, it could be worth a lot. Just my luck, it wasn't.

I put it on the table and reached back down into the box. Pandora tried to slow me down by jumping in and out of the box while I was trying to pick a book out.

I grabbed one book that was longer than the others were, making a face when I realized what it was. A photo album. They were virtually worthless—no one wanted to buy someone else's photos, but they *were* kind of fun to look at.

Pandora must have liked it because she rubbed her face on the edge as I flipped it open. I turned to the first page and my heart skipped. Staring me in the face was a younger version of Idris Bates.

I flipped through the book, which must have been twenty years old. There were pictures of a smiling Felicity and Gardner Bates—Derek and Carson's father—in happier times. There were pictures of Derek and Carson in their twenties, and a nice picture of Idris, Gardner, Carson and Derek all with their hands on a plaque. I squinted at the picture ... it looked like a family crest. Something about the picture niggled at my mind, but before I had too much time to think about it, Pandora distracted me by jumping into my lap and pawing at the book.

"Hey, don't rip the pages." I pushed her away and she jumped back to the ground with an angry meow, then resumed her box sniffing routine. I remembered Derek had come by the bookstore looking for family scrapbooks and albums his mother might have sold by mistake at their yard sale—this must have been one of them.

I'd have to take a trip up to the Bates mansion and return it. Maybe this time and I could talk to Idris about the bronzes. My natural curiosity was piqued about Felicity and the big crash that had made Derek rush me out of the house. Maybe I could find out what, exactly, she'd been practicing.

I put the photo album on the table and looked through the rest of the box to see if there were any more Bates scrapbooks or albums. I didn't find any, but I did see some interesting books that looked to be very early editions.

I picked one out and settled back in the chair, excitement causing my pulse to pick up speed. Early books were rare and could be worth a lot of money. I opened the book, carefully fingering the thin, yellowed pages. I could see foxing—brown stains of water damage—on the edges. That would affect the value, but the book had gorgeous, hand colored plates inside that would make up for it.

Pandora got bored with sniffing the box while I was studying the book. She trotted over to the living room and started to bat around one of her cat toys. The toy made a familiar jingling noise that stirred a memory, stealing my attention from the book I'd been studying.

I'd heard that noise somewhere else recently—where?

It came to me in a snap. Emma had been hiding something that made a similar noise behind her back at the church.

Emma had gray hair.

Emma had mentioned the church's desperate need for money.

Lavinia had some sort of secret that had to do with the church.

"Could Emma be the killer?" I said out loud.

"Meow!" Pandora went crazy, throwing the ball up in the air and pouncing on it. It was almost as if she was trying to tell me something. Too bad I had no idea what that something was.

"It doesn't seem like she would be the killer."

"Mew." Pandora stopped her antics and stared at me. I picked her up and cuddled her in my lap, stroking her soft fur.

"Little old ladies don't clobber other little old ladies and push them down the stairs, do they?"

Pandora answered by purring and kneading her razor sharp claws into my arm.

I didn't know what that meant, but I did know one thing ... I was going to pay Emma a visit and find out why both Lavinia and Ophelia had lied about lighting candles at the church and what—if anything—that had to do with

Lavinia's murder.

Chapter Twenty-Three

The next morning, I contemplated my plan of attack over peanut butter toast. I wanted to visit Emma at the church and find out Lavinia's secret and I also wanted to take the photo album to the Bateses and, hopefully, to find out about the bronzes.

The problem was that I didn't want to leave the shop closed too long. I'd been opening late, taking a long lunch and leaving early a lot lately and I didn't want to put customers off. Lavinia might have been murdered, but I still had to earn a living.

I decided to visit the Bateses during lunch and the church later in the afternoon. I didn't usually get too many customers after three, so I'd close early and still be able to get to the church before Emma went home for the night.

I finished my toast, eyeing Pandora who was lounging lazily on the sofa in the living room. It was probably best for me to leave her here, since I'd be in and out of the shop all day.

I opened the drawer where I kept the catnip and Pandora immediately jerked her head up, her eyes slitting open and zoning in on the drawer. She leaped down from the couch and padded over.

I took a pinch of dried herbs out of the catnip bag and sprinkled it on the floor. She sniffed, then made a gleeful meow and threw herself on her back, rubbing and rolling in the pile of herbs.

I stuffed one of her favorite toys full of the catnip and threw it. She sprang up, pouncing sideways and sliding into the wall, then scurried over to the toy, grabbing it in her mouth, tossing it in the air and catching it.

Satisfied that she was happily distracted, I grabbed the

Bates' photo album and made a run for the Jeep.

***

I got to the bookstore late and the regulars were waiting for me outside. I let them in and we had the usual conversation. Bing stayed behind when Hattie, Cordelia and Josiah got up to leave.

"I was wondering if you've gotten any good books in." Bing craned his neck to look behind the counter where I usually stacked the new books. "I'm starting up a collection of old leather-bounds. The older the better."

"Well, I got some books from Barry and there were a few old ones in there." I pointed toward the aisle where I kept the older books. "All my older ones would be over there."

"Great." Bing headed in that direction. He was an avid reader and liked to compile collections of antiques and then, eventually, sell them off. I guess it was an interesting way to make money out of a hobby.

The morning was filled with a whirlwind of customers and Bing must have left without a purchase as I never saw him again. I was distracted, waiting on customers and anxious to close up for lunch and get out to the Bates mansion.

I took the opportunity of the lunchtime lull to close up shop so I could take the photo album up to the Bates'. We didn't have drive-thrus in Mystic Notch, so I had to settle for eating a packet of cheese crackers that I picked up at the gas station.

I was just finishing the last one when I pulled into the Bates' crushed gravel driveway. The crackers settled like lead in my stomach as I looked at the foreboding mansion, remembering how Derek had rushed me out the last time I was there.

Maybe I wouldn't be welcome?

Glancing at the photo album on the seat beside me, I realized that was silly. Of course I would be welcome—Derek wanted the photo album. He'd made a special trip to my shop to ask about it.

Still, I felt the tingle of nerves bloom in my stomach as I

walked up the steps. The four-story mansion loomed over me, sucking all the sunlight out of the day.

It was chilly and grew even cooler in the shadow of the house. A shiver tickled my spine as I pressed the fancy white porcelain doorbell.

I waited.

The sound of the bell echoed through the house, but no one came to the door. Where was the fancy butler?

Maybe I should give him more time. The house was gigantic and if he was at the other end it would take a while to get to the door.

I waited, tapping my fingertips on the soft leather of the photo album.

No one came.

Impatience spread through me. My leg started throbbing. Was no one home? I'd come all the way out here and I hoped it wasn't a wasted trip.

I backed down the steps and looked up at the house. No signs of life. Sighing, I turned back toward the driveway when a movement over by the garage caught my eye.

Was someone there? I remembered Derek liked to tinker with cars. I took off in that direction.

The gravel crunched under my feet as I approached the garage, which was almost as big as my house. Made from the same granite block as the mansion, it had two stories and four garage bays. Three of them were closed, their green wooden doors blocking what was inside. The fourth stood open, revealing a white 1960s Triumph convertible.

I approached tentatively, wrinkling my nose at the smell of oil and metal. It was dark inside and I didn't see a soul. What was that movement I'd seen?

"Hello?" I ventured.

Clunk.

"Ouch!"

Derek slid halfway out from under the Triumph on a dolly. Rubbing his head, he frowned at me from his upside down position, then recognition lit his face.

"Willa! What are you doing here?" He slid all the way out, stood up and brushed the dirt from his blue mechanic's outfit.

"I thought you might like this." I held out the photo album and he pulled a rag from his pocket, using it to wipe the grease off his hands before taking the album.

A smile formed on his lips as he leafed through the book. "Well, I'll be..."

A noise came out of the dark recesses of the garage, startling both of us. Derek swung around toward it. Carson appeared, seemingly out of nowhere, a boyish grin on his face.

He casually crossed the other bays toward us, his hands in his pockets. My eyes had adjusted to the dark and I noticed a car occupied each of the bays. A Mini-Cooper in one, a pickup truck in another, and a long dark sedan, almost like a limousine in the last. I remembered seeing Felicity being chauffeured around by a driver and noticed some dark chauffeur's coats and caps hanging on knobs at the other end of the garage. Must be nice to have money.

"Carson, jeez, do you have to sneak up on us like that?" Derek closed the album and glared at his brother. I wondered if they didn't get along ... they always seemed to before.

"Hi, Willa," Carson said, ignoring his brother, his gaze falling on the photo album. "What's that?"

"An old family photo album I came across in my travels. Thought you guys might want it."

Carson came closer.

"Let's see." He held his hand out and practically had to wrestle it away from Derek. "I hope we didn't rush you out of here the other night ... mother can be a little overzealous in her ... umm ... experiments.

"What kind of experiments is she doing?" I felt my brows creep up my forehead. Experiments?

Derek shot a look at Carson, who was busy flipping the pages of the photo album.

"Oh, yoga and stuff ... you know." Derek waved a hand dismissively.

"These are great." Carson held the book up with one hand spreading the pages apart to show the picture of the two brothers with their father and grandfather. "Look at this great picture of us with Dad and Grandpa. Cripes, this album must be twenty-five years old."

"Yes, well, we don't need to keep Willa. I'm sure she's busy." Derek snatched the book away from Carson, who looked hurt.

"Where'd you get it?" Carson asked.

"It was in a box of books I acquired."

"Were there any other books of ours in with it?" Carson nodded toward the house. "Mother sold off some of our collection of older books and we'd like to get them back."

I shook my head. "There weren't any other photo albums or scrap books in there."

"Where's the box? Could we take a look?" Carson asked.

I frowned toward my car. "Well, I guess so..."

"Great!" Carson took off toward the car and Derek and I followed.

I opened the back hatch and the empty cargo bay reminded me that I'd been in such a hurry to rush out while Pandora was occupied with the catnip that I'd left the box at home. "Oh, sorry guys ... I left the box at home."

"That's okay. We don't need those old books." Derek's eyes darkened as he looked up at the mansion. "We have enough stuff in there. The photo album is one thing, but forget about all those old dusty books."

Derek steered Carson back toward the garage and I remembered I wanted to talk to Idris about the bronzes.

"Hey, I was wondering if I could ask your grandfather about those bronzes," I said. "I knocked on the door but no one answered."

Derek scowled up at the house. "Grandfather is very ill. We're not entertaining visitors in the house."

"Oh, okay." I felt disappointed about the bronzes, but maybe I could find out more about Felicity. "Maybe your mother remembers?"

"Mother?" No, I doubt it. She doesn't take much of an interest in that stuff." Derek reached into his pocket. "Thanks for bringing by the photo album. What do I owe you?"

I flapped my hand in the air. "Forget about it. I couldn't sell it to anyone else, anyway."

"Great. Then thanks for stopping by." Derek turned

around, dismissing me, and I watched the two of them walk back to the garage.

I had no choice but to get in my car and drive away, disappointment following me like a black cloud.

As the stone mansion grew smaller in my rear view mirror, I got the funny feeling that there was something strange about the Bates family, and it wasn't just because their house looked like it should be in a horror movie.

Chapter Twenty-Four

I took a detour on my way back to the bookstore. I wanted to get the box of books I'd left at home so I'd have some new stock for the store.

Pulling into the driveway, I trotted up the farmer's porch steps and opened the door, expecting to be greeted by an angry Pandora.

The box sat on the kitchen table, right where I'd left it. I hefted it up against my hip, noticing the odd silence in the house.

"Pandora?"

Silence.

She must be really mad. I pictured her silently glaring at me from the living room sofa, or maybe hacking up a hairball on my bed.

I peeked into the living room. No cat, just the sun glinting off the paperweight, which reflected the books from my bookshelf on its curved surface.

Putting down the box, I went over to get the one thing that would bring her running—a can of cat food.

I popped open the top. Usually, the sound would entice her from even the most remote part of the house, but this time she didn't come.

I made a lot of noise putting the food into a bowl, but still no Pandora. Glancing over at the cat door, I realized she must have gone out.

"Well, I'm sure she can take care of herself," I said to no one as I picked the box back up and headed for my Jeep.

The books shifted in the box on the seat beside me as I drove to the bookstore. I probably *should* let Derek and Carson look through them before I stocked them on my shelves. I knew there were no more photo albums or scrapbooks, but some of the books were ancient and if they'd had a book in a collection, it should probably go back to the family.

I didn't have time to go back there now, though. I wanted to open the shop for the full afternoon and hopefully make up for all the time I'd been taking off.

I parked in my spot behind the shop and dragged the box inside, setting it down behind the counter. Potential customers were already peering in the windows, so I hurried over to unlock the door and turn the sign to 'Open'.

Customers filed in immediately and I enjoyed a busy afternoon with almost record sales. Unfortunately, I didn't have any time to look at the books in the box or call the Bateses. I'd been so busy, I didn't even notice it was past five p.m. when the steady stream of customers died down.

The approaching dinner hour emptied the streets and I closed up shop, taking the chance to sneak away and visit Emma over at the church. I doubted she was the one that killed Lavinia, but she did mention she needed money and she *was* hiding something. If nothing else, maybe I could find out what secret Lavinia and Ophelia shared.

***

The white doors of the church loomed in front of me. They were big, standing about twelve-feet tall. And they were locked.

Oversized brass latches adorned the front. I pulled and tugged on them, but the doors wouldn't open. Did the church close? I thought it was always open.

I turned away from the doors, my shoulders slumping. I was batting zero in my investigation today—I hadn't been able to find out anything about the bronzes and now I wouldn't be able to talk to Emma, either.

"Mew."

I turned to my left and recognized the ginger-colored cat Pandora had had the altercation with behind the library. Come to think of it, I'd seen the same cat at Lavinia's funeral.

I crouched down and put my hand out.

"Here, Kitty," I crooned, trying to lure the cat over.

The cat looked at me with disdain, then turned toward the woods, walked a few steps, then turned back to look at me again.

"Meow."

The cat swung around and headed toward the woods again, pausing a second to look back over its shoulder at me, almost as if it was trying to get me to follow it.

Should I?

I hesitated on the church steps, trying to remember what was in that direction. I knew the church owned a lot of land in addition to the piece I was standing on where the church was built and the large parcel behind it where the cemetery was. The wooded area the cat was heading into was also part of the church property, but hadn't been developed yet.

The cat was at the edge of the woods now, looking back at me.

"What the heck," I said out loud, and started into the woods after it.

The dense woods blocked out most of the late afternoon sun and a damp chill settled on me as I followed the cat. Surprisingly, my leg didn't hurt. I hoped it was finally getting better.

The cat was following a path and we hadn't walked far when a rustling sound to my right caused my heart to jerk. I whipped my head toward it. Just another cat. I breathed a sigh of relief as I recognized the gray tiger cat as one that had been behind the library when I'd found the embosser.

I kept following the orange cat while the gray tiger kept pace over to my right, but at a safe distance. Just when I was starting to wonder if I'd made a mistake, an unkempt building appeared. It looked like some sort of storage building—large, with a door on the front but only one window on the side.

We were about ten feet away when the door opened slowly. My breath caught in my throat as Emma backed out of the building.

Emma whirled around, leaving the door open behind

her.

"What are *you* doing here? This is church property!" Her voice rose in a pitch of anger ... and maybe even a little anxiety.

Stainless steel bowls clanked together in her hands and I leaned sideways to see into the building behind her.

She stood her ground, legs firmly planted as if she was guarding Fort Knox. What was in there? A stash of crucifixes? Frankincense and Myrrh? What could possibly be so important in a church storage shed ... and what was with those bowls?

Elspeth appeared in the doorway and I sucked in another surprised breath.

"Elspeth?" My brows mashed together as I stared at my neighbor. What was *she* doing here?

"It's okay, Emma," Elspeth said sweetly. "Willa is a friend."

Emma eyed me dubiously as she stepped aside.

"Not many people know about this place." Elspeth held out her arm, beckoning me closer. "We try to keep it secret, because there are some that would do us harm. Your grandma was a big supporter, though."

"Supporter?" Apparently, I'd been reduced to one-word questions.

"Yes," Elspeth's radiant smile lit her face as she stepped aside. "Come on in and I'll show you."

***

The windows on either end let filtered light into the dim interior. It took a few seconds for my eyes to adjust. When they did, I stared in wonder.

"Cats?" I raised my brows at Elspeth.

The building must have been about sixteen by twenty feet. The entire perimeter was stacked with wooden platforms loaded with straw. Bales of hay were strewn about. An occasional wooden kindling box lay on the floor. A row of stainless steel bowls holding cat food and water lined the far end.

Cats lounged around the perimeter. Several of them ran

off as I entered. Others remained lounging, peering at me warily, coiled to spring up and run if I came too close. A few ignored me altogether. I recognized a couple of them from the day behind the library.

"These are feral cats," Elspeth said. "As you can see, we have quite a few that we try to keep warm and fed."

I crouched down, trying to coax one over.

"Most of them won't go near humans." Emma crouched down beside me, apparently warming to me now that she knew I had Elspeth's stamp of approval. She stuck out her hand and clucked.

A ball of black and white fur darted out from behind a bale of hay. It was the small black and white kitten with the tattered ear. She came over to Emma and licked her hand, then eyed me tentatively. I held my hand still and she ventured over, letting me pet her behind the ear.

"The friendly ones like her," Emma nodded toward the kitten as she scampered back behind the hay bale, "we try to adopt out to a good home. The others are too wild to adopt, so we provide shelter and food for them here."

Now I knew where Elspeth had acquired her growing collection of cats.

"Why in here?" I asked.

Elspeth and Emma looked at each other. Elspeth's face grew sad.

"Unfortunately, there are some who would harm our cause," Emma said.

"Really? Why?" Being an animal lover myself, I couldn't imagine who would oppose feeding starving animals.

"Some people in this town think the feral cats are dirty and will drive away the tourists that come to spend money," Emma said.

"So we hide back here." Elspeth looked around the room. "We've had to move the operation to different buildings three times in the past few years."

"And there's been some from the 'opposition' that come sneaking around the church trying to find the location. That's why I might have seemed a bit unfriendly to you in the church the other day." Emma looked at her feet.

"That's understandable," I said. I remembered the jingly

object she'd been hiding behind her back. It had been a cat toy! That day, Emma had also said Lavinia donated to our causes. "Did Lavinia know about the cats?"

Emma glanced at Elspeth who nodded.

"Yes, she came twice a week to feed them and helped us out financially. In fact, she was here the morning she died," Emma said.

That explained why Lavinia lied about the candles—she was protecting the cats. Did that also explain why Ophelia lied?

"Would Ophelia Withington be one of the opposers?" I asked.

The look on Emma's face gave it away. "That woman! I hate to speak ill of anyone, but she was one of the worst ones. Once Pete died, it became an obsession with her. Pastor Foley discovered her skulking around the church ... she isn't a member, so I assume she was trying to figure out where we sheltered the cats. She said they got into some of the empty houses she was trying to sell and brought down property values—she wanted them all to be euthanized!"

My heart twisted as I looked at the cats. No wonder I didn't like her. Sure, she had seemed nicer since she'd been a victim of one of Pepper's teas, but who knew how long that would last? Besides, anyone who wanted to euthanize animals just because they brought down property values was no one to be friends with in my book. I found myself wishing, once again, that Ophelia was the killer.

Ophelia had been in town that morning, trying to find the cats. She'd provided an airtight alibi for the time of Lavinia's murder, but what if Emma had seen someone else in town that morning? She was out and about early enough and it was worth asking.

"Emma, was there anyone else around that morning ... the morning Lavinia died? Maybe someone else who was trying to uncover the cat shelter?"

Emma pressed her lips together. "The Bates family is another one of our opposers. At least, most of them are. I've seen that woman sniffing around in the woods trying to find the shelter, but not that morning. *That* morning I saw her son in that chauffeured car they come around in sometimes."

"Which son? Derek?" I'd known both Derek and Carson since we were little kids and found it hard to believe either of them would be cat-haters.

"I think so. Yes, it was Derek. I saw him sneaking around here early in the morning around six. I avoided detection by hiding behind a tree," Emma said proudly. "It was weird, though, because later on ... about seven ... I was all done with the cats and getting coffee at the cafe when I saw someone run out of the woods on the other side of the street—about a hundred feet up from the library—and jump into that fancy chauffeured car the Bateses have. It must have been him, but I have no idea what he would have been doing all that time."

"Maybe scouring the woods on both sides for the shelter?" Elspeth offered.

Emma shrugged. "Maybe. I'm just glad he didn't find it."

"But that would be a good sign. If he had to look on both sides, it means they don't really know where the shelter is now," Elspeth said.

"But you're sure you saw him?" I asked.

"Oh, yes. I wasn't that far from him in the woods, and who could miss that big old car they have?"

The car must have been the same one Ophelia had seen. I'd seen the car myself earlier that day in the garage. There was no question ... Derek had been in town at the time of Lavinia's murder. Should I add him to the suspect list? The only problem was, I wasn't sure if he met any of the other criteria. His family was rich as anything, so he certainly didn't need money.

I thought back to earlier in the day ... had he been wearing a ring? No, I was sure he hadn't been. Since Lavinia had mentioned it, I'd programmed myself to look at everyone's hands and I was sure I would have noticed.

But the truth was, he had been speeding away from town that morning. The only question was ... had he been speeding away in frustration because he couldn't find the cat shelter, or had he been fleeing because he'd just committed murder?

Chapter Twenty-Five

Pandora woke from a long sleep, stretching her legs out lazily. She slitted one eye open. Where was she? Rolling on her back, the soft blanket underneath cushioned her while she watched a rectangle of light play on the plywood floor.

Opening both eyes, she remembered chasing the mouse up into the attic where she'd promptly fallen asleep on the old blanket. The blanket had been Anna's and she often came up here to feel closer to her previous human. It comforted her.

But now it was time to get up—she knew she'd been asleep for a long time. Catnip always made her so tired. And hungry.

She rolled onto all fours, pushed her front paws out in a stretch that elongated her back, then shook and trotted downstairs.

The smell of savory salmon feast tweaked her nose as she approached the stairs. Had Willa come home? Her heightened senses told her the house was empty now, but she did vaguely remember hearing Willa call for her while she was sleeping.

In the kitchen, she had her answer. Willa had been here and conveniently filled her cat dish. It looked like her training of the human was beginning to pay off.

Sticking her tongue out tentatively, she licked the top of the food. It was a little dry indicating it must have been sitting out for a while. Normally, Pandora would turn her nose up at such an insulting meal, but she was unusually ravenous, so she dug in to the mound with gusto.

A glow in the living room caught her attention. It was

that thing *again—the globe on the coffee table that was apt to glimmer at odd times. She tried to ignore it—thinking it quite impertinent that it thought it could summon her so easily.*

Her eyes kept sliding over to the living room as she ate. So once she was done, she licked her paws, washed her face and then made her way over to see what the thing *wanted.*

Pandora slinked over to the coffee table, approaching it from the side, her gaze intent on the orb. It sparked with color, drawing her closer. She stood on her hind legs, reaching her front paw out tentatively to bat at the sphere.

Now that she was eye level, she could see what she thought were things moving inside. Movement like that was something no cat could resist and she leapt onto the coffee table—something Willa would not approve of—to get a better look.

She looked down into the orb, her eyes growing large, the pupils turning to thin slits as she stared inside.

There was *something in here ... it looked like the inside of Elspeth's barn. Pandora could see the other cats gathered around. They looked up at her from inside the ball and she had an irresistible urge to go join them at the barn ... she knew something was very wrong.*

***

It took only a few minutes for Pandora to run through the woods to the barn. The other cats were inside, just as she'd seen in the paperweight.

"What took you so long?" Otis admonished.

"I was sleeping." Pandora sat down and flicked her tongue over her back, washing herself as if she hadn't a care in the world. "Did you want something?"

"Things are coming to a head and we must keep the evil ones from getting what they seek." Inkspot's baritone rumbled from atop a hay bale.

Pandora wondered why he had to always be so vague. What evil ones and what were they seeking? "And...?"

Pandora didn't like the way the other cats were all looking at each other, as if they knew something she didn't and were afraid to tell her.

Snowball trotted over and sat beside her. "We think your human may be in danger."

Pandora's stomach twisted. "What do you mean?"

"Willa has the key ... they will try to take it from her," Truffles purred.

"What key?" Pandora wracked her memory ... had she seen Willa with a key?

"That's not important now. They're coming for it and we must come up with a plan to protect her," Otis cut in.

Pandora shot to her feet. Willa was in trouble and she had to help her. "What do you mean? Where?"

"I've got intel that leads me to believe they are going to Willa's house tonight," Tigger spoke up from the back of the barn.

Tonight! Panic clutched Pandora's heart. She had to get home and save Willa!

"Thanks!" Pandora turned and sped toward the barn door.

"Wait! We must form a proper plan!" Inkspot yelled after her.

"There's no time!" Pandora shot back.

"Impetuous fool will get herself killed." She heard Otis's disapproving tone as she shot into the woods.

Ignoring his words, she raced toward home as fast as she could, stopping only long enough to sharpen her shivs on the bark of a tree—she had a feeling she might need them to be razor sharp tonight. Her feline instincts were on high alert. Trouble was coming and she'd have to do whatever she could to stop it.

Chapter Twenty-Six

After talking to Emma and Elspeth, I stopped in at *The Mystic Cafe* for supper. I wasn't up for another English muffin jalapeño pizza and I didn't have anything else at home. Pandora would be mad, but I'd left the food out for her at noontime, so at least she wouldn't go hungry.

I sat by the window, watching the sunset and eating an Italian sub. If what Emma had said was true, I should add Derek to my suspect list. He was in town at that time, so he had opportunity ... but did he have motive?

So far, I had been operating on the theory that the killer was after the bronzes for financial gain, but what if there was another motive? I wondered if the police had come up with anything else, which made my thoughts turn to Striker.

I hadn't seen him since I threw up on his shoes and I wondered if he had been avoiding me. Chances were he probably never wanted to see me again.

"Easy come, easy go," I muttered to myself as I tossed out my sandwich wrappings and headed to my Jeep.

It was dark by the time I pulled into my driveway. The pitch-black moonless night enveloped my car as soon as I shut the headlights off. Ever since I'd reached my mid-forties, my eyes had been taking longer and longer to adjust to the darkness and tonight was no different.

Which was why I didn't notice anything wrong with my door until it swung open on its own when I tried to insert the key.

***

I stared into the dark interior of my house, adrenalin

shooting through my veins.

Was someone in there?

I strained to hear even the slightest noise, but the house was silent. Grabbing the baseball bat I kept next to the door, I inched my way in, flicking the light switch, then immediately lifting the bat behind my head, ready to swing at anything that came at me.

The house was empty. Or at least the kitchen was.

I'd left in a hurry. Maybe I hadn't closed the door fully?

I crept further into the kitchen where I could see into the living room and the heart-thudding scene turned my legs to jelly and answered my question.

The living room was a mess!

My large floor-to-ceiling bookcase had been pulled away from the wall and rested on its back on the floor. Books lay strewn in piles around it, their formerly pristine pages torn and creased. The cushions had been tossed from the sofa and chairs and lay about the room.

My heart thudded against my ribcage as I ran back to the porch, my fingers tapping Augusta's number on my cell phone.

Even though I was sure no one was still in the house, I sat on the porch and waited for Augusta to arrive. It didn't take long and within ten minutes, I was back in the living room with her, my stomach sinking at the sight of my ruined book collection.

"Did they take anything?" Augusta frowned at the overturned bookshelf.

I studied the pile, the feeling of being violated blooming in my gut. "Impossible to tell."

"What about the rest of the house?"

"I haven't looked. I saw the mess in here and called you right away."

"Okay, let me check it out." Augusta headed toward the stairs, peeking first into the dining room on the other side, and then headed up.

I was about to follow her when another car pulled into my driveway.

Striker.

He jumped out of the car, bounding into the kitchen. My

stomach lurched and I wondered if he was thinking about the last time he saw me—when I threw up on his shoes.

He didn't seem to be holding that against me now. He rushed to my side and it seemed like he was going to hug me until he stopped short, just inches away. Probably trying to keep his shoes at a safe distance.

"Chance, are you okay?" My heart warmed at the concern in his eyes.

I ran my hands through my curls. "Yeah, I'm fine. I came home and found my living room in shambles."

"Let's see." He led the way into the house and we entered the living room just as Augusta was coming down the stairs.

Striker eyed the mess. "Is that the extent of the damage?"

"I think so," Augusta answered. "Nothing out of place upstairs or in the dining room or kitchen."

"I don't understand," I said. "What would someone want in here? I don't have anything valuable or important. Do you think this has something to do with Lavinia's murder?"

Striker and Augusta exchanged a glance. Did they know something I didn't?

Striker shrugged. "You never know."

"But I didn't have any bronzes or anything on the shelf. Just books."

"Were any of them valuable ... or did you have any of those hollowed-out books that you can hide stuff in?" Augusta asked.

I shook my head.

"What about papers inside the books?" Striker asked.

"No, nothing." My stomach sank as I bent down to pick up one of the books. Glancing at the pile, I could see most of them were ruined. They weren't valuable, but I had kept them in pristine condition and now, with the pages folded and the spines stretched, they would never be worth anything.

But it wasn't just about the value of the books. I loved books and seeing them treated with such disrespect grated on me.

I placed the book back on the pile and it seemed to sigh

in disappointment.

"Did you hear that?" Augusta frowned at the pile.

"What?" I cocked my ear toward it and that's when I heard it.

The faintest, most pitiful meow I'd ever heard.

"Pandora!" I dug at the pile furiously. I'd assumed she'd run off when whoever broke in had ransacked the house. Had she been lying underneath the books, hurt the whole time?

My heart twisted as I uncovered a lump of gray fur.

Pandora lay on her side. The end of her tail bent at an impossible angle. Blood matted the fur on the side of her head. I reached out to touch her and she stirred slightly, then sighed and lay still.

Tears burned my eyes as I gently freed her from the pile.

Striker had knelt beside me and he reached out, touching her neck.

"She's alive!" He turned to Augusta. "Call Doc Evans, he'll open the animal hospital up for me."

Striker gently took Pandora from my arms and we ran for his car.

***

My heart crowded my throat and tears burned my eyes as I stared at Pandora's still form on the stainless steel exam table. Her shaved arm stuck out straight to the side, IV lines running from the needles that pinched her tender skin in several places. The side of her head had also been shaved, the long gash closed with ugly stitches.

"She took a beating. Put up a good fight, too," Doc Evans said. "But she'll be fine. Just needs some rest."

I nodded, unable to speak.

"She's in good hands." Striker put his arm around me and I nodded again, my eyes riveted on the still form of my cat.

I knew she was in good hands. Doc Evans was a pediatrician who had retired to become a veterinarian. He'd been a great pediatrician, but was even better with pets. Some said he had a calling for it. If anyone could mend Pandora, it was Doc Evans.

"You should get some rest, too. But I don't think you should go home alone," Striker said, turning me gently toward the door. "I called Pepper to come and get you. She said you could stay at her place."

"You did?" I croaked the words out, my throat raw with emotion. I felt a stab of jealousy—when did Striker get Pepper's number and how often had he been calling her?

"Yes. She said she'd be here any minute." Striker looked through the window of the examination room to the dark, empty reception area then back at me. "Will you be okay until then? I want to go back to your house and help Augusta inspect the crime scene."

"Sure." I opened the door and he followed me out into the lobby. Since it was after-hours, there was no receptionist, no customers waiting, which suited me just fine. I could use some alone time.

We stood looking at each other awkwardly. I wondered what Striker was thinking ... and why my stomach was flip-flopping.

Then the door opened and Elspeth swept in, breaking the spell.

"Where is she?" Elspeth's worried eyes darted between the three examining room doors.

"In here." I started toward the room Pandora was in. Striker gave me a wave and moved toward the door to the parking lot.

"Thanks," I called after him. He turned and nodded to me, then was gone.

Elspeth was already at Pandora's side, her hands lovingly caressing the cat's fur.

"What happened?" She looked at me with puckered brows.

"Someone broke into my house and ransacked my living room. Pandora must have been there. I found her like this, under a pile of books."

"Books?"

I nodded.

Elspeth's face hardened and she pressed her forehead against Pandora's, all the while crooning softly to the cat.

Pandora's tail lifted a fraction of an inch, the kinked end sticking straight up in the air. Her eyelids fluttered, then opened. She gazed into Elspeth's eyes as if the two of them were having some sort of telepathic communication.

Pandora put her paw on Elspeth's forearm and Elspeth nodded, then turned the paw gently in her hand. Pandora's claws shot out, revealing broken jagged edges.

"She fought the intruder," Elspeth squeezed her paw gently and I saw the pinkie claw pop out. My breath caught in my throat ... skewered on the claw was a scrap of navy blue fabric.

"That looks like the same fabric that was on the murder weapon. I should get Augusta to look at that." I pulled the fabric off, found a plastic baggie in one of the drawers, and deposited it inside.

Holding the bag up in front of me, I felt a spark of hope. "I don't know why the person who killed Lavinia would break into my house, but maybe this scrap of fabric will help the police figure things out."

"That's not the only thing that might help them," Elspeth said.

"What do you mean?"

"Judging by Pandora's claws, she fought hard. Your intruder couldn't have escaped being marked. Find the person with claw marks on their arm, and you may have found your killer."

Chapter Twenty-Seven

"You think the person who broke into your house was the same person who killed Lavinia?" Pepper's brow creased as she tucked the soft, mint-colored chenille blanket around my legs.

"Well, the color looked the same and it is a strange coincidence."

I'd called Augusta from the animal hospital and she'd come right away to pick up the navy blue piece of fabric. According to her, they hadn't found any clues to go on at my house. Striker had insisted on righting my bookshelf and putting the books back, which somehow made me feel all warm and fuzzy. Or maybe the warm and fuzzy feeling came from the tea Pepper was pumping into me as I sat tucked into an overstuffed chair, safe and warm inside her country cottage.

"But what's the connection?" She poured more tea into my cup.

"I have no idea, but now I'm starting to think the murder didn't have anything to do with the bronzes, and I got the impression Augusta and Striker might think so, too."

"Well, if it wasn't about the bronzes, then what?"

I shook my head and took a sip of tea. I don't know what Pepper had put in it, but it sure was relaxing me.

"Maybe if we look at the suspects, it will make more sense," Pepper said.

"Oh, that reminds me, I do have a new suspect since I last talked to you." I told her about my conversation with Emma.

"Derek Bates? But he always seems so nice." Pepper screwed her face up. "I can't picture him being a killer."

"True, but I can't picture Bing or Josiah being the killer

either."

"I hate to think it's any of them. Can't you come up with someone else?"

"I've tried and, other than Ophelia, who has an alibi, those three are the only ones who had means, motive or opportunity."

"But, which one of them had all three?"

"That's a good question." I chewed on my bottom lip while I thought about it. "All three of them were in town that morning, so they all had opportunity."

"And any one of them had the means to clobber Lavinia and push her ... you don't have to be too strong to do that."

"So, that leaves motive." I put my teacup down and snuggled into the chair. "And if the killer wasn't after the bronzes, we're not really sure *what* the motive is."

"It could still be financial," Pepper said. "You said they ransacked your bookcase. Maybe they were after a valuable book?"

"But, I don't have a valuable book."

"Not that you *know* of, but have you checked all those books lately? Maybe one became rare for some reason ... the author died or whatever. Or maybe you just never knew you had a rare one."

"Maybe." I did a mental inventory of my books. Some had been my grandmother's. I thought I knew the inventory pretty well, but maybe I'd missed a rare one.

"So who needed money?" Pepper asked.

"Not Bing or Derek ... maybe Josiah. He can't make much on the postmaster's pension."

"Josiah could probably use some extra money, but Derek's not rich, either." Pepper took my teacup and walked around the center chimney to the kitchen area. "Idris controls the Bates fortune and he doesn't hand money out easily, so Derek doesn't really have any of his own."

I stifled a yawn. "So it's between Josiah and Derek."

"Not necessarily." Pepper took a pillow out of the hall closet and started making up the sofa for me to sleep on, which was a good thing since my eyelids felt like someone had tied lead weights to them. "You can't forget about the clues. The navy blue cape, the ring and the gray hair."

"Josiah doesn't wear a ring. I have no idea if Derek or Josiah have a blue cape, but I know Bing does—his magician's cape. *And* he has gray hair and a ring."

Pepper screwed her face up. "I'm trying to think, but I remember Derek has dark hair. So, only Bing and Josiah have gray hair."

"This is confusing. It could be any of them." I moved over to the sofa, nestling under the soft covers.

"Or anyone else." Pepper tucked the blanket under the sofa cushion and pecked my cheek. "But it's late and you must be exhausted. Let's get some sleep and we can think more about it in the morning.

"Mmmhmm." I mumbled my response, almost fully asleep.

As I drifted off, my subconscious mind sifted through the clues and suspects. Visions of rings, capes and murder weapons passed before my closed eyelids. The pieces snapped into place just before I fell into the deep abyss of sound sleep.

Suddenly, I knew who matched all three clues ... and I had a good idea how to prove he was the killer.

Chapter Twenty-Eight

I leaned on the counter at my bookstore, tapping my finger impatiently on its polished wood surface. I'd come in early, after checking on Pandora, and set the wheels in motion.

Today, Lavinia's killer would be brought to justice.

Outside, dark clouds had settled over the mountain. The smell of rain permeated my senses and the humidity frizzed my hair and made my leg ache. I bent down to massage it, jerking my head up as the bells over the door tinkled.

"Morning Willa." Hattie and Cordelia, in matching purple raincoats sauntered in. Cordelia had an extra Styrofoam cup, which she handed to me.

"Thanks." I tipped the cup toward her, then took a sip.

The door opened again and in came Bing, followed by Josiah. I noticed they both wore trench coats, but that wasn't unusual given the rainy forecast. Josiah shrugged his off and took a seat on the couch, rolling his sleeves up. His arms were not marred with scratches, which supported my theory.

Josiah was not the killer.

Bing sat on the couch next to him. He didn't remove his raincoat. I glanced nervously at the big ring on his hand.

"I heard about the break-in at your place." Bing turned concerned eyes on me. "Are you okay?"

"News travels fast. I'm fine."

"And Pandora?" My heart warmed at the genuine concern in Hattie's voice.

"She'll be fine," I said. "Doc Evans is just watching her for another night."

"Oh, good," Hattie and Cordelia said in unison.

The door opened again and the four gray heads swiveled to see Augusta enter, her brows raised in question.

"Hi, everyone," Augusta turned to me. "I got your cryptic message. What's this about?"

I took a deep breath. "I think I know who Lavinia's killer is, and I'm going to prove it right now."

Augusta raised her brows.

Hattie and Cordelia gasped.

Bing frowned, his bushy white brows practically covering his eyes. "Now, Willa ...."

Josiah cocked his head, rubbing his chin. "You don't say."

Out of the corner of my eye, I saw a wispy swirl starting to form at the end of the cookbook aisle. Figures, Lavinia would show up now when I didn't need her.

I turned away from Lavinia's ghost in time to see Augusta roll her eyes at me.

"Willa, how many times do I have to tell you not to investigate on your own? If you have a theory about the killer, you should tell me and let the police do the proper investigation."

The door jingled open, saving me from having to answer, and everyone turned to see Derek Bates step inside the shop.

Lavinia's ghost was doing her best to distract me. I could see her out of the corner of my eye down at the other end of the store where she was gesturing and gyrating. You'd think she'd be happy I was getting ready to unmask her killer, but instead she looked concerned. I turned my back on her.

"Hi, everyone." Derek scanned the group uncertainly before resting his gaze on me. "Willa, you said you have a book for me."

"Hi Derek." I avoided his question. "I think you know everyone here."

"Umm ... yeah." He made a face and pushed a lock of hair back from his forehead, revealing the gray streak. "What's going on? Where's the book?"

"There isn't any book," I said.

"What?" What are you talking about?"

Derek was still standing by the door and I was on the other side of the couches. Everyone's heads were swiveling back and forth between Derek and me like they were watching a tennis match.

I decided to move in for the kill.

"Emma at the church told me she saw you skulking around here the morning Lavinia Babbage was killed."

Derek scrunched his face up. "What? When was that? ... Oh. Yes, I remember now. I *was* in town ... but surely you don't think I had anything to do with *that*?"

I looked down at his hand. Where was his ring?

Lavinia had made her way over to the counter and was gesturing at me again. I turned to the side, ignoring her.

Doubt started to bloom in my gut—maybe Derek wasn't the killer. But he *had* to be—the clues all led to him.

He was young and strong, with the means to clobber and push an old lady.

He was seen in the area at the time of death.

He needed money and knew about the bronzes in the library... if the bronzes were even still the motive.

Even though his hair was dark, he did have that streak of gray. Lavinia could have easily reached back and grabbed on to that exact spot of hair.

And, even though he wasn't wearing a ring now, I'd remembered what had niggled at me about the photo of him with his brother, father and grandfather holding the family crest in the photo album—they'd all been wearing matching family crest rings.

Not only that, but I'd seen a long black car in the Bates' garage—just like the one Ophelia described fleeing town that morning. And hanging next to that were dark driver's coats. Sure, I hadn't been able to make out the color in the dark, but I was willing to bet they were navy blue.

He could deny it all he wanted—the real killer usually did.

I noticed everyone was staring at me so I continued. "Isn't it true that you're in need of money? You don't have much of your own and your grandfather controls the family money."

Derek's face pinched and he shuffled his feet. "Well, yes,

but I don't see what—"

"And you knew about the valuable bronzes in the library," I cut him off.

"The ones grandfather donated? That you keep pestering us about?"

Lavinia was practically doing cartwheels on the counter. I ignored her—I was almost finished, and then we'd have this whole thing behind us and Lavinia could go off to wherever ghosts went off to.

I narrowed my eyes at Derek. "Where were you last night around six p.m.?"

"Huh? I was home ... just what is going on here?"

"My house was broken into by Lavinia's killer and I think you know *exactly* what is going on because you had means, motive and opportunity." I ticked the last three words off on my fingers.

"That's crazy!" The words exploded from Derek's mouth. "I didn't kill Lavinia or break into your house!"

"Really? Then explain why you were skulking around in the woods just before the murder and were seen fleeing town right after in your long black car."

A confused look passed over Derek's face. "Long black car? You mean the Lincoln? I never take that car ... and if you must know, I was bringing my cat to the vet that morning."

I remembered what Emma had said about Derek being one of the 'opposers' of the feral cat sanctuary. "Cat? I heard you didn't even like cats, so now I know you're lying."

"That's not true," Derek said. "The rest of my family doesn't like them, which is why I had to take Kitty to Doc Evans early in the morning. I keep him in my wing of the house ... away from the others. Anyway, he jumped out of the window of my Mini-Cooper on the way through town and ran into the woods. I was in there trying to catch him."

What? If that was true, it blew my whole case. The back of my mind wondered if Doc Evans could give him an alibi, but my mouth couldn't be stopped. "I think you're lying—covering up. That's what killers do."

"Willa—" Augusta tried to cut in.

"No. Wait." I held my hand up to Augusta. "I can prove it."

I took two long strides to Derek's side, grabbed his sleeve and pushed it up to the elbow, turning triumphant eyes to Augusta. "See!"

Augusta squinted at Derek's arm. "See what?"

I whipped my head back to look at his arm, my stomach sinking. There were no scratches. I pushed up the other sleeve only to find that arm was scratch free, too.

"But that's impossible," I said. "Pandora fought the intruder and Elspeth said they would have scratches on their forearm!"

Derek jerked his arms away. "Well, I'm not the one who broke in, which is why I don't have any scratches. And I certainly am not the one who killed Lavinia Babbage!"

And with that, Derek stormed out the door, leaving an embarrassing silence in his wake.

I looked around the room, my leaden stomach growing even heavier. Everyone was staring at me, even Lavinia, who stood behind the counter, hands on hips.

Josiah cleared his throat and pushed up from the couch. "Well, I should be going."

"Yep," Bing said.

"Us, too," Cordelia and Hattie twittered as the four of them fought their way to be first out the door.

Augusta gave me a look of disappointment, then wordlessly shook her head and disappeared out the door behind the others.

"Sorry..." I mumbled, staring at the closed door.

Had I accused Derek wrongly? It certainly seemed like I had. I'd wanted to reveal the killer and help Augusta out, but I'd only made a fool of myself and made Augusta mad. She'd probably never trust my instincts again.

And the worst part was that if neither Derek nor Josiah were the killer, that left only one person on my suspect list ... Bing.

Chapter Twenty-Nine

I looked around the empty bookstore. Apparently, even Lavinia was disappointed in me—she was nowhere to be seen.

Slipping behind the counter, I lowered myself to the stool, my shoulders slumping in defeat. Glancing down, I saw the box of books I'd put there yesterday.

Nothing like looking at old books to pick up one's spirits.

I rummaged in the box, picking out a thick book bound in soft brown leather. It was heavy—about four hundred pages, the edges dipped in gold leaf, almost completely worn off with centuries of use.

How many centuries? Certain that it was at least one hundred years old, I opened it up to search for a date.

It was a strange book. No publishing information could be found. The pages were thicker than most old books. They rasped as I turned them, the smell of old paper wafting up to my nose.

It was handwritten in what looked like an old quill pen. But the words weren't English ... at least not most of them. I could barely make out what it said, but they were organized with a list at the top and then a few paragraphs at the bottom. Like a recipe book.

With a start, I realized this must be one of the Bates' ancestors hand written recipe books and probably of value to the family, especially considering the exquisite binding, which must have cost a fortune. I wondered if the recipes were any good.

I really should return it to the Bateses, but I was too embarrassed to call Derek after what had just happened.

"Oh, I see you are finally getting a clue." Lavinia's ghost popped into view out of nowhere and I fumbled the book, almost sending it crashing to the floor, managing to save it at the last minute.

"Sorry, Lavinia," I said. "I really thought Derek was your killer."

"Why would Derek kill me?"

"For the money."

"Money? Haven't you figured out yet that this is about something far more important than money?

My brows mashed together. The truth was, I had been starting to think this had nothing to do with the bronzes. I just couldn't figure out what it *did* have to do with.

"You're holding the key right in your hand," Lavinia said as if reading my mind.

I looked down at the book which lay open in my lap. "This recipe book?"

"Those aren't recipes, Willa. That book holds something very important, and now you must protect it."

Her words made me uneasy. "Huh?"

"Sorry, I couldn't help you more earlier." Lavinia wrung her hands together. "The truth is, being a ghost isn't all it's cracked up to be. You aren't trusted with all the information up front. Anyway, I just now found out the real truth, which is why I was trying to get your attention when you were grilling Derek."

This was getting confusing. "So, you're saying this has nothing to do with the bronzes or money, but to do with this recipe book instead?"

"Not recipes, Willa," Lavinia bent down, her mouth close to my ear. "Spells."

"Spells?" I squinted at the book. "I guess spells could look like recipes. But that's ridiculous. Who would use these spells? Witches?"

Lavinia nodded solemnly.

"But, there's no such thing."

"Don't I wish it," Lavinia said. "Anyway, I cannot tell you how important this book is. There are forces of good and evil ... you don't want the evil forces to get a hold of it."

"But, how do I know who is good and who is evil?" I squinted up at her. I still wasn't even sure I believed the malarkey about spells and witches, but since I wasn't doing so well with my own theory, the least I could do was to hear her out.

"Oh, you'll know," she said.

"And you must be very, very careful," Robert Frost piped in from the purple couch where he was sitting with Franklin Pierce.

"Yes, Willa," Franklin added. "This is dangerous and important business and we don't want anything to happen to you."

Robert nodded. "We've gotten quite attached to you here in the bookshop. It just wouldn't be the same without you."

I was starting to feel like I was in a dream. Spells? Witches? Ghosts getting attached to me?

The three of them jerked their heads toward the door. Robert and Franklin swung back to look at me, their mouths forming round 'o's.

"Oh-oh," they said in unison before disappearing.

I turned to Lavinia who had a look of panic on her face. "Look out, Willa—my killer is coming. Remember, above all, you must protect the book!"

I looked back down at the book in my lap.

"I still don't understand what, exactly, is the big deal." I looked back up at Lavinia, but she was gone.

"Hey ..." I let my voice trail off. Leave it to a ghost to disappear with some vague warning and only half the answers I needed.

"Are you talking to someone?"

I whirled around at the sound of the voice, fingers of dread squeezing my heart when I saw who stood there ...

Bing Thorndike.

***

How did *he* get in? I hadn't heard the door jangle.

My eyes slid to his forearms, but he still had long sleeves, so I couldn't see the scratches Pandora had inflicted on him when he'd broken into my house. The break-in hadn't made sense last night, but now I knew the reason. I was holding it in my hands.

"Give me the book, Willa. I'll keep it safe." Bing reached out toward the book, the clunky gold Magician's Guild ring gleaming on his finger.

My mind whirled in confusion as Bing advanced on me, his face wore a smile that might have appeared friendly any other time, but looked menacing to me now.

I sat frozen on the stool. I couldn't give Bing the book—he was the killer! Handing the book over was the *last* thing I was going to do. Not just because I instinctively felt protective of the book, but I also feared he'd kill *me* once I handed it over.

Movement at the end of the inspirational books aisle caught my eye and I looked over to see Robert Frost pulling a book from the shelf.

Bang!

The sound of the book slamming to the floor distracted Bing and I ran toward the door.

"Willa! Wait! I'm trying to help you!" I heard Bing yell as I ran across the shop, the old book clutched to my chest.

My leg was burning, slowing me down. It seemed like I was running in chest-high water and my gut twisted as I realized it wasn't just because of my bum leg. Something strange was happening, as if time was slowing down.

I fought my way toward the door, a glance back over my shoulder showed Bing gaining ground. I closed my eyes, the sinking sensation in my chest overwhelming me ... I couldn't let Bing get me.

The memory of a book I once read surfaced. In the book, the hero could speed up time by turning the hands of their watch forward. *Too bad I don't wear a watch*, I thought, wishing with all my heart I had put one on that morning.

I looked down at my wrist. I *had* put one on! Not caring why I didn't necessarily remember putting it on that morning, I reached down and turned the small knob, the minute hand moving forward just as I felt Bing's heavy hand clutch my shoulder.

***

I was catapulted out the door onto the street, my face

crushed into someone's chest.

I pulled away, the taste of wool in my mouth and my heart racing as I looked up into the surprised face of Carson Bates. His car sat idling behind him at the curb, the back door still open.

Relief flooded through me.

"Carson, thank goodness." I glanced behind me to see if Bing was catching up. "You gotta help me! We need to get out of here."

His eyes flew up and he stepped aside, gesturing toward the open door. I launched myself into the car and he slid in beside me, closing the door behind him.

"Go!" I yelled at the driver, who raised his brow at Carson in the rear view mirror. Carson nodded and the car shot forward.

I twisted in the seat, looking out the rear window, past the long length of the trunk to see Bing shoot out the door of my shop onto the street.

I pulled my cell phone out of my pocket. I needed to call Augusta, although I wasn't sure what I was going to say. Somehow I didn't think telling her Bing had slowed down time to take a recipe book from me was going to impress her.

"Not so fast," Carson said as I started to punch the numbers.

"Huh?" I looked over at him.

The phone turned molten hot in my hand and I dropped it with a squeal, pulling my hand back. As I watched it melt on the floor mat, I held my already blistering fingers against my chest.

I looked from the puddle of my phone to Carson, my brows mashed together. My brain felt a little slow on the uptake. My heart thudded against my ribcage.

What was going on?

"Thanks, Willa." Carson reached across the seat toward the book in my lap. A glimmer of gold on his finger caught my eye—the Bates family crest ring. "I was coming for this, but you saved me the trouble. How convenient."

I pulled the book away, instinctively trying to hide it behind my back on the other side of him. He stretched around me to grab the book, the sleeves of his navy blue coat pulled back, exposing his forearms.

My breath caught in my throat—his arms were raked with scratches.

Chapter Thirty

The hard, musty floor pressing on my shoulder blades alerted me to the fact that I was lying down. Dampness seeped through my sweatshirt. A dank, earthy smell tickled my nose. I opened one eye, the dim flicker of light from the single bulb in the ceiling seared into my eyeball with a stabbing pain.

Closing my eye, I rolled on my side, blinking my eyes open again as I fought the wave of nausea that rolled over me. Once it passed, I stared at my surroundings in disbelief.

I'd heard rumors that the Bates mansion had a real dungeon, but I didn't believe them. Until now. Now I *had* to believe it ... because I was in it.

The stone walls in the cavernous room were void of windows, the only source of light coming from the one dim bulb sticking out of the screw-in socket in the ceiling directly above me. It was clear the addition of electricity had been an afterthought down here in the basement.

To tell the truth, the depressing atmosphere would have been more appropriately illuminated by the ancient torches that sat unlit in their iron holders in the wall. Given the dim lighting, I could see only about twenty feet in front of me, after which the rest of the basement was shrouded in foreboding dark shadow.

Seeing twenty feet in front of me was enough, though. Enough to see that I was in some sort of iron cage, the bars going from floor to ceiling, the door held shut by an old iron lock. The cage was empty except for me and a thin layer of straw in the corner, which I hoped wasn't supposed to be my bed.

How did I get here?

I pushed myself up from the ground. The stinging pain in my hand as it touched the floor jolted my memory of the car ride with Carson.

My stomach twisted. It was Carson Bates who had broken into my house and likely him who killed Lavinia. He wore a big ring. He rode in the dark black car. He had the same gray streak in his hair as Derek.

And, when I'd run into him on the street, he was wearing one of the coats I'd seen in the Bates garage. A navy blue coat with oversized storm flaps on the shoulders and back. Those storm flaps could easily have been mistaken for a cape in the shadowy figure Lavinia had seen as she fell down the steps.

My head started to ache along with my hand and my leg as I tried to remember what had happened. The last thing I remembered was Carson trying to take the book from me in the car. Seeing as how I didn't have the book now, he must have succeeded. Everything after that was a blank.

Did he knock me out, somehow? How had I gotten here? And where was I? I assumed it was the Bates' basement, but since I didn't remember getting here, I supposed it could be anywhere.

But what did it matter? No matter where I was, I needed to get out. Fast.

I walked over to the door and pushed. Naturally, it didn't budge—I couldn't be that lucky. I pulled on it with as much force as I could muster, but it was solid ... and locked tight.

I paced the perimeter of my ten by ten cell, studying the floor and ceiling to see if there were any cracks or openings I could wriggle out through. There were none. I tested every bar with my good hand until it stung from pulling on the chipped, rusty iron. None of them budged.

A sigh of frustration escaped my lips as I leaned against the wall. The hard, cold stones chilled my back as I sunk down to the floor.

My heart plummeted as I realized I was now trapped by the person who had killed Lavinia. I hugged my knees to my chest, put my head down and cried.

***

"Meow."

I lifted my head from the crook of my elbow, and brushed away hot tears. Did I just hear a cat? I thought about Pandora and my heart twisted.

Looking out at the edge of the darkness, I saw something slinking about. It *was* a cat. Not Pandora, though. This cat was white, with mocha colored markings.

"Here, Kitty," I put out my hand and made clucking noises.

The cat turned to face me, her pale blue eyes studying me intently as she crept closer.

She snaked her way throughout the bars and came to me, rubbing her cheek against my hand.

"Hi, there. Who are you?" I wondered. Was it Derek's cat? Now that I knew Carson was the killer, maybe Derek had been telling the truth. I wondered if Derek had been involved, too.

"Oh, well, what does it matter now?" I asked the cat as I found comfort in stroking the silky fur behind her ears.

As the cat's purring relaxed me, I worried what would happen to Pandora if I didn't make it out of there. I was glad she was safe at the animal hospital. If not for the break-in, she would have been at the bookstore with me and who knows what might have happened to her.

This brought my thoughts to what had happened in the store. It had all been about that old book. The book Lavinia had told me to protect.

I remembered how Bing had wanted the book, but I thought he was the enemy and ran from him. My stomach twisted ... I'd practically delivered the book right into Carson's hands, and now if something bad happened because of it, it was all on me.

I couldn't just sit here and let that happen. I had to do something.

I stood suddenly, causing the cat to let out a startled mew. I rushed to the door of my cell, the cat trotting in front of me, seeming to know where I was going before I even got there. I pressed my face against the bars, above the lock and looked down, trying to get a look at the lock opening.

The Bates mansion was over three hundred and fifty years old and the cell had probably been here for that long. The lock was original—a simple device that could be opened with a skeleton key. My years as a crime reporter had garnered me a lot of skills, not the least of which was basic lock picking.

I knew how to pick one of these. I just needed something long and straight. I searched my pockets, coming up empty.

"Damn!" My arms fell against my sides in frustration.

"Meow!" The cat had left the confines of the cage and was playing with what looked like a big dust ball. I watched as she batted it with her paw, sending it rolling and then pounced on it over and over again.

That gave me an idea.

Scanning the floor, I saw a long flat piece of metal that would make a perfect lock pick. It was too far for me to reach, but I might be able to use one of the tricks I'd learned from Bing to get the cat to do my work for me.

One of Bing's favorite tricks was to make things look like they floated in air. He used a fishing line for that, the line seeming invisible. I didn't have fishing line, but I had something Bing always said would work just as well—my hair.

The strands were thick, and the corkscrew curls made it look shorter than it actually was. I plucked a few strands out, pleased that I got two of the white ones, and tied them together. Then I picked a few pieces of straw from the corner and tied that to one end.

The dangling straw caught the cat's eye and she left her dust ball and trotted into the cell. Standing up on her hind legs, she batted at it.

"You like?" I squatted down and threw the straw end out. The cat skittered after it, pouncing on it. I jerked it out from under her and she skittered again.

I reeled in my new cat toy and went to the edge of the cell. Sticking my hand out through the bars, I tossed the toy out toward the metal piece. It landed just beyond it.

Perfect.

The cat pounced on the toy, her front paw hitting the metal piece and sending it sliding toward the cell. Not far enough, though. I jerked the piece toward me and she hit the metal again, inching it closer. A few more well-placed tosses and the metal piece was within reach.

"Thanks, Kitty." I stretched my fingers through the bars, ignoring the throbbing pain of my burned fingertips, and grabbed the metal piece.

Standing, I poked my hand out so I could put the metal into the lock. The cat sat on the other side of the door, staring at me intently.

I dug the metal piece around. Turns out it's a lot harder picking a lock from the inside. After about five minutes of fiddling, I heard a satisfying click.

I pushed the door and it swung open.

Chapter Thirty-One

I stepped out of the cell, my heart thumping as my eyes darted around the room, or at least the part of the room I could see.

Which way should I go?

My senses told me I was in a basement because the air had that dank, damp underground feeling. But there were no windows like a regular basement.

My stomach tightened as I looked into the dark. I had no idea what I would find there, but there certainly wasn't any way out from where I was standing.

I forged ahead.

The cat stayed with me, following by my side. I had no idea what I was looking for, but maybe I could find a door that led outside. Or upstairs. Although, if I was in the Bates mansion as I suspected, going upstairs could be fatal.

"Mew." I heard the soft sound behind me and realized the cat had stopped. I turned, barely able to make her white form out in the dark. She was standing next to the wall ... no, not next to it—half-way inside it!

I bent down to find a crack in the wall. It was about five inches, big enough for the cat to wriggle through. She disappeared behind it, the reappeared a few seconds later.

"Meow!" She jerked her tail at me.

"Sure, I'd love to follow you, but it's too small. Guess I shouldn't have had dessert last night." I stuck my arm through and tried to wedge my shoulder in. It just wasn't big enough.

I pulled my arm out ... or tried to. It was stuck.

"Meow." The cat weaved around my ankles.

"Yeah, thanks. This is just great." I jerked my arm and it

came free, but not before I felt the stones shift slightly.

Was it my imagination ... or had the opening widened?

I put my arm in again and this time more of my shoulder fit through. I wriggled and pushed. Pain shot through my bad leg as I used it for leverage, but it worked. The crack opened up enough for me to fit and I slid in.

I was in a narrow passageway. The cat flicked her tail impatiently before me as I stifled a sneeze from the dust tickling my nose. I could barely make out a set of stairs in front of me. At the top, thin slats of light that I assumed were coming from between the boards that made the passage allowed for minimum visibility.

Where was the light coming from?

The cat started up the steps and I followed.

We got to the top and there was an intersection. I peered through one of the lighted gaps into a large kitchen. It was empty, but the stainless steel appliances gleamed on top of black and white checked tile.

I limped a few more feet and peeked through another gap. This one revealed a sitting room decorated in pale blue. I realized I must have been in a secret passageway somewhere inside the house. All I needed to do was find a way out, hopefully in an unoccupied room with a door to the outside so I could make a clean get-away.

"Mew." The cat sat up ahead. Looking at me, then at the wall. At me, and then the wall. Clearly, she was trying to tell me something.

As I tiptoed up to her, I could hear voices. My blood chilled when I recognized one of them as Carson Bates.

The gap in the boards in front of the cat looked different from the others. It was a door. A secret doorway that led into the room. Pressing my face against one of the slats, I looked into an ornate library.

Bookshelves lined the walls. Two tufted leather sofas sat facing each other in the middle of the room. A large stone fireplace filled the opposite wall.

Idris Bates stood at the end of one of the sofas. Hadn't Derek said he was sick? He looked fine to me. Felicity sat on the sofa, her white, flowing dress spread out on the seat on either side of her. Carson stood at the fireplace.

"I can recreate these and we can turn things in our favor. We'll *own* this town." She pointed toward the coffee table, her wide sleeves fluttering around her wrists.

My eyes slid to where she pointed and my breath caught in my throat. The book Carson had taken from me lay on the table, the binding open to the middle, revealing the ink covered parchment pages.

"I don't know, Felicity. Your spells have mostly backfired, so far." Idris Bates looked at his daughter-in-law disapprovingly.

Carson coughed over by the fireplace, and the two other Bateses looked at him. "We need to make use of what's in the book if we plan to turn Mystic Notch to our side."

My eyes slid from Carson to the book. I had no idea what he meant by 'turn Mystic Notch to our side', but I had a pretty good idea it wasn't anything I would like. It all hinged on the book and I was the one that had screwed up and let Carson get ahold of it. If anything bad happened in Mystic Notch because of it, it would be my fault.

I had to make things right.

I was contemplating just how to do that when a hand clamped over my mouth and pulled me back down the passage, stifling the scream that tried to burst from my throat.

***

"Shhh ... I'm on your side."

Really? It doesn't feel like it, I thought as I clawed at whomever it was, my eyes darting wildly as he pulled me into a little alcove.

"I'll help you get the book."

That got my attention. I stopped struggling and tried to turn to see who it was.

"Promise you won't scream if I let go," he said. "If you do, the rest of them will come running and it won't be a good ending for you."

I nodded.

He let go, and I whirled around to see Derek Bates standing there with a hopeful look on his face.

"You!" I hissed.

He crossed his arms over his chest.

"I should be taking that tone with *you*," he whispered. "You accused me of killing Lavinia."

"Well, considering what I'm finding out about your family, I'm wondering if you had a hand in it," I whispered back.

The cat weaved around Derek's legs mewing softly. So, it *was* his cat. He must have been telling the truth about his reason for being in town the morning of Lavinia's death.

He saw me looking down. "Yes, this is the cat I was taking to the vets. Do you believe me?"

I nodded. "But your family ..."

Derek brushed his hand through his hair. "I didn't want to believe one of them could be the killer, even though I had my doubts. But now, with that book and all ... well, you can see why I rushed you out of the house the other day."

"Sort of," I said, still not sure what the Bates family was up to. Were they witches? And whose side was Derek on?

"I saw Carson sneak in with the book. I knew he had you downstairs. I was actually on my way down to let you out," Derek frowned at me. "How *did* you get out, anyway?"

"Would you believe magic? But not the black kind. I picked the lock and your cat led me to this passage. So you're not in on any of this with your family?" I still wasn't sure I believed him, but I had to ask.

"No." His face turned hard. "I've always been different. The black sheep of the family, so to speak. I tried to ignore their darker side—I suppose I love them in some way, but this thing with the book. I just can't let them unleash evil on Mystic Notch."

Unleash evil? That sounded bad. I was pretty sure I didn't want that to happen either.

"Okay, what do you suggest we do?" Just a few hours ago, I thought Derek was the killer and now I was considering joining forces with him. I didn't see that I had too many other choices.

"We need to get the book away from them. They think you are still locked up downstairs, so we have the element of surprise on our side."

"And just how do you propose we utilize that?"

"I have an idea." Derek glanced down the passage toward the library where we could still hear the soft hum of conversation. "Here's what we'll do."

***

My nerves tingled with anticipation as I stood at the secret door, looking into the library through one of the gaps in the boards. It looked like I was seeing the room through a tunnel and I realized that my view was between two books—the door must have been cleverly built into one of the bookcases.

I shifted my position to relieve the pressure on my leg as well as to be able to get a better view of the book on the coffee table. Reminding myself to breathe, I placed my hand—the one that wasn't burned—on the panel that would slide the door open while I waited for Derek to create the distraction that would allow me to slip into the room and steal the book.

Carson, Idris and Felicity were still discussing their dastardly plan of action, but I wasn't listening. I was too intent on waiting for the perfect moment.

"Fire!" I heard Derek yell and saw him rush into the library, standing in the doorway and pointing excitedly into the hall. "The kitchen's on fire! Everyone out!"

Carson ran out into the hall. Felicity sprang up from the couch and headed toward the door. Idris followed at a more dignified pace.

I pushed the panel, the door slid silently open and I stepped into the room, my eye trained on the book.

Idris had almost cleared the door when I was already halfway into the room. He must have remembered the book on the coffee table and he turned back toward it, his eyes growing wide when he saw me.

I ran for the book, noticing absently that a paperweight very similar to the one Elspeth had given me sat on the table beside it. Like my paperweight, this one glowed strangely, as if lit from inside.

Idris charged back into the room with surprising speed for a man his age.

A jolt of adrenalin surged through me—I knew I had to stop him. I grabbed the book and the paperweight, yelping as the paperweight seared my already burned fingers.

I aimed at Idris. Swinging the orb with all my might, I let go, watching in awe as electricity arced from my fingertips, circling the paperweight that exploded into a million pieces.

Kaboom!

My eyesight blurred. I felt the sensation of flying, then the weightlessness of falling. Hot air rushed past my face, then a bone jarring thud sent pain shooting through my body before everything went black.

Chapter Thirty-Two

A crushing weight on my chest made it hard to breathe and what little air I could get was tinged with smoke and the smell of charred wood. I opened my eyes, but it was dark. The debris I was pinned beneath made it impossible to move.

"Mew."

I tried to call out, but my voice was muffled by the debris.

"Mew ... mew ... mew ..." There was more than one cat out there. I found myself hoping they were good diggers as I tried in vain to push myself out of the pile of wood and stone I was buried in.

"Over here!"

Was that Striker?

I felt the pile shift and heard the noise of wood and stone being thrown aside. A shaft of daylight appeared and I turned my face to it, sucking in a lungful of clean air.

"Chance! Are you okay?" Striker's concerned face came into view and I nodded.

A large black cat poked his face near mine as Striker continued to dig me out. A Siamese traced its rough tongue on my nose. An orange tomcat sat off to the side, sizing me up. Weren't these Elspeth's cats? How in the world had they gotten all the way down here?

"Willa!" Bing Thorndike came into view, his eyes ringed with compassion. "Thank God you're okay."

"Is anything broken?" Striker asked.

I tried out all my limbs, wiggling my fingers and toes. Everything seemed to work. In fact, I was surprised my leg wasn't hurting more than it was. "I don't think so."

"Okay, hold on." Striker grabbed under my arms and

pulled me the rest of the way out.

"I'll take the book and keep it safe for you,' Bing said.

"Book?" I frowned in the direction Bing was looking and noticed I had an old book clutched to my chest. It looked familiar, but I couldn't quite place it. I knew it was important. Looking up at Bing's smiling face, I got the overwhelming feeling that giving him the book was the right thing to do.

I handed it over.

Bing took the book, holding it carefully, then gave me a knowing look and I felt like everything was all right even though I had no idea why.

"What happened?" Striker asked.

"I don't remember." My brows mashed together as I looked at the gaping hole in the side of the Bates mansion. There had been an explosion, obviously, but I didn't remember what I had been doing here in the first place.

"Let's get you checked out." Striker grabbed my hand and it exploded in pain.

"Ouch!" I pulled my hand back turning it over to reveal blisters and raw skin.

Striker's eyes clouded with concern, he reached for my hand again.

"Let me see." He looked it over gently. "Looks like you got a bad burn. I'm going to take you over to the ambulance and get this bandaged."

Putting his arm around me, Striker led me to the front of the house, which was loaded with police cars and an ambulance. I glanced back over my shoulder to where I'd been buried in the pile. It was out of sight of the main activity.

"How did you find me over there?" I wondered.

"The cats. I noticed a group of them and they were sniffing around the pile. That's why I investigated. Then once I got close, I smelled the peppermint and knew it was you."

My cheeks burned. Did the *Iced Fire* smell that strongly? I searched for the cats, but there were none in sight.

"Willa!" Augusta came running, her arms outstretched, enveloping me in a hug. After a few seconds she held me at arm's length, inspecting me. "Are you okay?"

"Yes. I'm fine." I looked over her shoulder where the Bates family was gathered near the front of the house, my stomach clenching as I remembered how I'd falsely accused Derek. "You're not mad at me because of this morning—"

Then I remembered seeing the scratches on Carson's arm and the ring. I grabbed Augusta's arm. "Carson is the killer!"

"I know, that's why we came." Augusta looked back at the Bates family and I could see an officer approaching them. "After you accused Derek it gave me some ideas. I took a look at the clues and realized you had the right family, but wrong brother."

"He was at the shop this morning." I wrinkled my forehead in concentration. "I don't remember much ... but he had the claw marks on his arm so he must have been the one that broke into my house!"

"I know." Augusta pulled the handcuffs from the back of her uniform. "Don't worry, we have enough evidence on him to get him for the break-in and Lavinia's murder."

Augusta turned and walked away just as Striker put something that stung on my hand.

"Ouch." I pulled away.

"This will help the burn." He pulled my hand back toward him, gently swabbing it with ointment, despite my protests.

"What were you doing up here, anyway?" he asked.

"That's a good question." I chewed my bottom lip. Why *had* I been here? "All I remember is that Carson came to the shop this morning. I saw the scratches on his arm and he was wearing a navy blue coat. But the rest is fuzzy. I might have been bringing them that book."

Striker's eyes clouded with concern.

"You don't remember? Did you hit your head?" He started feeling around my head. "Does this hurt?"

"No."

"I don't feel any bumps, but it's strange you don't remember. Maybe the trauma of the explosion." He looked at the house and then back to me. "What was that book, anyway?"

"I thought it was some old family book. I found it in a box with an old Bateses family photo album."

"So then, why did Bing take it?"

"Good question," I looked around for Bing, but he was gone. "I guess I was mistaken about it being from the Bates collection."

Over near the house, I could see Augusta putting the cuffs on Carson. He looked angry. Felicity was crying. Derek stood off to the side. Idris leaned on his cane, the picture of frailty ... except something niggled at me that he was anything but frail.

Striker turned me toward him. "You don't have to worry about them. Carson's going to jail. He's been unstable for a long time."

I thought about that. It was true he was a little strange when we were younger, but since I'd been in Massachusetts until recently, I didn't really know what he'd been up to all these years.

I watched Striker wrap a large gauze bandage on my hand. His gentle motions made my heart flutter. He secured the bandage, then put his hands on my shoulders.

"I hope you've learned not to get involved in any more investigations, or at the very least to not go off on your own." He looked over my shoulder at the gaping hole in the side of the Bates mansion. "As you can see, it can be very dangerous."

His gray eyes locked back on mine and I felt a flood of warmth at the genuine concern in them.

I nodded.

"Good. Well, I'm just glad you're okay," he said, leaning in toward me and kissing me on the lips.

My pulse skittered and my stomach flip-flopped, but this time I didn't throw up on his shoes.

Chapter Thirty-Three

I stood on the sidewalk in front of the bookstore. Pandora, who I'd picked up from the animal hospital on my way to work, lay in my arms. She must have missed me, because she was letting me hold her while she purred contentedly.

Doc Evans had assured me she would be fine with no permanent ill effects other than the kink in her tail, which she slapped against my arm lazily.

I looked up at the bright sun and closed my eyes. The storm system that had brought all the rain had moved out of the mountains and the next few days promised to be the sunny and warm New Hampshire spring days that I loved. Even the birds were encouraged, as was evidenced by their lively twittering in the bud-laden trees.

Since it was so nice, I was having the morning tête-a-tête with Bing, Josiah, Cordelia and Hattie outside instead of on the purple couches in my shop.

"Thank goodness you weren't hurt, Willa," Cordelia said as she reached over to stroke Pandora's head.

"Yes, that was a freak accident," Josiah added. "I mean, the gas explosion. Blew the front side of the Bates mansion clear off."

"Gas explosion?" I wrinkled my forehead at Josiah.

"Yeah, that's what blew the side off the Bates mansion. Well, you should know, you were there." Josiah studied me, rubbing his chin. "Why *were* you there, Willa?"

"Good question," I said.

Bing gave me a knowing look and I felt like we shared a secret about that morning. Too bad I didn't remember what it was.

"I don't know how you got caught in the rubble." Hattie

sipped her coffee. "But it's a good thing you weren't actually inside the house—you could have been killed."

I smiled and nodded. Inside the house? Why did I feel like I might have been in there? I shook my head—my memory of the day was still fuzzy and the truth was I had no idea where I was when the explosion happened.

"It's such a shame about Carson," Hattie said. "Felicity is crushed."

"She's kind of an odd one, don't you think, sister?" Cordelia asked Hattie.

"They're all odd, if you ask me," Josiah said. "But at least Willa was on the right track."

"Yeah, but I still don't get it. *Why* did Carson kill Lavinia?" Cordelia asked.

"Well, you know that boy's always been a little funny." Josiah tapped the side of his head. "From what I understand, Felicity sold some family books and he got it in his head they were in the library."

"Yeah, but why not just ask Lavinia? He didn't have to *kill* her," Hattie took a sip of coffee.

"Like I said, the boy ain't right," Josiah answered. "Rumor is that he claims he's innocent, even though the police have ample evidence. They say he was in the library looking for those old family books and Lavinia surprised him and he killed her. I hear he denies it, though."

"So, if Lavinia hadn't been in town early that day, she'd still be alive," Hattie mused.

My stomach crunched and I snuggled Pandora closer despite her protesting meow ... Lavinia had been killed because of her dedication to the feral cats.

"And he broke into Willa's house for the same reason," Josiah added.

"That's right. Maggie had picked up a box of books for me, and inside I found a photo album of the Bates family. When I brought it up to the Bates' house, Carson wanted to know if there were any other books in the box with it.

"I'd told him I'd left the box at home, but made a pit-stop that afternoon to bring the box to the store. Carson wouldn't have known that, though. He would have thought they were still at my house."

"Well, it's an interesting mystery, but I'm glad it's solved." Josiah looked at his watch. "And now, I must mosey off to the barber."

He nodded at us and turned to leave.

"We'll walk with you," Cordelia said. "Hattie needs to stop in the fudge shoppe."

"Not just me." Hattie swatted at Cordelia's arm. "You ate all the penuche last time."

I smiled as the three of them walked off, leaving me standing on the sidewalk with Bing.

Bing cocked a bushy eyebrow at me. "So, you don't remember much about what happened at the Bates mansion?"

I shook my head. "Not really, but there is one thing I remember. That old book ... were you looking for it too?"

"I looked all over town for it." Bing shifted uncomfortably then leaned closer to me. "We have to make sure it doesn't get into the wrong hands."

"You looked all over town?" I narrowed my eyes remembering how I'd passed him on the road on my way to Barry's. "So that *was* you at Barry's house the other day!"

"Yes," Bing said, then held up his hands at my look of alarm. "I wasn't the one that hurt him, though. I was there in time to save him. It was Carson that knocked him out. He was there looking for the book."

I remembered how Barry had said the books were out of order in the box. And Carson lived further out than Barry so I wouldn't have passed him on the road.

"What's so important about this book, and why do you want to keep it from Carson?" I asked Bing. "I thought the Bateses had it to begin with and Felicity sold it off by mistake."

Bing pressed his lips together. "Apparently, Felicity didn't realize the value of what she'd sold. She always was kind of ditzy and old Idris doesn't keep her well-informed. Anyway, as you know, the book wasn't at Barry's. He should suffer no ill effects from his fall."

"That's right. The book was in the box Maggie had left on my porch. The one with the Bateses family scrapbook."

"We searched all local book acquisitions and even your home earlier, but that must have been before Maggie dropped the box off."

My brows rose. "You searched my house?"

Bing looked at me apologetically. "Now, don't get all upset, we were just trying to nip things in the bud before everything blew up ... no pun intended. You never even knew we were there, and of course we would never do anything to hurt you."

"But when did you do that?" The memory of the night of deep sleep after eating Elspeth's pie surfaced. Was Elspeth in on this? She certainly did have some unique qualities, like conjuring up butterflies, and she did seem to have an odd way of understanding animals. "I don't understand ... who is this *we* you keep talking about and what is this really all about?"

Bing took a deep breath. "You'll understand all that in time, Willa. For now, you know what you need to and Mystic Notch will go on as it has."

A warm smile bloomed on Bing's face as he surveyed Main Street, but I hardly had time to notice. A swirly mist had started to form outside the shop door and that could only mean one thing.

"Now, if you don't mind, I must be going," Bing said, pulling my attention from the mist long enough to see him start across the street. "See you tomorrow, Willa."

"See ya." I wasn't satisfied with his lame explanation, but didn't have time to go after him. I turned my full attention on the mist discovering, much to my surprise, there were two figures.

As the ghosts started to solidify, my attention was pulled away, yet again, by the trio of women walking down the sidewalk toward me. Pepper and Elspeth walked toward me side by side with, much to my dismay, Ophelia Withington following behind them.

"Pandora, it's so good to see you all fixed up!" Elspeth kissed Pandora on the head and tweaked her tail. Pepper rubbed her neck.

Pandora, her eye on the mist swirls that only she and I could see, wriggled in my arms to get down. I gently placed her on the ground.

"And it's good to see you all fixed up, too." Elspeth gestured toward my bandaged hand.

"Yes, I was pretty lucky," I said, glancing toward the misty swirls.

Pepper hugged me. "I'm so glad nothing bad happened to you."

"Thanks," I said to Pepper, then slid narrowed eyes over to Opheila. What was *she* doing here? I hoped she wasn't going to cause some kind of trouble about me having Pandora in the bookstore.

"Mew." Pandora, on the other hand, didn't seem to have any worries as she batted and swirled at the misty figures. My brows pulled together ... was that Robert Frost and Franklin Pierce?

It was! Which was odd, because the two of them never left the bookstore as far as I knew.

"Willa?"

I turned back to Elspeth and Pepper. "What?"

"I was just saying that Striker did a great job with your hand," Pepper gave me a knowing look and I felt my cheeks burn.

"Yes, he did." I glanced nervously at Ophelia who alternated between casting strange glances at Pandora and fiddling with something under the lapels of her wide red cape that flapped in the wind.

"That's my cat, Pandora," I said glancing back to see Franklin Pierce poke playfully at the gray cat. "She's not feral."

"Oh, dear, Willa. I'm afraid you might have heard the worst about me." Ophelia pressed her lips together. "I must apologize for acting so badly, but you see, I just wasn't myself."

"Yes, it seems Ophelia has come to a new understanding." Elspeth stepped aside as she said it and I noticed that whatever Ophelia had been doing under her cape involved something furry.

A head popped out of the top of her cape and I gasped, recognizing it as the black and white kitten with the tattered ear.

"You adopted a cat?" I stared at Ophelia incredulously.

"Yes!" Ophelia beamed, as she cooed to the little kitten snuggled inside her cape.

"It seems Ophelia had a change of mind about the feral cats," Elspeth said. "She even donated some money to help fund the shelter."

"I wonder what changed her mind," Pepper cut in, raising a brow at me and purposely taking a sip of tea from the china cup she'd brought with her.

My eyes slid from Pepper to Ophelia and back again. Had Pepper's tea concoction really changed Ophelia from nasty to nice? Maybe there was something to Pepper's herbal obsession, after all.

"Not only that, but did you hear? The library is donating the sale of one of the bronzes to help build a new shelter for the feral cats." Elspeth said. "Lavinia would have liked that."

I remembered Lavinia telling me that Ophelia had scoured the library already. I'd thought she'd been looking for the bronzes, but I guess it had something to do with cats. Or maybe she thought Lavinia was hiding information about the cats there ... either way, it didn't seem like it mattered much now.

Out of the corner of my eye, I saw another swirly mist starting to form over by the door. It was Lavinia ... and she had luggage. I watched as she pecked Robert, then Franklin, on the cheek. Then she turned to me, mouthed the words 'thank you', bent down to pet Pandora and promptly disappeared.

Robert and Franklin looked sad for a few seconds, then Franklin put his arm out, gesturing for Robert to precede him, and the two of them disappeared back into the bookstore, leaving Pandora frowning at the closed door.

"Well, we're off to get cat supplies." Elspeth started down the sidewalk.

"I do hope we can be friends now." Ophelia stuck her hand out and I shook it.

"Sure," I shrugged at Pepper who favored me with a cat-that-ate-the-canary smile.

A sheriff's car pulled to the curb with Striker at the

wheel.

"Hi, Eddie," Pepper waved at him, then turned to me. "Gotta get back to my shop. See you later."

She wiggled her eyebrows at me before turning and heading off in the direction of her shop. I walked toward the car, Pandora at my heels.

"Hey, Chance." Striker smiled the smile that made his dimple show up and my heart fluttered.

"Hi." I smiled back remembering our kiss.

Pandora meowed and Striker leaned his head out to look down at her. "Hello, to you, too."

We stood there awkwardly for a few seconds. We hadn't really had a chance to talk since that kiss and I felt unusually tongue-tied. My thoughts turned to his shoes. I never did apologize for throwing up on them.

"Listen, I wanted to say how sorry I was for ruining your shoes the other day when I ... you know."

Striker laughed. "Oh, don't worry. Something tells me you'll have plenty of chances to make up for it."

And with that he winked and drove off before I could say another word.

"Meow." Pandora rubbed her face against my ankle and looked up at me, her intelligent eyes taking on more of a green tint in the bright sunlight.

I stared down at her. It almost seemed as if she was trying to tell me something, and I wondered, not for the first time, if my cat knew more about what was going on, than I did.

***

Like this book?
Sign up for Leighann Dobbs' newsletter and
be the first to know about new releases.
Early birds get them for the lowest possible price!
http://www.leighanndobbs.com/newsletter

BAKE, BATTLE, & ROLL

Chapter One

"According to Chef Dugasse, your pie crust is too thick," Lexy's assistant Deena said as she fitted a sheet of dough into a pie pan taking care to flute the edges the way Lexy had shown her.

Lexy glanced up at her as she worked the marble rolling pin over the dough, pounding it a little harder than necessary.

"I don't think *Chef* Dugasse knows his pie crusts," Lexy replied pushing down the anger she felt and wondering for the umpteenth time why she had agreed to fill in as pastry chef at the rustic lakeside resort.

When her grandmother Mona Baker, or Nans as Lexy called her, had phoned with the offer, it *had* sounded like fun ... at first. The current pastry chef had been taken ill, they were desperate for a temporary replacement—and they were willing to pay very well for it.

Still, Lexy wasn't sure why she had accepted. She had her own bakery to run where *she* was the boss and didn't have to listen to a pompous overpaid head chef berate her baking. But the promise of a free two week vacation in a rustic cabin with her fiancé, Jack, had won her over ...

... And she had regretted it every day since.

"How's this?" Deena stood back, indicating the pie plate.

Lexy tilted her head, inspecting the work. Deena had a part time job in the kitchen for the summer and Lexy had been training the enthusiastic teen on various baking techniques. Deena reminded Lexy of herself at that age—full of energy and eager to learn everything about baking. Training her was one of the few things she'd enjoyed about the temporary job and Deena was turning out to be a quick study.

"That looks great." Lexy squatted down so that her eyes were level with the table, then turned the pie plate and pointed to one section. "It's a teeny bit higher here."

Deena looked at the pie plate from table level and nodded. "Oh yeah. I can see that from this angle."

Lexy shrugged. "It just takes practice. You did a really good job for your first try."

Deena beamed with pride. "Thanks. If you ask me, Chef Dugasse is just being a jerk. Your pie crust is delicious."

Lexy agreed. Chef Dugasse *was* a jerk. He had been a thorn in her side since she took the position. She wasn't the only one that thought so, either. Most of the staff was at odds with him and it was no wonder with the way he was always yelling and screaming at them.

But he was world renowned, and his food was excellent, so he could do as he pleased and the resort kept him on.

Lexy glanced around the kitchen. The resort itself dated to the 1940s, but the kitchen had been recently renovated. Billed as a rustic-campy get away with five star dining, the meals had to be cooked to perfection so the kitchen, which sat inside a gigantic antique log cabin structure, was top notch.

It would be a pleasure to work in it ... if it wasn't for the domineering presence of Chef Dugasse.

Dugasse's voice thundered from the other side of the kitchen as if sensing Lexy's thoughts. "Theeze eggs are not up to our standards! You vill throw them out and start over!"

Lexy turned in the direction of the screaming. Dugasse was in a white chef's outfit complete with a tall hat. His six foot frame carried a three foot wide body, his gigantic bulk towering over a terrified first year cook, Thomas, who cowered in the corner. She watched as the head chef picked up the warming tray full of scrambled eggs and dumped them in the trash, then stormed off toward the back door that led outside.

Lexy saw Sylvia Spicer, Dugasse's long suffering sous-chef, rush over to soothe the cook's ruffled feathers. Sylvia's eyes shot daggers at the retreating back of the head chef before she started toward the door after him.

Lexy turned back to Deena who was still looking in the direction of the cook, wide-eyed with terror and her heart clenched for the poor girl. Lexy didn't see why Dugasse had to run the kitchen this way, almost everyone was terrified of him and it created an unpleasant work environment.

"Uh hum ..."

Lexy turned toward the throat clearing noise to find one of the chefs, Brad Meltzer, standing next to her. Brad worshipped Dugasse and the head chef often took advantage of that by sending Brad to do his dirty work, which Brad appeared to delight in.

Brad was as thin as Dugasse was wide. He had narrow, beady eyes and a pointed face which made Lexy think of a weasel. He didn't seem to like Lexy very much, which was fine with her since the feeling was mutual. Lexy raised an eyebrow at him.

"Dugasse says you have to make the cornbread for the *Chili Battle*." Brad jerked his head toward the back of the room where Dugasse had just disappeared.

"Excuse me?"

"The *Chili Battle*. They have it every year and it's a huge deal. The winner gets their own chili label to be sold nationally in grocery stores. Everyone knows Dugasse has a prize winning chili recipe so he's a shoe in. But he needs a cornbread side and that's where you come in."

Lexy felt her cheeks growing warm, anger causing her pulse to pick up speed. Having your own chili label was worth a lot of money, not to mention the branding opportunities for the chef. But she didn't see why *she* should have to put in extra hours to help make *him* rich and popular—not someone as mean spirited as Dugasse. She was sure he wouldn't do the same to help her if the tables were turned.

"That's not part of my job. I'm up to my eyeballs in pies and desserts here. I don't have time to make cornbread so that Dugasse can win some contest." She punctuated the chef's name by slamming her palm on the counter a little bit harder than she probably should have.

Brad's eyes grew wide. He took a step backwards and

spread his hands at his sides. "Hey, I'm just the messenger."

Lexy swiveled her head toward the back of the room. Dugasse wasn't there—he must still be outside.

"Sorry, Brad. I know that. But I'm sick and tired of being bossed around by Chef Dugasse." She spun on her heels and started toward the kitchen door. "And I'm going to put a stop to it once and for all."

***

Lexy felt the eyes of the entire kitchen staff drilling into her back as she stormed over to the door. A blast of cold air from the giant freezer that stood next to it did nothing to cool her anger as she ripped the screen door open and stepped outside.

It was still early in the morning, but the heat of the day was starting. Lexy's hands clenched at her sides as she stood just outside the door ready to lay into the head chef.

Where was he?

Her eyes darted around the area, her heart pounding with anger. Straight ahead the woods full of tall pines was empty except for birds and squirrels. Normally, Lexy would delight in watching them scamper and fly about, but this morning she was too mad to notice.

To her left was a short path that led to the parking lot, to her right the dumpster, surrounded by the stench of rotting food.

Did he go somewhere with Sylvia? She'd thought she had seen the sous-chef head out here after him, but where could they be? Lexy cocked an ear to listen for their voices but didn't hear anything except the flies buzzing around the dumpster.

Tentatively, she picked her way around the end of the large metal container. She peered around to see if they were on the other side, her breath catching when she saw a pair of chef's clogs. But instead of the soles lying flat on the ground, they were sticking up as if the person were lying down.

Lexy raced to the other side of the dumpster. Her heart

lurched up into her throat when she saw what lay on the other side. Chef Dugasse, lay on the ground—a big, shiny mahogany handled chef's knife sticking straight up out of his chest.

Lexy threw herself down beside him, her anger at the chef forgotten. "Chef Dugasse?"

No response.

Her mind whirled. What should she do? Should she pull the knife out and try to stop the bleeding?

Lexy realized she should check for a pulse. She placed her fingers on his neck.

Nothing.

She bent over him, putting her ear to his mouth to see if she could hear him breathing.

Nothing.

She tried his wrist.

Nothing.

Lexy sat back on her heels with a sigh, realizing there was nothing she could do.

Chef Alain Dugasse was dead.

***

A scream pierced the air, interrupting Lexy from digging her cell phone out of her pocket. She whipped her head around to see Sylvia Spicer standing just behind her, hands over her mouth, eyes wide.

"You killed him!" Sylvia rushed over to Dugasse's other side, slapping his face and lifting his arm.

"What? I did *not* kill him. I found him like this." Lexy narrowed her eyes at Sylvia who had given up on the face slapping and arm lifting and was now staring at her over the chef's body.

"Where were you?" Lexy asked.

"Me? I was in the kitchen." Sylvia turned her attention back to the chef. "Should we hide the body?"

Lexy stared at the sous-chef as she pulled out her cell phone. "Hide the body? We can't do that. We have to call the police."

"Right, of course, I don't know what I'm saying." Sylvia

pushed herself up and backed away from the body as if she just realized what it was.

Lexy made the 911 call while Sylvia paced back and forth, a whiff of musky perfume teased Lexy's nose every time the sous-chef walked by.

"Did you kill him?" Sylvia asked after she had hung up the phone.

"No. Of course not." Lexy studied Sylvia's worried face as she paced back and forth, wringing her hands. "Did you?"

Sylvia stopped and looked at Lexy. "Me? I wasn't even here."

"But I saw you come out after him." Lexy gestured toward the dead chef. "Right after he reamed out Thomas about the eggs."

Sylvia's brow wrinkled and she shook her head. "No, I didn't. I was in the freezer, cooling off. I was really mad so I went in there otherwise I *might* have killed him."

Lexy's teeth worked her bottom lip. She *could* have gone into the freezer, it was next to the door. And Lexy hadn't actually seen her come outside.

"But you have blood all over your shirt." Lexy pointed to Sylvia's chef's coat which was smudged with red. *Had it been that way before she knelt next to the body?* Lexy couldn't remember, she had been too distracted.

"So do you." Sylvia nodded at Lexy's shirt. Lexy looked down and her heart froze. She *did* have blood all over her —much more than Sylvia.

"Well, of course I do. I bent over him to see if he was breathing."

Sylvia stared at her. "Well, if you did kill him, you did all of us a favor."

Lexy rolled her eyes in exasperation. "I didn't do it."

Sylvia looked off toward the road as the sound of sirens split the air in the distance.

"Well, I don't care whether you did or didn't kill him, but my advice would be to get your ducks in a row."

"Why is that?" Lexy wrinkled her forehead at the other woman.

"Because I don't think the police are going to be very understanding when I have to tell them that I came out here to find you leaning over a dead body with blood all over your shirt."

Chapter Two

It didn't take long for word to get around and the kitchen staff crowded outside to see what was going on. Lexy was doing her best to keep them back from the crime scene when the police arrived.

"What's going on here? Don't you people know this is a crime scene? Haven't any of you ever watched TV?"

A short, round man flashed a badge and the crowd parted to let him and his entourage through. He stopped short when he saw Lexy and Sylvia with their matching blood stains.

"And who might you be?" He ping-ponged his dark eyes between the two women, his brows slightly dipped in a question.

Lexy stepped forward and introduced herself, Sylvia followed suit. The man's handshake was firm. He introduced himself as Detective Payne and the man beside him as his associate, Detective Wells.

They made an odd couple. Wells was over six feet tall, where Payne must have been only five foot six. Wells looked to be in his late twenties, Payne nearing sixty complete with partial balding and a protruding stomach. Wells looked professional in a dark blue tailor-made suit. Payne looked like a dork in a light blue polo shirt, and blue and red plaid Bermuda shorts.

"So you two found the victim?"

"Not me. She did." Lexy's stomach lurched as Sylvia pointed to her.

Payne swiveled his eyes toward Lexy. "So that's how you got the blood on you?"

"Yes. I saw him lying there and rushed over to see if I could do some sort of first aid. I must have gotten the blood on me then." Lexy's stomach churned as she looked down at her shirt.

"Hmm ..." Payne cut his eyes toward Wells, then walked back to the edge of the dumpster and looked at the kitchen door. "So, why were you out here, on this side of the dumpster?"

"What?" Lexy furrowed her brow at him, then remembered why she had walked around the dumpster. "Oh, I came out looking for the chef."

Payne raised his brows. "Do you normally find him behind the dumpster?"

"No." Lexy bit her lip. This wasn't going good. Maybe she should stop talking now, before she got herself into trouble. "I thought he would be just outside the back door. But when I didn't see him there, I peeked around and that's when I saw his shoes."

Payne scrunched up his face and walked over to the kitchen door. He made a big show of looking around, then came around the side of the dumpster.

"Oh yes." He nodded, pointing the pencil he held in his hand at the shoes. "They stick right out."

Lexy did a half smile and nodded as Payne came back over to them.

"And you?" Payne fixed his attention on Sylvia. "How did you get the blood on you?"

"I came out and saw chef on the ground and ran over to him to try to revive him. I didn't realize that Lexy had already determined he was dead."

Payne looked up at the sky, pursed his lips together and tapped them with the eraser end of the pencil.

"Yes, but what made *you* come all the way over to this side of the dumpster?"

Lexy saw a cloud pass over Sylvia's blue eyes and her brows wrinkle slightly. "Well ... I ..." She looked toward the door, then back at the body. "I came outside to have a word with Chef Dugasse and heard the commotion over here, so naturally I came over to see what was going on."

Commotion? Lexy didn't remember making any commotion.

Someone jostled Lexy's elbow—apparently a crime tech

who was trying to do their job of cataloguing the scene. It was getting crowded around the body and Lexy shuffled closer to the dumpster to give them room.

Payne looked around, wrinkling his nose as if suddenly becoming aware of the crime scene investigators swarming the scene and the stench of the dumpster.

Payne pointed to Lexy and Sylvia. "Let's finish this inside," he said jerking his head in the direction of the kitchen. He turned and started toward the door, almost tripping over an investigator that was scouring the ground for evidence. Wells fell in step behind him.

Lexy exchanged a raised eyebrow glance with Sylvia and followed them inside. The kitchen staff, who had been gathered in a circle, quickly dispersed to their various stations as soon as they entered the kitchen. Lexy realized that with Dugasse gone, Sylvia was now in charge.

Payne rambled over to the least crowded spot in the kitchen—the table where Lexy had been rolling the pie dough—and leaned against it. Wells stood to the side as if awaiting orders.

Payne looked down at a small spiral bound flip pad he had taken from his pocket when they were outside.

"Now, where were each of you when the murder happened?" Payne poised his pencil above the paper and widened his eyes at Lexy.

"Oh, I was right here. I was rolling pie dough and I saw chef over there." Lexy pointed to the end of the kitchen where she had seen Dugasse yell at Thomas. "Then I saw him go outside. I didn't go out until a few minutes later and found him with a knife in his chest."

"And someone saw you here?"

"Yes, several people. My assistant Deena and another chef, Brad."

Payne scribbled on the pad, then turned to Sylvia. "And you?"

"Well, I'm not sure exactly when he was murdered, but I went over to Thomas after Dugasse yelled at him, then I went into the freezer for a few minutes. When I went outside, he was already dead."

Payne's eyebrows mashed together. "Who is this

Thomas?"

"He's one of our cooks." Sylvia looked around the room, then spotted Thomas by the sink and pointed him out to Payne. Payne gave Wells a slight nod and the other man headed off toward Thomas, presumably to harass him with his own line of questioning.

"And why was Mr. Dugasse yelling at him?" Payne pronounced the chef's name as de-gassey and Lexy stifled a giggle.

"It's pronounced *doo-gah-say*," Sylvia said.

Payne made a face. "What?"

"The chef's name. It's pronounced *doo-gah-say*," Sylvia repeated, then continued. "He didn't like the eggs Thomas had prepared, thus the yelling."

"And did this chef yell a lot?"

Lexy and Sylvia both nodded.

Payne looked up at the ceiling and tapped the eraser end of his pencil on his lips. "So, would you say he was unpopular?"

Lexy and Sylvia nodded again.

"And who would have wanted him dead the most?"

Lexy looked around the kitchen. The rest of the staff, who had been craning to hear what was being said, suddenly developed a keen interest in their various tasks. She felt a shiver run down her spine. The head chef had just been murdered, yet everyone was going about their business as if nothing had happened. Then again, the resort couldn't shut the kitchen down. The meals were included in the price for paying guests so the food service had to continue uninterrupted.

No one liked the recently departed chef, but would anyone here have disliked him enough to kill him? She turned to look at Sylvia. If they didn't bring in anyone from the outside to replace Dugasse, she'd benefit the most. *Was a head chef's position worth killing over?*

She shrugged. "No one really liked him that much, but I don't think anyone here would kill him."

Payne tapped his pencil on his lips while he looked around the room. He narrowed his eyes at Lexy and Sylvia, his gaze moving to their bloodstained shirts.

"You were both out there with the body. Either one of you could have had time to thrust the knife into the chef ... or both of you together. It only takes but a second."

Lexy's stomach dropped, anger flaring at the detective. But then she realized he was only drawing the logical conclusion ... she'd probably think the same thing herself. Except she knew that *she* didn't do it. Sylvia, she wasn't so sure about.

Payne twisted his face into a grimace, making exaggerated sniffing noises. "What is that smell? Is something burning?"

Lexy sniffed. She *did* smell something burning. She whipped her head in the direction of her ovens, her heart clenching when she saw smoke streaming out of them.

"My pies!"

She ran to the ovens and jerked the doors open. A dark cloud of smoke billowed out. She shoved her hands in some oven mitts and batted at the smoke. Choking and coughing, she reached inside the oven and brought out twin flaming pies.

She dumped the pies in the sink, running water on them to douse the embers.

"You bake the pies?" Payne gestured to the other pies on the counter, the ones that weren't blackened hunks of coal.

"Yes, I'm the pastry chef here." Lexy tore off the oven mitts and tossed them on the counter, her spirits sinking. She'd have to work fast to get the right number of pies out in time for dinner and Payne was taking up valuable time.

"What kind of pies are these?"

"Huh?" Lexy scrunched her face at the detective who gestured at two of the pies she had finished earlier which were cooling on the counter. "Apple and blueberry."

"And this one?" he asked pointing to one in the back.

"Lemon meringue." Lexy wondered what this had to do with the dead chef.

Payne tapped his lips with the eraser end of his pencil. "May I?"

Lexy's brow creased deeper. Was this guy for real? He wanted a piece of pie? Now?

She nodded slowly.

Payne reached over and grabbed a chef's knife, cutting a large slice of pie. He looked at the knife as he pulled it out.

"This looks similar to the knife that killed your chef." Lexy's stomach clenched as Payne turned his dark eyes on her. She glanced over at her knives, her shoulders relaxing when she realized they were all there.

"Well, all my knives are accounted for, so it wasn't one of mine that killed him." She nodded toward the knife rack on the counter, then remembered the mahogany wood on the handle. "Besides, that knife had a mahogany handle ... mine are rubber."

Payne narrowed his eyes at the knife, then grabbed a plate from a stack of clean ones beside him and plopped the pie on it. His eyes darted around the counter, looking for something to eat the pie with. Lexy held out a plastic fork hoping to speed up the process and get rid of him.

"Mmm...'s good," he mumbled around mouthfuls. Lexy shuffled her feet impatiently.

"Detective ... the murder?" Wells appeared at Payne's side, eyeing the piece of pie he was demolishing.

"Right," Payne said, swiping a gob of meringue from the plate with his sausage-like finger and then licking it off. He put the plate down and consulted his flip pad.

"Chef Dugasse was murdered." He announced the obvious, looking up from his pad. "And someone in this room is most likely the killer."

All work in the kitchen ceased. All eyes turned to Payne.

"How do you know that?" Lexy asked.

"Well, you all had opportunity." Payne looked around the room. "Since you were all here in the kitchen, anyone could have slipped out to do the killing."

"But what about motive?" A voice from the other side of the kitchen cut in. Lexy cringed, recognizing the voice as her grandmother's. It would be just like Nans to run on down here upon hearing there was a murder. Her grandmother had an odd hobby. She investigated murders and, judging by the gleam Lexy saw in the older woman's eyes, she was right on top of this one.

Payne's eyes lit up. "Very good Ma'am. Who here wanted the chef dead?"

His question was met with silence.

"No one? You all loved the chef?"

Most of the staff looked down at the floor, some shuffling their feet and many of them murmuring, "no".

"You all didn't like him, then?"

Lexy saw Brad step forward. He gave her bloody shirt a pointed glance.

"Some of us liked him, but many didn't. Especially her." Lexy's heart lurched as Brad pointed straight at her. "In fact, right before Chef Dugasse was murdered, I heard her say she was going to put a stop to being bossed around by him *once and for all*."

Chapter Three

It took an eternity for Payne and Wells to leave. The short detective bombarded Lexy with a series of questions, then warned her not to skip town before demanding her blood stained chef's shirt as evidence.

Lexy glared over at Brad who watched them with a satisfied smirk on his face before she changed her shirt and put on one of the kitchen aprons.

Somewhere in the middle of questioning Nans had left, but not before demanding Lexy's presence once she was done with her baking. Her grandmother seemed practically giddy with delight and Lexy figured she'd probably have the large rustic cabin she shared with two of her friends turned into some sort of command center to use for running the investigation by the time she got there.

Lexy got busy rolling out dough. She needed twenty pies for the dinner service and all that questioning had taken up valuable pie-making time. She worked at breakneck speed since she didn't want to waste the whole day in the kitchen.

"I can't believe Brad ratted you out like that," Deena said, cutting her eyes toward Brad.

Lexy pursed her lips. "Yeah, what a jerk." Then looking up at Deena's wide eyes, she added, "I didn't kill him."

"Oh, I know that," Deena said, then leaned across the table and lowered her voice. "Do you think it was someone in here?"

Lexy glanced around the kitchen. Sylvia had easily slipped into the role of head chef and was overseeing the food preparations. She had to admit that Sylvia was much more pleasant than Dugasse. Could she be the killer?

Everyone else seemed to be focused on their job. No one

was acting like they had just stabbed someone.

"I don't know. The police seemed to think so, but it could have been anyone, really."

"Yeah, someone could have come from the woods and killed him. I bet a guy like that had a lot of enemies," Deena said as she turned to put two more pies in the oven.

Lexy glanced out the kitchen window at the large section of woods behind the dining lodge. Someone *could* have come from the woods. There were several paths out there.

"I heard he was behind the dumpster. What was he doing there?" Deena started pouring the filling into more pie shells.

Lexy bit her bottom lip. "I don't know."

What *was* he doing behind the dumpster? She'd assumed the chef had gone out for a smoke, but usually the smokers stayed right outside the kitchen door. There would be no reason for him to go behind the dumpster ... unless he was lured there or had some sort of secret meeting and didn't want to be seen.

Lexy finished rolling out the last of the pie dough, cut it into two circles, and quickly fitted them into pie plates for Deena to fill.

"Can you fill these and bake them, then set them to cool? I need to take off," Lexy said as she untied her apron.

"No problem." Deena nodded, getting to work with the pie filling.

Lexy bunched up her apron and threw it in the clothes hamper as she headed toward the door.

She was in a hurry to get to Nans. This case had a lot of angles to it and she'd feel much better if someone competent was looking into it. She didn't know if she trusted the pie eating Detective Payne, but she *did* know that Nans and her friends were good at solving crimes. They'd even helped the police department back home—where her fiancé, Jack, was a homicide detective—solve several cases.

Plus, she figured, it couldn't hurt to do some investigating of her own. It might help solve the case more quickly and she wanted to make sure the real killer was caught ... especially since *she* seemed to be the one that was at the top of Payne's suspect list.

***

Lexy stopped outside the dining hall, taking a deep breath to calm herself from the stresses of the morning. She was no stranger to dead bodies. In fact, she seemed to come across them frequently, much to the dismay of her fiancé ... and the delight of her grandmother. But still, it was never pleasant to find someone dead ... or to become the number one suspect.

Starting down the hill, she tried to push the image of Chef Dugasse with a knife sticking out of his chest from her mind. Instead, she focused on the scene in front of her.

The dining lodge was at the top of a hill with panoramic views of the rest of the resort. Lexy looked out over the pristine lake which was dotted with kayaks and canoes. Sunlight glinted off the deep blue waters. The peaceful sound of chirping birds filled the air and the smell of pine permeated her nostrils adding to the tranquil scene.

The resort was all about nature and relaxation. The roads were dirt, more like paths and people rarely drove cars on them—only to get to their cottages and to leave the resort. Most people walked or drove small golf carts inside the complex and the absence of the drone of car engines added to the peaceful feeling.

Quaint, rustic cottages painted in reds, blues, whites and greens—their shutters with cutouts of pine trees sat along the roadways. Most of them had porches complete with rockers and the yards were bursting with colorful displays of flowers. Lexy could see hammocks swinging in the breeze and wished she had time to relax in one.

Turning left on Aspen Lane, she headed toward Nans' cottage which was one of the largest in the resort. It sat at the very end of the street and had a huge front porch on which Nans and her three friends, Ruth, Ida and Helen were waiting.

"Lexy, are you okay?" Ruth hugged her.

"Come inside dear, we made some tea." Helen held the door to the cottage open and ushered Lexy inside.

"Tell us all about finding the body." Ida scooted a chair out from the wide pine table that sat next to a large window on one side of the room, indicating for Lexy to sit.

Ruth appeared at her side with a steaming cup of tea and then all four ladies took their seats around the table, staring at Lexy with wide, excited eyes.

Lexy sipped her tea and looked around the room. It resembled the squad room from an episode of *Castle*. There was a giant white board with a picture of Chef Dugasse on it and different columns of information. Papers were piled up on a nearby desk. Nans' iPad was charging on the coffee table.

"Where did you guys get that?" Lexy waved at the white board.

"Oh, Norman brought us to Staples and helped us with it," Ida said referring to her fiancé who had accompanied her on vacation. They had a small cottage near the lake while Nans, Ruth and Helen shared this one. Lexy and Jack had their own cottage a few streets over, which they shared with Lexy's white Poodle mix, Sprinkles.

The thought of her dog made Lexy smile and she glanced at her watch. She'd better hurry, she wanted to take Sprinkles for a walk before dinner and she should spend some time with Jack ...

"Tell us everything you know about the murder." Nans interrupted Lexy's thoughts.

"There's not much to tell. I went out to talk to Chef Dugasse—I had seen him go outside earlier. When he wasn't outside the door, I looked a little further and I saw his shoes on the other side of the dumpster, toes up. I ran over and there he was with a knife in his chest."

"You didn't see anyone else, or hear anything?"

Had she?

"I'm not sure, I was so distraught at finding him like that, I really wasn't thinking."

"So he was already dead?" Helen went over to the white board.

"Yes, I think so."

"And what time was that?"

Lexy gnawed on her bottom lip. "I'm not sure, I didn't

look at my watch or anything, but it was probably about five or ten minutes before I called 911."

Lexy pulled her cell phone out of her pocket and looked through the sent calls. "The 911 call was sent at eight twelve."

Helen wrote the time on the white board.

Nans got up from her chair. "So, you went out the door and looked for the chef?"

"Yes, I already said that."

Nans held up her finger. "When you didn't see him, you looked around the dumpster." Nans mimed looking around an imaginary dumpster in the middle of the room.

"Yep." Lexy nodded.

Helen scribbled something on the board.

"Then you saw his shoes and ran around to the other end of the dumpster?"

"Yeees ..."

Nans ran around the imaginary dumpster, threw her hands up in mock surprise and then knelt on the ground. "Like this?"

Lexy nodded and sipped more tea.

Ida went over beside Nans and looked down at the imaginary body. "You checked his pulse—he was dead. What else did you do?"

Lexy shut her eyes, trying to remember exactly what happened. "I checked his pulse—his neck and wrist and then I leaned over to see if he was breathing ... and that's when Sylvia came out."

"Sylvia, the sous-chef?" Ruth wrinkled her brow at Lexy.

Lexy nodded.

"She was out there?" Ruth asked.

Lexy nodded again.

"Won't she get the head chef position, now that Dugasse is dead?"

Another nod.

"Then she could be our killer!" Ruth went over to the white board and added Sylvia's name under the 'Suspects' column.

"Which direction did Sylvia come from?" Ida asked

Lexy pursed her lips. "She came from behind me ... I

didn't see exactly where, but I assumed she came out the kitchen door."

"But she could have been hiding on the other side of the dumpster after killing the chef," Nans said.

The ladies murmured their agreement.

"She had means, motive and opportunity!" Helen punctuated the last word by jamming the cap onto her white board marker.

"Well now, let's not get too excited," Nans said. "We can't call the case closed without doing a proper investigation."

"Right." Helen took the cap off her marker and posed her hand over the white board. "Who else do we have for suspects?"

Everyone looked at Lexy.

"What?"

"Who else would have wanted your chef dead? Did he have enemies?" Nans asked.

"He was mean to everyone in the kitchen, but I don't think that would be a reason to kill him ... unless he really pissed someone off. He *was* yelling at Thomas right before he was killed but Thomas didn't leave the kitchen." Lexy's eyebrows mashed together. "But I did see Sylvia heading toward the door after the chef."

"Aha! So she *was* out there," Helen said.

"Well, she said she was in the freezer. The freezer door is next to the door that leads outside. I didn't actually see her open either of the doors." Lexy shrugged.

"But she could be lying," Nans pointed out.

"Sounds like we'll have to do some digging to see if anyone besides Sylvia would have had motive." Ida picked up the iPad and powered it on. "Are there any surveillance cameras in the kitchen? Ones we could use to see exactly where Sylvia *did* go?"

"I don't think so. The kitchen is pretty old and low tech. But I can ask Thomas, he might have seen where she went," Lexy offered.

"What about the murder weapon?" Ruth asked.

"It was a standard chef's knife," Lexy said. "Thankfully all of mine are accounted for, plus the handle on that knife was different from mine."

"*Yours* are accounted for, but were anyone else's missing?" Nans wrinkled her brow at Lexy.

"I don't know." Lexy bit her lip trying to picture the kitchen. Most of the chefs had their own personal set of knives, too bad she hadn't thought to look to see if anyone was missing one.

"You should check that out tomorrow," Ruth said. "In the meantime, we'll see what we can dig up online about Chef Dugasse and ask around about any potential enemies."

"What did you think of the detective in charge of the case?" Nans turned to Lexy.

Lexy made a face. "Not much. He seemed more interested in eating pie than finding the killer ... which he seemed convinced might be me."

"Well, don't you worry. We'll find the real killer in no time, isn't that right, girls?" Nans turned to Ida, Ruth and Helen who all nodded.

Lexy stared at the four women, their cheeks flushed with excitement. She had to hand it to them. They were in their 80s and still sharp as a tack. With several successful investigations under their belts, they'd had great success solving murders back home. They'd even given themselves a name—*The Ladies Detective Club*.

Lexy felt a momentary pang when she realized this was supposed to be a vacation for them and she was causing them to have to work when they should be relaxing on the beach.

"I really appreciate you guys doing this, but I don't want to ruin your vacation," Lexy said taking her tea cup to the sink.

The ladies looked at each other and Nans spoke. "Don't be silly. Vacations are nice and all, but to tell you the truth, we were getting kind of bored."

"Yeah, we need to keep our brains active," Ruth said.

"Who wants to lie on the beach when we could be tracking down a killer?" Ida rubbed her hands together.

"That's right," Helen said. "Now you run along and let us get to work."

Lexy felt her shoulders relax. She smiled at the women. "Thanks, I *do* feel a lot better knowing you guys are on the case."

She was in the middle of hugging them when the chirping of birds erupted from her pocket. She dug out her cell phone and her heart clenched. It was Jack.

She'd been dreading explaining the morning's events to him. He took a dim view of her getting mixed up in murder cases, and they'd had more than one fight over her investigating cases with Nans and the *Ladies Detective Club*. This time she was going to have to put her foot down.

She was a prime suspect and didn't want to depend on the bumbling Detective Payne to find the real killer. She hated to do anything that would jeopardize her vacation with Jack … or their engagement … but she was determined to investigate this one with Nans and the ladies, whether Jack wanted her to nor not.

Chapter Four

"... and I seem to be the prime suspect." Lexy studied Jack's handsome face as she steeled herself for a lecture on the dangers of getting involved in murder investigations.

She felt her brows knit together as Jack smiled at her. He'd listened patiently while she'd relayed the morning's events, including the part about how Nans had turned her cottage into a crime investigation center. She'd expected him to be mad, but he was sitting there as calm as could be, changing out the reels on his fishing pole.

"So, you don't trust this detective ... what's his name?" Jack asked.

"Payne. Do you know him?"

As a homicide detective himself, Jack knew a lot of the other detectives in the state. Lexy was hoping that if Jack knew Payne, he might be able to get some information on the investigation.

Jack shook his head. "Never heard of him. But if you and Nans are on the case, I'm sure you'll ferret out the real killer."

Lexy stared at him. "You're not mad?"

"Why would I be mad?"

Lexy narrowed her eyes. "Usually you get mad when I get involved in these types of things with Nans."

Jack put down his fishing rod and came over to her, putting his hands on her upper arms.

"Lexy, I've come to realize that you're going to do what you are going to do no matter what I say. I can't fight it. So, I'll just have to trust that you won't do anything dangerous." He put his thumb on her chin, tilting her face up to look at him. "Right?"

"Right." Her heart melted at the look of concern in his

eyes. He bent his head, brushing his lips against hers and her stomach flip-flopped. She snaked her arms around his neck, pressing herself against him.

"Woof!"

Her dog, Sprinkles, jumped at her leg, stealing her attention from Jack. Lexy reluctantly released Jack and bent down to pet the little dog who was pawing at her calf.

"Hi Sprinkles. You want to go for a walk?"

The dog barked, jumped in the air and spun around.

"I guess that's a yes." Jack laughed. "Let's leash her up and take her out. I have a few hours before evening fishing."

Lexy crossed their small cabin and picked Sprinkles' harness and leash off the hook by the door, then put them on the small white dog which was quite a feat considering that Sprinkles was wiggling and jumping the whole time.

"Where do you want to go?" Jack asked.

"Well, if you don't mind, I wanted to check out the trails behind the dining hall. Payne thinks the killer was someone in the kitchen, but the murderer could have come from one of those trails. There are several that lead right to the dumpster area."

"So you're thinking Dugasse might have had a rendezvous with someone, or he was lured back there?" Jack opened the cottage door for Lexy and Sprinkles tugged her outside.

"Exactly." Lexy's heart soared. Jack seemed eager to help with the case which was a huge win for both the case and their relationship.

"Okay, let's take this trail." Jack indicated a trail next to their cottage that led up the hill and Lexy started toward it.

Sprinkles led the way, prancing eagerly up the path, stopping every so often to sniff something. Lexy was grateful for the tall pine trees that provided a cool respite from the hot afternoon sun. She breathed in the thick woodsy smell, watching the chipmunks scurry through the leaves. Her flip flops slapped the backs of her heels as they navigated the path.

She'd walked this path before, but she'd never really paid

attention. She looked at the slats of sunlight that filtered through the trees and realized the whole forest was a warren of trails.

"There's so many paths, the killer could have taken any of them."

"True, but the trick is finding which one is most likely. That's assuming the killer did use one of the trails to make his getaway."

"Well, what do *you* think? If this was your investigation, what would you do?"

"The paths are one angle to investigate. But I'd start where I always do—with the family." Jack glanced at Lexy. "Did Dugasse have a wife?"

"I'm not sure." Lexy pursed her lips trying to remember if she'd ever heard of a wife or any other family.

"Well, if he did, that's a good place to start. Then find out if he had any enemies, look into his finances. That's all pretty standard, I'm sure Nans has that covered." Jack smiled down at her.

They walked in silence for a few minutes, stopping with Sprinkles whenever she found something interesting to sniff or wanted to mark her territory. Lexy wondered how the dog seemed to have an endless supply for territory marking.

Lexy could see a small clearing up ahead. "Isn't that the dining hall?"

"Yeah, let's check it out."

Lexy turned in that direction and Sprinkles was only too happy to lead the way, her nose twitching in the air as she smelled the aroma of roasting meat from the kitchen.

Lexy stopped at the head of the path. She could see the dumpster about twenty feet away, roped off by yellow crime scene tape.

"So, that's the scene of the crime," Jack said it as a statement.

"Yeah, he was lying right there." Lexy shivered and Jack put his arm around her.

"I'm sorry you had to find him like that. It must have been awful for you."

Lexy shrugged. "Well, it wasn't fun, but I guess I must be

getting used to finding bodies since it didn't affect me nearly as much as the others."

Jack cocked an eyebrow at her but didn't say anything.

Lexy looked around the area where four paths met. "So, Detective ... which path is the most likely?"

"Well, the path we just came on leads out to the street near our cottage. The killer could have run down the path and no one would have noticed." He pointed to the path across from them. "That one goes parallel to the parking lot, I think."

"Yes, and you can see most of it from there, so the killer probably didn't take that one. Plus you have to go past the kitchen door and someone would have probably noticed him."

"That leaves these two paths here." Jack pointed to two trails that forked off deeper into the woods.

"I don't know where those go. Should we take one?"

"Well, if I was running the investigation, I'd have my people scouring each path for evidence." Jack frowned at the crime scene tape over by the dumpster. "But it looks like Payne is only searching the dumpster area."

Lexy's brows knit together. It seemed like Payne wasn't even covering the basics. Another reason to investigate it herself.

"Do you know if he had his people look at the paths?" Jack asked.

"I don't know but I can ask around. Maybe I will suggest it to him."

"Yeah, I'm sure that will impress him," Jack said dryly, then started down one of the paths. "Let's take this one and see where it leads. Keep a close eye on the ground and see if you can pick out anything unusual."

"Unusual? Like what?"

"A button, a scrap of paper, a shoe print. Anything that wouldn't naturally be there."

Lexy followed him down the path. She stared at the ground looking for a clue which was difficult with Sprinkles pulling her this way and that. After a few minutes, they came to a dead end.

Lexy's stomach dropped.

"That's it? The path just ends?" She looked around for another path, but found only thick woods—too thick to walk through.

"I guess the killer wouldn't have taken this one." Jack shrugged and started back the way they had come.

"If he did take a path, then it must have been the fourth one," Lexy said.

Jack stopped and looked at his watch. "Maybe, but I need to get back and get my fishing gear ready to go fishing this evening. I don't think it's a good idea for you to walk that path alone this close to dusk. Maybe we could walk it another time?"

Lexy felt her back go stiff, her shoulders tense. She hated being told what to do, but Jack was right. It probably wasn't smart to follow the path a killer might have taken alone.

Jack pulled her over to him. His right hand massaged her neck, melting all the tension she had felt a moment ago.

"Besides..." His left hand traced the waistband of her shorts. She sucked in a breath, her stomach tingling as he pulled the shorts away from her stomach just an inch and peered down. "I was hoping to get a look at your tan lines before I head out."

Chapter Five

Lexy woke up early the next day. She had to make five batches of brownies and several dozen cannoli and she wanted to get a head start. Plus she wanted to get in early to get a good look at the knife situation.

She entered by the dining hall front door, then went through the double stainless steel doors that separated the dining room from the kitchen. The doors opened to the end of the kitchen opposite from her baking station. Taking her time walking down the middle, she glanced around at each chef's station feeling more disappointed the further she went. It looked like all the knives were in place.

Donning her apron, she gathered, flour, cocoa, eggs, salt, vanilla, sugar and butter and brought them over to the giant mixer on the counter. Unlike her bakery where she usually made small batches, the dining hall was set up to feed large groups of people at once. The kitchen was used for cooking in bulk and she could mix gigantic batches, then pour several pans of brownies and bake them at once.

Deena came in just as Lexy was measuring the last of the ingredients into the gigantic mixing bowl.

"Is that for the brownies?" Deena stood on her tiptoes to peer into the bowl.

"Yep. I came in a little early to get things started." Lexy turned on the mixer. "But this will work out good because we can put the brownies in the oven and then get straight to work on showing you how to roll the cannoli shells."

Lexy felt a smile tug the corners of her mouth when she saw the teen's eyes light up. She remembered back to when her biggest worry was learning to roll the thin pastry correctly, unlike today when she had to worry about things like being arrested for a murder she didn't commit.

Lexy checked the mixer to make sure everything was mixed thoroughly. The smell of chocolate wafted up and her stomach nagged her that she hadn't eaten breakfast. She shut the mixer off and wrestled the bowl out of the stand.

"I'll pour and you can hold the pans."

Deena grabbed the side of an oversized brownie pan while Lexy struggled with the heavy bowl, somehow managing to pour the batter in without dropping the whole thing. They repeated the process for four other pans, then Deena ran them to the oven which Lexy had already preheated.

Lexy turned toward the fridge, intending to get the cannoli dough she had made the day before and bumped right into Thomas.

"Oh, sorry—I didn't see you." She put her hand on his arm to steady herself. "I hope you are doing okay after ... you know ... yesterday."

"Oh yeah. That was disturbing." The young man stepped back from Lexy, his eyes darting around the kitchen.

"Yes. Well, chef didn't have any right to yell at you like that."

Thomas' face turned red. "Surely, you don't think that I ... I—"

"Of course not." Lexy interrupted him. "I know you didn't even leave the kitchen. But I was wondering ..."

Thomas raised his brows at her.

Lexy leaned closer to him and lowered her voice. "Did you see where Sylvia went after she talked to you?"

Thomas wrinkled his face, sucking in his bottom lip and running his teeth over it. "I don't remember. I don't think I was watching her ... I was too busy trying to get more eggs made for breakfast."

"Oh. Okay, thanks," Lexy said.

Thomas nodded and scurried off. Lexy continued on to the fridge. She let out a sigh as she searched for the dough. If Thomas didn't see where Sylvia went maybe someone else did. But who?

Deena was waiting at the table when Lexy returned with

two balls of dough. She handed one to the teen. They floured the table and their rolling pins, then started rolling the dough.

"You didn't happen to notice where Sylvia went yesterday ... after that whole incident with Thomas, did you?" Lexy asked.

Deena stopped rolling, her brow creased in concentration. "No, I wasn't looking that way. But I think my friend Jules was over near there. I can ask her if you want."

"That would be great." Lexy felt her heartbeat pick up speed a notch. She remembered being a teen and how they used to gossip about everything going on in the kitchen. The teen network here could be a valuable resource and she had an "in" with Deena. "Actually anything you can find out about that day ... or Chef Dugasse would be helpful."

"Okay, sure. I'll ask around." Deena looked up from rolling the dough and whispered, "On the sly."

"Thanks," Lexy said, giving her dough one final pass with the rolling pin.

"I like to roll the dough about one eighth inch thick." Lexy held up the edge of her dough as an example. "That will make the shells nice and crispy."

Deena nodded rolling her dough to the same thickness.

"Okay, good." Lexy grabbed a round stainless steel cookie cutter from a drawer and handed it to Deena. "Now cut the dough with this ... that will make the shells."

Deena pressed the cookie cutter into the dough, cut a circle, then placed it down again as close to the previous cut as possible so as to make the most use of the dough they had rolled out. Lexy felt a swell of pride—she'd taught her well.

Lexy cracked an egg into a little bowl and beat it with a metal whisk, then added a teaspoon of water and beat it some more. She grabbed the cannoli form—a round stainless steel tube that was about one inch across.

When Deena was done punching out the dough, Lexy picked one of the circles up.

"Okay, this is easy. You just take the dough and wrap it

around the cylinder." She wrapped the dough so just a tiny piece of the edge overlapped.

"Then you take the pastry brush, brush some egg wash on the edges and press them lightly together so it doesn't come unwrapped when you fry it." She illustrated with the brush then handed the form to Deena.

"Now you try it," Lexy said.

Deena gingerly picked up a form, then a circle of dough. Lexy watched her wrap it, a little off center but still not bad for a first try. She was dipping the brush in the egg wash to help wet the edges when she heard a familiar voice behind her.

"Looks like we're having cannoli for dessert!" Nans navigated the kitchen, carefully stepping on the rubber mats. Ida, Helen and Ruth followed along behind her.

"Hi!" Lexy greeted the ladies. "What brings you here?"

"Oh, you know, we were in the neighborhood ..." Nans gave the kitchen a sweeping glance, then leaned in toward Lexy and lowered her voice. "We were wondering if you made any progress."

Lexy frowned. "Not really, but I'm working on it. Do you guys want some brownies? I'm just about to take them out of the oven."

Nans held her hands at chest level, palms out. "None for me, thanks."

Ruth, Ida and Helen shook their heads. Lexy narrowed her eyes at them. It wasn't like the ladies to turn down a dessert.

She left Deena to the cannoli shells and went to the oven. She was bent over, trying to lift the large pan out when she sensed someone behind her. Straightening, she spun around, her heart jumping when she saw Brad standing there.

"Can I help you?" she asked in a not very friendly way.

"I see you're still here even after yesterday," he said.

Lexy put her hands on her hips, anger pulsing in her veins. "And why wouldn't I be?"

"Well, it's just that it's awfully suspicious that you stormed off after chef yesterday and then he ends up dead ... with his blood on your shirt." Brad glanced over toward her knife set.

"Yes, my knives are all there," Lexy said taking the brownie pan out of the oven and slamming it on the counter. "So my knife was *not* the one that killed Dugasse."

"Really?" Brad raised an eyebrow at her. "It sure seemed like you were mad. And you had the opportunity. You could have used any of the knives from the kitchen ..."

Lexy ignored him, turning back to the oven.

Brad glared at her. "What's a'matter? Don't have a snippy answer for that one eh?"

"Don't you have some work to do?" she shot over her shoulder.

Brad started toward the front of the kitchen then turned back to Lexy. "Enjoy what time you have left in the kitchen ... I heard Payne is here and he might be ready to make an arrest."

Lexy's heart clenched. Surely Payne didn't have any evidence to arrest her with?

"What was that all about?" Nans stared at Brad's retreating back.

"I have no idea. Yesterday he made a big deal out of telling Payne that I had stormed out after Dugasse vowing to stop him once and for all ... or something like that."

"And did you?"

Lexy cringed. "Well, I guess I did ... but I didn't mean I was going to stop him by killing him!"

"Oh, so you didn't kill him?" A voice behind Lexy made her jump and she whirled around coming face to face with Detective Payne in a white polo shirt and a new pair of plaid Bermuda shorts—these in purple and yellow.

"No. I. Did. Not," Lexy said, taking another tray of brownies out of the oven and slamming them on the counter.

Payne's eyebrows went up. "Are these brownies?"

"Yes."

He rubbed his hands together. "Are you going to cut them?"

"Yes."

Payne grabbed a plate from the stack near the sink and

held it out to Lexy who felt her mouth hanging open. Was he serious? She was about to give him a piece of her mind when she remembered Nans' old saying about catching more flies with honey then vinegar. Maybe if she kept giving the detective pastries, he wouldn't want to arrest her.

She took the plate, grabbed a knife—not a chef's knife like the one that killed Dugasse, a smaller one—and cut neat rows in the pan. Then she removed an extra-large brownie, put it on the plate and handed it to Payne, forcing herself to smile in the process.

"So, Detective ... what brings you here? Do you have more questions?" Lexy asked after he'd taken a few bites and mumbled his approval.

"Mmmm ..." Payne put the plate down and blotted his lips with a tissue he took from his pocket. "Yes, of course. I did come here for a reason. It seems some new evidence has come to light."

Lexy's stomach clenched. "It has?"

"Yes." Payne turned to face the rest of the kitchen and raised his voice. "There is a new suspect ... someone who has been seen sneaking up to the kitchen on several occasions."

The kitchen grew silent, everyone stopping their tasks and turning to look at Payne. Lexy's heart thudded with anticipation.

"And that person is in the room right now." Payne slowly looked at everyone in the room, his pencil poised in the air as he surveyed the area.

"Who is it?" someone asked.

"It is ..." Payne suddenly stopped, then whirled in the direction of Nans and her friends. He stabbed his pencil out toward them.

"Ruth Weston!"

Chapter Six

Payne's words hit Lexy like a punch in the gut and she whirled around to look at Ruth along with everyone else in the kitchen.

Ruth's hand fluttered around her throat, her face turning an unhealthy shade of red.

Nans, Ida and Helen all said "Ruth!" at the same time.

Lexy turned back to Payne. "That's got to be some sort of mistake. Why would Ruth be sneaking up to the kitchen?"

"It is no mistake. I have it on good authority." Payne picked up the plate and shoved the rest of the brownie in his mouth.

Lexy narrowed her eyes at the room wondering who would have said such a thing. Her gaze came to rest on Brad who was leaning against the sink, arms crossed on his chest, a smirk on his face.

"Ruth, tell him that's not true," Nans said.

"I ... well ... I can't," Ruth stammered.

"What? Why can't you?" Nans asked.

"Because," Ruth looked down at the floor, "it's true."

"What?" Ida gasped. "But why would you be sneaking around here?"

Ruth's chest heaved as she took in a deep breath. She looked up at Nans. "I was sneaking rolls."

"Rolls!" Helen said sharply.

Ruth's face turned even deeper red.

Lexy's brow creased. "Why would you have to sneak up to the kitchen for rolls?"

"Oh, it's this darn Paleo diet. It's killing me!" Ruth said.

"What? What Paleo diet?" Lexy cut her eyes to Nans.

"We've been on the Paleo diet. You know eating like a cave man? It's supposed to be very good for you and help slow down aging. God knows we can use all the help we can get in that area," Nans said.

"So, we're sworn off baked goods. We agreed to eat only meat, fruits, nuts and vegetables. Didn't we Ruth?" Helen turned to Ruth whose face got even redder.

That explained why they didn't want the brownies, Lexy thought.

"But what's that have to do with Chef Dugasse?" Lexy asked.

"Nothing," Ruth said. "I didn't even know the chef. I was just sneaking over for rolls. Jules would give them to me."

Lexy looked at Payne. "This seems pretty flimsy. Why does that make Ruth a suspect?"

"My source told me she was very sneaky like she didn't want to be seen. In my book, that's suspicious."

"Well, maybe Jules can corroborate Ruth's story."

"Which of you is Jules?" Payne bellowed out into the room.

A young, blonde girl stepped forward, her eyes flitting around the room.

"I am," she squeaked.

Payne made circling motions with his pencil. "Well, tell us. Did you give Ruth the rolls?"

"Yes, she came the past three mornings. Early. Said not to tell anyone."

"And did she fraternize with Chef Dugasse?"

"No, sir." Jules picked at the strings fraying from her apron pocket. "She just poked her head in the door and asked for a couple of rolls and some butter."

"At the back door?" Payne pointed his pencil to the door that led out to the dumpster.

Jules nodded.

Payne turned to Ruth. "And did you see Chef Dugasse ... or anyone else out there?"

"No." Ruth shook her head.

Payne looked up at the ceiling, tapping the eraser end of his pencil on his lips in the familiar gesture that Lexy took to mean he was "thinking".

"What time was this?" he asked.

Ruth glanced at the other ladies. "I wanted to eat the

rolls and get back before Helen and Mona got up so I always came at seven thirty on the dot."

Payne did more pencil tapping on his lips. "The medical examiner places the time of death between seven forty-five and eight fifteen. So that would be too early to kill the chef ... unless you lurked around the dumpster, killed him and then went back to your cottage."

"That's impossible." Nans cut in earning a raised eyebrow look from Payne. "We have our alarms set for seven fifty am precisely and Ruth was already there when mine went off. So she wouldn't have had time to kill the chef and get back to the cottage."

Ruth turned to Nans, Ida and Helen. "I'm so sorry if I let you down. But I just couldn't go without bread!"

Helen grabbed her hand. "That's okay, Ruth. To tell you the truth, I snuck a Mounds bar the other day."

"I ate some animal crackers at the beach," Nans added.

"And I snuck one of Norman's scones," Ida confessed.

"Ladies! Ladies!" Payne waved his arms. "Let's stick to the morning of the murder."

Nans, Ruth, Ida and Helen turned their attention back to Payne.

"Now, you came from the parking lot to the back door?" Payne asked.

Ruth nodded.

"You didn't come up the path by the dumpster?"

"No."

"And did you see anything unusual while you were there?"

Ruth scrunched up her face. "I'm not sure this has anything to do with your investigation, but the parking lot is usually quite empty at that time of morning ... except yesterday there was a very unusual car in the lot. It stuck right out.

Payne made impatient circling motions with his pencil. "Are you going to tell us what it looked like?"

"It was a pink Cadillac. I've never seen one before. It was quite striking."

"Who here has a pink Cadillac?" Payne said looking around the room.

No one fessed up.

"No one knows who owns such a car?"

Everyone shook their head. Payne scribbled in his notebook. Lexy tapped her foot impatiently.

"Are we done here?" Lexy asked.

"Not quite ..." Payne eyed the brownies.

"But Ruth is free to go, right?" Nans asked.

"Yes, I suppose she is in the clear," Payne said reaching into his pocket and producing a business card which he handed to Ruth. "If you remember anything else that might be useful, give me a call."

Ruth took the card and the women started toward the door with Nans miming instructions to Lexy to meet her at their cottage when she was done.

Lexy tried to go back to cutting the rest of the brownies only to be interrupted by the annoying detective.

"I do have some bad news for you," he said to Lexy. "Sylvia Spicer says she found you standing over the body so if there's anything you want to tell me ..."

Lexy felt her cheeks grow warm, she glanced over at Sylvia her stomach tightening with anger.

"Why would I kill him?" She turned back to Payne. "If you ask me, Sylvia had more of a motive—with Dugasse gone, she gets promoted to head chef ... and *I* saw *her* heading in the direction of the door right before I went out and found him dead."

Payne's brows shot up, he scribbled in his book. "She said she was in the freezer."

Lexy shrugged. "Well wouldn't you say that, too, if you didn't want to be suspected of murder?"

Payne tapped the eraser on his lips. "Yes, I guess I would."

He reached over, took another brownie and then started in the direction of the door. After taking two steps, he turned around jabbing the brownie in her direction.

"I still have more clues to put together, but I'd say it doesn't look so good for you. I've done some digging and I know you've been involved in other murders."

Lexy started to protest and he held his hand up to silence her.

"I know, you were never charged with any of them, but it seems rather suspicious to me that you're always around when a dead body shows up." He leaned in toward her, his dark eyes drilling into hers. "I'm going to be looking into you very carefully. Rest assured that if you had something to do with *this* murder, your detective boyfriend won't be able to get you out of it this time."

Chapter Seven

It was noon by the time Lexy and Deena stuffed the last cannoli shell with her sweet ricotta recipe. She threw her apron into the bin, said good-bye to Deena and grabbed a cannoli on her way out the door.

She took the same path to Nan's cottage as she had the day before. This time she was more focused on the sweet creamy pastry than the scenery. The hours spent over the Fry-O-Lator had paid off. The shell was perfectly crunchy. They were sure to be a big hit at tonight's dinner. Speaking of which, Lexy realize she'd better hurry if she wanted to have some beach time with Jack before they had to come back to the dining hall to eat.

She shoved the rest of the cannoli in her mouth, wiped her hands together and sprinted the rest of the way to Nans.

The four ladies turned as Lexy tapped lightly on the screen then let herself in. She glanced at the white board and noticed they had added a column labeled 'clues' and put 'pink Cadillac' under it and had updated the 'Dugasse' column with the time of death.

"Did Payne say anything enlightening after we left?" Nans was all business.

"Not really." Lexy sunk into the old slip covered sofa that faced the white board and studied the columns.

"Let's go through the board and you can tell us about any new information," Nans said to Lexy.

"Did you find out about any enemies or any rumors about Chef Dugasse?"

Lexy shook her head. "Nothing so far. I have Deena asking around. You know how teens are, they see a lot more than the rest of us."

Nans nodded, then pointed to the 'Crime Scene' column. "Do you know what they might have found for evidence?"

"Other than the knife? No. But Jack said, if it was his case, he would be scouring the trails for evidence and it doesn't look like Payne is doing that. We walked a couple of them yesterday and didn't find a thing, but there's one more I want to check out ... maybe you guys could go with me?"

"Sure," Nans said, looking at the others who nodded their agreement.

"I wish we knew if they found anything out by the dumpsters," Helen said. "It sure is a lot easier investigating these things when you have an 'in' at the police department."

Lexy nodded her agreement. Back home, Jack usually knew everything about the cases they were working on and he would give them tidbits of information. She didn't think they'd be getting the same courtesy from Payne.

Nans pointed at the murder weapon column on the white board. "This knife could be a clue ... if we could verify whose knife it is."

Lexy shrugged. "Most every chef has a set of knives, but I did notice that knife was a very high end one with a mahogany handle. I haven't seen any like that in the kitchen but I'll keep looking."

Ida stepped out from the other side of the board and tapped her finger on the heading of the next column, 'Sylvia'. "This is probably where we should focus our efforts."

"Yes, she seems to be our most likely suspect," Nans agreed.

"She claims she was in the freezer, that she never went outside until after I found him," Lexy said. "Thomas, the chef she was talking to right before the murder said he didn't see where she went, so I can't place her at the scene ... yet."

"She stands to gain the head chef spot and she probably hated him just as much as anyone," Helen pointed out.

"I bet when she saw him yelling at the other chef, it was the straw that broke the camel's back and she got so mad that she ran out there and shoved the knife into his chest!" Ida clasped her hands together and arced them in the air in front of her, making stabbing motions.

Ruth nodded. "Pent up aggression for how he treated everyone."

"A crime of passion," Helen added.

Helen's words triggered something in the back of Lexy's mind. "Or maybe ..."

The four women raised their eyebrows at her.

"What if there was more going on with Sylvia and Dugasse than just a chef and sous-chef relationship?" Lexy asked.

Nans eyebrows shot up. "Did you see something to indicate that?"

"Well, sort of. I did see them in some conversations that seemed to be more personal then professional. I didn't think anything of it at the time, but now ..."

"A lover's quarrel!" Ida's eyes lit up.

"Well, I don't know. It's one thing to look into, I guess. There's another thing too." Lexy's brow wrinkled. "When Sylvia saw me with the body, she asked if we should hide it."

"Hide it?" Nans said. "Why would she ask that if she didn't kill him?"

"I have no idea," Lexy said. "And then there's the matter of Brad."

"Who's Brad?" Helen asked.

"Another one of the chefs. He's the one that told Payne I had stormed off to 'stop Dugasse once and for all'. *And* he was needling me today about being the killer." Lexy pressed her lips together. "I have no idea why he would do that, unless he just hates me."

"It could be a love triangle!" Ida said.

Lexy made a face. "I'll have to ask around and see if anyone else noticed anything."

"Meanwhile, I'll add Brad to the board." Nans added his name under the 'Suspects' column.

"There's another thing to consider," Ruth said. "How did his body get *behind* the dumpster?"

"He might have been dragged there to buy some time for

the killer. If the feet weren't sticking out he might not have been found until hours later." Nans pinched her nose with her thumb and forefinger. "The smell of the dumpster would have masked any smells from the body."

"And that would imply the killer wanted to get far away ... so maybe it wasn't someone from the kitchen," Helen said.

"Or, he was lured to the other side of the dumpster by the killer, who stabbed him, then took off down the path," Ida added.

"Either way, that indicates we should also consider suspects that weren't in the kitchen," Nans said.

"Which ties in with what I found online." Ruth held up the iPad.

Lexy's eyebrows shot up. "What did you find?"

"Well, it seems your chef was involved in some sort of chili contest," Ruth said.

Lexy nodded remembering Brad's order that she make the cornbread was the catalyst for her finding Dugasse in the first place. "Yes, I know."

"Well, it seems this chili contest can be quite lucrative and it's very competitive ... some newspaper articles describe it as 'cutthroat.'"

"Why?" Helen asked.

"The usual reason. Money. The winner gets a national brand so not only will they get the money from chili sales, but their name will become a household word which will lead to other endorsements, cookbooks etc. ..." Ruth looked up at them. "Winning that contest could be worth millions."

"Did he ever talk about the contest? His rivals, or anything?" Nans asked Lexy.

"I never heard him say anything." Lexy spread her hands wishing she'd paid more attention to Dugasse, the truth was she kind of zoned out whenever he started droning on.

"Well, that's something to look into then." Ruth crossed to the board and added 'Chili Contest' to the list.

"And that brings us to the pink Cadillac." Helen pointed to the words on the white board.

"Too bad we can't ask Jack to just look that up in the

database," Ida said.

"Well, luckily a pink Cadillac is unusual, so I'm going to start by doing a search on newspaper articles. Then if that doesn't pan out, I'll hack into the motor vehicles database." Ruth looked up at them and widened her eyes, putting her hand over her mouth. "Ooops ... I mean I'll look elsewhere."

The other women laughed, then gathered behind Ruth to look over her shoulder as she searched.

After a minute she said, "Got it!"

She held the iPad up. "Here's a picture of the exact same car I saw in the parking lot. The article is about a semi-celebrity that's staying in the area at the Sheraton Hotel. You know the fancy five star one, on the side of the mountain?"

"Yes," Nans, Ida, Helen and Lexy all said. Everyone knew that hotel. It was the height of luxury.

"Well, apparently she loves pink. Pink car. Pink clothes. Pink purse. Even a pink dog."

Lexy wrinkled her brow and bent closer to the iPad. Sure enough, it showed a middle-aged blonde with gigantic pink sunglasses holding a furry dyed-pink Pomeranian.

"What's that have to do with our case?" Nans wondered.

Lexy grabbed the iPad and scanned the article. Her heart jerked in her chest when she looked at the caption under the picture. She sucked in a deep breath and looked up at the four women.

"The owner of the pink Cadillac is Victoria Dugasse ... Chef Dugasse's wife."

Chapter Eight

"Thanks for making the cake, Lexy," Nans said as she slid into the backseat of Ruth's gigantic Oldsmobile beside Lexy.

Lexy looked down at the red velvet cake on the seat beside her. She'd had to cut her beach time with Jack short to make it yesterday afternoon and he'd been unusually understanding. In fact, he seemed strangely disinterested in the case and the fact that she was a murder suspect.

"Lexy?"

"Oh sorry, I was just thinking how Jack seems only interested in fishing, he didn't even care that we were going to visit Victoria Dugasse today. Normally he'd have all kinds of warnings about butting into police stuff."

Ida turned in the front seat to face her.

"Oh, that's how they get. When it comes to fishing they become obsessed. I know Norman is. He has only fishing on his mind ... well that and one other thing." Ida winked at Lexy who shifted uncomfortably in her seat, unwanted pictures of Ida and Norman bubbling up in her mind.

Ruth maneuvered the car out of the resort and headed up the highway. Lexy wondered how she managed—her eyes barely cleared the top of the steering wheel. Lexy tested her seatbelt to make sure it was fastened properly.

"Do you really think she'll buy our ruse of wanting to give our condolences?" Helen asked.

"I don't see why not. It's the proper thing to do," Nans replied. "Besides, we'll make it seem like we are on official business from the resort, then she'll be more likely to talk to us."

"Hopefully we can get her to open up enough to tell us where she was that morning," Ida said. "Because if she wasn't in the kitchen ..."

"... She could have been out by the dumpster with Dugasse." Nans finished the sentence.

"Well I doubt she's going to tell us she killed him." Lexy cringed as Ruth turned into the parking lot for the hotel, her back tires going up over the curb and crushing a bed of petunias.

"No, but hopefully we'll be able to tell if she's hiding something," Nans said as Ruth parked the car.

Everyone got out. Lexy grabbed the cake and followed the four women into the gigantic hotel, happy to have gotten there in one piece.

The lobby was sumptuous. Lexy's sandals sunk into thick carpeting in a dark blue and gold pattern as she walked past the giant marble table that held a vase of flowers which must have been six feet tall and three feet wide. A crystal chandelier sparkled above the flowers.

Nans walked past the oak paneled front desk and straight to the elevators. Ruth had somehow gotten the room number so they knew just where to go. They rode the elevator up to the eighth floor, turned left and walked the fifty feet to room 845.

Nans knocked on the door. Lexy heard the safety chain slide, then the door opened a crack. A baby blue eye peeked out at them.

"Yes?"

"Mrs. Dugasse?" Nans asked.

"Yes." The door swung open to reveal a tall blonde who raised her perfectly plucked eyebrows at them. Lexy noticed she was wearing an expensive pink silk sleeveless shirt and white capri-length pants. Her bare feet sported petal pink painted toenails and gigantic pink diamonds glittered in her ears.

"We're from Lakeshore Resort. We'd like to express our condolences," Nans said as Lexy shoved the cake in Victoria's face.

"Oh. Do come in." The door swung open and they stepped inside while introducing themselves.

"Please call me Victoria," their host said as she took the cake from Lexy. "Would you like a piece?"

"No thanks," Nans said and the rest of them shook their heads.

Victoria put the cake on a sideboard and gestured them further into the opulent suite. They settled in the living room—Victoria, Nans and Ida picked out chairs while Ruth, Helen and Lexy shared the sofa. The room was decorated with French provincial furniture in off white. Pink curtains and throw pillows accented the white upholstered sofa and chairs. Lexy wondered if the hotel just happened to have a pink room or if Victoria had redecorated.

A white Pomeranian with pink tipped fur pitter patted into the room.

"You dyed your dog's fur?" Lexy asked.

"Yes, well, just the ends." Victoria picked the tiny pooch up—a girl Lexy assumed by the pink bow—kissed the top of her head, then set the dog on her lap. "My hairdresser says it is quite safe."

A motion to Lexy's left caught her attention. She turned her head and felt her eyebrows shoot up. It was a maid, in a black and white uniform. Who has a maid in a hotel room?

"Oh Myra, why don't you bring us some lemonade." Victoria glanced at Nans and the rest of them who nodded. "Six lemonades, then."

Myra disappeared and Nans put her hand on Victoria's arm. "We're so sorry about the loss of your husband."

"Thank you." Victoria dabbed at her eyes with a tissue even though there were no tears. Lexy noticed that pink and white diamond rings were stacked on almost all of her fingers. Her wrist displayed a flashy Rolex watch.

"You knew Alain?" She asked after the appropriate amount of eye dabbing.

Nans nodded. "We enjoyed his food. Lexy here is the pastry chef in the kitchen at the resort."

"Chef Dugasse will be missed," Lexy said forcing a smile at Victoria, then crossing her fingers behind her back and hoping not to get struck by lightning.

The maid came in saving Lexy from having to say anything more. She handed out crystal glasses filled with lemonade—pink lemonade, of course.

With the formalities dispensed, Nans got right to the point. "You were there that morning, right?"

Victoria's eyes went wide. "Well ... I ..."

"I noticed your lovely pink car," Ruth said. "It's quite distinctive ... hard to miss."

"Oh, yes. I suppose I was there. Earlier." Victoria took a sip of lemonade.

"To see your husband?" Nans asked.

"Yes."

"And you had a fight." Nans persisted.

Victoria's eyebrows mashed together. "How did you know that?"

"Oh, one hears things ..." Nans waved her hands. "It must be very disturbing to you to have been fighting right before he ... well, you know."

"Yes, it is very sad for my last memory to be of that fight. Although I doubt Alain would feel the same way."

Nans looked at Victoria over the rim of her lemonade glass. "Why do you say that?"

"Because, Alain was having an affair."

***

Nans eyebrows shot up. "An affair? What makes you say that?"

Victoria shrugged. "He had been sneaking off at around two in the morning on several nights. He thought I didn't notice that he got up early and left."

"And you confronted him about that?" Ida asked.

"Yes, of course. I used it as leverage to stop him from curtailing my spending." Victoria waved her hand around the room. "I need to be kept in the manner to which I've become accustomed."

"What did he say when you confronted him?" Lexy asked.

"He denied having the affair. Typical cheater." Victoria studied her frosty pink nails. Lexy noticed that she didn't seem very upset about the affair or his death.

"Do you have any idea *who* he was having the affair

with?"

"Nope. It could have been anyone," Victoria said.

"So, you were using the knowledge of the affair as leverage to keep your spending habits, but why? How would that help you?"

"It's all in the prenup. Alain would lose a lot of money if he had an affair."

Lexy saw Nans exchange glances with Ida, Ruth and Helen.

"But, if you killed him, then you'd get to keep all the money either way," Nans said.

Victoria's back stiffened.

"Is that what you think? That *I* killed him?" She dumped the pink pooch on the floor and shot out of her chair. Storming over to the door, she held it open gesturing for them to leave.

Lexy took the hint and got up from her chair as did Nans, Ruth, Ida and Helen. They filed out the door.

Victoria stood in the doorway and watched them go.

"And for your information," she yelled after them, "I didn't need, or want to kill him. The truth is Alain would have made even more money after he won the *Chili Battle*. So, you see, he was worth much more to me alive than dead."

***

"She didn't seem too upset about her husband being dead," Lexy said once they were strapped into Ruth's Oldsmobile and heading back to the resort.

"But she sure got upset when she thought we were accusing her of killing him," Ida added.

"That doesn't necessarily mean she killed him." Ruth looked at Lexy in the rear view mirror.

"I doubt she is the killer," Nans said. "If Dugasse was going to become even richer because of winning the *Chili Battle*, it wouldn't be in her best interest to kill him."

"Unless he was going to divorce her and leave her out in the cold," Ida ventured. "Maybe that's what they argued about."

Lexy pressed her lips together. "I wonder who he was sneaking off to see in the early morning. That seems like an odd time to meet a secret lover."

"I bet it was that Sylvia Spicer. They had a lover's spat and she killed him," Ruth said.

Lexy blew out a whoosh of air. "Maybe. There's a lot of things we still need to look into. Like where that other trail leads and if Sylvia really *was* in the freezer when Dugasse was being stabbed. *And* we need to find out more about this chili contest. How come everyone is so certain that Dugasse was going to win?"

"Good question," Nans said. "We do have our work cut out for us."

Ruth rolled down her window and stuck her hand out to signal for the turn.

"Ruth, you know that most everyone uses the directionals on the steering column now, right?" Ida turned around and rolled her eyes at Nans, Helen and Lexy in the back seat.

Ruth ignored her and made the turn, almost clipping the outer corner of the sign for the resort.

"Do you want me to drop you off at your cottage, Lexy?" Ruth asked.

Lexy glanced at her watch. "Actually, why don't you drop me off at the dining lodge? I have to make tarts today, but I'm going to do a bit of poking around first ... to see if I can get any of these questions answered."

Chapter Nine

Ruth dropped Lexy off at the main entrance to the dining hall. The dining room was empty at this time of day and Lexy skirted her way down the cedar log wall, in between the rustic tables, and past the giant window that had a panoramic view of the lake. She turned left at the two story stone fireplace, then ducked into an obscure hallway that led to the restaurant offices.

Lexy stopped at a large office. Prescott Charles, the restaurant manager, was sitting at his desk in a crisp white short sleeved shirt and light blue tie. Lexy tapped softly on the door.

Prescott looked up from the paperwork he had been studying. "Hi, Lexy. Come on in."

He half stood indicating for Lexy to sit in a faux leather chair across from his desk. Lexy noticed a musky scent lingering in the air as she entered the room. It niggled something in her memory, but she didn't have time to dig deep enough to figure out what it was.

"So, what can I do for you?" Prescott steepled his fingers together, his light green eyes questioning her from behind his mahogany desk. Behind him, Lexy noticed a wall of bookshelves filled with various books on subjects ranging from restaurant management to log cabin building to decorating. Family photos of Prescott with his wife and kids dotted the shelves.

Lexy shifted in her chair, suddenly thinking maybe this wasn't such a great idea. Prescott raised his brows.

"Um ... Well, I was wondering if there's any type of surveillance in the kitchen. You know cameras that record what's going on," Lexy said.

"Surveillance? Why would you want to know about

that?"

"Well, umm ... Detective Payne seems to think I'm his best suspect for Dugasse's murder and I was thinking the cameras would prove I was in the kitchen when it happened," Lexy lied. She didn't want to tell him the real reason was that she wanted to know if Sylvia Spicer really *was* in the freezer like she claimed. She didn't want to cast any aspersions on Sylvia if she was innocent.

"We don't have anything like that in the kitchen," Prescott said, avoiding eye contact with her.

"Oh, okay." Lexy got up to leave, then turned at the door. "You didn't happen to notice anything strange going on with Sylvia Spicer and Chef Dugasse, did you?"

Prescott jerked in his chair. His elbow hit a cup full of pens and they spilled out on to the floor. He bent down to pick them up and Lexy walked back to the desk and squatted down to help.

Prescott looked at her from under the desk. "Why do you ask that? I didn't notice anything." His voice was choppy, nervous.

"Well, it's probably nothing, but she said something kind of funny to me when we were out at the dumpster after I found Dugasse." Lexy handed him the pens she'd gathered and they both stood up.

"What was that?" Prescott wrinkled his brows at her.

"She asked if we should hide the body."

Prescott sucked in a breath, his eyes going wide, the pencil holder clattering to the floor, pens spilling out all over again.

"What?" He stared at Lexy, his face growing red. He reached up to loosen his tie.

Lexy had a momentary pang of guilt. She felt bad talking about Sylvia ... but it was true and asking around might be the only way to find out what really happened.

"She was probably just so distraught ..." Lexy bent down to help with the pens again but Prescott waved her off.

"I can pick these up." His eyes slid to the door inviting her to leave. "Please close the door behind you."

"Okay, well ... thanks," Lexy said, not sure what she was thanking him for.

She backed out of the office, closing the door quietly behind her. She stood there for a minute, thinking about Prescott's reaction. *Why had he been so nervous when she asked about Sylvia and Dugasse?*

A faint rustle in the hallway behind her and the scent of musk caught her attention. She whirled around. The hallway was empty, but she had turned just in time to see the doorway to the first office slowly closing.

She crept over to the door which was open just a crack. Someone was standing just behind it. Hiding. Lexy reached out, grabbed the knob and wrenched the door open, her heart jerking wildly in her chest as she looked up into the face of Sylvia Spicer.

***

Sylvia stood in front of her, eyes wide, mouth forming a surprised "Oh." She held something behind her back. A chef's knife? Images of herself as the next victim flashed through Lexy's mind and she took a step backward into the hall.

"What are *you* doing here?" Lexy asked.

"What are you?" Sylvia's eyes darted around the room and out into the hall.

"I came to ask Prescott about ... something." Lexy leaned to the left to get a view of what Sylvia had behind her back.

Sylvia whipped her hand out from behind her back in one fluid motion and Lexy's heart jumped into her throat.

"I came to drop off this invoice," she said, indicating the piece of paper she'd been holding behind her back.

Lexy's shoulders relaxed and she leaned against the doorjamb. Sylvia shot nervous glances at Prescott's door.

"Hey Sylvia, I was wondering something," Lexy said.

"What?"

"When we were out by the dumpster, you said something about hiding Dugasse's body. Why would you say that?"

Sylvia's eyes jerked over to Prescott's door again before she louvered them back at Lexy.

"I did? I must have been so distraught that I didn't know what I was saying." Sylvia shrugged. "Why would I want you to hide the body?"

"That's what I was wondering," Lexy said, then she narrowed her eyes at Sylvia. "Did you get the head chef job ... to replace Dugasse?"

"Yes. Prescott ... I mean, Mr. Charles promoted me to head chef."

"Congratulations. So it looks like Dugasse's death was good for you in that respect. But I bet you miss him."

Sylvia wrinkled her brow and Lexy leaned in closer, lowering her voice. "I heard you were very close with someone here."

Sylvia's face turned red and her eyes did more darting around. "I don't know what you are talking about."

"Well, you know sometimes men in a position of power can be very attractive ... even if they *are* married." Lexy gave Sylvia her best 'you can confide in me' look.

Sylvia's eyes grew wide. "What did you ..."

"Well, sometimes things go wrong and people get hurt. And that might cause the wounded party to do something they wouldn't normally do ... you know out of passion."

Sylvia glared at her. "Are you implying *I* killed Chef Dugasse because I was mad at him?"

"Oh no, I'm just saying bad things can happen sometimes when you get involved." Lexy's heart leapt into her throat when she saw the menacing look on Sylvia's face.

"I don't know what you're talking about but I do know that Dugasse got what he deserved ... it just wasn't at my hands." Sylvia spat out the words, then brushed past Lexy and stormed off down the hall in the opposite direction of Prescott Charles' office, the invoice apparently forgotten.

Lexy stared after her wondering what she meant by 'Dugasse got what he deserved'. *Was Dugasse involved in something that got him killed?*

Lexy stood in the hall, her lips pursed going over her exchange with Sylvia when she thought she saw a shadow moving under the door to Chef Dugasse's office.

Who would be in there?

She crept down the hall. The door was open just slightly and she craned her neck, her heartbeat picking up speed at what she saw inside. Brad Meltzer had one of the desk drawers open and was rummaging through it.

Lexy held her breath. She stood off to one side and prayed Brad wouldn't look over and see her. She watched as he pawed through the drawer, then moved on to the next drawer, then the next and finally started leafing through cookbooks that were stacked on the desk.

What was he doing?

Lexy stepped closer to the door and pushed it open. Brad jumped away from the desk, jerking his head in her direction. His eyes narrowed when he saw Lexy standing there.

"Looking for something?" Lexy asked.

She saw a ripple of anxiety cross Brad's face, then he composed himself and looked down at the desk.

"I needed the schedule ... chef made it out on Monday." Brad picked up the sheet of paper that had been lying in plain sight on the desk and then started out of the room brushing past Lexy who was standing in the doorway, arms crossed against her chest. She stared after him as he went off down the hallway toward the kitchen.

Looking back into the room, she felt an icy chill run up her spine. All of Dugasse's notes and personal effects were in here and, in light of the fact that he had been murdered, she didn't think anyone was supposed to be in his office ... much less rummaging around in the drawers. The schedule was important, but it had been sitting on the top of the desk, surely Brad didn't need to rummage around to find it.

Which begged the question ... what exactly *was* Brad looking for?

Chapter Ten

Deena had the day off, and Lexy was able to whip up the tarts for that evening's dessert at record speed since she didn't have to take time out for giving instructions. Once finished, she threw her apron in the laundry basket and headed off for some well-deserved beach time.

At her cottage, she changed into a white and blue striped one piece and threw on a long sleeved white shirt as a cover-up. Tossing Sprinkles a treat, she shoved a towel in her oversized beach bag and headed down to the small beach at the end of her street.

The beach was dotted with colorful blankets and beach umbrellas. Kids played at making sand castles, parents sat in beach chairs next to coolers and teens ran through the water laughing and diving.

Lexy spotted Jack lying on a lounge chair about ten feet from the edge of the water. She slipped off her flip flops to feel the warm, course sand on her feet and started toward him.

"Hi handsome, is this spot taken?" Lexy spread her towel down beside Jack who peered over the top of his book at her.

"I suppose you can sit here, but only until my wife comes down."

Lexy laughed, then bent over to kiss him before plopping down on the towel.

"So how was your visit with the widow?" Jack asked.

"Interesting." Lexy dug in her beach bag for suntan lotion. "She said Dugasse was worth more to her alive than dead."

Jack raised an eyebrow. "How so?"

"Well, he was a shoo-in to win that *Chili Battle*. You

know, the one they are having here at the fairgrounds." Lexy pointed in the direction of the open field in the middle of the resort. "Anyway, I guess winning that means you get a lot of money thrown at you."

"Hmmm." Jack pursed his lips.

"Oh, and she also said that she thought Dugasse was having an affair because he snuck out in the wee hours of the morning."

"But she was there the morning he was killed, right?" Jack asked.

"Yes, but she said she didn't kill him."

"They all say that." Jack dog-eared a page and then closed his book. "But she might have a point about him being worth more money. Does she have an alibi?"

Lexy's brows mashed together. She dumped out the contents of her bag, still unable to find the suntan lotion. "I don't know. She didn't seem very hospitable after Nans practically accused her of killing Dugasse, so we got out of there fast."

Jack laughed. "Well, maybe you could check the hotel. Or maybe Payne has already done that. The room keys record when people come and go so if she was back in her room at the time of death, it would show that."

"Well, I don't think Payne is going to share any of that information with me. He's not as nice as you are with that sort of stuff." Lexy grabbed the copper colored bottle of sun tan lotion and opened the top. Squirting some on her arm, she started rubbing it in. "But I don't think the wife is the killer."

"Oh, why not?"

"I ran into Sylvia Spicer when I was at the dining lodge and she was acting really funny. Nans and the ladies were thinking she might be the one Dugasse was having an affair with, so I kind of hinted around about that and she got really mad."

Jack chuckled. "Well, wouldn't you, if someone was hinting around that you had an affair and murdered someone?"

"Yeah, probably." Lexy pressed her lips together. Maybe Sylvia *was* only reacting to her accusations. "But I found out some other strange things today too."

"What?" Jack took the bottle from her and started rubbing lotion on her legs, venturing into parts that were already covered by her suit and causing her to almost forget what she was saying.

"What? Oh ... when I was at the dining hall I talked to Prescott Charles, the manager, and he was acting kind of strange about the whole Dugasse thing and then I caught Brad Meltzer sneaking around in Dugasse's office!"

Jack finished with the lotion and looked at her. "Well, it sounds like you have a lot of things to follow up on before you can get a picture of what is really going on."

"Right." Lexy bit her bottom lip. There *was* a lot to figure out ... could she, Nans and the *Ladies Detective Club* handle all that?

"You know what I'd do?" Jack prompted.

"What?"

"I'd start with one clue and follow it through to the end. Knock off each of your questions one by one until they are all resolved and then you'll know the truth."

"You make it sound so easy." Lexy opened her bag and started putting the contents that she had spilled on her towel back inside it.

"It's not that hard if you take it one at a time," Jack said. "Did you ever get back to that other trail?"

"No, I was planning on doing that later today. Wanna come?"

"I wish I could, but I'm going fishing." Jack peered over his sunglasses at her. "You're not going alone, I hope."

"Oh no, Nans and the ladies will be with me so I'll be perfectly safe."

"That's great. I'm *sure* you won't get into any trouble with them," Jack said dubiously as he pushed his sunglasses up on his face and flipped over on his stomach.

Lexy leaned back on her elbows and watched the lake lap at the shore. A little bird ran along the edge of the water pecking for food. Out on the lake, people paddled on kayaks and canoes. The occasional motor boat sped by in the deeper waters. It was calm. Relaxing.

Lexy's stomach twisted to think a murderer could be

running loose right in this very resort. And, since Payne didn't seem to be doing a very good job, it might be up to Lexy and the *Ladies Detective Club* to catch the killer.

Chapter Eleven

Lexy had just finished showering and was wrestling Sprinkles into her harness when Nans, Ruth and Helen appeared at her cottage door.

"Where's Ida?" Lexy asked.

"Oh she begged off," Nans said.

"Claimed she had to do something with Norman before he went out fishing tonight." Ruth giggled.

Lexy made a face and held her hand up. Considering Ida's comment earlier that day about the two things fishermen were interested in, she didn't want to know anymore.

"Will you guys be okay? This could be a long walk and a lot of it is uphill." Lexy realized the three women were clutching their giant patent leather old ladies purses. "You're not bringing those purses, are you?"

"We bring these everywhere," Helen said.

"They're loaded up with all kinds of useful items," Ruth added.

"You never know when something in here is going to come in handy." Nans opened her purse and angled it toward Lexy.

"They look heavy," Lexy said. "Why don't you leave them here and you can pick them up on the way back? You'll be able to walk the path easier without them."

The three women looked at each other. Nans held her purse out by the handles as if judging the weight, then nodded.

"You may be right, dear," she said and put her purse on the table. Ruth and Helen did the same with theirs.

"Okay, let's get this show on the road." Nans opened the door, leading the way outside.

They followed the same path Lexy and Jack and followed the other day. When they got to the top of the hill, Lexy had to stop to catch her breath.

"You guys don't even seem winded." She stared at Nans, Ruth and Helen.

"Oh, that's nothing," Nans said. "We do yoga, Pilates and water aerobics ... a little hill like this is child's play."

"Maybe you should consider joining us in our regular workout." Ruth frowned at Lexy. "You seem a bit out of shape.

Lexy looked down at her slim body. *Out of shape?* Well, sure she was a bit winded after the climb but she still *looked* good. At least that's what Jack had said down at the beach.

"You're not in your twenties anymore," Nans added looking her up and down. "And you won't be able to keep that cute shape without having to work at it for long."

"Yeah, you don't think our girlish figures come without a price, do you?" Helen ran her hands up and down the sides of her body and everyone laughed.

"Okay, where's this path?" Nans asked.

"Over here." Lexy pulled Sprinkles to the end of the path and walked the short distance to the back of the dining hall where the trails intersected.

Nans glanced over at the dumpster, still marked with crime scene tape. "Is that where ...?"

"Yep, that's where I found him." Lexy shivered despite the warm afternoon air.

Ruth walked right up to the crime scene tape. "Maybe we should take a little look around. The police may have overlooked a clue."

"Good idea," Helen said. She held the tape up while Nans and Ruth scooted under, then ducked under it herself.

The smell of old fish, sour milk and rotting cabbage assaulted Lexy and she pinched her nose shut.

"Can you guys hurry up?" she said, except it came out as 'hubby up'.

Nans bent down, scuffing at the debris under the dumpster with her shoe. "Come take a look at this."

Ruth and Helen bent over to take a look. Lexy pinched

her nose even tighter and got as close as she dared, craning over the crime scene tape to see what they had found.

"Is that ...?" Ruth asked.

"I do believe it is," Helen replied.

Nans worked at something with her shoe, sliding it out from under the dumpster. She pulled a kleenex out of her pocket, then bent over to pick up the item. She stood holding it in the air, careful to touch it only with the kleenex.

"Is that blood?" Lexy asked. The item Nans held up looked to be a swatch of fabric—plaid flannel. It was about one inch square and a rust colored smear on it that looked suspiciously like blood. *But, whose blood?*

"I think so," Nans said. Wrapping the fabric in the tissue, she slid it into her pocket.

"Is that Dugasse's blood?" Ruth asked.

"It could be. But the fabric was wedged under the dumpster so it could have been there before he was murdered."

"Or it could have come from the killer."

"I wish we had our own forensics lab." Nans pressed her lips together. "I don't trust that Detective Payne not to fumble this up. He didn't even find that fabric when he searched the area!"

"True. He seems like a dope," Ruth said.

"I don't see anything else. Do either of you?" Helen asked.

"Nope. Let's move on," Ruth answered and the three of them scurried under the crime scene tape and then joined Lexy at the intersection of the paths.

"So which path?" Nans looked at Lexy.

"Well, this one goes to the front parking lot so I doubt the killer used that one," Lexy said pointing to the path on the left. Then she turned and pointed to one of the middle paths. "And this is the only other one I haven't walked on."

"Well, let's go!" Ruth started in the direction of the path in a power walk and Lexy trotted after her.

"We should slow down and look for clues ... you know anything unusual," Lexy said remembering Jack's advice.

"Yes, we know what clues are, dear," Nans teased.

They walked leisurely letting Sprinkles make her various pit stops. They were only about twenty feet down the path when Sprinkles found something she must have thought was irresistible. Lexy tugged on the leash, but Sprinkles insisted on sniffing whatever it was she had found under a small shrub.

"What have you got, Sprinks?" Lexy bent down to investigate hoping it wasn't a dead animal. It wasn't. Lexy picked it up and held it out for the ladies.

"What is it?" Nans narrowed her eyes at the thin strip of leather with stainless steel spikes sticking out of it.

"I think it's a bracelet," Ruth said.

Lexy wrapped it around her wrist and it snapped closed with magnetic clasps on each end. Ruth was right. "Who would wear a bracelet like this?" Lexy asked.

"Maybe one of the teenagers?" Nans said. "Their ever changing fashions always baffle me."

"Maybe." Lexy put the bracelet in her pocket and started forward. "I'll just keep it ... it could be a clue."

The ladies nodded and followed her down the path. Like the previous day, the tall trees provided welcome shade. The birds chirped, chipmunks scurried in the leaves and the smell of the woods made the walk relaxing and pleasant. Until they came to a section that became very dense ... and dark.

Lexy hesitated, looking at the others. "Is it getting dark out?"

"No, it's just the woods are really thick here." Nans looked back behind them. "The trail narrows, but it keeps going."

Nans forged ahead and Lexy followed. They had to walk single file since the trail was so thin and dense forest on either side made it impossible to stray. They walked in silence, Lexy's nerves getting more jittery with every step.

Nans stopped abruptly and Lexy almost rammed into her.

"There's a clearing up ahead." Nans pointed. Lexy craned around her to see. It looked like the path ended in a clearing with a small camp in the middle.

"Let's check it out," Helen whispered.

They scuffled up to the end of the path where they could get a better view of the small house. A picnic table sat in between the path and the camp and there was a large campfire pit in front of it. Six motorcycles were lined up next to the house. No one seemed to be there except a large Boxer dog that lay snoring on the porch.

Nans motioned for them to crouch down behind a bush and they all obeyed.

"I wonder who stays here?" She whispered.

Lexy shrugged. "Do you think they take the path to the dining hall?"

"I don't know. Someone does."

The Boxer lifted its head and started sniffing.

Sprinkles sniffed too and wiggled around. Lexy pulled the dog tight beside her. "Shhh.."

Lexy's heartbeat kicked up a notch when she saw the Boxer get up from his place on the porch. He lifted his nose in the air, sniffed, then turned in their direction.

Sprinkles started to growl.

The Boxer started walking toward them.

Lexy shushed Sprinkles again.

The Boxer came even closer and Sprinkles let out a yelp, then darted out from behind the bush, yanking the leash out of Lexy's hand and running in the direction of the Boxer.

Lexy jumped up, her heart jerking in her chest.

"Sprinkles come back!" She started off toward the dogs ready to grab Sprinkles from the clutches of the menacing Boxer. Sprinkles stopped in front of the Boxer and the two dogs calmly started sniffing each other.

Lexy felt her shoulders relax, then the door of the cabin exploded open and two burly guys in leather vests burst out. One of them had a shotgun and the other a knife.

Lexy's heart pounded against her ribcage as the largest guy—the one with the bandana on his bald head and spider tattoo on his neck—pointed the shotgun at her.

"Who are you?" he demanded.

Lexy's mouth went dry. She tried to swallow but it was like drinking sandpaper.

"I told you we should have brought our purses." She heard Nans whisper from behind the shrub.

The big guy narrowed his eyes in the direction of the shrub. "Who's that? Is someone behind that bush?"

Lexy looked back over her shoulder and her heart sank as she saw Nans, Ruth and Helen all stand up, their hands held up next to their heads, palms out.

"We're just some little old ladies from the resort." Nans nodded at Lexy and Sprinkles. "I was just taking my granddaughter and her dog for a walk."

The two guys cut their eyes to the dogs who had gotten around to sniffing each other's back ends. Lexy thought the dogs seemed to be making friends a lot easier than their owners.

"Hey, looks like Brutus found a friend," the smaller guy said.

The big guy narrowed his eyes at the dog, lowering the gun slightly then jerked it back up in Lexy's direction. "Who sent you?"

Lexy's brows mashed together. "Sent me? No one."

The two guys exchanged a glance. The smaller guy put his knife away and shrugged.

"They're grandmas," he said pointing his chin in Nans direction.

The big guy nodded, but kept his gun trained on Lexy. "I suggest you take your dog, get on out of here and don't come back."

Lexy ran over and grabbed Sprinkles leash. "Right. No problem. Sorry."

She turned and sprinted back toward the path, making sure Nans, Ruth and Helen got away ahead of her.

She glanced back over her shoulder every twenty steps and her heart didn't stop racing until they were a full five minutes away.

"What was that all about?" Nans asked.

"I'm not sure but it seemed like a gang of unfriendly bikers to me," Ruth answered.

"Do you think they could have had something to do with Chef Dugasse's murder?" Helen asked.

"I bet they either had something to do with it, or they

know something," Lexy said.

"Just because they are bikers and acted like they didn't want us in their camp is no reason to assume they are killers," Nans admonished.

"It's not just that." Lexy pulled the bracelet she'd found at the head of the trail out of her pocket and held it up in front of her. "The guy with the knife had this exact same bracelet on and, since this one was found only twenty feet from the dining hall, I think it's safe to assume one of them has been to that kitchen at least once before."

Chapter Twelve

Lexy dipped her spoon into the thick custard and brought it to her lips. The sweetness from the sugar and the unmistakable flavor from the real vanilla bean she'd added danced on her tongue. The creaminess of the custard was like velvet in her mouth. Perfect.

She pulled over a tray of the small puff pastries she'd made to house the custard and set the bowl of chocolate she'd drizzle on the top next to her. Spooning the custard into a piping bag, she picked up a pastry, squeezed some custard inside then set it on another tray. She continued until she had one tray completed, then spooned the chocolate on top for a perfect set of miniature bite-sized éclairs.

She popped one into her mouth letting the flavorful explosion thrill her taste buds. They were just the way she wanted. She pulled another tray of puff pastries over and started repeating the process.

As she filled the pastries she thought about the previous evening's excursion with Nans and the ladies. Could the biker gang have something to do with Dugasse's murder? Why would Dugasse be involved with them? It didn't make any sense.

She was trying to figure out how she could find out more about the bikers and what they were doing there when a grating voice cut into her thoughts from across the room.

"Miss Baker, what a surprise to find you here in the kitchen instead of pestering suspects."

Lexy's stomach tightened as she watched Detective Payne make his way over to her. He wore his usual plaid Bermuda shorts and had his spiral bound notebook and pencil in hand. His eyes slid from hers to the tray of éclairs.

"I have no idea what you mean," Lexy said feigning innocence.

"You went to visit Victoria Dugasse?" He raised an eyebrow at her.

"My grandmother and I paid our condolences."

"Hmm ... well, she seemed to think you were doing more than that." Grabbing an éclair from the tray, he stuffed it into his mouth before continuing. "I'd appreciate it if you left the police business to the police ... besides the wife didn't to it. The hotel records show that she was in the hotel gym at the time of death."

Lexy's eyebrows shot up. That was one person she could cross off her suspect list. She decided to test out Payne to see how much he knew.

She leaned closer to him and lowered her voice. "So, she didn't kill him because of his affair with Sylvia Spicer?"

Payne's forehead collapsed in a network of wrinkles. "Spicer? What makes you think they were having an affair?"

"They seemed awfully close. In fact Sylvia came right out after I found him and was very upset."

"Well, of course she would be upset. Her boss was dead." Payne glanced around the room looking for Sylvia, no doubt. "Maybe you are just implicating Sylvia because she has the damaging statement of finding you leaning over the dead body."

Lexy pressed her lips together and leaned even closer. "Well, there is the matter of her getting promoted."

Payne nodded. "Yes, yes. We know all about that. We *are* the police you know. But Spicer wasn't having the affair with Dugasse."

"How do you know that? The wife told us he was sneaking off."

Payne waved his hand around dismissively. "Sneaking around does not necessarily mean an affair. Like I said, you should leave the detecting to the detectives. You are, after all, one of the suspects."

Lexy felt irritation spark in her chest. Why did Payne keep defending Sylvia and insisting that Lexy was a suspect? It was becoming clear that she was going to have to dig out the clues herself if she wanted to get her name off his radar.

"So I have your word you will leave this Chef Martino Marchesi alone?"

Lexy's heart skipped. Who was Chef Martino Marchesi?

Payne must have caught her confused look. "Don't try to play dumb. I know that you already know Marchesi is the favorite to win the *Chili Battle.*"

"*Chili Battle?*" Lexy's brows mashed together. Did Dugasse's death have something to do with the *Chili Battle*?

Payne flapped his arms in exasperation. "Look Baker, you're still high up on the suspect list, but I'm working to cover all the bases and make sure I get the real killer. If you continue to meddle in this case I will have no choice but to stop you ... even if I have to throw you in jail."

Payne grabbed another éclair, popped it into his mouth and pointed the eraser end of his pencil at her and said, "Consider yourself warned."

Then he turned on his heel and stomped off toward the exit.

***

Lexy finished the éclairs as fast as she could and then ran down to Nans' cottage.

"You guys won't believe it ... I just found another clue!" Lexy burst through the front door of the cottage. Nans, Ida, Ruth and Helen were seated at the table shoveling cheeseburgers onto large plates of salad.

"Would you like a cheeseburger salad?" Nans asked.

Lexy narrowed her eyes at the plates. "No buns? Are you guys back on the Paleo diet?"

Nans waffled her hand over the table. "We're just trying to cut down on the carbs."

"Did you say something about a clue, dear?" Ida speared a piece of lettuce, a tomato and then a chunk of burger and brought it up to her mouth.

"Yes. Payne came to the kitchen to yell at me about

visiting Dugasse's wife and he let a clue slip. Something about another chef that was connected with the *Chili Battle* contest."

Nans narrowed her eyes. "I knew the chili contest had to figure in here somewhere. What was the chef's name?"

Lexy pursed her lips together wishing she had written the name down. "It was Italian sounding ... I think it was Martin Parcheesi. Does that ring a bell with anyone?"

The ladies looked around at each other shaking their heads.

"No, but we can Google him." Ruth got up from her chair and went over to the iPad. Lexy watched as her fingers tapped on the screen.

"I don't find any Chef Parcheesi. Let me look up this chili contest."

Nans, Ida and Helen munched away at their salads while Lexy went to look over Ruth's shoulder.

"So, is this Parcheesi guy another suspect? Along with the wife, the sous-chef, and the bikers?" Helen asked.

"Seems like we're really piling them up." Ida cleaned the last of the salad out of her bowl and brought it to the sink.

"Actually, the wife has been cleared. Payne let it slip that she has an alibi for the time of the murder," Lexy said.

"Oh good." Ida walked over to the white board. "I'll cross her off the list then."

"Do you mean Chef Martino Marchesi?" Ruth looked up at Lexy.

"Yes!" Lexy snapped her fingers. "That's it!"

"Well, he is involved with the *Chili Battle*. He's one of the front runners," Ruth said.

"So Payne thinks he might have killed Dugasse to win the contest?" Nans stood up and brought her and Helen's bowls to the sink.

"He just warned me to stay away from him. He didn't say why but he said I should stay away from the suspects, so I assume Marchesi is one." Lexy watched Ida write 'Marchesi' on the whiteboard in the suspect column.

"Seems a little drastic to kill someone to win a contest," Helen said.

"Apparently not if you are this Marchesi guy." Ruth

tapped the iPad with her finger. "He has ties to organized crime and there's some articles here that put him in a questionable light."

Nans raised her brows. "Is he here in town now?"

"I'd have to check local hotels," Ruth said.

"Do you think he could have some involvement with those bikers we saw yesterday? Maybe he hired them to do his dirty work or something," Helen offered.

"Maybe." Nans studied the white board. "What about Sylvia? Did you find anything more about her supposed affair with Dugasse?"

"That's another thing Payne said. He seemed sure Sylvia was not the one having the affair with him. But she acted so strangely when I confronted her yesterday," Lexy said.

"Well, I wouldn't necessarily take what Payne says as gospel." Ruth rolled her eyes. "He doesn't seem that competent if you ask me."

Lexy nodded. "You can say that again. I think I might need to have another talk with Sylvia."

"Yes, and we need to figure out if Marchesi was in town when Dugasse was murdered *and* talk to those bikers to find out why the bracelet was near the dining hall," Helen said.

"How are we going to talk to the bikers?" Lexy asked. "They didn't seem very friendly when we were there yesterday."

"Oh, don't worry. I think I have that covered." Nans winked at Lexy. "Meet us here tomorrow at two p.m. and I'll show you how to get even the most adversarial suspect to open up."

Chapter Thirteen

Lexy paced back and forth in her small cottage. Nans and the ladies were at bingo and Jack was out fishing. Which left her with too much alone time on her to think about Dugasse's murder.

Sprinkles lay on the floral cushion that was fitted to the seat of the green wicker rocker. Her eyes followed Lexy as she went back and forth.

"If the killer was this Chef Marchesi, then how come no one saw him in the kitchen?" she asked the little dog.

"Did he hide out by the dumpster and wait for Dugasse to come out? Or maybe he lured him out there?"

She looked at Sprinkles who raised an eyebrow.

"I still think Sylvia Spicer is up to something. She's been acting way to jumpy."

Sprinkles let out a little bark.

"And she asked about hiding the body!"

Sprinkles beat the side of the rocker with her tail.

"Do you have to go out?"

The little white dog jumped off the rocker and ran to the door. Lexy saddled the dog up in her harness and led her out through the porch and into the woods beside the cottage.

It was dusk and the air had cooled considerably. It was a perfect summer night, with peepers peeping and flowers perfuming the air. Lexy looked up and sighed at the perfectly round moon and abundance of bright stars.

Sprinkles rummaged around in the leaves and pine needles and Lexy's thoughts turned to Brad Meltzer rummaging around in Dugasse's desk. Just what *had* he been looking for?

She had to admit, she'd never liked Brad. He always

seemed like he was pulling something over on you. But just because he was a pompous jerk didn't mean he was a killer.

Still he *had* tried awfully hard to make her look guilty in front of Payne and he *was* looking for something in Dugasse's office. She didn't fall for that excuse of him looking for the schedule. Surely he would have seen it right on the desk. No, he was up to something, Lexy was sure of it.

She glanced up the hill at the dining hall. At this time of night it would be empty. All the meals had been served and cleared, and the chefs and waitstaff would have gone home.

Maybe *she* should poke around in Dugasse's office herself. If she discovered what Brad had been looking for, that could be a valuable clue—maybe even the clue that cracks the case.

Lexy dragged Sprinkles inside and changed into a pair of black jeans and a black tee-shirt. She tied her hair up in a ponytail, then slipped on a pair of black Keds sneakers. Grabbing a small flashlight, she slipped out her front door and headed up the path to the dining hall.

***

Lexy fingered the key to the kitchen's back door in her pocket.

Should she?

It wasn't too late to turn back. But she did have a key, so it wasn't like she was breaking and entering. Just entering. If anyone asked, she could just say she had to check on some stuff for the next day's desserts.

She slid the key into the lock and clicked the door open.

The kitchen was dark. Lexy didn't want to turn any lights on so she switched on her small flashlight and angled it at the floor.

Her heart thumped loudly in her chest as she made her way down the back passageway that led to Dugasse's office. The passage was more of a storage corridor. It had no windows and was pitch black, but she didn't want to risk going through the dining room with its giant windows to get to the main hallway.

Rounding the corner to the main hall, she found Dugasse's door closed. Her heart squeezed.

What if it was locked?

She reached out for the knob, turned it slowly and then breathed a sigh of relief when it twisted open. She cracked the door and slipped inside, closing the door behind her.

As she approached the desk, she could hear Jack's voice in her head telling her how dangerous it was to come here alone. But he'd also said she should check each clue one by one and this was the perfect time for her to look here. She might not get another chance.

With a shrug, she pushed Jack's nagging voice out of her head, opened a drawer and pointed her flashlight inside. She hunted around in the drawer for a few minutes but found nothing except old papers, pencils and pens.

She moved to the next drawer and came up empty with this one too. Lexy chewed on her bottom lip as she looked around the room. It wasn't surprising that she hadn't find anything in the desk drawers, she'd already seen Brad look in there and he hadn't found what he was looking for.

Maybe she should look somewhere that Brad hadn't already looked?

A filing cabinet in the corner captured her attention. She opened a drawer, slowly so as to not make any noise. Putting the flashlight in her mouth, she leafed through the folders, feeling deflated when all she found was old recipes.

Recipes? Her heart pinged.

Could Brad have been looking for a recipe? *The* recipe. The one for Dugasse's famous chili that everyone thought was going to win him the contest? Maybe Brad had plans to enter the contest on his own with that recipe. Winning the contest would be life changing for a low-level chef like Brad, but was it life-changing enough to kill Dugasse for?

A sudden noise in the hall startled Lexy causing her to drop her flashlight which turned off when it hit the floor.

Who would be here at this time of night?

Lexy's heart hammered against her ribcage as she

dropped to her knees and groped for the flashlight. Her hand connected with the cold metal and she clutched the light in her fist.

Then she crouched under the desk and waited.

***

Lexy held her breath expecting someone to burst in the room at any second. She waited several minutes listening to only the sound of her own heartbeat thudding in her ears before she climbed out.

Was someone in the hall?

She crept over to the door and put her ear to it but didn't hear anything. No light came in under the bottom of the door. She cracked the door open slowly and peeked out. Nothing.

Pulling the door the rest of the way open she slipped out into the hall. She was just about to head out the way she had come when a light at the other end of the hall caught her eye. It was coming from under Prescott Charles' door. Someone was in his office!

Lexy tiptoed back down the hall and stood to the side of his door. Shadows moved in the light that spilled out from underneath and she could hear the low murmur of voices. She leaned closer, straining to hear.

"... Killed him ..."

"You ..."

Snatches of conversation drifted out from the office and Lexy pressed even closer. *Were they talking about the murder?*

"... No ... stabbed ..."

Lexy felt her heart jolt ... they *were* talking about the murder. *Who was in there?* She stepped up next to the door, her heart lurching when a floorboard gave her away with a loud groan.

The voices in the room stopped and she froze in her tracks.

"Is someone out there?" She heard a woman say from inside the room.

"No one should be here at this time of night." A man's

voice this time, laced with panic.

Lexy's mind whirled. Should she make a run for it, or stay still?

The door jerked open causing her heart to plummet.

Lexy's eyebrows mashed together as her eyes registered the scene in front of her. Sylvia Spicer stood directly on the other side of the door, her beige silk shirt untucked and rumpled. Prescott Charles stood close behind her, his eyes wide, face turning beet red.

"You!" Sylvia pointed at Lexy who backed up a step. "What are *you* doing here?"

Lexy felt like a kid caught with her hand in the cookie jar until she realized she wasn't the only one who wasn't supposed to be there.

"Me? What are the two of *you* doing? I thought I heard you talking about killing Chef Dugasse."

Lexy blurted it out without thinking then realized maybe she shouldn't have said it. If they really were the killers then they'd already killed once and there wasn't much to stop them from killing her. Lexy felt a pang in her stomach as she realized no one knew where she was.

"I didn't say *I* killed the chef, I asked Prescott if *he* killed the chef." Sylvia looked down, noticed her rumpled shirt, turned red and started smoothing it and tucking it in.

"Why would he kill Chef Dugasse?"

Sylvia and Prescott exchanged a look. Lexy wondered if she should make a break for it.

"I wouldn't ... I didn't ... but ..." Prescott stammered.

"What is going on?" Lexy demanded.

Sylvia sighed and turned to Prescott. "We might as well tell her. She's so nosey, she's not going to stop until she finds out the truth and it's better that we give her the real story."

Nosey? Lexy's back stiffened and she raised her eyebrows waiting for the 'real story'.

Sylvia ran her fingers through her blonde hair and looked at Lexy. "You were right about me having an affair."

Lexy's eyebrows shot up. She *knew* it!

"But it wasn't with Dugasse," Sylvia added.

Lexy's eyebrows fell back down and mashed together.

"It was with Prescott." Sylvia turned to Prescott and he nodded.

Lexy felt her mouth fall open. She ping-ponged her eyes back and forth between the two of them. "But why did you act so squirrelly about Dugasse's death?"

Sylvia sighed, collapsing into the guest chair. "Dugasse found out about our affair and he threatened to blackmail us."

"So when he ended up dead ... we each thought the other might have done it," Prescott added.

"So that's why you asked about hiding the body?" Lexy turned to Sylvia. "But why would you think I would want to hide it?"

"I don't know what I was thinking. When I saw him dead, I panicked."

Prescott put his hand on Sylvia's shoulder. "So you see, we were acting strange because we were covering for each other."

Lexy narrowed her eyes. "That's what you *say*, but how do I know the two of you weren't in on it together?"

"We both have alibis."

"You do?"

"Yes," Sylvia said. "Justin was in the freezer at the same time I was that morning. We discussed the way Chef had yelled at Thomas."

"And I was in a meeting with eight other people," Prescott added.

Lexy felt her stomach deflate. Sylvia had been her best suspect and now she'd have to find someone else. But who?

"Hey, what are you doing here this time of night, anyway?" Sylvia interrupted her thoughts.

Lexy felt her cheeks grow warm. "Oh, umm ... well, I caught Brad Meltzer going through Dugasse's office the other day and I wanted to see what he was up to."

"Meltzer? He's been acting really strange since Chef Dugasse died," Sylvia said.

"How so?"

"Like a jerk. I mean he was always kind of a jerk but now

with chef gone, he's being rather disrespectful and refusing to do the tasks I give him."

"Do you think he wanted the head chef job?" Prescott asked.

"Maybe. But since I was the sous-chef, he would know that I would be the likely candidate for that job. I can assure you, I won't be making *him* the next sous-chef."

"Maybe he is just upset at Dugasse's passing. He really seemed to adore him," Lexy suggested.

Sylvia pressed her lips together. "I don't know. He followed Dugasse around but he didn't seem to admire him ... It was more like he was stalking him."

"You don't think he had anything to do with Dugasse's murder, do you?" Prescott asked.

"I don't think he could have been the killer," Lexy said. "He was standing right in front of me about the time the chef got murdered. Or shortly after. I would think he'd have had blood on him ... or been unsettled. But he wasn't."

"Well I don't know who could have done it ... if it wasn't you." Sylvia looked pointedly at Lexy.

"It wasn't. You have more of a motive than I do." Lexy's voice rose along with her anger.

"Ladies!" Prescott cut in. "Let's say it wasn't either one of you. Who would have had the strongest motive?"

"Maybe the wife?" Sylvia answered.

"According to Detective Payne, the wife has an alibi," Lexy said.

Sylvia sighed and glanced at Prescott. "I just hope the killer is found soon so people don't dig too deep into the goings on here and find out about us."

Prescott cleared his throat. "Yes, umm ... Lexy. I hope we can keep each other's secrets."

"Secrets?"

Prescott gestured out into the hall. "We won't tell that you were in here after hours looking around if you keep quiet about our relationship."

Lexy stared at the two of them. The last thing she needed was someone telling Payne she was sneaking around in here—it would make her look guilty of something. And since she didn't really care about their affair she figured that was a good deal.

"Sure, I'll keep quiet. But I might need your help."

"With what?"

"Victoria Dugasse said her husband kept sneaking out at night presumably to meet his lover," Lexy said.

Sylvia and Prescott shrugged. "So?"

"I thought he was meeting Sylvia, but if he wasn't, then where was he going and who was he meeting?" Lexy asked.

"I would have no idea." Prescott spread his arms, palms out and shrugged.

"Wait a minute," Sylvia said. "I might."

Lexy raised her brows at the other woman and gestured for her to elaborate.

"A couple of nights ago when I was leaving here after ... umm ... meeting Prescott, I noticed someone cooking in the kitchen. I'm pretty sure it was Dugasse."

Lexy felt her heartbeat kick. "Did you see anyone else with him?"

Sylvia's cheeks turned pink. "I didn't want anyone to know I was here, so I didn't go near the kitchen, but I'm sure I heard him talking in there."

"That's odd. Why would he meet his secret lover in the dining hall kitchen and cook?" Lexy wondered.

"Stranger things have happened," Prescott said. "I can tell you one thing though—if we can figure out who he was meeting, we may have found our killer."

Chapter Fourteen

Lexy cracked one eye open just as the sun was just starting to rise. She closed her eye and rolled over, stretching her back. Feeling the weight of someone staring at her, she opened both her eyes and looked straight into a pair of deep brown orbs which were gazing at her with expectant adoration. Sprinkles.

Lexy felt her lips curl in a smile and reached out to pet the dog who reacted by leaping off the bed and running circles on the floor.

"Okay, okay. I'll get up," Lexy whispered, then swung her legs over the bed.

She padded into the small kitchen, filled Sprinkles' bowl with dog food, then set it down. Lexy leaned against the counter while Sprinkles dug into the food. She was excited to tell Nans what she had learned from Sylvia and Prescott the night before, but it was too early—she wouldn't have time to pop over there before work so it would just have to wait until their meeting at two.

Suddenly in a hurry to get to the kitchen and get her baking done for the day, Lexy grabbed Sprinkles' leash and dashed outside with the dog who quickly did her business then ran back inside and jumped in bed with Jack.

Her dog duties accomplished, Lexy threw on a tee shirt and jeans, planted a kiss on Jack's sleeping cheek and then headed off to the kitchen.

She hurried up the path, the tantalizing smell of bacon blanketed the resort causing her mouth to water. Slipping inside the back door, she took a detour past the griddle where the bacon was sizzling and grabbed a piece, crunching it into her mouth before continuing on to her area.

She assembled the flour, butter, sugar, baking powder, salt and milk for biscuits she would use as the basis for a strawberry shortcake that would be served for dessert at that evening's dinner. She was just measuring the last of the ingredients into the giant mixing bowl when Sylvia appeared at her side.

"I've done some poking around and no one here knows who would have been in the kitchen late at night," Sylvia said in a low voice.

Lexy glanced around the kitchen. Only about half the staff was in, but she wouldn't have been surprised if no one else admitted to knowing anything either.

"Where's Brad?" Lexy's brow creased as she looked around for the irritating chef.

Sylvia checked her watch. "He's not in yet."

"Oh, well it probably wouldn't help to ask him, but I think we should try to keep an eye on him between the two of us. I'm making up the biscuits and whipped cream for strawberry shortcake, but I have to leave around one thirty," Lexy said.

Sylvia nodded. "I'll keep my eyes and ears open."

"Open for what?" Deena asked as she came up behind them.

A look of panic crossed Sylvia's face.

"Anything that might have to do with Dugasse's murder," Lexy offered, putting Sylvia at ease and answering the teen's question.

"Oh." Deena looked at Sylvia suspiciously. As head chef, Sylvia was probably too much of an authority to be trusted from Deena's point of view and Lexy found herself wishing the other woman would leave. She could see that Deena was bursting at the seams to tell her something.

It must have been Lexy's lucky day because Sylvia turned away from the counter and said, "Well, back to work," as she headed off toward the front of the kitchen.

As soon as Sylvia was out of earshot, Deena whipped her head back around to Lexy. "I may have found something out that will help you."

Lexy felt a flutter of excitement in her stomach. "Great. Let's start this batter up and then get the ingredients for the flavored whipped creams. Then you can tell me."

Lexy indicated for Deena to finish measuring the ingredients into the bowl while she got heavy cream from the fridge. She stopped by the pantry for some sugar and flavored extracts so that she could make some flavored whipped creams for people to put on their strawberry shortcakes. The shortcake, cut up strawberries and whipped cream would be refrigerated separately and then assembled at the last minute before dessert.

She dropped the ingredients on the counter next to the mixer that was already beating the dough.

"These will be easy. We're just going to make three bowls—one vanilla, one coconut and one almond flavored. So we'll just whip the cream, sugar and extract together." Lexy handed the brown vanilla extract bottle to Deena. "You do the vanilla."

Deena followed Lexy's lead, matching her measurements and adding the extract carefully. They picked up their bowls and whisks and started hand whisking the cream.

Lexy raised her eyebrows and glanced around to make sure no one could hear them. "So, what did you find out?"

Deena pressed her lips together, her arm quivering as it worked the cream in the bowl.

"You have to promise not to tell anyone." She looked solemnly at Lexy.

"I promise."

Deena glanced around. "Some of the kids ... we hang out on the trails at night. Sometimes we have a bonfire. But anyway, one of them told me that she saw a guy coming up the trail and being let in the back door of the kitchen. And it happened more than once."

Lexy stopped whisking, her heartbeat picking up speed. "What trail?"

"One of the middle ones. Not the one that goes to the parking lot or the one that ends up by the cabins."

"Do you know what time of night?"

Deena made a face and lowered her voice so that it was barely audible. "Don't tell anyone but it was a few hours after midnight ... my friend snuck out of her cabin. Her parents don't know."

Lexy's heart beat even faster—that was the same time Dugasse's wife said he was sneaking off. "Did she say what he looked like?"

"She didn't really have a description. She said he looked big and tough. And one thing was strange."

"What's that?" Lexy's brows creased together as she started whisking the cream again.

"He wore a thick leather jacket—a biker jacket. She said he must have been real hot in that in the middle of summer."

***

Lexy and Deena hurried through making the whipped cream, a batch of blondies and some moon pies. By the time she left it was quarter to two. She rushed down the path to Nans and burst through the front door to find all four women of the *Ladies Detective Club* sitting around the table drinking tea.

Nans peeked at her watch. "How nice of you to join us, I thought maybe you might not make it for our little excursion."

Lexy felt her face flush. "Sorry, I had to finish the baking. But you'll be glad you didn't leave without me because I have some interesting news."

Four sets of gray eyebrows shot up.

"Do tell," Ida said.

"Last night, I went back to the dining hall to look in Dugasse's office," she started.

"Alone?" Helen interrupted.

Lexy felt a twinge. "Yes, I know it was a bit dangerous but I wanted to see if I could figure out what Brad was looking for."

"And did you?"

"Not really, but I found something very interesting."

"What's that?" Nans asked.

"Sylvia Spicer and Prescott Charles," Lexy said, proud of her late night discovery.

"What about them?" Ruth asked.

"They were there … in the middle of the night … in

secret," Lexy said. "It turns out Sylvia *was* having an affair, but it was with Charles—not Dugasse."

"Ohhhh."

"So, she didn't kill him in a fit of passion?" Ida looked disappointed.

"No," Lexy said. "And they both have alibis that can be corroborated by other people."

"Well, darn. We sure are running out of suspects." Helen went over to the white board and erased Sylvia's name.

"So what was Brad looking for in Dugasse's office?" Nans asked.

"I don't know." Lexy shrugged. "The only thing in there is recipes ... so I was wondering if he could be looking for that famous chili recipe."

"Ha! Things are all starting to point to that chili contest. It usually comes down to money." Ruth shook her head knowingly.

"Maybe ... or maybe not," Lexy said. "I also found out something that might tie the bikers to Dugasse."

"Oh?"

"My assistant told me that the teens hang out in the woods there behind the dining hall and one of her friends said she saw a man that fits the biker's descriptions being let in the back door of the kitchen."

"By Dugasse?"

"She didn't say but it was in the middle of the night about the same time that Dugasse's wife said he was missing from home."

Helen scrunched up her face. "Why would a biker be meeting Dugasse in the middle of the night?"

"Maybe they were having an affair!" Ida wiggled her eyebrows, apparently delighted with the thought.

Lexy scrunched her face together, the image of Dugasse and a burly biker having an affair in the kitchen made her queasy.

"Well, I guess we'll find out soon enough." Nans stood up and went over to the fridge. "Are you guys ready to go make some new friends?"

"I guess so," Lexy said, "but I'm curious ... what is it that you think will get them to talk to us?"

"Why, one of my famous mile high apple pies, of course," Nans said, bending over and grabbing something out of the fridge. She turned around holding out a beautiful golden-crusted apple pie.

"No man alive has ever been able to resist my apple pie, and I'm sure these biker gentlemen are no exception."

Chapter Fifteen

They stopped by Lexy's cottage and Nans got Sprinkles into her harness while Lexy changed clothes.

"Do you have the bracelet that you found on the trail the other day?" Nans asked.

"I think so." Lexy looked around the room for the jeans she had been wearing that day. She found them in a pile on the chair and dug into the front pocket producing the bracelet.

"Here it is." She held it up and Nans reached out and took it.

"You never know when this might come in handy," Nans said, putting it in her pocket. Then she grabbed the pie off the table where she'd set it when they came in and led the way out the front door.

The five of them walked the same path they had the other day. They each took turns holding the pie.

"What, exactly are we hoping to learn from this excursion?" Ida asked and Lexy remembered she hadn't been with them the other day.

"Well, at the end of the path is the biker camp we told you about. In light of the bracelet Lexy found and what Deena told her, it seems pretty likely they are involved or they know something," Nans said handing the pie to Ruth.

"Are they dangerous?" Ida asked.

Lexy chewed her bottom lip. "Well, they did have a knife and a gun ... but they didn't seem too keen to use it on us."

"But they also weren't that happy to see us." Ruth handed the pie to Helen.

"Which is why I baked the pie, to sweeten them up," Nans said.

"Do you think they killed him?" Lexy asked.

"I'm not sure what the motive would be," Nans answered. "But he could have been having an affair with the biker that was visiting him and they had a falling out."

"I can't picture any of those tough bikers being gay." Helen handed the pie to Ida.

"Maybe Dugasse was having an affair with one of the bikers' girlfriends and they had it out over her?" Ruth offered.

"Either way, the best thing to do is just make friends and then use our investigative skills to find out the truth," Nans said taking the pie from Ida.

They got to the clearing where the camp was and Lexy's stomach twisted up in a knot.

The same dog was on the porch and he lifted his head when he heard them approach. Lexy hesitated but Nans forged ahead, walking right up to the door and knocking. Lexy followed, watching as Sprinkles and the Boxer re-acquainted themselves.

The door jerked open and Lexy's heart surged into her throat. A large, bald man growled at them from the other side of the door. Inside Lexy could see five other bikers gathered around a table. She recognized the big guy with the gun from the other day. He came over to the door and peered out at them.

"It's those grandmas!" Another guy said from inside.

The two guys stepped out onto the porch and closed the door behind them.

"What do you want?" The first guy eyed them suspiciously, then glanced over his shoulder at the closed door.

Lexy's heartbeat skittered. *What was he hiding in there?* She could smell something cooking in the air and wondered if they had a meth lab or some other illegal operation going on inside.

"Did *he* send you?" The guy from the other day asked.

"What? No, we told you no one sent us," Nans replied.

"So you aren't in cahoots with that chef?"

Cahoots?

"What chef? Dugasse?" Ruth asked.

The two guys looked at each other. "You know Dugasse?"

Lexy's heart flipped. "We did."

"And you're not from the other chef?"

"Noooo." Nans drew the word out.

One of the guys looked down at the dogs who were laying side by side watching the conversation.

"Looks like our dogs get along like old friends," he said.

Nans shoved the pie up in their faces. "And we just want to be friends, too."

"Is that apple?" the biggest guy asked.

Nans nodded and his eyes lit up. "That's my favorite."

He glanced at the other guy. "Should we let them in?"

The other guy shrugged. "Okay, but if we find out you are up to something you'll be sorry."

He opened the door and they shuffled in. The bikers that were sitting around the table all stood up and a round of introductions ensued. They *seemed* like regular guys ... except for the abundance of leather and tattoos. And the names like Snake, Weasel and Rat.

Lexy gave herself a mental warning not to get too comfortable around them—one of them might have killed Dugasse.

The cabin was one large room with a counter and sink unit on one wall, a big picnic table in the middle, and an old sofa and mismatched chairs on the opposite side of the room. A fridge sat against a wall behind them and a stove was at the end of the counter. One of the guys was at the stove stirring the steaming pots with a wooden spoon.

Nans went to the counter and set her pie down. "Do you guys want a piece? I'm famous for it you know," she said proudly.

Snake and Rat practically fell over themselves getting a knife for her. Nans cut the pie and Rat held out paper plates for her to dish the slices out on. He passed them around with plastic forks and the guys dug in.

Snake rolled his eyes back in his head. "This is so good. Just like my Gam used to make."

"Thanks," Nans said. "You know Lexy here is the baker at the resort. She makes the best desserts. I don't recall ever seeing you guys eating there."

"Oh, this isn't part of the resort," Rat said as he crunched down on a piece of pie crust.

"Oh, it's not?" Nans screwed up her face. "That's funny because I know at least one of you has been to the kitchen."

Everyone stopped chewing and stared at Nans. Lexy's stomach dropped. Her muscles tensed.

"What makes you say that?" Rat asked.

"Well, someone saw one of you walk right down the path and go in through the back door late at night," Nans answered.

The seven guys all looked around at each other. Chairs creaked as they squirmed in their seats.

Nans held up her hands. "Now don't get all nervous. If one of you was having an affair with Dugasse we certainly won't tell."

Snake shot up out of his seat. "What?!"

Lexy's heart leapt and she moved to get between him and Nans.

"I'm not saying any of you killed him," Nans continued, then reached in her pocket. "But we did find this bracelet right at the head of the trail not twenty feet from where he was killed."

"Now you look here old lady," Weasel said advancing on Nans, the veins in his neck straining against his spider web tattoo.

"Wait!" Rat jumped up from his chair and grabbed Weasel's arm.

Weasel shook off Rat's arm. "We can't let her say stuff like that about us."

"It's okay," Rat said holding up his hand. "That bracelet is mine."

"You were the one having an affair with Chef Dugasse?" Ida stared at Rat.

Rat shook his head. "I wasn't having an affair with Dugasse, but I did go there to meet him. Several times."

"But why?" Nans asked.

"Because he was my father," Rat looked down at the ground, his eyes moist. "He was teaching me to cook."

Chapter Sixteen

"Dugasse was your father?" Lexy stared at Rat. "But I didn't even know he had any kids."

"No one knew. We actually just found out a few months ago ourselves when my mother died. They weren't married and she never told me who my father was until right before she passed. The funny thing is, I always wanted to be a chef ..." Rat let his voice trail off, looking out the window toward the path that led to the dining hall.

"A chef?" Ida sized him up.

"Yeah, you don't think bikers have regular jobs? Snake here is an accountant, Weasel's an architect and Stone owns a coffee franchise," he said waving his hand at the others as he talked about them.

Lexy felt her eyes widen as she looked at the men—dirty, unshaven and loaded in leather and tattoos. She couldn't imagine hiring an accountant named Snake or an architect named Weasel.

"These aren't our real names," Snake said catching her incredulous look. "I'm Arty, and that's Devon, James, Zander, Ricky and Rusty. The other names are just our biker nicknames."

"And we clean up real good," Weasel said looking down at himself.

"So you didn't kill Dugasse?" Ruth said to Rat, aka Ricky.

"No, of course not."

Ida let out a sigh of frustration. "Well if it wasn't the wife, and it wasn't Sylvia Spicer and it wasn't one of you, then who the hell *did* kill him?"

Rat rubbed his face with his hand. "That's what *I'd* like to know."

"Did he have any enemies? Did he mention anyone he

thought might want to harm him?" Nans asked.

"Well, there was this one other chef that Dad said was threatening him. He wanted to buy Dad's chili recipe for the *Chili Battle* and when Dad refused, he got pretty mad."

"Chef Marchesi?" Ruth asked.

"Yes, that's him!" Rat narrowed his eyes at her. "How do you know him?"

"We don't." Ruth shook her head. "But we heard he was a rival for the chili contest and Payne mentioned him as a possible suspect."

"Is that who you thought sent us?" Lexy asked.

"Yes. We knew he wanted to get his hands on the recipe and thought he might send someone to try and take it ... but we thought it would be by force, not with pies." Snake chuckled.

"And you guys have the recipe?" Nans raised her brows.

Rat nodded. "Dad and I were going to enter the chili contest together but now that he's gone, I'll enter it myself ... in his honor."

"We're cooking up a test run now." Snake pointed to the stove. "Would you like a taste?"

Nans went over to the stove, lifted one of the lids and stuck her nose in. "Oh, this smells good."

Snake and Weasel handed out bowls and everyone lined up at the stove where Rat proudly ladled out the chili.

Lexy took her bowl over by the window and brought the spoon tentatively to her lips. It *was* good—sweet and with just enough of a spicy kick.

"This is delicious," Ida said.

"Umm." Helen, Ruth and Nans agreed.

"I don't get why this Marchesi guy would kill Rat's dad over a chili recipe," Snake said.

"Well, everyone seems to think Dugasse's chili would win the contest and winning that contest could be worth millions." Nans slurped the rest of her chili.

"Millions?" Rat's eyebrows mashed together.

"Yeah, your father didn't tell you?"

"No. He just seemed happy that we were working on something together," Rat said looking even sadder than before.

"The good news is that now *you* might be the one to win that contest," Helen said.

"And the millions," Ruth added.

"Unless Marchesi gets to you first," Nans cautioned.

"We can't be certain he's the killer," Lexy said.

"No, but he certainly had a motive," Nans replied. "And right now he's the best candidate we have. We just have to prove he did it."

"How can you do that?" Rat asked.

Nans shrugged. "We've caught killers before. Usually we just snoop around and something always comes up. I don't see why this would be any different."

Ida turned to Rat. "What time do you start setting up for the *Chili Battle*?"

"We get our assigned spots tomorrow night and we can set up our tables and canopies then," Rat said.

"The next day, the contest grounds open at noon. We can start cooking then and the general public is allowed in around 4 pm," Snake added.

"Boy, it sure would be great to get in early and snoop around his tent," Ruth said.

Rat looked at her and snapped his fingers. "I know! You can meet us tomorrow night and we'll get you in with V.I.P. visitor passes ... if you want."

"Oh that would be perfect!" Nans put her chili bowl in the sink and started washing the dishes.

"Oh, hey, you don't have to do that ... you're a guest." Snake took over the job of dish washing and Nans raised her brows at Lexy who shrugged.

"I feel much better knowing you guys are helping find out who killed my dad," Rat said. "I didn't have a lot of confidence in that detective Payne."

"Neither do we, actually," Nans replied.

"So he knows about you then." Lexy cut her eyes to Rat.

"Yes, he was here the other day," Rat said. "Weasel's cousin is on the police force here but he didn't know I was Dugasse's son. I guess Payne figured that out on his own somehow."

Lexy raised a brow. Maybe Payne wasn't as much of a bumbling idiot as he appeared to be.

"Well, I guess we better get going." Ida pushed herself up from the table where she'd found a seat in between Stone and Rusty.

Lexy noticed the men exchanging a look and her muscles tensed. *What was that about?*

Rat raised his eyebrows at Snake and Snake nodded.

"Is something wrong?" Lexy ventured, her nerves on high alert.

"No ... we just ..." Rat looked at the others. "Should we?"

"Should you what?" Nans stood near the door, her hand on the knob.

"Yeah, go ahead." Snake and the others nodded at Rat.

"Well, I was wondering if you ladies would like to go with us to biker bingo tonight ... it's a lot of fun, the biker camps from all around the lake go and tonight's the big game where you can win the grand prize."

"Oh, that sounds like fun!" Nans raised her brows at the other ladies. "Do you want to go?"

Ruth, Ida and Helen nodded. The women loved bingo and never passed up a chance to get in on a big game.

"What's the grand prize?" Ida asked.

Snake's eyes lit up. "A Harley."

"Count me in!" Ruth said. "I always wanted a Harley."

Chapter Seventeen

Lexy didn't go to biker bingo. Partly because she wanted to spend the time with Jack, but mostly because she didn't want to have to explain to him how they'd befriended a gang of bikers. He'd been really understanding about her crime solving activities on this trip and she didn't want to push her luck.

Jumping into the shower, she washed her hair then fluffed it dry letting the natural wave take over before changing into a short turquoise colored sundress. By the time Jack got back from fishing, she had beer in the cooler, steaks on the grill and Jack's favorite coconut cream pie in the fridge which was, strangely enough, located on the porch.

She was sitting in one of the rockers on their screened-in porch enjoying the view of the lake through the trees when Jack joined her, fresh from the shower. He'd given his hair a rough towel dry so it stuck up around his unshaven face. The rumpled hair and stubble gave him a handsome bad-boy look, causing Lexy's pulse to beat a little faster.

She handed him a beer from the cooler and he sank into the second rocker. Sprinkles adjusted her position so that she was lying on the floor in between the two rocking chairs and Jack bent down to scratch behind her ears.

"How was fishing today?" Lexy asked, hoping the subject of fishing would distract Jack enough so he didn't ask about *her* day.

"Good. I caught a four pound bass, which beat Norman's best catch of three point eight pounds." Jack smiled. "Plus a few smaller bass and some pickerel."

"You're really getting into vacation mode ... too bad we only have a few more days here."

"Yep. I haven't relaxed this much on vacation in years. But it will be good to get back home and back to work." Jack ran his finger lightly up Lexy's arm sending tingly shivers down her spine. "Until we go on our next vacation ... just the two of us."

"Next vacation?" Lexy's eyebrows mashed together.

Jack tilted his head at her. "Our honeymoon? We *are* getting married, right?"

Lexy laughed. "Oh, sorry. Yes, of course ... but I guess there's a lot of planning before that can happen."

"Well, I think you should start planning right away, as soon as we get back."

Lexy's heart lifted at the thought. They'd been engaged for several months, now, but sometimes it seemed like Jack might be having second thoughts. He sounded so sure about it now that Lexy figured she'd just been acting silly and vowed to put the plans into action right away.

"How is the Dugasse case going?" Jack pulled her out of her thoughts.

"Well, it wasn't the wife." Lexy watched Jack pad out to the grill in his bare feet and flip the steaks over. The smell of grilling meat combined with the sizzling sound they made when he flipped them caused her mouth to water.

"How do you know?" he asked through the screen.

"Payne said she had an alibi."

"He shared information with you?"

"Only by accident." Lexy grimaced. "He came to the kitchen to lecture me about bothering suspects and let it slip that the wife wasn't the killer."

"Well that sounds familiar." Jack returned to his rocker and laughed as he settled back in with his beer. "So do you think it was the other chef ... Sylvia?"

"She wasn't having the affair with him and she also has an alibi." Lexy felt a pang of guilt in not telling Jack the whole story about Sylvia's affair with Prescott Charles but it wasn't relevant to the murder case and she'd promised not to tell.

"So you're out of suspects?" Jack raised a brow at Lexy, then grabbed the platter and headed out to the grill.

"No, we have one other." Lexy got up and started setting

out plates and a salad on the small table they had set up for eating on.

"Who is this other suspect?" Jack prompted as he dished steaks onto their plates.

Lexy glanced out the window to make sure no one else was around. "Another chef—one who was threatening Dugasse about his chili recipe."

Jack's eyebrows shot up. "I didn't know he was getting threats. That sounds like something to investigate. I hope Payne is aware of that."

"I'm sure he is." Lexy put a small chunk of steak in her mouth and it practically melted on her tongue. She rolled her eyes back in her head. "Nummy ... this is sooo good."

Sprinkles put her paw on Lexy's foot and stared at her as if to say "don't forget to give me some." Lexy's heart surged and she threw her a small piece.

"Anyway," Lexy said. "Dugasse's son said this Marchesi guy—that's the other chef—tried to buy the chili recipe and when Dugasse refused he got mad."

"Wait ... Dugasse has a son?"

Lexy nodded. "Yeah, I guess it was kind of a secret ..." She let her voice trail off not wanting to get into the details of how *she* found out about the son.

"Speaking of the chili recipe ... are we going to the big *Chili Battle* tomorrow night?" Jack asked.

"Of course. It should be interesting, considering what happened to Dugasse." Lexy purposely forgot to tell him about Dugasse's son entering the contest with the recipe.

"That's for sure. And I heard there were going to be fireworks after. How about we bring a big blanket and spread it out on the hill? We can gorge ourselves on chili and then lay back and watch the fireworks."

"Sounds good." Lexy's stomach flipped wondering how she'd manage to eat chili with Jack and stalk Marchesi at the same time.

Jack finished off the last of his steak and salad, then took a long pull on his beer.

"The thing is, I'm not really sure how to go about getting clues that prove Marchesi is the killer," Lexy said, wiping her plate clean and stacking it on top of Jack's.

Jack leaned back and took another sip of beer. "I would try to establish a timeline ... where was Marchesi when the murder happened? Do you think he did it himself or did he have an accomplice?"

Lexy pursed her lips. "I don't know, I hadn't thought about it."

"One technique we like to use is to simply follow and observe ... we do it with suspects or people that seem to know too much about the case. Usually something shakes out. Criminals like that are dumb and all it takes is watching them a bit to find a clue."

Lexy settled back in her chair. She'd have to have Ruth find out where Marchesi was staying and then maybe one of them could follow him around while Lexy was working tomorrow morning.

"But you need to be careful if you follow this guy around ... he could be a killer. You'd be smart to leave that part to Payne." Jack's eyes drilled into hers as if he was reading her thoughts.

"Oh, of course," she said, then stood up and walked to the fridge, thinking to distract him from giving her the usual lecture about messing in police business with his favorite coconut cream pie.

She opened the door, enjoying the blast of cool air. "I have your favorite pie for dessert," she said, looking at him over the top of the door.

Jack got up and walked over to her, pulling her out from behind the door and closing it. He slid his arm around her waist, dragging her to him. He dipped his head, his lips brushing lightly against hers.

"Actually, I had something else in mind for dessert."

Chapter Eighteen

Lexy was halfway through frosting a batch of miniature cupcakes when Nans, Ruth, Ida and Helen showed up in the kitchen the next morning. She glanced nervously out the window, half expecting to see a shiny new Harley in the parking lot.

"How was biker bingo? Did you guys win anything?"

"Ida won a hundred dollars, Helen got a gift certificate for a pedicure and Ruth and I got skunked." Nans shook her head.

Lexy made a face. "A gift certificate for a pedicure? Who would have thought bikers would want that as a prize?"

Nans shrugged. "I guess one of the bikers has a salon and he donated it."

"So you didn't win the Harley?" Lexy eyed Ruth.

"No." Ruth laughed. "I guess I'll have to make do with my Oldsmobile."

"Probably safer," Lexy offered.

"For everyone," Helen added and Nans and Ida snickered.

"But we did get the V.I.P. passes," Ruth said to Lexy. "We're supposed to meet Snake, Rat and the gang at the field around five."

"Okay." Lexy checked her watch. "I'm tied up here this morning but I was thinking it might be smart to follow Marchesi around today. If he is the killer and he's still after the recipe, he might do something suspicious."

"Good idea. I'm sure he must be in town by now for the contest," Ida said.

"Did you ever look into that?" Nans asked Ruth.

"Not yet. Shouldn't be too hard though." Ruth leaned in and said in a low voice, "I have a great program that hacks the hotel guest databases."

"Easy peasy. We'll just find out where he is then stake out his hotel and put a tail on him if he leaves." Lexy thought Nans looked quite pleased that she'd been able to fit lots of police jargon in that sentence.

"Okay, but don't confront him. He could be dangerous," Lexy said, then wondered if she'd been listening to Jack too much.

A splash of vibrant color at the front of the kitchen caught her eye and her heart sank when she saw Detective Payne in a bright pink shirt and pink, white and blue plaid shorts making his way down the aisle toward her.

"What is it?" Nans turned to see what was causing the look of distaste on Lexy's face. "Oh. Well, time for us to go."

Nans, Ruth, Ida and Helen turned abruptly and scooted off in the other direction before Lexy even had time to say good-bye.

Payne smiled at the cupcakes, then frowned at Lexy. "Miss Baker, I hear you've been making the rounds."

"The rounds?" Lexy tried on her best wide-eyed innocent look. "I have no idea what you mean."

Payne narrowed his eyes at her then grabbed a little cupcake and shoved the whole thing in his mouth. He brought the spiral notebook and pencil out of his pocket.

"I think you know we have a new suspect," he said, studying her reaction. A glob of blue frosting rested on the corner of his mouth.

Lexy raised an eyebrow. She didn't point out the frosting.

"It seems Dugasse had a son," Payne announced.

"I knew that," Lexy said. "But the son didn't kill him."

"Oh really? And how do you know that?"

Lexy pressed her lips together. She was already in enough trouble with Payne and didn't want to tell him she'd scouted out the biker camp on her own or that she'd found the bracelet at the head of the trail.

"Rumors around the kitchen." She waved her hand around the room.

Payne looked at the ceiling and tapped the eraser end of his pencil on his lips. The glob of frosting quivered but stayed in place.

"Seems like you know an awful lot about this murder ... for someone who isn't really involved."

Lexy's stomach sank. Whenever she talked to Payne she seemed to get herself in more trouble. All the more reason to investigate this herself, she thought.

Payne picked another cupcake off the tray and shoved it in his mouth. This one with chocolate frosting. "I trust you'll be going to the *Chili Battle*?"

Lexy nodded. *What an odd thing for him to ask.*

"Good, then all my favorite suspects will be in the same area at once."

And with that he turned and walked off leaving Lexy to wonder what he meant.

***

The fairgrounds at Lakeshore Resort where the *Chili Battle* was being held was a giant field with barns at one end. Today, a big section was roped off and Lexy could see canopies being set up in rows. Two men in khaki shirts guarded the entrance.

Nans pulled the V.I.P. passes out of her giant purse and handed them out so each of them could show their ticket and be let inside. Since the event wasn't open for the general public, there wasn't a lot of people, but those that were there seemed to be quite busy.

It was sectioned off into booths each about ten by twenty and with a post that held boxy electrical outlets. The contestants were setting up their tents and tables and getting their cookware in order. Lexy remembered that Rat had said they weren't allowed to start cooking until noon tomorrow. She figured most of the contestants wanted to make sure they had everything in good order tonight so they could get right into cooking first thing the next day.

"So you didn't find out anything today when you followed Marchesi?" Lexy said once they were far enough away from anyone who might overhear.

"No," Nans said. "It was boring. Helen fell asleep in the

back seat."

"He stayed in the hotel and went out once to the grocery store. Bought a lot of beans," Ida added.

"But you got a good look at him, right? So you'll recognize him if you see him here."

"Oh we got a good look," Nans said, craning her neck to scan the area. "But I don't see him here."

"How about we go logically down the rows and check out each booth?" Ruth asked.

"Okay, we'll start at this end." Lexy pointed to a booth in the corner. "Then go up and down the rows."

They started toward the end and Lexy felt a tingle at the base of her neck. *Was someone watching her?* She turned around but didn't see anyone. Probably just nerves about what might happen if they have a run-in with Marchesi, she thought.

They walked the rows methodically. Lexy noticed a lot of the contestants had special canopies with their names. Probably not unusual considering the amount of money at stake. She wondered if some of them were professional contestants or just people that liked to make chili.

Nans stopped in front of a booth that had a tropical looking canopy with "Chilin' Chili" written on it in scrolly letters. The canopy was turquoise and pink and the contestants inside had matching aprons. Even their crock pots were turquoise.

"This looks like a fun booth," Nans said.

One of the aproned contestants smiled over at Nans. "It is. We even give out small margarita samples." She nodded to the stack of cups.

A second lady glanced up. "Be sure to come back tomorrow for the tasting ... and vote for us!"

Nans winked at Lexy as they continued down the row. "I know the first place I'll be heading to tomorrow night."

They passed more interesting booths. "Hot to Taught" was manned by teachers and "It's a Gas" claimed to have the hottest—and gassiest—chili in the contest.

As they walked the rows, Lexy couldn't shake the feeling of being watched. She kept looking behind her, but didn't see anyone.

They found Rat, Snake and the others in a booth in the third row. Nans rushed right over and Lexy watched the four older women exchange high-fives with the six bikers.

Lexy noticed their tent was a plain white color with Dugasse written in script on an awning that hung on the front. The guys wore plain black aprons and Rat shuffled around inside, placing items in one spot, then moving them a few seconds later.

"What's that for?" Ruth asked pointing to a large grill they had set up in the corner.

"We're going to warm the cornbread up on it so it will be lightly grilled." Rat smiled proudly. "It's going to be the best cornbread in the contest."

"Over here we have the crockpots ... this is where we'll start the beans in the secret sauce right at noon." Snake pointed to a table with rows of mismatched crockpots on it. Lexy wondered if the boys had attended every yard sale in a ten mile radius to amass the odd collection.

"And over here we'll cook up the meat." Weasel walked over to a stove plate that sat on another table.

"Then we mix it all together with vegetables and put it back in the crockpot to simmer for a few hours," Rat said.

"Sounds like you guys have it all worked out." Nans looked around the booth, then lowered her voice. "Have you seen Marchesi?"

"No, we were afraid he might come by and bother us, but nothing so far. I'm not sure he even knows who we are." Rat shrugged.

"But if he tries anything, he'll be sorry," Snake said, pointing to a stack of baseball bats in the corner.

"I heard his booth was in the very last row," Rat said.

"We should go check it out. He doesn't know who we are so maybe we can interrogate him and get him to slip up," Ida said.

Lexy mashed her brows together. "Interrogate him? That might not be such a good idea."

"Oh, I didn't mean in an obvious way, dear," Ida said. "You know us old ladies have a way of interrogating people without them realizing it."

Lexy gave a half nod. She had to admit, being an

octogenarian did have its advantages, one of which was that people paid little attention to what you asked and tended to spill their guts before they even realized what they were saying.

Nans clapped her hands together and started toward the aisle. "Shall we?"

Ruth, Ida, Helen and Lexy said a quick good-bye to the bikers and followed her out. She made her way down to the end of the row and skipped over the next one heading straight for the last row of booths. Lexy followed along, ignoring the feeling that she was being watched.

She rounded the corner to see Nans standing in front of one of the booths.

"Here it is." Nans pointed up at the awning which said Marchesi in block letters along with a black and white line drawing of the chef.

"No one is here." Ida looked deflated.

Lexy glanced around. The booth was blocked off, with tables set up around the edges where one would normally enter. The back had tables too and those were loaded with high tech stainless steel crockpots and racks of spices. On one of the tables close to them was a picture of Marchesi in his chef's uniform in the kitchen.

Lexy picked up the picture. "So this is him?"

Nans looked over her shoulder. "Yep. Looks like he's in his restaurant or something."

"Who's that other guy next to him?" Helen asked.

"I don't know ... wait a minute." Nans grabbed the picture from Lexy and held it close to her face.

"It couldn't be ..." Her voice trailed off as she set the picture down and dug in her purse. She produced something wrapped in a tissue, her eyes lighting up as she unwrapped the tissue and looked inside.

"It is!"

"Is what?" Lexy asked.

Nans laid the object flat in her palm and Lexy recognized it as the bloodied scrap of fabric she'd found under the dumpster.

"The pattern on this fabric matches the pattern on that guy's shirt in the picture ... exactly." Nans emphasized the last word by stabbing her index finger at the man standing next to Marchesi in the picture.

Lexy squinted, comparing the two fabrics and her stomach lurched ... Nans was right.

Ida gasped her eyes riveting between the scrap of fabric and the picture. "That's it! He's the killer!"

***

"Shhh!" Nans looked at Ida. "This doesn't *prove* that he's the killer ... just that he has the same shirt."

"Actually, we don't even know that swatch is *from* the killer," Lexy said.

"It could have been there before the murder," Ruth reminded them.

"We probably shouldn't have taken it." Lexy's stomach sank. "Now Payne will have no way to tie this to the scene of the crime."

"Yeah, it's unlikely that he'll believe us if we suddenly come forward and say we found it there," Ruth said.

"Maybe the best thing to do is to give this to Weasel. He had a cousin on the police force. He might know what to do about it."

Nans frowned down at the swatch. "Yeah, probably. I guess we'll just have to find some other evidence or get Marchesi to admit to it."

"Too bad we couldn't catch him trying to steal the recipe or threatening Rat and the gang."

"Does he even know that Rat is Dugasse's son?"

"Not according to what Rat said earlier," Lexy answered.

"So, for all we know, he thinks he's got the contest all tied up since Dugasse is dead," Ruth said.

"Which is good because when killers think they are in the clear, they tend to let their guard down," Ida added.

"Well, let's get this swatch back to Weasel." Nans wrapped the fabric back in the tissue and put it in her purse. "We can come back to the booth tomorrow when Marchesi is sure to be here and see if we can get him to admit to being the killer ... or at least having his henchman do it."

As they turned to head back down the aisle, Lexy's heart jolted when she caught a glimpse of someone ducking out of sight at the end of the row.

"Hey! You!" She ran toward the person but when she got to the end no one was there—just a crowd of people milling about the area looking in the various booths.

"Damn!" She stopped and waited for Nans and the ladies to catch up.

"What is it?" Nans asked.

"I thought I saw someone watching us." Lexy stood on her tip toes scanning the crowd. "I've had the feeling someone has been following us all night."

Nans pursed her lips together. "Interesting ... why would someone follow us?"

Lexy shrugged. "I don't know, but I'm willing to bet it has something to do with Dugasse's murder."

Chapter Nineteen

Lexy kept herself busy the next day making extra batches of brownies and cupcakes to keep her mind off the chili contest that night. She was jittery with the feeling that *something* was going to happen and a little nervous at what Nans might do to try to expose Marchesi.

She'd expected detective Payne to show up and read her the riot act about the swatch of fabric. The bikers had been happy to hear about how they had found it and the picture that showed Marchesi's friend wearing it. Weasel had even whipped out his cell phone and tried to call his cousin on the spot, except there'd been no cell phone service.

Payne hadn't graced the kitchen with his appearance by the time Lexy was done with her kitchen duties and she breathed a sigh of relief. She didn't know if that meant he just didn't know about it yet or if she was off the hook, but either way she wasn't going to have to deal with him today … at least not until they could get a confession or some other clue from Marchesi later on that night.

Rushing to her cottage to change, Lexy wondered how she was going to get away from Jack to go to the Marchesi booth. Jack wouldn't approve of Nans interrogating him and she certainly wasn't going to let Nans and the ladies go without her. God only knew what kind of trouble they could get into.

She showered and changed into a blue tank top and faded jeans. She fed Sprinkles and dug out a big blanket for them to sit on to view the fireworks which were supposed to start shortly after dark.

Lexy felt the corners of her lips curl in a smile thinking of how romantic it would be to lay on the blanket with Jack and watch the fireworks … and also of how leaving Jack on the blanket to 'save their spot' would provide the perfect excuse for her venturing off with Nans.

***

By the time Jack finished showering, Nans, Ruth, Helen, Ida and Ida's fiancé Norman had come to collect them. They put Sprinkles in her harness and then they all started off toward the field.

"I figure Norman and Jack can get some chili and then save our spots on the blankets." Ida winked at Lexy. Apparently the older woman had the same idea Lexy did.

They made their way into the event and walked around to a few booths. Lexy wasn't surprised when Nans went straight to the "Chilin Chili" booth and grabbed margaritas for everyone. The salty tang of the drink flirted with Lexy's taste buds as the pungent tequila soothed her nerves.

The air was filled with a festive vibe and the smell of spices. Lexy felt good walking hand in hand with Jack and surrounded by her grandmother and friends, but she still couldn't shake that niggling feeling that she was being followed.

"It's getting crowded up on the hill." Ida pointed to the hillside which was starting to fill up. "Why don't you and Jack grab some chili, then take the blankets and save us a seat? Us girls wanna walk around a little more."

"Okay by you?" Norman asked Jack who nodded. Jack and Norman both loved fishing and the two of them had spent most of the vacation doing just that and becoming close friends in the process.

Lexy knew Jack wasn't much for milling around in crowds so he was more than happy to take the blanket and Sprinkles and set out for more spacious territory. He gave Lexy a quick peck on the cheek and off they went.

"Now, let's get down to business," Nans whispered after they were out of hearing range. She turned and walked briskly toward the very last row where Marchesi's booth was. Taking a detour to breeze by Rat's booth, she stopped only long enough to wish him good luck, then continued on to the last row.

Lexy felt a jolt of apprehension as they turned into the last row. The crowd had thinned and it made her feel exposed. She got that hair standing up feeling on the back of her neck again and wished she'd had two—or more—margaritas.

Her heartbeat picked up speed as they approached the Marchesi tent. The crowd seemed oddly disinterested in it which was strange considering Marchesi was supposed to have one of the best chili recipes. As they got up closer to the tent, Lexy found out why.

The tent was closed.

"What the heck?" Nans turned around to face them her arms extended at her sides, palms out.

"Is anyone in there?" Lexy tried to lift one of the flaps but the tent was buttoned up tight as a drum. She managed to lift a corner flap to get a peek inside.

"It's empty." She shrugged at Nans and the ladies.

"Well, where could he be?" Ruth looked around.

"Maybe out killing someone else that he thinks might steal the win from him," Ida whispered.

"Let's look inside." Nans tugged on the corner of the flap that Lexy had opened and a few more snaps unsnapped making the opening big enough for them to squeeze in.

Lexy's heart pounded against her ribs as she followed Nans inside. She looked around at the tables—crockpots were simmering and the tent smelled deliciously like molasses and spices. She noticed Chef Marchesi had all the most expensive equipment from the stainless steel crockpots to the high tech convection ovens. Everything was top notch right down to the premium mahogany handled knife set.

Lexy's stomach lurched and she sucked in a breath as she stared at the knife set ... the handles were identical to the knife she'd seen sticking out of Dugasse's chest.

"What is it?" Nans turned to her.

"This knife set—it matches the one that killed Dugasse." Lexy pointed to the set. "And it's missing the chef's knife."

"It's too bad you're so nosey."

Lexy whirled toward the sound of the familiar voice, her heart jerking in her chest when she saw who it was.

Brad Meltzer ... and he had a gun pointed right at Nans.

Chapter Twenty

Lexy's heart hammered in her chest. Too late, she realized they'd made a mistake coming into the closed off tent—no one could see them. But would they hear her over the din of the event if she screamed?

"Don't even think about screaming or the old lady gets it," Brad said as if reading her mind.

"Old lady?" Nans bristled at Brad.

"Shut it!

Brad let out a low whistle and a flap on the other side of the tent opened. A large man wheeled in dollies stacked with boxes and burlap sacks. Lexy's blood froze when she recognized him as the man with the plaid shirt in the picture—the killer.

Nans, Ida, Ruth and Helen stood frozen in their tracks

Lexy's heart jerked as Brad started toward the ladies. She lunged toward Brad to prevent him from getting to them, but plaid shirt came at her from the left. She turned to the left, leaping at him to catch him off guard but he lowered his head and smashed into her mid-section sending her plummeting to the ground.

She kicked out and heard a grunt as her foot connected with hard bone. His knee. It merely slowed him for a second and he reached out and grabbed her by the hair, pulling her head back.

Lexy felt his arm squeeze around her neck as her clouding vision registered Brad advancing on Nans and the ladies. She struggled against him but he was like a brick house.

She tried to cry out for Brad not to hurt Nans but the hold on her throat was too tight.

And then everything went dark.

***

Lexy opened her eyes but she couldn't see a thing.

She was rolled up in something and she was moving. Then, the movement stopped. She strained to hear something—anything—that would give her a clue as to where she was but all she could hear was the sound of her heart thumping in her ears and heavy clanking metal. Like chains.

Next thing she knew she was falling, a fall which ended in an explosion of pain in her right shoulder and hip. Then the sound of a door slamming shut and more metal clanking.

Where was she?

She tried to sit up but was restrained by whatever it was that held her. She wiggled, feeling the coarse fabric that was loosely around her. Raising her hands up, she realized she wasn't rolled up in something ... she was in a burlap sack!

Fumbling for the top, she managed to push it open and poke her head through. She was in what looked like some sort of dark, windowless shack. She could barely make out four large sacks lying beside her.

Nans!

She wriggled out of her sack and ran over to the one beside her. She could hear grunts from inside and see movement—at least they were alive. She undid the strings and looked in.

"Where the hell are we?" Nans blinked up at her.

"I have no idea. In some building."

"Hey, help me out of here," A muffled voice said from one of the other sacks and Lexy rushed over to free Ruth while Nans unwrapped Ida. Helen managed to get out of hers by herself and they all stood looking around.

"What is this place?" Ruth asked.

"Anyone have a light?"

Helen rummaged in her purse, producing a box of matches. Lexy took them, striking one against the side. The smell of sulfur spiced the air and the match provided a swatch of light which Lexy used to look around the place.

"It's some sort of storage shed." She walked toward the rows of shelving looking at the boxes. Bringing the match closer to a box, she read the writing ... her heart seized and she dropped the match stepping on it as fast as she could.

"Shit!"

"Lexy, dear. There's no need for that kind of language," Nans said.

"This place is full of fireworks! I could have blown us up." Lexy's hand shook as she picked up the match.

"Oh, this must be where they store the fireworks. I think the ones they are using for tonight are already set up though so these must be extra," Ruth said.

"Why do you think they brought us here?" Ida asked.

"I heard Brad say something about getting us out of the way until after the contest when they can dispose of us." Helen rubbed her hands on her upper arms.

"Well, I don't know about you guys, but I'm not going to wait for them to come and *dispose* of us," Nans said.

"Let's see if we can ram the door open." Ruth went over to the door and pushed her shoulder against it. It didn't budge.

"Let me try." Lexy took a few running steps and leapt into the door. It opened a tiny crack, but the door was solid and secured by something. She remembered the sound of metal chains.

"I think it's chained shut. We'll never get it open." Lexy felt her stomach drop. How were they going to get out of there?

Lexy pressed her ear to the door. She couldn't hear anything.

"Does anyone know how far we are from the field?"

A chorus of "no's" answered her.

She pounded on the door. "Help!"

Ida stared at her. "Lexy, I doubt anyone can hear us. The killers aren't *that* stupid ... are they?"

"Wait a minute." Nans turned around and squinted at the shelves. "Gimme those matches ... I want to see what we have to work with here."

"No way. You could blow this thing sky high and us with

it!" Lexy shoved the match box into her pocket.

"How about we just use the flashlight app on my cell phone?" Ruth held out her phone and everyone stared at her.

Lexy felt her eyebrows shoot up to her hairline. "You have a cellphone? We can just call someone for help!"

"Oh right." Ruth fiddled with the phone. "Ughh ... no cell service."

"Damn!"

"Shine the flashlight over here," Nans said.

Ruth pointed the end of her cell phone at the shelf and a beam of light illuminated the boxes. Nans walked down the rows, telling Ruth where to point. Finally she found a box she liked and picked some firecrackers out of it, then brought them back to the front of the shed.

"Ida do you have a tube of lipstick?" Nans asked.

"Sure." Ida rummaged in her purse, then produced a gold colored metal lipstick.

"Thanks," Nans said. "Does anyone have any duct tape?"

Helen reached into her purse. "Right here."

Nans grabbed the duct tape and Lexy watched in fascination as she ripped the lipstick out of its container and threw it on the floor.

"Hey, what are you doing?" Ida frowned down at the lipstick. "That's my favorite shade—coral passion."

"All for a good cause," Nans said as she ripped open the fireworks pouring the powder into the lipstick container top, then jamming the bottom on. "Lexy, see if you can find a nail and something hard to pierce a hole in this."

"Oh, I have some nails in my purse," Ruth offered.

Lexy found a large rock in the corner and set the lipstick on the floor. She took a nail from Ruth and balanced it on top, then bashed it with the rock to pierce through the metal.

"Perfect." Nans ripped off some duct tape with her teeth and used it to seal the tube closed, then she threaded the fuse from the fireworks into the hole Lexy had made in the top.

Nans held the modified lipstick out to show them. "Well, who wants to light it?"

"Light it? That thing could blow us up!" Lexy stepped back.

Nans waved her hand. "Oh, don't be silly. There's not a lot in here. I figure we wedge it in the crack of the door and it will be enough to blow the lock off and we can get out of here."

Lexy felt her stomach drop as she looked at Ruth, Ida and Helen. It sounded dangerous to her, but waiting around for Brad and plaid shirt seemed pretty dangerous too.

"Okay." she shrugged and cracked the door open. "Stick it in."

Nans stuck the lipstick in the crack and Lexy let go so the force of the door would hold it in place.

"You guys stand back." She motioned to the other side of the room as she took the matches from her pocket.

Holding her breath, she struck the match then backed up as far away from the lipstick as she could while still being able to touch the match to the fuse. Her heart leapt into her throat as it caught and she ran back to where Nans and the ladies were huddled. She turned away from the door and covered her ears.

Boom!

The door blew open and the five of them tumbled out of the shack coughing and batting at the thick smoke that hung in the air.

Lexy tilted her head to the side, trying to get the ringing in her ears to stop. It started to subside, but was replaced with a low drone which got louder and louder until she realized what it was ... motorcycles!

Rat, Snake, Weasel, Bug and Spike came roaring out of the woods behind them.

"Get on! Marchesi's getting away!"

Lexy looked at Nans and the ladies who shrugged and then hopped on the back of the motorcycles as they raced off in the direction of the chili contest.

Lexy looked back over her shoulder as they sped off and her heart clenched.

"The shed door, it's on fire!" she shouted.

Rat glanced back over his shoulder but kept racing

forward. "We don't have time to go back. Marchesi's making a run for it!"

Chapter Twenty One

Lexy felt the sting of bugs smacking her face as they raced over to a wooded patch directly behind Marchesi's tent. As they approached, she could see the fat chef, Brad and the guy in the plaid shirt making a run across the field toward the woods.

Something moved at the edge of the contest area and Lexy's eyes widened when she saw Detectives Payne and Wells racing across the field along with another uniformed officer after Marchesi.

Rat and the gang pushed their bikes to go even faster and Lexy felt her heartbeat racing along with her as they gained on the chef.

Marchesi was getting closer to the woods but Payne was gaining ground as Lexy and the bikers flew out into the clearing. They aimed their bikes toward Marchesi who jerked his head over his shoulder in their direction, his mouth forming a surprised 'O' as he saw the five motorcycles racing toward him.

With a final push, the motorcycles flew across the field and circled around Marchesi and his accomplices preventing their escape. Marchesi dodged and weaved trying to make it to the woods but the bikes were too quick for him and cut him off at every turn.

And then, just when Lexy thought she'd seen it all, Detective Payne made a running leap. He flew through the air in a colorful blur of pastel shirt and plaid pants, landing right on Marchesi and bringing the big chef to the ground.

Wells and the uniformed officer wrestled with Brad and the third man while Payne whipped out his handcuffs and locked them on Marchesi's wrist.

"Chef Martino Marchesi ... you're under arrest for the murder of Alain Dugasse."

Lexy jumped off the bike and approached Payne. "So, he really is the killer?"

"Not the actual killer, but the mastermind behind it." Payne turned to Brad and the other man. "And those are his accomplices."

"So one of them killed Dugasse?"

Payne nodded. "Marchesi sent Brad to work in the kitchen in order to get close to Dugasse and try to get the recipe. When it became clear that wasn't going to work, and Marchesi's threats didn't scare the chef, Brad lured Dugasse out to the dumpster somehow where the other gentleman was waiting to kill him."

Lexy felt a shiver despite the warm weather. The killer had been out there lurking behind the dumpster that morning and anyone could have stumbled across him.

"I think Brad might have been trying to frame you for it," Payne said to Lexy.

"Yeah, and for a while it seemed like you were going to believe him." Lexy narrowed her eyes at Payne. "So how did you figure out what really happened?"

"Actually, it was all thanks to you." Payne stood, heaving Marchesi up off the ground. "After our talk the other day, I had you followed ... you led us right to the clues in Marchesi's tent."

"The knife set?"

"Yep, that and the scrap of fabric your grandmother found tied the whole case together. Then we just waited for him to come back to the tent here to arrest him. He ran as soon as he saw us but ... well, you know the rest."

"So you knew we were here in the tent? Why didn't you help us?" Lexy fisted her hands on her hips.

Did Payne actually let Brad kidnap them?

"Unfortunately, my guy lost you, so I didn't know you had been kidnapped until these gentlemen here called me." Payne thrust his chin toward Rat and Snake. "Surely you don't think I'd *let* the bad guys kidnap you and your grandmother?"

Lexy frowned. *Would he?*

"Wait. How did Rat and Snake know we got kidnapped?"

Rat overheard her and walked over. "We got worried when you guys didn't come back so we did a little snooping around. We saw Brad and that other guy bringing some really big sacks of beans to the shed."

Snake joined them. "We thought that was pretty strange and after we asked around and found out it was the fireworks storage it clicked in that they had put you in the sacks!"

Rat laughed. "But it looks like you guys didn't really need us to rescue you."

Lexy felt the corners of her mouth curl and she looked at her grandmother. "Yeah, Nans and the ladies have a lot of tricks up their sleeves ... or should I say, in their purses."

"I'll say." Snake shook his head. "I never would have thought of a lipstick bomb."

"Well, I hope all this didn't ruin your chances in the chili contest," Lexy said to Rat.

"I have some of the other guys handing out the chili." Rat looked at his watch. "But I better get back there and make sure everything is in place for the judging!"

Lexy watched him and Snake rush off toward their bikes as Wells and the other officer took Marchesi from Payne.

"We would have figured it all out without you Miss Baker," Payne said. "But I do appreciate you helping to speed things up. That being said, I hope you will be going back to your bakery in Brook Ridge Falls soon ... where you will be out of my hair. If you want to meddle in the police business of your boyfriend, well that's his problem."

At the mention of Jack, Lexy's heart lurched.

How long had she been gone?

"Right. Nice meeting you too." She stuck her hand out at Payne who shook it and then she ran off to gather Nans and the ladies.

"We better get back to the blanket before Jack starts asking questions." She tugged on Nans arm.

Nans raised an eyebrow. "Oh, you don't want to tell him about our exciting excursion?"

"Well, it's not that I want to lie or keep things from him, but sometimes it's better if he doesn't know every little detail."

"I agree," Ida said. "We girls have to keep a little mystery in the relationship."

"Well, let's get a move on then." Nans hooked arms with Lexy and Ruth. Ida and Helen joined in on either end. "I want to get back there in time to see who wins the *Chili Battle*."

Chapter Twenty Two

"Where have you been? Your chili is cold." Jack wrinkled his brow at Lexy as she plopped down on the blanket beside him.

"Oh, we were just walking around. Lost track of time," She said, feigning intense interest in the chili so he wouldn't ask for any details.

"What's with your hair? It's all wild." Jack reached up and picked something out of her hair, then held it in front of his face. "A beetle."

Lexy's hands flew up to her hair, fluffing and brushing away any other bugs that might have gotten trapped in there. "It's the humidity."

Jack leaned over sniffing her hair. "You smell like gunpowder."

Lexy's stomach tightened.

"That smell must be from one of the grills in the tent," she squeaked.

Her heart crunched as Jack frowned at her.

"Shhh." Nans saved her from further scrutiny. "They're judging the chili now."

Lexy put her bowl down and Sprinkles jumped on it like she hadn't eaten in days. Lexy didn't mind—turns out cold chili isn't that tasty.

She shielded her eyes from the setting sun and squinted toward the stage. The judges were sitting behind a table and the three finalists stood before them. Her heart surged for Rat who was one of the finalists.

She strained to listen as the judges made comments on each of their dishes. Rat got extra brownie points for his cornbread.

"Yay!" Nans clapped her hands together.

The judges droned on.

"Just get on with it," Ruth muttered after several more minutes of chili talk.

"Come on Rat!" Ida yelled.

"Rat?" Jack wrinkled his forehead at Lexy who grimaced.

"Long story," she said patting his leg and her stomach flip-flopped as he took her hand in his.

Finally, the judges got down to tallying up the votes. One of the judges stood up, retrieving a giant check that had been leaning against the tent wall behind them.

"And the winner of the fifth annual *Chili Battle* is ..."

Lexy held her breath while the judge paused for effect.

"In honor of the late Chef Dugasse, his son, Rick Monroe!"

The field erupted in applause. Lexy, Nans, Ruth, Ida and Helen clapped and high-fived each other.

"Way to go!" Nans yelled.

Helen let out a loud wolf whistle.

Ida sucked down a margarita and Lexy craned her neck to see behind the older woman, wondering if she had a stash of them.

Amidst the din of the applause and whistles, Lexy thought she heard the distinctive sound of bottle rockets. The applause started to die down and she realized it *was* bottle rockets along with a series of loud bangs.

Jack swiveled his head around, looking at the sky. "Why are they starting the fireworks *now*? It's still light out."

Lexy's heart skipped and she exchanged a look with Nans remembering how the fireworks storage shed had been on fire when they'd roared off on the motorcycles.

Lexy flinched when she heard another round of loud bangs and saw flashes of light in the sky.

Jack's forehead wrinkled as he looked up. "I hope that wasn't the finale ... you can hardly see anything."

"Oh, I bet that was just a little preview." Ida giggled, sloshing part of her margarita on Lexy.

"Hey, isn't that your detective friend?" Jack pointed down toward the parking lot and Lexy swiveled her head in that direction, glad to have something distracting Jack from the fireworks.

In the parking lot, Payne and Wells were stuffing Marchesi, Brad Meltzer and their accomplice into separate police cars.

"Yes," Lexy said. "He's arresting the killer."

"So, it *was* that other chef?" Jack asked.

"Yep, guess so." Lexy smiled at Jack.

Jack brushed his lips against her forehead and she felt her stomach flip at the tender gesture.

"I'm so proud of you," he said.

Lexy narrowed her eyes. "Why?"

"Well, you're up here and the arrest is happening down there."

Lexy glanced down at the parking lot. "So?"

"So, that shows you're finally learning to leave the dangerous stuff to the police." Jack took both her hands in his. "Isn't it much easier ... and less dangerous this way?"

Lexy glanced over Jack's shoulder at Nans who made a 'zipping up the lips and throwing away the key' motion, then turned back to Jack.

She smiled up at him, her heart melting at the love in his eyes, her stomach suffering a twinge of guilt for not telling him *exactly* the whole truth.

"Yes," she said. "Yes it is."

***

Join Leighann's mailing list and get in on the early bird specials to get her latest books at the lowest price:
http://www.leighanndobbs.com/newsletter

A ZEN FOR MURDER

Chapter One

Claire Watkins tossed a dead rose stem from her spacious garden into the small wheelbarrow just as the sun made its appearance, splashing the blue Atlantic Ocean with a wash of pink.

Sunrise was her favorite time of day. It was quiet. Peaceful. To her, the hours before her little town of Crab Cove on Mooseamuck Island, Maine, woke up and the hubbub of tourist and local activity started were the most precious hours of the day.

Stretching, she winced at the slight pull in the muscles in her lower back and the popping sounds that crackled from her spine. Even so, Claire felt grateful that she enjoyed relatively good health for her seventy years, which she attributed to the strict natural health regimen she'd adopted in the past decade.

She'd never tire of looking at the panoramic view from her stone cottage, perched three-quarters of the way up Israel Head Hill on the small island off the coast of Maine. She'd grown up in this house and returned in later years to tend to her ailing father. Now, she lived here alone. Which suited her just fine.

Sucking in a deep breath of salty sea air, her gaze drifted from the ocean that stretched in front of her to the cove below, with its picturesque fishing boats on her left. Claire couldn't imagine living anywhere else.

She closed her eyes, letting her breath out slowly as she enjoyed the early morning island sounds.

The happy chirping of chickadees, wrens and nuthatches in her garden.

The familiar cry of gulls in the distance.

The soothing sound of the surf lapping at the shore.

The angry yelling and cursing coming from the road below.

Claire's eyes flew open.

Angry yelling and cursing?

That wasn't a normal, early morning sound on the island. She cocked her head, honing in on the direction of the noise. It sounded like it was coming from the scenic vista that overlooked the cove. She hurried to the patio in the corner of her yard that looked down on the vista.

Claire's father had installed the patio years ago in order to make the most use of the yard and its views. The property fell away drastically at the edge of the patio, so they'd put up a heavy-duty railing for safety. Claire could just barely see the road from her vantage point. She leaned precariously over the railing, the cliff falling away below her. Her brows rose when she saw who was causing the ruckus.

Norma Hopper, the island's resident artist, had setup her paint-splotched, wooden easel in her usual spot. For as long as Claire could remember, Norma had started the day at that very spot, where she painted the island sunrises that she was famous for and which sold to tourists like hotcakes in the summer.

But today, her canvas was blank. Instead of painting, she was engaged in a heated argument with Zoila Rivers. The two women were squared off, facing each other, Norma with her hands on her hips, Zoila waving a piece of paper in Norma's face.

Snatches of angry words drifted up and, although Claire couldn't make out exactly what the words were, she could tell something serious was going on.

Norma stood rigid, the immense brim of her straw hat, which Claire had always suspected she wore more to keep people out of her space than to ward off the sun, stuck out like a quivering awning.

Zoila, in contrast, was a whirl of energy, shuffling her feet and waving her arms. Claire didn't know Zoila very well. The psychic had come to the island just over a year ago and, while some people didn't believe in her abilities, Claire had thought she was well-liked.

It wasn't unusual to see Norma acting angry. She was naturally abrasive, but everyone liked and respected her. Despite the artist's gruff demeanor, Claire had fond memories of Norma, who she'd known since she was a little girl growing up on the island. When Claire had returned a few years ago, she'd rekindled that friendship as an adult.

Claire knew Norma's usual, angry facade, though, and this wasn't it. Not only that, but Claire's training as a criminal psychologist made her an expert in body language ... and the body language of these two women told Claire this was no trifling matter.

As far as she knew, though, Zoila Rivers and Norma Hopper were only passing acquaintances. She couldn't imagine what could possibly cause them to argue so vehemently.

Claire pushed back from the railing and pulled her sweater tight around her to ward off the late spring chill that seemed to suddenly permeate the air. Then, she put her pruning shears away and rushed into the house. She'd better hurry and get ready for what the day may bring. Her intuition told her something unusual was afoot on Mooseamuck Island.

***

Further up Israel Head Hill, Dominic Benedetti sat on the patio of his condo, his great, bushy eyebrows drawn together in a disapproving 'V' as he regarded the cannoli on the plate in front of him. It wasn't the confection, so much, that drew his objection but the uneven placement of the tiny, chocolate-chip garnishments. Five on one side and six on the other.

Does no one take pride in their work anymore? he wondered as he picked it up and took a small bite.

The creamy pastry coated his tongue and he nodded. Almost as good as his Nonna made.

Almost, but not quite.

Nothing was quite as good as it had been in his youth, especially not the home-made Italian food he'd enjoyed or the culture of his close Italian neighborhood in the north end of Boston.

But then, one couldn't expect things to stay the same forever.

He sighed, his heart twisting as he looked past the French doors into the living room where the picture of Sophia, his late wife, sat in its sterling silver frame. They'd shared forty-five years and two children together, and though cancer had taken her from him almost two years ago, the loss still felt fresh and raw—like a big hole had been cut right out of him.

He wrenched his eyes from the picture and looked back down at the cannoli, his appetite fading as his memory rehashed those last few weeks with Sophia.

She'd made him promise to live a good long life. He'd agreed because it seemed to give her peace. But the truth was he didn't want to live a good long life—not without her. In the end, though, he'd tried to honor that wish. Which was why he'd come to Crab Cove—a place where they'd spent many happy vacations with their children. The kids were grown now and Sophia was gone, but Dom still loved the quaint New England island.

Living on the island had taken some of the sting from his loss and he had to admit he *had* started to enjoy himself a little. He'd even indulged himself in a few things Sophia wouldn't have approved of—like eating dessert for breakfast.

He sighed and bit into the cannoli again. When Sophia's death had dulled his zest for life, he'd retired from his investigative consulting practice to come up north and lick his wounds. Adjusting to his new life hadn't been easy and he had to admit, now that time had dulled some of the pain, he was getting a little bored.

He listened to his parakeets, Romeo and Juliet, chirp away inside the condo while he finished off the pastry. He had been lonely at first, but the birds helped keep him company and the other residents of Crab Cove had made him feel right at home.

Dom allowed himself a thin smile as he mused about his newfound celebrity status on the island. Apparently, they didn't get many folks who had 'made the papers' up here, and Dom had made them plenty as a consulting detective on high profile cases down in Massachusetts.

But that was in his old life. Now, he had to amuse himself by finding runaway cats and lost sets of keys. Still, he did have a spectacular view from his condo, high atop the hill. One could have a much worse retirement.

He carefully wiped the crumbs from his lips and glanced to the east, over the vast Atlantic, to where the sun kissed the very edge of the ocean.

Time to start the day.

Dom was just about to rise out of his chair when a movement further down the hill caught his eye.

Claire Watkins.

It wasn't unusual that she'd be out in her garden at this time of day, but what she was doing out there *was* unusual. Quite unusual, indeed.

His eyes narrowed as he watched her lean over the railing. Clearly, she was straining to see something below. Dom wished her stone cottage was not blocking the view, because judging by the way she was positioning herself precariously over the railing, he could tell it must be something of the utmost interest.

Dom's eyebrows started to tingle with electricity—a feeling he recognized well and one he hadn't felt in a long time. For most of his adult life, his bushy eyebrows had been overly sensitive. He knew from experience that this sort of tingle meant something big was about to happen. As an investigator, they'd been a valuable asset—and to think his daughter had wanted him to trim them when he retired!

He watched with interest as Claire pushed off from the railing and hurried inside her cottage.

Then he, too, hurried inside, a spring in his step.

He carefully cleaned off his plate and dried it, putting it away on top of the stack of same-sized plates and patting the edges to make sure they were aligned perfectly. Romeo and Juliet twittered and peeped. He stopped in front of their cage on his way to the bedroom and the two birds became quiet.

Romeo fluffed up his green and yellow feathers and sidestepped along the perch toward Dom. Juliet remained in the corner, preening her white and aqua tail.

The birds' normal chattering was mostly gibberish, but every so often, Romeo surprised Dom by uttering an almost perceptible word in his high-pitched parakeet voice. Romeo looked sideways at Dom with one of his bright, black eyes and squalked,"Zoorious."

"Indeed, my little friend," Dom said as he clipped a millet spray to the side of the cage. "It certainly is *very* curious."

Chapter Two

Chowders Diner was a Crab Cove mainstay and a favorite of the locals. Tucked away on a side-street, it was not often found by tourists, which was fine with the island residents. It had the best food in town and they preferred to keep it to themselves.

The diner had been around since the 1930s. Originally run by prominent Mooseamuck Island resident Josiah Chase, it had been recently purchased by a newcomer—Sarah White. Claire had taken an immediate liking to Sarah, who she figured to be in her early thirties. Sarah was a pretty blonde, a bit too serious for her young age. Claire could tell that serious demeanor was caused by a dark secret.

Claire didn't know what the secret was, but she knew Sarah thought she was keeping it well-hidden. She was probably right, for the most part. If not for Claire's training, she wouldn't have suspected it, either. She'd tried to draw it out of Sarah on a few occasions, but it seemed Sarah wasn't ready. That was okay, Claire wanted to help, but she knew from experience that a person had to be ready before they could be helped.

Claire sat at the usual speckled Formica table by the window, where, on most mornings, her regular crowd gathered to start the day. These were the people she was most close to on the island—people she'd grown up with as a kid. They were more like family to her than mere neighbors ... well, most of them were.

The exception was Dominic Benedetti. Dom was a fairly new addition to their 'group' and Claire didn't know if she was happy about this. She'd known him in her previous life as a criminal psychologist in Boston, where they'd often been called in to consult on the same cases. Back then, they'd had a working relationship she could only describe as grudgingly respectful.

It wasn't that she didn't like Dom—he was a nice enough guy, on a personal level. But on a professional level, the two of them had gotten along like water and oil. Oh, sure, he was an excellent detective with uncanny skills of deduction, but their methods were so different that they often found themselves butting heads.

Claire had spent most of her life studying human behavior, so when called in on a case, that was what she used to solve it—the behavior of the people involved. Dom, on the other hand, insisted on using only facts. It had caused a lot of professional arguments between them, yet they'd always seemed to get their man in the end.

But that was a lifetime ago. They were both retired now, and Claire had vowed to forget about their professional disagreements and try to make friends with the man who now sat across the table from her.

Claire watched a swirl of steam curl up from her cup of red rooibos tea as she listened to the others at the table chat about island gossip. Claire's thoughts drifted to the argument she'd seen between Norma and Zoila just a few hours earlier and her chest tightened with anxiety.

Her eyes slid to the doorway. Where *was* Norma?

Usually, the ornery artist joined them here when she was done with her morning painting. Claire glanced at the clock over the counter—it was almost ten o'clock. Norma should be done painting by now, but if she wasn't here—

"What do you think, Claire?" Tom Landry's question pulled Claire from her thoughts and she looked up to see Dom scrutinizing her, which only heightened her anxiety.

She quickly looked away from Dom and addressed Tom. "Think of what?"

"I was saying how egg production on my free-range chickens is way up this spring," Tom said. "They say increased egg production is a prediction of good summer weather."

"Well, hopefully it doesn't mean your chickens are going to be running around my garden again," Mae Biddeford admonished him. "Last year, they nearly ruined my blueberry bushes and I need those berries for jam."

Tom tilted his head, narrowing his eyes at her. "My chickens provide good fertilizer for your berry bushes and you know it."

Mae huffed and Claire suppressed a smile. Tom Landry and Mae Biddeford were both past eighty. They'd grown up next door to each other and each now lived in the very family home they'd grown up in. Tom's was a small working farm with goats, chickens and a few cows. Mae's property boasted acres of fruit trees and bushes. The two of them had an ongoing feud, rumored to have started in kindergarten. They bickered constantly, but Claire suspected they secretly had the hots for each other. If only she could get *them* to realize it, too.

"Besides, it looks like you have plenty of berries." Tom pointed to a large bag sitting on the floor beside Mae's seat. "I assume that's filled with jam."

"Yes, I'm trading it to Florence Ryder for a permanent," Mae huffed.

Claire cringed and caught her best friend, Jane's, eye. The islanders often traded goods or services instead of paying money. It was an old tradition started by their grandparents and, since most of the regulars were from families that had been on the island for generations, they continued the tradition. But Mae went a little overboard with her jams and most everyone had more jam than they could possibly use. Claire and Jane had a running joke about it and Jane winked back at Claire in acknowledgment.

"I see Crabby Tours has opened up early this year," Jane said, changing the subject from jam to more seasonal matters.

"Probably trying to get a jump on Barnacle Bob's fleet this year," Alice James said, her knitting needles clacking together with a metallic beat as she stitched furiously. Alice was always knitting something ... most of which she traded as eagerly as Mae traded her jams.

"Seems like those two are opening earlier and earlier." Tom referred to the rivalry between the boat lines, who both ran whale watches, lobstering cruises and pleasure cruises in the summer.

They'd had a rivalry going on for decades and for the past several years, it seemed each had tried to get a jump on the other by opening for business first. Not that there was any shortage of customers for the cruises. Mooseamuck Island was a popular tourist destination, and soon the population of the island would quadruple. And a favorite tourist pastime was going on one or more of the cruises.

Jane sighed. "I suppose so, but that means tourist season is just around the corner and my job is going to get a lot busier."

As postmaster of the Island, Jane had it relatively easy from September to June, when it was just the locals. But handling mail for all the summer residents and tourists could be a lot of work. Jane usually had to hire temporary help.

"True. But it is good for the economy," Alice pointed out.

"Still, I just wish Crab Cove didn't get so crowded," Mae complained.

Claire's attention drifted over to the doorway as the others discussed the pros and cons of the upcoming wave of tourists. Still no sign of Norma.

"Waiting for someone?"

Claire jerked her attention back to the table to answer Dom's question. "What makes you ask that?"

Dom shrugged, his dark eyes looking at her curiously. "You keep looking at the door is all."

"Oh, no. My mind was just wandering." Claire's eyes narrowed at him. Just what was he getting at, anyway? He was staring at her expectantly, as if he knew something. And then it hit her—somehow, he must know about the fight she'd witnessed.

Claire remembered that he had a view of the cove from his condo at the top of the hill. Had he seen Norma and Zoila fighting? No, he couldn't have. She'd been on his patio before and knew he could only see as far as her garden from his place—her cottage blocked the scenic vista. And, since she could barely hear the two women, she was sure he couldn't have heard them, either.

He'd probably seen her straining over the railing, though. But why would that pique his interest? It wouldn't pique the interest of a normal person, but then Dominic Benedetti wasn't exactly what Claire would classify as a normal person. He was a born investigator with keenly honed instincts, and his instincts were probably kicking in right now.

Somehow, Claire knew it wouldn't do to have him digging into whatever was going on with Norma. Dom didn't *know* Norma like she did and he might misinterpret things. What those things were she didn't know, since she had no idea what was going on herself.

She couldn't help but glance at the door again. This time, much to her surprise, it flew open and ten-year-old Gordie Glenn skidded inside, his cheeks flushed with excitement.

The hubbub of noise ceased and everyone in the diner turned expectantly toward the door where Gordie stood, his eyes darting from one patron to the next.

"Gordie? What is it?" Alice prompted.

Gordie's eyes lighted on Alice. His mouth opened and then closed. Claire's heart filled with worry. Was something wrong with Gordie or one of the other kids? And then Gordy finally blurted it out.

"There's been a murder at the zen garden!"

Chapter Three

The zen garden was part of the meditation area in Mooseamuck Island's public gardens—a twenty-acre tract of conservation land with an ocean view. It was startling to hear about a murder in the most peaceful place on the island. There hadn't been a murder on Mooseamuck Island in over twenty years. Everyone in the diner was shocked ... and interested.

So, naturally, most of them headed on out to the garden to see for themselves. Some rode bicycles—a normal form of transportation on the island—and others carpooled.

Claire hitched a ride with Tom and sat quietly wedged in between him and Jane in the front of his pick-up truck.

Would it be Norma lying dead up there?

Gordy hadn't known who the victim was—he'd only heard about it on the ham radio. Robby Skinner, current chief of police and Claire's nephew, had called in to the mainland, requesting help. By Claire's estimation, it would take about thirty minutes before the mainland police could get their boat out, so they had some time before they would inevitably be shooed away from the crime scene.

They jumped out of Tom's truck and headed down the path where she could already see her nephew flapping his arms, trying to keep people away from the scene.

"Hey, Robby. What happened?" Dread clutched at Claire's heart as she craned her neck to peek over her nephew's shoulder.

"Murder is what happened." Robby's eyes reflected desperation and she felt a tug at her heart. She knew he'd never secured a murder scene before and she felt bad for him. But not bad enough to stop straining to see who it was lying in the sand. Her eyes raked over the body and relief washed over her.

Then concern.

The body wasn't Norma. It was Zoila.

Robby tried to block her view "You know you shouldn't be here."

Claire tore her eyes away from the body and looked at her nephew. He was a decent cop, but he *was* a small-town cop, which was perfect for their little island where most of the crime consisted of minor infractions. Even then, he sometimes consulted with her on cases and she figured she'd helped him solve a good number of them.

"Sorry, Robby. This is big news, though, and you can't keep the regulars away." She glanced behind her at the small crowd that had gathered. It was mostly the regulars from the diner, but a few others had straggled in. "I figure it was better to come up and see if I could help out."

"Thanks." Robby's cheeks flushed and he kicked the dirt with the toes of his shiny, police-issue boots. "I had to call back to the mainland for the homicide crew. I'm not trained to investigate a homicide on my own. Until then, I gotta keep the scene secure."

"Of course. No one expects you to have that kind of expertise," Claire soothed. "I'll help keep the others back."

Her eyes drifted over his shoulder again and she took in the murder scene. The contrast of the still body lying in the peaceful circles of sand was startling. Not to mention the bloody mess that was Zoila's face. She'd been beaten, not shot or stabbed. But with what? Claire noticed the blood soaking into the sand beside the body, which was wearing the same outfit she'd been wearing during her fight with Norma.

And where was Norma?

Claire glanced around but didn't see her anywhere in the crowd.

"My word!" Mae gasped. "Who would do such a thing?"

Claire turned to see Mae's face had gone pale, her hand covering her mouth.

"That's a very good question." Dom raised a brow at Claire, as if she might know something.

Claire narrowed her eyes at Dom. "Yes, it is." She put her

arm around Mae and walked her over to a bench out of view of the scene.

Why had he looked at her that way? She didn't know who would kill Zoila. Well, she had seen Zoila fighting with Norma, but Norma wasn't a killer. She wrinkled her brow, remembering the piece of paper Zoila had been waving in Norma's face ... she didn't have that paper in her hand now.

Maybe she'd delivered the paper before her meditation. Or maybe the killer had taken it.

Claire watched Dom as he walked around slowly, just outside the confines of the yellow crime scene tape. At the edge of the zen garden, he squatted and tilted his head, studying the scene from a lower angle. He nodded, his lips pursed together in a thin line. Then he smoothed his eyebrows, stood and continued his walk to the other side of the garden.

Claire handed Mae over to Jane and wandered to where Dom and been. She squatted in the same spot. What had he found so interesting? The body lay crumpled, the legs at an impossible angle. The circles had been raked in the sand recently and were still almost perfect ... except for one smudged area.

A shoe print!

She looked closer. The print was distorted, but it looked large. Probably a man's shoe. One of the rocks was out of place, too, and—

A flurry of activity behind her broke her concentration and she turned to see the crowd parting, as if Moses were coming through.

Except it wasn't Moses. It was Detective Frank Zambuco, and he did not look pleased.

***

If there was one word Claire would use to describe Detective Frank Zambuco, it was overbearing. Or maybe annoying. Probably both. The man exuded an amount of energy unusual for his age, which Claire guessed to be about sixty—though it was hard to tell, given the ever-present scowl that normally contorted his face.

He whirled onto the scene, barking instructions, tapping his sausage-like fingers and whistling under his breath. His rumpled, blue, button-up shirt and stained, tan chinos were evidence he had no one at home to dress him. She was not surprised. She figured no woman would be able to put up with him for very long.

"Out of the way. Out of the way," Zambuco bellowed as he swatted his way toward Robby. "Don't you people know you are interfering with a crime scene?"

The crowd shrank back from him and he eyed them with beady, dark eyes. "Now, don't go too far any of you. You might all be suspects. At any rate, I'll want to question some of you." He turned to Claire. "Especially you."

"Me?"

"Yep, you seem to be the ringleader often enough."

"Well, I just came up with the others. I don't—"

"Right." Zambuco put his hand up to silence her and turned to Robby. "What have we got here?"

"Looks like she's been dead a few hours." Robby turned to look at the body. "It's Zoila Rivers."

"Rivers?" Zambuco's eyes narrowed. "Wasn't she some kind of fortune teller?"

"Psychic," Jane cut in.

Zambuco's left brow ticked up and he glanced at Jane. "Right. Psychic."

Zambuco walked over to the crime scene tape, lifted it and slipped under. He spent the next few minutes wandering around the scene, whistling to himself as he looked things over. His actions appeared to be aimless, but Claire knew they were anything but. Detective Zambuco might come off like a goof, but he was actually a very good detective. Which made her nervous because if Norma *was* somehow involved in this, he would find out.

Claire shook her head to clear her thoughts. *What was she thinking?* Of course, Norma had nothing to do with Zoila's death. She was sure once she talked to Norma, the argument would be explained and it wouldn't have anything to do with this.

Suddenly, Zambuco turned sharply toward the

bystanders. "Which one of you found her?"

"I did." The tremulous voice came from the corner and Claire looked over to see thin, gray Sam Banes, head gardener, raising his hand tentatively.

"And what were you doing here?" Zambuco asked.

"I'm the gardener. I came to make sure the rakes were out. People are always taking them."

Zambuco looked around, presumably for the rakes. "And were they?"

"Oh ... I don't ..." Banes looked around. "I guess not. I forgot about them when I found Ms. Rivers."

"Ms. Rivers? You mean you knew her?"

"Of course. She comes here most mornings to meditate." Banes's face crumbled and he looked down at the ground. "Or *did*, I should say.

"And did you see anyone else this morning?"

"No, sir, but I was on the other end of the gardens, tending to the annuals. I just drove over in my truck." Banes pointed to the white and green Moosamuck Islands Public Works truck visible at the end of the path.

Zambuco nodded, then whirled around, his eyes scanning the small crowd. "And what about the rest of you? Did anyone see anything amiss up here?"

They shook their heads, almost as one.

"Okay. We need to get you people out of here and process this scene." Zambuco pointed at one of the detectives that he'd brought with him. "Smithfield, you get their names and numbers. Oh, and I want you to halt all boat traffic leaving the island, *including* the ferry."

"Whyever would you want to do that?" Mae asked.

Zambuco stopped what he was doing and glared at her, then stabbed his finger in the direction of the body.

"Judging by the coagulation of the blood, Ms. Rivers was murdered only a few hours ago. It's early in the season and I happen to know there's only three ferries a day right now. The first one doesn't arrive for another twenty minutes ... which means the killer is still somewhere on this island and I don't want him to get away."

Chapter Four

Dom went back to *Chowders* with the others, his mind mulling over what he'd observed at the crime scene. The method of murder had been brutal, which indicated there was an emotional element.

But why chose a public place like the zen garden?

It must have been the only opportunity that presented itself to the killer. Dom was certain the killer must have needed to silence Zoila right away—Zoila Rivers knew something and someone else didn't want her to talk.

Dom had observed the crime scene closely and noticed a few things that seemed strange. He had them catalogued in his photographic memory for future inspection. He'd also observed Claire's odd response to the body. She had seemed shocked, which would have been appropriate for a regular person, but with Claire's training and the number of crime scenes she'd attended, it was out of place. Dom was certain Claire had found something startling about the body—whether it was something on or around the body or the mere fact that it was Zoila, he didn't know.

Even now, Claire was acting strangely. He noticed her slight hesitation when Tom and Jane got out of the truck in the parking lot. Almost as if she were reluctant to join them in the diner.

"Surely, he can't stop us from leaving the island!" Alice said as she pulled a skein of light blue yarn out of her tote bag.

"Or the tourists from coming *to* the island," Tom added.

"That's right," Jane said. "I doubt the town council will allow that, and I think they have the final say."

"A killer on the island." Mae shivered and turned her wide, brown eyes to Dom. "Who do you think it is?"

"It must be a tourist. A stranger," Alice cut in, directing her words at Dom. "I mean, it couldn't be one of us islanders, could it?"

Dom preened his left eyebrow as he felt an ember of excitement start to glow in his chest. Just like the feeling he used to get when he was an active consultant. Before Sophia got sick and he retired. When life was exciting.

"It could be anybody," Dom replied. "Does anyone know if she had any enemies?"

They all looked at each other and shrugged.

"None that I know of," Tom said.

"Me, either." Jane added.

"Perhaps she became privy to sensitive information through her work," Dom suggested. "She was a psychic, so she might have discovered information someone didn't want known."

Mae's brows shot up. "That's true. Maybe she had a vision about something bad that someone did."

Dom nodded wisely. "Yes, it could be. The police will probably want to check her latest clients. If she had sensitive information on someone, it stands to reason that person might be mad or upset. Can you think of anyone who has been acting strangely?"

Another round of shrugging occurred between everyone. Everyone except Claire, that is. Dom noticed that she kept glancing toward the door while she fidgeted in her chair.

Dom pressed his lips together. "It could be an old feud, too. But Zoila wasn't from the island, right?"

"Oh, no," Alice said to Dom. "She moved here about two years ago. Not long after you did. Bought old man Barrett's cabin up, near the conservation land."

"She said the old hunting camp had the perfect ambiance for her psychic readings," Jane added.

"And was she well-liked?" Dom asked.

Tom shrugged. "Well enough. She kind of kept to herself. Though I'm told plenty of townsfolk snuck up to the camp for a reading or two, at times."

Dom smoothed his eyebrow. An old hunting camp? Secret meetings? This was getting better and better. But if Zoila lived in a remote camp, why wouldn't the killer just kill her there?

There was only one reason—the killer must have not had time to wait until Zoila went home to that cabin. Which probably meant something had happened earlier in the morning. Something unusual.

He stole a glance at Claire. Maybe even something that would cause Claire to lean over her railing for a better look.

He didn't have time to think about what that might be, though, because just then, the door opened and Detective Zambuco stormed in.

***

Zambuco's brows zoomed up when he spotted the crew at the table. He strode toward them, grabbing an empty chair and pulling it across the floor, then shoving it in between Dom and Jane before folding his tall frame into it.

Everyone at the table scooted their chairs around to make room.

"I'll have a root beer. Lots of ice," Zambuco said to Sarah, who had come over to take his order. Then he turned his sharp eyes to the rest of the people at the table. "So, what do you people think? Got any ideas who did it?"

"Us?" Jane's brows rose. "How would we know who did it?"

Zambuco tipped back in his chair and looked at Dom. "What about you, Benedetti? I know you've investigated quite a few crime scenes in your day. You must have an opinion."

Dom smiled patiently. "True. But I'm retired now."

Zambuco snapped his chair back to the ground, accepting the glass Sarah handed him.

"Let's hope you stay that way. I don't need you people meddling." Zambuco looked pointedly at Claire. "Especially you."

"Me?" Claire looked at him innocently.

"Yes," Zambuco said as he crunched an ice cube. "I know how you like to give your opinion even when it's not wanted."

Dom's lips curled up in a smile. He agreed with that. In fact, he had to stop himself from nodding so as not to hurt Claire's feelings.

Zambuco continued on. "Seeing as I have you all here, I'd like to get the ball rolling with some questions."

"Okay," Claire answered, and the others nodded their assent.

"Did any of you notice Ms. Rivers acting out of the ordinary this week?"

His question was met with silence. In fact, the entire diner was silent as the other patrons were carefully eavesdropping on the conversation. Dom figured that by now, word had spread about the murder, and everyone knew Zambuco was here to investigate it.

"So, no one noticed anything?" Zambuco persisted.

Everyone at the table shook their heads. The customers at other tables bent their heads together, whispering, probably asking each other the same question.

"Did she take on any new clients or have a falling out with any regular clients?"

Claire pressed her lips together. "I don't think any of us know much about her client list."

"Do any of you use her services?" Zambuco asked.

The diner was filled with more silence. The only sound was the clinking of ice cubes as Zambuco chugged down his root beer while everyone at the table looked each other over. Even though the people on Mooseamuck Island were like family, they still liked to keep their private lives private. Dom wondered if anyone at the table *had* used Zoila's services and was afraid to mention it.

"Well, I certainly didn't," Mae said finally.

Tom shook his head. "Not me."

Alice's knitting needles clacked faster. "Nope."

Claire, Dom and Jane shook their heads.

Zambuco studied them with intelligent, bird-like eyes, then waved at Sarah and pointed to his glass for a refill. "Banes said Ms. Rivers meditated there every morning. Was that well-known?"

"Oh, yes, I would say so," Mae said. "Everyone knows

everyone else's habits here on the island."

Sarah appeared at Zambuco's elbow and filled up his glass. He looked down into the glass thoughtfully, swirling the ice around. "So, then most anyone on the island could have done it. Even someone at this table."

Mae gasped. "Well, it certainly wasn't one of us!"

"No?" Zambuco chugged down the second root beer. "So, no one here had a beef with Ms. Rivers?"

"No." Claire spoke for all of them.

Zambuco tapped his fingers on the table. "And no one has anything to add?"

"No," they chorused.

Zambuco rose out of the chair and turned to address the rest of the diner patrons. "What about the rest of you? Does anyone know who might have wanted Zoila Rivers dead?"

Silence.

"Okay, then." He turned back to Dom's table. "I want you to all stay accessible. I might have more questions."

"Well, we can hardly go anywhere, since you've stopped the ferries," Mae huffed.

Zambuco screwed up his face. "I may not be able to get that to stick. But at least for now, we have everyone contained here on the island. If we figure out who the killer is, it will make it easier to catch him ... unless he's already fled on a private boat."

Don watched Zambuco march toward the door, practically knocking over Kenneth Barrett who was on his way in. Kenneth shrank back from the detective, who nodded a half-hearted acknowledgment before disappearing out into the parking lot, leaving the entire diner staring in his direction.

A blush of pink tinged Kenneth's neck as he noticed everyone still looking in his direction. "So, I guess you've all heard."

"Yep." Several people answered.

"It's scary thinking there's been a murder here." He said the word 'murder' gingerly, as if the very word coming off his tongue might mar his cleft-chinned, preppy good looks.

As Dom watched Kenneth make his way to the counter, the din of the diner slowly came up to its normal volume. Now, everyone was talking at once—asking the same questions.

Who could have killed Zoila?

And why?

Kenneth pushed a glass pie plate aside and leaned over the counter, directing his next words to Sarah. "I came over as soon as I heard. I hope this doesn't spook you too much. Our little island doesn't usually have any violent crime."

Dom noticed Sarah's lips curl in a smile, but the smile didn't reach her eyes. She was being polite, though Dom suspected Kenneth wanted more than a polite smile from the pretty diner owner.

"Oh, I'm fine." She waved her hand dismissively. "Where I come from murders happen all the time. Besides, from what I hear, it sounds like the killer had a reason to target Zoila. It's not like there's a maniac around randomly killing people."

"I should hope not!" Alice's knitting needles stopped in mid-purl.

"Yeah, I heard that, too. Anyway, I was wondering if you could send Ben down with an order later today," Kenneth said.

Sarah's face puckered into a frown. She glanced toward the back. "Ben's not in today."

"Oh?" Kenneth frowned.

"He took the day off."

Dom noticed Kenneth looked put-out. Like most wealthy people, he was used to getting what he wanted, when he wanted. But on Mooseamuck Island, options were limited. Especially those for take-out delivery.

Ben Campbell worked for Sarah doing dishes, light food prep, cleaning and delivering food that he carried in the basket of his bicycle. Dom smiled at the thought of Ben, and Sarah's kindness toward him. Ben was a grown man, but not mentally capable of holding a 'regular' job. Sarah had trusted him and taken the time to train him, and he had flourished with his new responsibilities which turned out to be incredibly important seeing as Ben's mother, Anna, who had cared for him his whole life now lay dying in the hospice center on the mainland.

Dom's stomach tightened as he thought of Anna. He hoped Ben hadn't taken the day off because his mother had taken a turn for the worse. But if she had, he knew the islanders would rally around Ben and make sure he was taken care of. Most everyone on the island seemed to think of the sweet-natured young man as an extended member of their family.

Kenneth leaned sideways on the counter, so he could see both Sarah behind the counter and the others seated in the diner.

"I saw Zambuco leaving. Does he have any leads?" he asked, apparently not sharing any of Dom's concern about Ben's welfare.

"He didn't seem to," Jane answered.

"Sounded like he thought it might be a client," Mae added.

"Oh. A client," Kenneth nodded. "Right. Maybe someone got mad at one of her readings. She doesn't always see pleasant things."

"How do you know that?" Claire asked. "Did you use her services?"

"Who? Me? No." Kenneth waved his hands. "But I've heard from others. In fact, now that I think of it, she did seem upset yesterday when she called me out to the hunting camp."

"Why did she call you out to the camp?" Claire asked.

Kenneth shrugged. "She wanted to renovate it. She was asking me some questions about it yesterday. As you know, that camp had been in my family for generations and she wanted some history on how it had been added to over the years. Anyway, she seemed a little off, but I didn't really think much of it at the time."

"Off?" Claire looked at him with interest. "How so?"

"Anxious or upset, I guess."

"Did she say that anyone or anything in particular had upset her?" Dom cut in.

"No. Like I said, we didn't talk about that. So, I'm afraid I don't have any clues as to what would have upset her." Kenneth leaned back over the counter to address Sarah. "You be sure and call if you need anything."

"Thanks. I'll be fine," Sarah assured him.

Kenneth nodded, then pushed off and headed toward the door which opened, revealing Shane McDonough, fourth generation islander and local handyman.

"Hey, Shane might know something," Kenneth said as the two men passed each other. "Didn't I see you heading out toward Zoila Rivers' place yesterday?"

"What? Yeah, I was out there. Why?" He looked around the diner, obviously confused as to why everyone was looking back at him.

"She was murdered this morning," Mae blurted out.

"What?" Shane's handsome face scrunched up in surprise.

Dom watched Shane's reaction carefully. It seemed genuine enough, but then human nature was more Claire's department than his. Dom preferred to stick to hard, cold facts, and one fact was that Shane had seen Zoila yesterday. He stole a glance over at Claire and noticed that she, too, was studying Shane's reaction.

Shane walked to the counter. "Wow, that's crazy. Anyone know why she was killed?"

"Nope," Jane answered.

"What were you doing out there?" Claire asked.

"What?" Shane looked confused at her question, then his face cleared. "Oh, she asked me to give her an estimate on fixing that stone fireplace. Some of the mortar is loose and a few stones fell out. I can't imagine why anyone would kill her. Are they sure it was murder?"

"Absolutely," Dom said.

Shane leaned over the counter, concern on his face as he looked at Sarah. "You okay?"

Sarah smiled at Shane. A genuine smile this time, Dom noticed.

"Yes, I'm fine." She produced a paper lunch bag from behind the counter and handed it to Shane. Shane reached for his wallet, but Sarah held up her hand to stop him. "Nope. It's on the house. Repayment for helping me fix the oven yesterday."

Dom smiled to himself. It seemed that all the eligible bachelors in town were falling over themselves with concern about Sarah. He could see why they would want to protect her. She had a vulnerable quality about her. But he could tell Sarah White was a woman who could take care of herself.

Dom himself had become very fond of her. Not as a suitor—those days were long gone for him and he was too old for Sarah. His interests were more of a fatherly nature. She was alone, with no family on the island, and so was he.

Which reminded him. At his insistence, Sarah was trying her hand at Italian pastry baking. She prided herself on her dessert selection and wanted to broaden her horizons. Dom had shared some of his Nonna's recipes with her. He wanted to help her out, but he also had a selfish motive—he normally had his pastry shipped from Boston's north end and it was getting rather expensive. Having a source that would help feed his Italian pastry addiction right on the island would be convenient and economical.

The first dish she was trying was one of Dom's favorites—ricotta pie—and she had promised to have a test pie ready for him today. With all the excitement, he'd forgotten.

Dom got up and went to the counter just as Shane was leaving with his paper bag.

Sarah turned her attention from Shane and flattered Dom with a smile—a real one that reached her sparkling, hazel eyes. "I bet you're expecting your pie, aren't you?"

"I've been holding my breath waiting for it," Dom teased. He stepped closer to the counter and felt something gritty under his feet. He looked down to see sand, which was odd, because Sarah kept the place spotless. That was one of the reasons he liked the diner so much. His gaze went to the door that Shane was just now closing. The carpenter must have tracked the sand in.

"Here it is." Sarah was holding up a vanilla-colored pie. The edges were perfectly golden brown and it looked dense and firm.

Dom took the pie from her. It was heavy, just as it should

be. He lifted the plastic lid and delighted in the sweet vanilla scent that wafted out. "This smells *delizioso.*"

Sarah fixed him with a stern look. "Now, I'm expecting you to tell me the truth. No lying to spare my feelings. If it's good, I'll think about offering it to my customers."

"I will give it my full attention tonight and you will have my honest opinion tomorrow," Dom promised.

Another customer caught Sarah's attention and Dom turned back to the table.

"Well, I gotta take off," Claire said, just as Dom slid his pie onto the table. Then she stood, pulled a ten out of her pocket and slid it under her mug. "This should take care of my part plus a tip, but I'm sure you all will let me know if I owe anything."

Dom watched Claire hurry out of the diner.

"Well, she certainly rushed off abruptly," Mae said as she sipped her tea.

"Yeah. I guess she had somewhere to be," Tom added.

Dom glanced out the window in time to see Claire's little brown Fiat whip out onto the road. She did seem to be in a hurry, which made Dom wonder … just where was Claire rushing off to?

Chapter Five

Claire had patiently waited for the right time to leave the diner, and finally she was on her way to the harbor. She had to talk to Norma, but she didn't want to just rush off and raise anyone's suspicions ... especially Dom. For some reason, she couldn't shake the feeling that he was watching her.

Detective Zambuco had clearly been looking for someone who had a problem with Zoila, and she wanted to get to Norma and find out what was going on between the two of them before Zambuco did. She just hoped she was the only one who had seen them fighting.

A pang of guilt stabbed at her as she pulled her car into the small parking lot in the quaint shopping area next to the Crab Cove harbor. She wasn't used to keeping information from people, and it had been difficult to keep quiet about the fight she'd seen between Norma and Zoila earlier that day—but her loyalty to Norma had won out. The woman had been almost like a mother to her when Claire's own mother had died when she was a teen, and she couldn't give up any information that might incriminate her. Especially since Claire knew Norma would never have killed anyone.

Claire felt certain Norma would have a good explanation —maybe even one that would help reveal the identity of the real killer.

Claire hurried past the shops, with their weathered clapboard siding. The cove, with its selection of stores, was a big tourist mecca and, even though it was still early in the season, there were quite a few tourists browsing. Claire paid them no mind as she breezed past the *Harbor Fudge Shoppe*, *Mim's Boutique*, and *Sandy's Beach Jewelry*.

She stopped in front of Norma's studio, *Hopper Gallery*, her stomach plummeting with disappointment—the lights were off and the studio was empty.

She stepped closer to the large, glass window, cupping her hand over her eyes to look inside. Norma's colorful paintings lined the walls, their gold frames adding a rich tone to the room. But Norma wasn't anywhere to be seen in the small space. Claire adjusted her position to look to the only other room in the studio—the bathroom—but the door was open and that, too, was empty.

Where could she be?

"If you're lookin' for Norma, she done took off in Bryan's boat a couple hours ago." The voice startled Claire, and she turned to see Jeremiah Woodward standing at her elbow.

"What?" Claire squinted at the old man.

"Yep, she commandeered Bryan's boat and sped out toward the mainland."

Claire's heart froze as she thought about Zambuco's warning—that the killer might flee in a boat.

"What was she going to the mainland for?" Claire asked.

"Didn't say."

"When was that?"

Jeremiah scrunched up his face and looked to the sky. "Well, the sun was over theyah'." He pointed to a spot left of where the sun was now. "So, I guess that was about eight or nine o'clock."

Claire looked at her watch. It was almost noon. They'd discovered the body about an hour ago, and Zambuco had said it was a few hours old. She wasn't sure how reliable Jeremiah's estimation of time was. The timeline was tight, but Norma taking off in the boat might actually prove her innocence if she wasn't on the island at the time of death. But then again, if the death happened before that, it could make her look guilty. Especially if she didn't come back.

"Whatcha all gawkin' at?" Norma's raspy voice came from behind and Claire's heart flooded with relief. Norma hadn't *fled* the island—she'd probably just gone for painting supplies or something. Even though the island had a small grocery store and hardware store, some things just couldn't be purchased there—including some of the paints and supplies Norma used for her artwork.

Claire turned to Norma and smiled, despite the older woman's grouchy demeanor. Norma looked from Claire to Jeremiah, her wide-brimmed hat casting a sinister shadow over her face, which was pulled down in an unpleasant scowl.

"Norma, I thought you were over at the mainland," Claire said.

"Oh, and *who* told you that?" Norma glared at Jeremiah.

"Sorry, I didn't know it was a secret," Jeremiah stuttered, wilting under her gaze. "It seemed like it was right important that you get there."

"Now, Jeremiah Woodward, you be minding your own business." Norma rapped her cane on the ground loudly and Jeremiah jumped. Then, she whirled on Claire. "And what do *you* want?'

Claire wasn't fazed by Norma's seemingly harsh treatment. She was used to the artist's gruff exterior and she didn't let that upset her, because she knew somewhere inside was a heart of gold. Sometimes you just had to look really hard for it.

"I came to talk to you." Claire slid her eyes over to Jeremiah, the movement negating the necessity for her to add the word 'alone'.

"Hrmphh. Well, be quick about it" Norma hung the cane on her arm. Its ivory bull-dog faced handle stared out at Claire through its red, garnet eyes while Norma fished for the key to her studio. "I have a commissioned painting I need to finish and don't have time for idle chit-chat."

"Ahh ... well ... I'll leave you ladies to it," Jeremiah backed away from them. Claire got the impression he was happy to be escaping.

Norma shoved the door open and gestured for Claire to precede her into the cramped studio—which Claire did, deftly avoiding the stacks of canvases that leaned against the walls as her nose adjusted to the smell of turpentine and oil paint.

"So, what do you want?" The old, wooden floor creaked as Norma walked the perimeter of the studio, looking at her paintings and ignoring Claire.

Claire was glad to see that Norma was acting normal—not at all like someone who had beaten another person to death just hours ago. But what else had she expected? She already knew Norma didn't do it.

Claire gave a mental head shake and looked up to see Norma assessing her with intelligent, dark eyes, the brows of which were slightly raised in question.

"You haven't heard about Zoila?"

Claire saw Norma flinch just slightly. Probably not enough that anyone else would have noticed, but Claire was trained to watch for those tell-tale flinches. The mention of Zoila's name had hit a nerve.

"What about her? No one should pay attention to what she has to say. The woman is mad." Norma stabbed her cane into the floor to accentuate the last word.

"Really? Why do you say that?"

Norma narrowed her eyes at Claire. She was too sharp to be tricked into giving anything away. "Why do you ask about her, anyway?"

"She was murdered this morning."

Norma's eyes widened. "Murdered? By whom?"

Claire noticed that Norma's reaction seemed to register genuine surprise. At what, exactly, Claire didn't know—the murder itself or the fact that Claire was asking. "They don't know who did it."

Norma let out a sigh and lowered herself onto the wooden chair behind the old metal desk, the only piece of furniture in the room.

She rested her cane against the side of the desk, then leaned her elbows on the surface, steepling her hands in front of her. Claire noticed her hands were dotted with red paint ... at least she hoped it was paint. She stepped closer to get a better look and noticed there was blue, white and brown dots, too. It wasn't unusual for Norma's hands to be dotted with paint—she was, after all, a painter.

"So, you came all the way here to tell me?" Norma asked.

"Well, yes." Claire didn't know what she had been expecting. Maybe she was hoping Norma would tell Claire how her and Zoila had fought about some benign matter that would obviously have nothing to do with her murder.

But she didn't. Instead, she said, "Why come all the way here? You thought finding out about it from someone else might be too much for a fragile old lady?"

"Well, no." Claire hesitated. Norma was anything but fragile. "I saw you fighting with Zoila this morning."

"And you think *I'm* the one who killed her?"

"No! Of course not. I just thought if you explained what it was about, then I could make sure Zambuco ruled you out as a suspect."

"Explain it to you?" Norma's eyebrows crept up to her hairline. "I don't think I need to explain myself to you. And what were you doing spying on me, anyway?"

"I wasn't spying. I could hardly avoid it. I could hear you from my garden."

"What were you doing up at the crack of dawn?"

"I always get up for sunrise. Anyway, if I heard you, someone else might have heard you, too, so it's best if you tell me what you were fighting about."

Norma's face hardened. "Well, if you heard us, then you must know what it was about."

"I only heard shouting. I couldn't make out what you were actually saying. Then I looked down and saw Zoila waving some kind of paper in your face. What was on that paper?"

"That's none of your business," Norma huffed.

"Look, I'm not trying to pry into your business," Claire reasoned. "Zambuco is looking for people to put on his suspect list—people who had an argument with Zoila. I'm just trying to get our ducks in a row, in case he starts looking in your direction."

Norma crossed her arms over her chest and stared at Claire. "Well, it was personal. I can't say what it was about."

Claire sighed. "So you can't tell me what you argued about or what was on that paper. Not even a hint."

"It's not for me to say what we talked about."

"Well, if you could just tell me the general subject—"

Norma shot out of her chair. "This is getting tiresome. I don't have to tell you what we talked about and I'm not going to."

"Yeah, I get that. But if you don't tell me, I can't help. And where did you run off to—"

"Enough!" Norma came out from behind the desk, took Claire's shoulders and turned her toward the door. "Now, I need you to leave. I have business to tend to."

Norma opened the door and pushed Claire out. Claire turned to face her friend. "But I'm only trying to help."

"I don't need any help. Now, shoo." Norma made shooing motions with her hand, shut the door in Claire's face and snapped the lock.

Claire stood on the steps, boiling over with anger, a seed of doubt sprouting in her gut.

What was the big secret Norma had with Zoila?

She stared through the glass window at Norma, who stood with her back to Claire, apparently inspecting a piece of art she had hanging on the back wall. Claire's fists clenched in frustration. She didn't know what the big deal was, but she knew Norma hadn't killed Zoila, and if her friend wouldn't help clear herself by telling Claire what the argument was about, then Claire had only one course of action.

She'd have to find the real killer before Norma ended up in jail for a crime she didn't commit.

Chapter Six

Dom laid down his fork with a satisfied sigh as he finished the last bite of a small sampling of Sarah's ricotta pie. It was creamy and sweet—just the way he liked it. He leaned back in his chair, remembering how his Nonna would sometimes add lemon or chocolate chips to the batter.

He closed his eyes, an excitement building inside him as he reflected on the morning's events. The fact that he wasn't on the police force or being called in as a consultant didn't dampen his enthusiasm. He felt more alive than he had in a long time—he had a real case to work on, and he knew exactly how to go about finding the killer.

Opening his eyes, he absently watched Romeo and Juliet twitter and preen in their cage while he mentally constructed a 'to-do' list. First off, he'd have to compile a list of suspects. But how would he do that without the authority of the police behind him? He couldn't very well commandeer Zoila's customer list to find out who she spoke to yesterday.

Romeo flew to the side of his cage to sharpen his beak on the cuttle-bone Dom had clipped inside. He peeked over the oval, chalk-like bone at Dom and let out a loud squawk.

"Squabin!"

"Good thinking." Dom nodded at the small bird. Zoila had talked to both Kenneth and Shane about renovating the cabin yesterday. Even though they weren't clients, Dom figured that was as good a place to start as any. Over the years, he'd learned to never leave any stone unturned. Even the most routine interview could reveal a vital clue.

A tap at his back door interrupted his thoughts, and he

looked over to see Mae Biddeford, holding up a jar filled with something green.

Dear Lord, not another jar of jam. Dom glanced at his cupboard, already full to the brim with the jams that Mae forced on him almost every day. He pasted a smile on his face and opened the door.

"Hello. I thought I would bring you a jar of my famous zucchini relish." Mae shoved the jar toward him hopefully.

Not jam. Relish. As if he didn't have a dozen or so jars of those, too.

"Why, thank you." Dom took the jar, then upon noticing how Mae was hovering in the doorway, he opened the door and gestured to his kitchen. "Won't you come in?"

"Okay." Mae practically sprinted over the threshold. "I won't stay but a minute."

Dom hoped she would only stay a minute—he had lots to do.

He put the jar on the counter and turned to her expectantly. After a long career as an investigator, Dom knew when someone wanted to tell him something, and he could tell Mae Biddeford had something she was dying to get off her chest.

"It's been quite an exciting morning." Mae glanced sideways up at Dom, who nodded but didn't say anything while he waited patiently for her to get to the point.

Mae worried her bottom lip, then glanced at the back door. She leaned toward Dom conspiratorially, and in a low voice asked, "Will you be investigating it?"

Dom smoothed his eyebrow and pretended to think about it. "Do you think I should? Detective Zambuco is already on the case."

"Pshaw." Mae waved her hand. "What does he know? He's from the mainland. We need an islander here to do the case justice."

Dom was surprised at how proud he felt to be considered an 'islander', but he wondered if Mae was just buttering him up. He sensed she had something she wanted to tell him about the case, so he decided to give her the perfect opportunity. "Well, I wouldn't know where to start. I don't think Zambuco will share Zoila's client list with me."

"I may be able to help." Mae's eyes twinkled with excitement.

His bushy brows crept upwards. "Really?"

She nodded. "Yes. Well, I don't know if this means anything, but I happen to know that Velma and Hazel were seeing Zoila quite regularly. Their appointments were on Tuesdays."

"And yesterday was a Tuesday," Dom added. He pressed his lips together, picturing the elderly spinsters, Velma and Hazel, who ran the *Gull View Inn*. They were sweet, gentle souls. "You don't think they had something to do with Zoila's death, do you?"

"Oh, no. But they might know something. Those two might seem dotty, but they don't miss a trick. And I know they were there yesterday because they stopped by Tom Landry's for eggs after and I overheard them talking from my garden." Mae looked at him sharply. "I wasn't eavesdropping or anything. I was tending to my raspberry bushes and their voices carried."

Dom chuckled to himself and turned toward the door. "Well, that certainly is helpful information. I will pay them a visit and see if they can shed any light on things."

Mae puffed up, satisfied she'd done her duty. "Glad to be of help. I'll just be on my way, then."

Dom opened the door and bid her goodbye. As he closed the door his excitement in the case turned to a pang of insecure doubt. What if he had lost his investigating skills? What if he was too old, or couldn't remember the right way to go about it?

It had been years since he'd investigated anything, and if he screwed up and his information sent the wrong person to jail, he'd never forgive himself.

Then again, if he didn't investigate and the wrong person went to jail because he wasn't there to give his input, he'd never forgive himself, either.

It was better that he investigate, Dom decided. He hurried to clean up the plate from his ricotta pie. He had four places to visit and he didn't have a minute to waste if he wanted to fit them all in today.

Chapter Seven

Even though the police were no longer there, the meditation garden still bore the mark of a violent crime. Yellow crime scene tape surrounded the area where the body had left an unmistakable impression in the sand.

Dom could see evidence that they had taken a cast of the lone footprint. Something about it bothered him. It looked out of place, marring the pattern of the concentric circles that had been traced in the sand.

It was hard to believe a violent murder had happened in such a peaceful place. Dom had never meditated the regular way, much less by the use of a zen garden, but he could see how immersing oneself in the repetitive motion of drawing patterns in the sand could be relaxing. Especially up here, where the air was filled with the fresh smell of the forest and the chirping of birds. It was a quiet place—a good place for reflection.

Dom doubted it had been this quiet earlier in the morning. The condition of the body told him that Zoila had struggled. Had she cried out? She must have ... but why had no one heard her?

"Can't go in they'ya."

Dom turned to see the gardener, Banes, standing beside the trash barrel, a scrunched up Coke can and an empty white bag in his hand. "I know. I was just looking."

Banes squinted at Dom. "Hey, ain't you that famous detective from Boston?"

Dom straightened with pride and preened his tingly left eyebrow.

"Well, I could hardly claim to be famous," he said modestly.

"Well, I heard about 'ya." Banes nodded toward the

crime scene area. "I bet you got some ideas on who killed her."

"I'm afraid I don't. Not yet, anyway." Dom raised a brow at Banes. "What about you?"

"Me?" Banes took a step backward. "Why, I have no idea."

"And you didn't see anyone up here or hear anything this morning?" Dom ventured.

"No, sir. I was on the other side and I'm a little hard of hearing. I was actually a bit late on my rounds this morning. Had to clean up horse poop on the trail." Banes scrunched up his face. "Otherwise, I might have been here when ... well, you know."

Dom nodded. "So, just what are your tasks here?"

"Well, I usually come up and rake the garden." Banes pointed toward the sandy area. "I make sure there are no leaves or pine needles on the sand."

"Do you make these circles?" Dom indicated the intricate series of circles that radiated from the stones that seemed to be placed at random in the zen garden. It reminded him of the waves that radiated from a rock tossed into a pool of water.

"Yep. To start. The way it works is the people come and make their own circles with the rake. That's part of the meditation. But each morning, I come up and rake them out to start the day. It's kind of fun, really."

"And the rakes. Do you supply those?" Dom asked.

Banes sighed. "Yes. We have to keep a supply of them, because sometimes people walk off with them."

"And this morning, the rake was missing."

"Yep." Banes looked over at the crime scene and shuddered. "I guess it might have been the murder weapon."

"Could I see one of these rakes?"

"Sure, just let me throw this out." Banes indicated the trash he held in his hand. As Dom followed him to the trash can, he noticed the white bag was a take-out bag from *Chowders*.

"Do you get a lot of trash up here? You'd think the islanders would respect it more," Dom said.

"Didn't use 'ta, but it's happening more and more now." Banes tossed the trash in the can and shrugged. "Kids."

Dom frowned at the trash. He could see the crushed soda can being tossed out by reckless kids, but he wondered if kids would be bringing take-out bags from *Chowders* up here. He didn't think so.

He tore his attention from the trash and joined Banes at the small storage shed. The gardener unlocked the door and reached inside, producing a strange-looking wooden rake.

"There's a couple of different kinds of rakes for zen gardens, but this here's the kind of rake we use." Banes handed it over for Dom to inspect.

It wasn't too heavy and of simple construction. A handle with a metal piece at the end. One side of the metal was flat and the other had a series of short, sharp tines protruding from it.

"The flat end is used to smooth out the sand, and the end with the tines is used to make the swirls and patterns around the rocks in the garden," Banes added.

Dom fingered the tines thoughtfully. With enough force, they could have caused the injuries that had killed Zoila.

Had the killer used the zen garden rake for his murderous act? And, if so, what had he done with it afterwards?

***

The Barrett family had settled Mooseamuck Island back in the 1600s and had once owned most of the land. Over the years, parcels had been sold off, and even the old family hunting camp—the first structure on the island— had been sold by Kenneth to Zoila, less than two years ago.

The Barretts had kept the best piece of land for themselves, which included a mansion—the largest house on the island—situated on a point of land that was surrounded by the Atlantic Ocean on three sides.

Dom pulled his Smart Car around the circular drive and got out. A fountain splashed melodically in the middle of the driveway as Dom walked to the home's impressive, double-wide oak doors. He rang the bell.

After a few seconds, the door swung open and a man in a black jacket looked out at him.

"Yes?"

Dom stared back. *A butler, in this day and age? People still have them?*

"Hi," Dom said. "I'd like to see Kenneth Barrett, please."

"Master Kenneth is in the stables around back." The butler leaned out onto the step and pointed around the left side of the house, where Dom could see a fancy carriage house.

"Okay. Thanks." Dom turned and headed toward the stables, enjoying the view of rolling hills giving way to the cliffs and the Atlantic below. As he neared the carriage house, he heard a loud clatter and then cursing. Peeking his head in, he saw Kenneth in one of the stalls, standing amidst a messy pile of wooden-handled stall mucking tools.

"Ahem." Dom cleared his throat and Kenneth snapped his head up.

"Oh. Hi. I wasn't expecting anyone."

"You muck out the stalls yourself?" Dom asked incredulously. He couldn't picture Kenneth, who looked like a male model with his swoop of blond hair, blue eyes and Kirk Douglas chin doing this type of work.

Kenneth shrugged. "Sometimes. I find this type of work keeps me grounded."

Dom nodded, inhaling the earthy scent of leather, hay and horse manure. He noticed that even the stables had the air of the 'well-to-do'. The saddles and bridles neatly hung on the walls were of the finest quality. Even the barn implements piled in front of Kenneth had matching gold and maroon adornment on the handles—a color combination that was repeated in the rosettes on the bridles and the coat of arms that hung over the doorway.

"What can I do for you?" Kenneth worked his way out of the stall and motioned for Dom to follow him down the aisle. A palomino snickered as they passed her stall, her blonde mane swaying like corn silk as she bobbed her head up and down. Kenneth stopped for a minute to stroke her velvety nose. Dom noticed the horses were in tip-top shape. This one was freshly groomed, her saddle shined and polished.

"In the diner, you mentioned that you talked to Zoila yesterday and she seemed agitated. I wanted to ask you more about that," Dom said.

Kenneth stopped and frowned at Dom. "Why? The police have already been here."

"Of course," Dom replied. "But I'm not with them."

"Oh, no? Then why are you asking?"

"Let's just say I want to make sure us islanders get a fair shake. Zambuco isn't from the island, so ..." Dom let his voice trail off, taking a moment to glance down at Kenneth's shoes. They were square toed—not a match to the footprint at the zen garden. Then again, this surely wasn't his only pair of shoes.

Kenneth stared at him for a few seconds, then Dom saw something change in his eyes. He nodded and spread his arms. "I don't know much. Like I said, Zoila lived in my family's old hunting camp. She was doing some minor renovations and found some pictures she wanted to give me. She also wanted to keep the history, so she asked me to come out and go over the various additions to the camp. She was interested in what year each room was added ... that sort of thing.

Dom gave an encouraging nod. "And ..."

"Well, that's it. I went out and showed her where the original camp was, then each section that had been added."

"You said she seemed agitated."

Kenneth's eyes darkened. "Oh, right. She did. She kept looking around, like she was expecting someone or something."

"Oh, really? And did anyone come?"

"No. It's pretty remote out there. The conservation land abuts three quarters of that lot." Kenneth's brows scrunched together. "Well, now that I think about it, someone rode by on a bicycle up the path that goes through the conservation land. She seemed really spooked about that."

"Who was it?"

"Just the Flannery kid. She relaxed once we saw who it was, but when we heard the bike coming, she seemed agitated." Kenneth hesitated, then added, "I just figured she was probably waiting for Ben to come back."

"Ben?"

"Yeah, Ben Campbell. The guy who works for Sarah. I saw him peddling away on his bike, like he was being chased by a demon on my way out there."

Dom's eyebrow twitched and he reached up to smooth it. "How interesting. Did she mention what he was doing there?"

"No. I assume he must have delivered some food up to her."

"Or he could have been a client."

"I suppose." Kenneth's face darkened. "Hey, you don't think—

Dom held up his hand, cutting him off. "Oh, no, I don't think. Not until I have all the facts, anyway. Right now, I've just begun to gather them."

"Okay, right. Wouldn't do to jump to conclusions."

"Nope. But you've been very helpful."

"Sure, anytime."

Dom turned to leave, walked a few steps, then pivoted around again. "Say, did you see anyone coming up to her place when you were leaving?"

Kenneth frowned. "Now that you mention it, yes, I did. I was driving away and passed Shane McDonough at the end of the road."

"And what time was that?"

Kenneth frowned. "Well, I'm not sure, but I wasn't there long. I guess it must have been about one o'clock."

"Okay. Thanks." Dom turned and left for good, this time, getting into his Smart Car and pulling around the fountain, then out of the driveway. As he pulled out onto the road, he saw Claire Watkins's brown Fiat taking a left into the driveway.

Dom waved and smiled, despite the feeling of irritation that swept through him. He was certain Claire was visiting Kenneth for the same reason he was. He was annoyed that

Claire was investigating Zoila's murder. He didn't need her butting in with her touchy-feely methods.

Then again, joining forces with the woman might not be such a bad idea. Though she was annoying to work with, they had done good work in the past and her assistance had been vital in solving quite a few of the cases they'd been on together. Not only that, but he was convinced Claire Watkins knew something and his instincts told him what she knew was a key piece on the puzzle of who murdered Zoila Rivers.

Chapter Eight

Claire eyed the silver Smart Car with irritation. She should have known Dom would be investigating. That was exactly what she didn't want. She was afraid he would misinterpret what was going on, with his 'stick to the facts' attitude. He was too rigid in his ways and Claire had a feeling this was a case where you had to consider the human aspect.

She knew the islanders better than Dom and would be able to interpret the clues more accurately with that knowledge. A feeling of dread settled on her as she parked next to the fountain. She just hoped she could find the killer before Dom or Zambuco went off half-cocked and arrested the wrong person.

Kenneth came round the side of the house as she was walking toward the front door. A scowl darkened his face when he saw her.

"I should have known you would show up," he said.

Claire frowned at him. Kenneth was in his mid-forties—a spoiled rich kid that Claire didn't have much use for. She'd never had much to do with him and judging by the rude comment he just slung at her, she'd been right not to.

"Why do you say that?"

"It's just that you seem to always wheedle your way into any criminal activity on the island. Sometimes, I wonder if your nephew actually solves any cases or if you do it for him."

Now she remembered. Kenneth and Robby had been rivals on the football team in high school. She'd have thought Kenneth would have forgotten about that by now. Claire chose to ignore his comments and get down to business.

"Have you been out riding?" she asked, indicating the horse dung on his boots.

"Earlier. I was just in the barn tidying up." He continued toward the house. "I know you're not here to make small talk. You're here to butt into the Zoila Rivers investigation."

"Well, I don't think *butt in* is the right phrase. I just want to make sure Zambuco doesn't arrest the wrong person."

She thought she saw Kenneth's face soften. "That's what Benedetti said, too."

"Yeah, I bet. So, what did you tell him?"

"Nothing, really. Because I don't know anything. I went over to talk about the cabin and she seemed agitated." He hesitated, then added, "Benedetti did seem rather interested when I told him Ben had been there."

Claire's brows mashed together. "Ben Campbell? You don't think Dom could suspect Ben?"

Kenneth shrugged. "He is a little odd."

"He's not mentally capable of murdering someone. He's almost like a child and one of the sweetest people I know." Claire's heart constricted thinking of the sweet, lovable Ben as a murder suspect. And what was even worse, Ben's mother Anna lay dying in hospice. He was all alone in the world, except for Norma who was Anna's best friend and cared for Ben like he was her own.

What if there was some odd piece of circumstantial evidence tying Ben to the murder, and Benedetti and Zambuco tried to pin it on him? Claire couldn't let that happen, even if it meant joining forces and 'playing nice' with Dominic Benedetti.

Kenneth was staring at her expectantly. "Is that all you wanted?"

"Did you see anyone else there?" Claire asked.

"Yep. Like I told Benedetti, Shane McDonough was pulling in as I pulled out."

"So, was Benedetti heading over to talk to Shane?"

Kenneth shrugged. "I guess so. Are you going to follow him over there?"

Claire didn't like his snooty tone, but she didn't bother to answer. She had already turned around and was heading for her car.

***

Luck smiled upon Dom as he drove through town on his way to the *Gull View Inn*. Shane's truck was parked at *Chowders,* offering a perfect opportunity to question Shane about his visit to Zoila, tell Sarah how much he enjoyed the ricotta pie and find out more about Ben.

It was mid-afternoon, so the diner was practically empty. Dom went straight to the counter. From his vantage point, he could see Shane fiddling with the large, stainless steel oven in the kitchen. The carpenter was on his knees, his feet out behind him. Dom took the opportunity to make note of his shoes. They had a round toe, like the footprint, but he noticed something distinctive about them—the tread was almost all worn off.

Had the footprint in the zen garden shown no treads?

Dom couldn't remember whether it did or not, and he had a momentary pang of uncertainty about his detecting skills. Back in the day, he would have had all that information catalogued in his sharp memory. Then again, he'd also had the advantage of being able to look at the police reports to refresh that memory whenever he wanted.

He caught Sarah's eye. She smiled, and came to stand on the opposite side of the counter. "Hey, Dom. Did you try the pie?"

"It was *delizioso!*" Dom pressed the tips of his fingers to his lips and then spread them apart in the air.

"So, you think I should start serving it here?"

"I sure would buy them if you did. In fact, I wouldn't mind ordering one special right now."

"I'll get right on that." Sarah grabbed the napkin-wrapped silverware from under the counter and placed it in front of Dom. "What can I get you?"

"Well, actually I came to talk to Shane."

Sarah's brows ticked up and Shane looked back over his shoulder from his position in front of the oven. "Me?"

"Yes. I just have a few questions about Zoila."

"Oh, are you investigating the murder?" Shane pushed himself up from the floor and wiped his hands on a kitchen towel as he walked over to the counter.

Dom shook his head. "Not officially, but I figured I could look into it in case Zambuco comes to the wrong conclusion."

"Oh, well, that's probably a good idea," Shane said. "I don't really see how I can help you, though."

"Earlier this morning, you said you'd been out at her place yesterday."

Shane narrowed his eyes. "That's true. Like I said, she wanted an estimate on the chimney and some of the renovations on the camp."

"And what did the renovations entail?"

"She wanted the kitchen modernized and that old fieldstone fireplace repaired. There were some loose rocks in it." Shane's voice took on an edge of agitation. "What's that got to do with her getting murdered?"

"Probably nothing," Dom soothed. "I'm just trying to be thorough."

Shane ran his hands through his thick, dark hair. "Oh, well, I don't see how this can help."

Dom smiled. "I'm just trying to get an idea of what was going on on her last day. Did she seem upset at all?"

Shane's eyes slid to the left, his brow creasing. "Upset? What do you mean?"

"Did she act angry or on edge?"

"No. She seemed fine to me."

Dom pressed his lips together. "Kenneth said he saw her right before you and she seemed anxious."

Shane looked at Dom strangely. "Kenneth Barrett?"

Dom nodded. "He was there right before you. Said he passed you on the way out, actually."

"Oh, that's right. I do remember seeing him drive by. I didn't realize he was coming from Zoila's."

"What time were you there?" Dom asked.

Shane looked down at the floor, then back up at Dom. "I'd say it was around three thirty or four o'clock."

"Are you sure?"

"Yep. I don't watch the clock or anything, but I headed

over when I was done at the Kirkpatricks', and that had to be after three."

Dom frowned. He could have sworn Kenneth said he'd seen Shane earlier. "And you were at the Kirkpatricks' this morning?"

Shane's eyes got even narrower. "No. And I don't like what you are insinuating."

Dom shrugged. "I'm not trying to insinuate anything, just trying to figure out where everyone was this morning. So, where were you?"

Shane's neck reddened, but he held his temper. "If you must know, I was at the Durants', repointing the brick on their chimney."

Dom noticed Sarah intently watching the conversation, her eyes pivoting nervously back and forth between Shane and Dom. He turned his attention to her.

"And what about Ben?"

Sarah's eyes widened.

"What about him?" Her voice rose defensively.

"Did he deliver sandwiches to Zoila?"

"Zoila? No, she never ordered from here."

Dom's brows shot up. "Really? But Kenneth saw him peddling away from Zoila's yesterday. Did he know her?"

Sarah and Shane exchanged a glance. "I don't think so. I mean, not any more than anyone else on the island."

"And Ben does do deliveries for you, right?"

"Yes, he delivers between eleven thirty and one thirty every day, after he finishes his morning tasks in the kitchen. I could hardly run the place without him, now." Sarah's voice rose proudly, like a teacher praising the accomplishments of a favorite student.

"Where is Ben now? Doesn't he usually work today?"

Sarah crossed her arms over her chest. "Yes, but he called in sick."

"Oh, really? Does he do that a lot?"

"No, but when you're sick, you're sick." Sarah glared at him, and Dom wondered if he'd be getting that ricotta pie after all. "I hope you're not implying that Ben had something to do with this. He couldn't. He doesn't have a mean bone in his body."

"Oh, no," Dom held is hand up. "I don't have any suspects, yet. I'm just trying to get the timeline straight."

"Well, that's good." Sarah relaxed. "And besides, Ben couldn't have done it."

"Why not?"

"He visits his mother every Monday, Wednesday and Friday morning. I don't even think he was on the island when Zoila was murdered."

Dom's eyebrows tingled. There were quite a few inconsistencies starting to appear in this case, between what he'd heard from Sarah, Shane and Kenneth. Someone wasn't being totally honest, but the question was ... which one of them was lying, and why?

Chapter Nine

The *Gull View Inn* was the quintessential Maine bed and breakfast. A sprawling, white Victorian with green shutters, it had a white trellised archway covered in lush rose vines that led to the generous, white wrap-around porch, also covered in rose vines. It was too early in the season for blooms, but the porch was alive in green leaves.

Dom sat in one of the white, wicker rockers on that very porch, being catered to by Velma and Hazel, the two spinsters who ran the Inn.

It was almost pleasant. Not like the interviews he'd conducted when he was on the job, Dom thought, as he gazed out over the vast waters of the Atlantic, watching the sun dance on top of the waves. The gulls cried in the distance and ice cubes clinked in his lemonade glass as he rocked lazily.

"I still can't believe it." Velma's white bun bobbed as she shook her head. "A murder, right here on the island."

"I know," Hazel replied. "It's disturbing."

Dom studied the two women, thinking they looked more excited than disturbed.

"You don't think we are in danger, do you?" Velma asked.

"Oh, no," he assured them. "We'll find who did it soon enough. In fact, you might be able to help."

"Us?" Hazel wrinkled her brow, her green eyes sparkling. "Oh, I don't see how."

"I heard the two of you had seen Zoila for a reading yesterday," he ventured.

Hazel looked at Velma who nodded. "Yes, we did. We saw her regularly."

"Did she say anything unusual, or seem out of sorts when

you saw her yesterday?"

Hazel shrugged. "No, I don't think so."

"What did you talk about?"

Velma held a plate of iced gingersnaps in front of Dom, who eagerly accepted. "Well, I hope you don't think we're odd, but we talk to my daddy through her ... you know, about running the inn."

"You do?" Dom knew the inn had been in Velma's family for generations and that she'd inherited it when her father passed away decades ago.

"Yes, he still gives me great advice."

"You didn't see anything out of the ordinary when you were there?"

The two women looked at each other and shrugged. "Nope."

"Did she act any different than other times you'd been there, or seem agitated or nervous?"

"She did have a hard time channeling Daddy. She said her energy wasn't in tune or something," Velma said. "But honestly, I don't think she was a very good psychic."

"Why not?" Dom asked

"Well, if she was, you'd think she would have been able to see her own death and takes steps to avoid it from happening."

Hazel pressed her lips together. "I don't think it quite works like that, Vel. Remember how she said only certain things were revealed, and sometimes she didn't know exactly what they meant."

"Oh, right, like the time she thought Daddy was telling us to serve fruitcake at Christmas," Velma said.

Hazel chuckled. "Yes! But he really meant that your cousin Chris was a fruitcake!"

Velma nodded. "We had twenty fruitcakes we had to get rid of that year."

They all laughed, and then Velma's laughter stopped abruptly as her eyes moved to something just beyond Dom's shoulder.

Dom turned around, his stomach sinking when he saw Zambuco standing behind him.

"Well, isn't this nice." Zambuco nodded at Velma and

Hazel, then narrowed his eyes at Dom.

Dom smiled. "Detective Zambuco, it's so nice to see you. What brings you here?"

Zambuco plopped down, uninvited, in a rocker. "Probably the same thing that brought you here."

"Me? I was just drinking lemonade and chatting with Velma and Hazel."

"Uh-huh." Zambuco eyed the three of them suspiciously.

"Ginger snap?" Velma handed the plate to Zambuco.

"Don't mind if I do." Zambuco grabbed a cookie from the plate with his giant hands and bit into it, crumbs falling on his shirt, and Dom guessed he either didn't notice or didn't care since he made no move to wipe them away.

"Now, Hazel, where are our manners. Let's get the detective a lemonade," Velma twittered.

"Lots of ice, please," Zambuco called after Velma, who had immediately sprinted for the front door.

The three of them were silent while they waited for Velma. Dom listened to the seagulls while Zambuco's thick fingers tapped a rhythm on the arm of his chair.

Velma returned with the drink. Zambuco looked at it and nodded.

"Thanks," he said, then chugged down most of it.

"Now, what can we do for you, Detective?" Hazel's keen eyes watched Zambuco as he bit into another cookie.

"Well, if you haven't given all the good information to Benedetti, I'd like to know what you can tell me about Zoila Rivers."

"Oh, we don't know much. Like we told Dom, we go there every Tuesday to talk to Velma's daddy about business matters."

"Velma's daddy?" Zambuco scrunched his face up. "He's still alive? And what was he doing at Zoila's?"

Velma laughed and swatted at Zambuco's arm. "No, silly, she channeled him. We talked to his spirit."

"Oh." Zambuco gave Dom a sideways look and rolled his eyes, as if he were wondering if the two elderly women were nuts and whether or not he should trust any information he got from them.

Dom simply shrugged.

"And what was her demeanor?" Zambuco continued.

"She seemed fine. Same as always," Hazel said.

"Well, she did have a hard time channeling, like we were telling Dom," Velma added.

Hazel nodded. "Thats right. Said her energy was a little off."

"But then, Daddy came through and told us to think about running a clambake on the first Sunday of the month." Velma turned to Dom. "What do you think about that?"

"That sounds like a fine idea." Dom took a sip of his lemonade. He was down to the bottom of the glass—the best part, where all the sugar was.

"We could serve steamers and corn, and—"

"Ahem." Zambuco cut Hazel off. "Did she mention anything in particular that was bothering her?"

Velma and Hazel both shook their heads. "Nope."

"She didn't mention having a disagreement or argument with anyone?"

Velma's forehead creased. "She didn't mention anything yesterday when we saw her ... but she *did* have a fight with someone this morning."

"She did?" Both Dom and Zambuco leaned forward, their attention focused on Velma.

"Velma!" Hazel said sharply.

Velma looked stricken. "Oh, dear ... I guess I shouldn't have blurted that out."

"Who did she have the fight with?" Zambuco asked.

Velma chewed her bottom lip, her eyes going from Hazel to Dom to Zambuco. "I can't say. I mean, I wouldn't want you to get the wrong idea about the person she fought with."

"Well, now you *have* to tell me," Zambuco said. "Otherwise, it would be considered withholding information and there might be dire consequences."

Velma's eyes widened. "You mean I could go to jail?"

"You won't have to go to jail," a voice cut in from the porch steps and Dom turned to see Claire Watkins. "And Zambuco won't force you to rat out your neighbor, either."

"I won't?" Velma's shoulders relaxed with relief.

Claire walked over to them and stood in front of Zambuco, her hands fisted on her hips. "No, Velma, you won't have to because I saw the fight, too. And I'm sure someone else did as well, so eventually, Zambuco will find out who Zoila argued with."

"For crying out loud, someone just tell me who it was before I throw the lot of you in jail!" Zambuco said.

Claire paused, then sighed. "Fine. I'm sure you'll find out soon enough. The person Zoila had an argument with was Norma Hopper."

Chapter Ten

Zambuco squinted up at Claire. "Norma Hopper? That mean old painter lady?"

Claire's gut twisted. She hadn't wanted to tell Zambuco it was Norma, but she couldn't stand him threatening Velma. She didn't want poor Velma to have to bear the burden of being the one who told him, so Claire had blurted it out. Anyway, he'd probably find out from someone else and this way, she could watch his reaction and try to temper the news.

"She's not mean," Claire said defensively.

"That's true," Hazel added. "She just acts that way. Once you get to know her, you realize she's not that bad."

Velma nodded. "That's right. We've known her our whole lives. She's crotchety, but she's not a killer."

"What did she and Zoila argue about?"

"I don't know." Velma pointed to her ear. "My hearing isn't as good as it used to be."

"Me, either. I could just tell they were yelling." Hazel looked up at Claire. "Do you know what they were arguing about?"

Claire shook her head. "No, I saw them from my garden. I could hear voices but couldn't make out the words."

Zambuco narrowed his eyes. "You ladies wouldn't be withholding information from me, would you? Because I'm pretty sure you had the opportunity to tell me this before Watkins."

Clair grimaced. "I didn't think it was relevant, because Norma isn't the killer."

"Really?" Zambuco glared at her with sharp, dark eyes. "And what else haven't you told me because you don't think it's *relevant*?"

Claire held up her hands. "Nothing, I swear."

Except the fact that Norma left the island early this morning.

"Well, it looks like I'll be paying a visit to Norma Hopper." Zambuco pushed up from the chair.

"You're wasting your time," Claire said.

"Maybe."

"Do you have any clues that even point to her?" Claire asked, seeing the perfect opportunity to try and find out what clues the close-mouthed detective actually did have.

Zambuco picked his glass up from the small table beside his chair, tipped it to his lips and took in a mouthful of ice cubes, which he crunched noisily. "We have the footprint down at the lab. Of course, we are still missing the murder weapon, which I'm hoping will be found on the killer's premises."

"The rake?" Dom asked.

"Maybe. Anyway, the last thing you people need is to know what the clues are." Zambuco pointed his index finger accusingly at Dom and then Claire. "I know the two of you can't help but stick your noses in, but remember, you're both *retired* now. I wouldn't want to have to arrest you on obstruction charges and don't even think about withholding pertinent information again or you may find yourself in the cell next to your friend."

Zambuco slid one last warning look at Claire and Dom, bowed to Velma and Hazel and then stormed off the porch.

***

"Oh, dear, I hope I didn't get Norma in trouble." Velma's hands fluttered nervously in her lap. "I didn't even think ... I mean, he asked and I just answered."

"It's okay," Claire soothed. "He was bound to find out sooner or later, and better he hear it from us than someone who might not like Norma as much."

"But now I wonder ..." Hazel's voice trailed off as she watched Zambuco's car speed off. "You know how obstinate Norma can be. I hope she doesn't do something stupid and get herself arrested."

"That's exactly what I was thinking," Claire said. "That's why we need to figure out who did this before Zambuco jumps to any conclusions. That's why I came here, actually—to see what you knew."

"We don't know anything, really," Hazel said. "We were just telling Dom that our weekly visit with Zoila was uneventful."

Velma looked regretful. "Unfortunately, we don't have any clues as to who killed her."

Claire turned to Dom. "So you *are* looking into this."

He nodded slightly. "And apparently, you are as well."

"Yeah, kind of like old times." *Old times she'd rather not relive.*

"Almost," Dom said. "Except this time, we don't *have* to work together."

It was true. When they were on the job as paid consultants, they didn't have a choice. But now, they didn't have to join forces. Although Claire knew they would get the job done faster—and probably better—together. It was just so *annoying* to have to put up with Dom's insistence on only considering hard, cold facts when she knew her assessment of the human factor was accurate.

Claire sighed and plopped down into the chair Zambuco had just vacated. She might regret this, but she could really use Dom's help. If Norma was going to be as tight-lipped with Zambuco as she had been with Claire, he might misunderstand and take that to mean she was guilty. Teaming up with Dom offered the best chance to find the killer fast ... before Zambuco could gather evidence against Norma.

"But we could work together if we wanted." Claire looked at Dom out of the corner of her eye.

"We could," Dom said cautiously. "But as I recall, you used to get very irritated with me."

"And you with me." Claire bit into a ginger-snap, swirling the spicy-sweet taste around in her mouth. "But maybe for the good of finding the murderer, we could try to work together again."

"Well, we did catch quite a few bad guys back in the day,"

Dom said proudly, over the rim of his lemonade glass

Claire noticed a familiar flicker in his eyes—a spark of light from deep within. The same spark she used to see when they were on a case. Back then, his eyes would light up with excitement. She remembered how that light had been extinguished when his wife got sick. Now, it was back and Claire felt her heart soar for him. She realized this case was about much more than just finding a murderer for him ... and maybe it was for her, too.

"So what do you say? Can we work together?" Claire stuck her hand out.

Dom regarded her hand cautiously, then nodded and extended his own for a firm shake. "Yes, I think we can."

Velma and Hazel, who had been following the conversation, silently picked up their lemonade glasses and held them out so the four could clink rims.

"Here's to the two of you finding the killer so we can all sleep at night!" Hazel said.

"Here! Here!" Velma added.

Claire's stomach twisted as she clinked glasses with the others. Would she and Dom be able to work together to convince Zambuco Norma wasn't the killer and set him on the path toward the real murderer? Claire sure hoped so, because from where she was sitting, if she didn't know Norma the way she did, she'd be putting her at the top of the suspect list, just like Zambuco was probably doing right now.

Chapter Eleven

Dom loved sitting at the docks down in Crab Cove and watching the boats glide in and out of the small harbor. Right now, however, his attention was on Claire, who sat beside him recounting how she had witnessed the fight between Norma and Zoila that morning.

"So that's why you were leaning over your railing like that?" Dom snapped a pistachio out of its shell and popped it into his mouth.

Claire's brow creased. "You saw me?"

"Yes, I was on my patio. Could hardly miss you leaning over like that. I wasn't sure if you would fall down the hillside or not."

Claire laughed. "Well, I have to say I *was* glad Daddy spent the extra money to have those railings cemented in."

"So, what were they fighting about?"

Claire's face darkened. "That's the thing. I couldn't hear what they were saying, just that they were yelling. Zoila had a paper in her hands and she was waving it in front of Norma."

Dom's eyebrows tingled. "A paper? What kind of paper?"

Claire scrunched up her face. "I'm not sure. I mean, they were pretty far away."

"Was it writing paper? Or newspaper? How many pieces?"

Claire closed her eyes and tried to remember. For once, she wished she had Dom's eye for detail. "I think it was one piece. It looked old."

"Hmmm. She didn't have any piece of paper when she was killed. At least, I didn't see one at the scene." Dom leaned back in the chair and looked out at the cove. From where he sat, he could see the row of shops to the left. Mae

Biddeford was walking down the sidewalk purposefully. He watched her go into the seafood store with three jars of purple jam clutched in her hand—grape, Dom assumed. He popped two more pistachios into his mouth. "Any idea what was on it?"

Claire shook her head.

Dom stared out at the cove. He was beginning to regret his decision to team up with Claire—so far, she hadn't produced much valuable information. But there was still time. "Did you ask Norma about it?"

"Yes. She practically threw me out of her studio. Didn't want to talk about it."

Dom munched his pistachio thoughtfully. "So, after the fight, Norma went right to her studio? Did anyone see her?"

"Well, she didn't actually go *right* to her studio ..."

Dom turned sharply to Claire. "Where did she go?"

Claire sighed and looked out over the cove. "She took one of the boats."

Dom's brows shot up. *Now they were getting somewhere.* "She left the island?"

"Yep."

"Where did she go in the boat?"

"She wouldn't tell me."

Dom picked another pistachio out of the thin, pink and white striped bag as he thought about the murder weapon. Could Norma have taken it out to sea to dispose of it? If she had, someone would have seen her with it. "Did anyone see her leave the island?"

"Yes, she borrowed Bryan's boat and Jeremiah Woodward saw her."

"Did they see if she had the zen garden rake with her?"

"The rake? Why would she have that?"

"We think it was the murder weapon."

Claire's back stiffened. "Oh, so you think she was disposing of it. Well, I can assure you she wasn't doing that, because she isn't the killer."

Dom settled back on the bench. He remembered that in the cases they'd worked together in the past, he could always count on Claire's assessment of the suspects as being spot on. He respected her opinion in that area, but he wondered if her judgment was clouded by her friendship with Norma.

"How can you be so sure that Norma didn't kill Zoila?" Dom asked.

"I *know* her. She's not the type. Plus, she seemed shocked when I told her how I'd seen them fighting and that Zoila had been murdered hours later."

Shocked about the murder, or shocked Claire had witnessed the fight? Dom wondered.

"We can't go on emotion. We must go with the facts and solid clues. Of which we have very few," Dom said. "We need to find out what the police know about this footprint."

Claire chewed her bottom lip. "Maybe I could get my nephew to tell us. He owes me for all the cases I've helped him with."

"And we should try to reconstruct Zoila's morning, and probably the prior day."

Claire smiled. "Just like old times."

"Exactly. Except we don't have the benefit of the police badge and associated clout."

"That makes it more challenging. But we have an advantage in that we know the people involved. We might be able to get more information than the police because they trust us." Claire settled back on the bench. "So, let's see. We know Zoila argued with Norma and then went to the meditation garden. But we don't know if she had a stop in between."

"We could ask Norma if she knew where Zoila went after the argument," Dom offered.

Claire tilted her head. "We could, but she might not tell us. For some reason, she is being exceedingly closed-mouthed. We should ask around to see if anyone was up at the zen garden that morning, and if they saw anything."

"I talked to Banes." Dom told Claire about his conversation with the groundskeeper and the bag from *Chowders*.

"It sounds like you think the bag from *Chowders* could be significant? Why is that?"

"Banes said the kids leave trash sometimes, but I don't think kids would have a take-out bag from *Chowders*. They usually eat junk food."

Claire scrunched up her face at him. "So, you think the killer ate at *Chowders*?"

"Not necessarily. I talked to Shane and Sarah after Kenneth, and they acted very strange when I asked about Ben."

"Why would you ask about Ben?"

Claire had shifted in her seat to face him and Dom knew she was going to be upset, but he had to mention the clues as he saw them.

"Kenneth said he was at Zoila's yesterday and I know he does delivery for *Chowders*. There was a *Chowders* bag up near the crime scene..." Dom shrugged, letting his voice trail off.

"Ben wouldn't leave trash up there!"

"Not normally ... but if he was fleeing a murder scene, he might."

Claire's cheeks burned. Her face turned incredulous as she stared at Dom. "You can't seriously suspect Ben? You know he couldn't kill anyone and I can assure you from a psychological standpoint, he's not capable. Besides, *why* would Ben want to kill Zoila?"

"That's the big question. Why would anyone. If we could answer that, we'd have our killer. Besides, it seems that Ben has an alibi."

"He does?"

"Yes, Sarah said he visits his mother on the mainland on Wednesdays and I don't think he would have been on the island when she was killed."

That's right, Claire thought. How had she forgotten that? Of course Ben could not have done it. She felt a pang of worry—she'd noticed herself getting more and more forgetful and hoped it was just a normal sign of aging and not something more sinister.

"Right. Well, I can assure you it wasn't Ben or Norma," Claire said in a clipped tone. Then, she calmed down and gave the situation some thought. It was better to act professionally, not emotionally. "We need some more leads to follow. Are you sure Banes didn't see anyone else up there or hear anything? You'd think Zoila would have screamed."

"No. He was cleaning up horse poop on the trails and he said he doesn't hear very good," Dom said. "As far as I know, no one else has come forward to say they were there that morning."

"*Meow!*"

Dom looked down to see a large Maine Coon cat weaving in between Claire's ankles. Claire reached down to pet the cat's head.

"Is that your cat?" Dom asked.

"No. She's a stray, but she comes to my garden sometimes, and I always leave something out for her. I call her Porch Cat."

"Oh. I've seen her on my patio. I wondered who owned her. She seems to stroll by in the afternoon, most days." Dom tossed a pistachio to the cat. She looked up at him with suspicious green eyes, sniffed the pistachio disdainfully, then rubbed the side of her head on Claire's calf while she presented Dom with her back end.

Claire laughed. "I guess she doesn't like pistachios. I think most of the neighbors feed her—she's well fed. I think she makes the rounds, and I've seen her sunning herself in the gardens up at the conservation area."

"Near the zen garden?"

"Yes. Too bad she can't talk," Claire said. "She probably knows a lot about what's going on around the island. She might even know who killed Zoila."

"*Meow!*" The cat looked up at Claire, then glared at Dom before continuing on her path along the length of the dock.

"That's exactly what we need. Someone who might have seen something but didn't realize it was important, so they didn't come forward," Dom said.

"Yeah. But preferably someone who can actually talk," Claire replied.

Dom watched the cat amble lazily down the wooden dock toward the shops, thinking what a great source of information it would be, with the run of the island and no one censoring their conversations around her. The cat would be privy to all sorts of information.

A light blinked in Dom's brain, and he thought of someone else who might be in a similar situation but could actually communicate with them. "Kenneth said the Flannery kid rode his bike past Zoila's yesterday on his way through the conservation area. Do the kids ride through there a lot?"

"I think so. I remember Robby saying he has to give them a talking to a lot because the bikes are wearing down the paths."

"Maybe one of them saw something and was too scared to say so, or didn't realize it might be significant," Dom suggested.

"Could be. We should definitely ask around," Claire agreed. "If I was being called in as a consultant, I'd know exactly what to do next. But now that we aren't with the police, things need to be handled differently. What do you suggest we do?"

Dom was glad Claire was asking his opinion instead of dictating the tasks. Maybe this partnership would work out, after all. "I say we talk to Norma and find out just what Zambuco is up to. We might be able to figure out what he is thinking and anticipate his next move by the questions he asked her. Maybe you can talk to your nephew and see if he will give us any insider information on the case."

"Sure, I can do that. I don't know what he'll share with me, but every little bit helps and I feel like we had better get to the bottom of this ourselves before Zambuco comes up with the wrong conclusion and arrests the wrong person."

"And the real killer gets off scot-free." Dom glanced over at the shops in time to see Mae coming out of the fish store with a brown paper package in her hand. Apparently, she'd traded jam for fish. Life was going on as normal here on Mooseamuck Island—the islanders seemed to be unconcerned that a killer was running around loose.

An icy finger danced up his spine, causing an involuntary shiver as Dom wondered if Zoila would be the only victim, or if the killer was already busy planning his next murder.

Chapter Twelve

"And what do you two want?" Norma glared from her desk at Dom and Claire, who stood just inside the doorway of her studio.

"We're trying to help you," Claire said softly. "Zambuco's coming by. He found out you had a fight with Zoila."

"Already been by," Norma snapped. "Asked a lot of annoying questions, just like you did."

Dom stepped inside the small studio and Claire followed behind him, then shut the door. The sun filtered in from the large window in the front, highlighting the bright colors of Norma's paintings that hung on every inch of wall space. The closed-in space intensified the smell of oil and turpentine, and Dom stifled a sneeze. "What, exactly, did he ask?"

Norma waved her hand in the air dismissively. "Oh, you know. Where was I this morning? What did I fight with Zoila about? Did I kill her? The usual interrogation stuff."

"And what did you tell him?" Dom asked.

"I told him it was none of his business, just like it's none of yours."

Claire flapped her hands against her sides in frustration. "We're just trying to help. If you tell us what this is all about, we can try to figure out who the killer is and get Zambuco off your back. But when you remain silent like this, you're making it seem like you *did* kill Zoila."

Norma pushed herself up from her desk and took a few steps toward them. Dom looked down at her feet and noticed she wore men's work boots with round toes. The image of the footprint left in the sand at the zen garden drifted to his mind.

"Is that what you think?" Norma thumped her cane on

the floor loudly. "That I killed her?"

"No, of course not," Claire soothed.

"Well, I didn't." Norma crossed her arms over her chest. "But I'm also not going to tell anyone what the argument was about or where I went. That information is confidential."

Dom and Claire exchanged a frustrated glance.

"Can you at least tell us what you think Zambuco was getting at? Did he mention any evidence or what he thought a motive might be?" Dom asked.

"He seemed to think that Zoila might have seen something in one of her readings. Some sort of premonition, and whatever it was, someone didn't want her talking about it."

"Is that what you were arguing about? A premonition she had?"

Norma shook her head. "No. And I'm not exactly sure Zambuco is barking up the right tree. See, Zoila had made a strange discovery, and if it was true ... well, let's just say there's someone on the island who might not like it very much."

Dom's eyebrows tingled. "Enough to kill her?"

"Maybe." Norma glanced out the window and Claire's heart twisted as she noticed Norma's eyes were moist. Was she about to cry? She'd never known the older woman to shed a tear before.

Claire reached out and rubbed Norma's arm. "Then why don't you tell us what it is? We can help."

Norma pressed her lips together, then looked at Claire with clear, determined eyes. "I wish I could, but sometimes one has to honor their word above all. Even if it means becoming a murder suspect."

***

"Well, that wasn't very helpful," Dom said as they walked down the sidewalk past the quaint Crab Cove shops after leaving Norma's studio.

Claire chewed her bottom lip. "Why won't she tell us? It doesn't make sense. Is she covering for someone?"

"Maybe she is trying to throw up a smoke screen."

"You mean like to throw us off track? Why would she do that if she wasn't guilty?" Claire stopped walking and looked over at Dom. "You don't really think it *is* her, do you?"

Dom looked up. Two gulls flew overhead, their raucous cries piercing the air. "A lot of the clues do point to her, but still, I can't see it. And there's too many unanswered questions. We need to find out what was on that paper and where it is now."

"Not to mention the murder weapon."

"And the footprint. I couldn't tell what kind of shoe it was, but it looked like a large boot with a rounded toe."

"A man's boot?" Claire asked hopefully.

"It could be either, and let's not forget some women wear men's boots." Dom glanced back at Norma's studio.

Claire's phone burst out in eerie science fiction music, and they both jumped. Cell phone reception was spotty on the island and they weren't used to phones blaring out at random times. She pulled it out and looked at the caller ID. "It's Robby. I'd better answer it."

Claire walked away a few paces, and Dom stared out at the harbor. The scene usually calmed his nerves, but it wasn't very calming now. Too many thoughts were clamoring for attention in his head. And a murderer was on the loose. He noticed the ferry pulling up to the dock. Just as they had suspected, Zambuco wasn't able to stop the ferries for long, which meant the killer could have easily slipped off the island. That might make finding him harder unless the killer was an islander, because if it was, their absence would soon become suspicious. Everyone knew everyone else's habits on Mooseamuck Island, and if someone deviated from the norm, there was sure to be talk about it.

Claire joined him again, her face grim.

"Did he tell you anything of interest?" Dom asked.

"He was reluctant to divulge too much information, but I did manage to get one clue about the footprint out of him. I had to promise to bake him an apple pie, though."

"Oh? What was the clue?" Dom's eyebrows started to

tingle, and he unconsciously smoothed them with his fingertips.

"They couldn't make out the model of shoe, but they did find some interesting tiny pieces of shell in the impression. Jonah crab shell."

Dom's high hopes deflated, and his eyebrows stopped tingling. "Crab shell? I hardly think that will help narrow things down. This place is loaded with crabs. That's why it's called Crab Cove."

"Not Jonah crabs. Those are only found in one remote place on the island. It's off the beaten path so hardly anyone ever goes there, but it has a nice view of the lighthouse and I know one person who manages a visit at least once a week."

"Oh, really?" The tingling started up again. Dom didn't need to ask who the person was, but he did anyway. "Who?"

"Norma."

Chapter Thirteen

Claire thought about Zoila's murder as she pinched the spent blooms from the purple petunia that hung from her back porch. The sun was just starting to set behind her as she took her last look of the day out over the Atlantic. It was unusually calm, which Claire thought was funny given the hectic events on the island.

Her thoughts turned to the information Robby had given her and her gut tightened. Just because there were crab shells in the shoe imprint *and* Norma was known to go to that stretch of the island didn't mean she was the killer. Lots of people wore work boots with round toes. And lots of people could have gone there, though Claire knew most people didn't bother because the beach was all rocky and there were nicer places that were easier to get to.

Norma had implied someone else might want to silence Zoila ... but who? And why wouldn't Norma tell them? It didn't make sense. Norma knew something, and the fact that she wouldn't tell anyone didn't bode well for her.

"Meow."

Claire looked down to see the stray Maine Coon looking up at her with curious, green eyes. The cat had something in its mouth and Claire bent down to see what it was.

"Hi, there." Claire rubbed between the cat's ears and was rewarded with a loud purring. The cat spit out the object— a shiny green leaf. Claire picked it up and then turned it over curiously.

"Where'd you get this?" she wondered. It was a smooth, winterberry holly leaf. The plant was very rare in this part of Maine. In fact, Claire knew of only one place that it grew. "Have you been to Anna's garden?"

"Meow."

Claire stood with the leaf still in her hand. Anna Campbell was an avid gardener, just like Claire—at least she had been, before cancer made her so weak she couldn't do anything but lay in bed. Thinking of Anna, who lay in hospice on the mainland with only a few weeks—maybe even days—left to live, reminded her of Ben and her heart clenched for him.

She thought about how Ben's name kept coming up in the investigation. That had to be a coincidence—Claire was sure sweet, simple Ben couldn't be involved.

Dom had said that Sarah and Shane acted strange when he asked them about Ben, and Kenneth had seen Ben speeding away from Zoila's. She rubbed the smooth leaf in between her thumb and forefinger, her forehead creasing with worry. Ben was under a lot of pressure, with his mother being sick and off the island. That pressure could make him act strangely ... but murder? No. Claire didn't think so. He would have no reason to kill Zoila.

Claire knew Anna and Norma were best friends. In fact, Norma had promised Anna she would look after Ben once Anna was gone. Though Ben was a grown man in his fifties and could function on his own for the most part, his simple outlook and limited capabilities sometimes made people think they could take advantage of him. Norma would protect him from that ... but was she protecting him now?

There had to be more to it. Something was going on, but Claire was sure neither Norma nor Ben had anything to do with Zoila's death. She needed to find out who was up at the zen garden that morning, and it looked like her best bet was to talk to some of the kids around town and see if they'd noticed anyone. She made a mental note to seek them out before she met Dom at *Chowders* in the morning.

"*Meow!*"

Claire looked down to see the cat sitting at her door expectantly.

"Oh, I see. You're looking for your saucer of milk, are you?"

The cat flicked its ears and looked from Claire to the

door, and back to Claire.

Claire laughed. "Okay, you win."

She went inside and poured some milk into a small bowl, which she left outside for the cat to drink at her leisure. She considered inviting the cat inside, but she never seemed to want to come in. Maybe when the weather got colder she would accept the invitation. It might be nice to have another living creature in the house to snuggle with on the long winter nights.

Claire snapped on the light beside her favorite oversized chair that sat next to the big stone fireplace in the sitting room of her cottage. It was too warm for a fire, but sitting next to the hearth made her feel cozy.

She picked up the crossword puzzle she'd been working on and settled into the chair, grabbing her half-moon reading glasses from the side-table. Then she opened the drawer of the table and peeked inside hopefully. She was in luck—a tiny piece of dark chocolate sat inside the drawer, right where she'd hidden it. She picked the piece out and unwrapped it, savoring the slightly bitter taste of the chocolate. It was an indulgence she allowed herself because of the many health benefits, and she often placed small squares of chocolate in various places around the house, usually forgetting just where she'd put them. It was always a nice surprise to find one.

She finished the chocolate and turned her attention to the crossword. Just a few more words and it would be complete. Then she would turn in early ... she needed to get a head start tomorrow if she wanted to get ahead of Zambuco before he came to the wrong conclusion.

***

Further up Israel Head Hill, Dom sat in his kitchen, a plate of ravioli on the table in front of him. He'd tried his hand at making them ... rolling out the pasta dough and placing a spoonful of ricotta filling inside. They weren't as good as his Nonna's or Sophia's, but they were okay.

He ate carefully, cutting each ravioli exactly in half, and eating one half then the next while he reflected on the events of the day. Working with Claire might not be so bad. Sure, she used emotion too much, but he had to admit getting an insight into how people thought and what motivated them to act a certain way could be fascinating. And she did come in handy given her connection to the police, even though Robby hadn't given them too many good clues.

He thought about the one clue they did get—the crab shells found in the footprint impression. Something didn't sit right with that. How could they know for sure who had been to that part of the island? Dom wasn't sure if the footprint was too smudged to be able to pinpoint the exact size and model of shoe. He'd have to wait to find out.

A chattering from the birdcage caught Dom's attention and he looked up to see Romeo preening Juliet's aqua and white feathers. A feeling of sadness descended on him—the birds reminded him of what he'd lost when Sophia died.

He balanced the last piece of ravioli on his fork and brought it to his mouth. No sense in looking back. Sophia was gone now, and he'd better make the best of the rest of his life, just like he'd promised her he would. And besides, he did have something to look forward to—Zoila's murder case. For the first time in years, he felt hopeful again, as if a dark shroud was being lifted and he could finally see clearly. He just hoped he was up for the task.

His eyebrows tingled, and he smoothed them out as he thought about the many questions yet to be answered.

What was Norma hiding?

Why had Sarah and Shane acted so strangely?

Was Ben involved somehow?

Most importantly, what had Zoila discovered that someone wanted so desperately to keep quiet that they killed her?

Another disturbing thought poked into Dom's mind—Zoila might have told someone what she'd discovered and, if that was the case, the killer's work might not yet be done.

Romeo scuttled over to the edge of his cage and watched Dom intently.

"Are you looking for a treat?" Dom picked a small piece of spinach out of his salad bowl, taking care to make sure it had no dressing on it, and held it up to the cage.

Romeo looked sideways at the spinach with his bright, black eyes, and then reached over with his tiny beak and pulled the leaf through the cage. He chewed it quickly, then flew to the side of the cage, clinging onto the grates and looking right at Dom.

"*Burber Peepon*," he squawked.

Dom smiled. Romeo's words were getting easier for him to understand, but he wasn't sure if it was because the bird was talking better or his ear was becoming more accustomed to the sounds. Either way, the bird had an uncanny way of saying the right word at the right time.

"That's right, my little friend." Dom fed another piece of spinach to the bird. "We have yet to find the murder weapon ... and when we do, will it lead us to the murderer?"

Chapter Fourteen

Chowders was abuzz with locals finishing up their breakfast when Claire slipped into the seat across the Formica table from Jane the next morning.

"Morning." Jane slid a tea cup in front of Claire. "Where have you been?"

"I was talking to some of the island kids." Claire glanced down the table and nodded at Dom, who tipped his coffee cup toward her in acknowledgment.

Beside her, Alice's knitting needles stopped clacking. "About the murder?" Did one of them see something?"

"Unfortunately, no." Claire shrugged and glanced at Dom. "Just Ben joyriding down the trails."

"Joy riding?" Mae's brows puckered together. "Ben's usually so careful. I haven't known him to go fast down those trails. It's dangerous."

"Maybe he's getting reckless with his worry for Anna," Tom suggested.

The table fell silent as they all thought about Anna, and how her death would affect Ben.

"I guess it's up to us to look after Ben now," Alice said. "Along with Norma, of course."

"I heard Zambuco searched Norma's place last night," Mae added.

Claire's heart pinched. "Searched it? For what?"

Mae shrugged. "Evidence, I guess. Maybe the murder weapon. I heard they haven't found that yet."

Tom Landry frowned at Mae. "Surely, you don't think Norma did it, do you?"

"Of course not." Mae gave him a disgusted glare, then turned to Dom and Claire. "What do you guys think? You *are* investigating it, aren't you?"

Claire looked at Dom. What *did* they think? Usually, they wouldn't discuss clues with anyone during an ongoing investigation, but this one was different. They weren't officially working with the police. Still, she didn't know how much they should share. Then again, they didn't have much information to share, anyway.

Alice's knitting needles clacked away as she looked at them slyly. "I heard from Velma that you two have teamed up, just like when you used to work together before."

"We have, but we really don't know much," Claire sighed.

"Well, who are your suspects?" Mae looked from Dom to Claire expectantly.

Dom cleared his throat. "We don't actually have any suspects. We've been trying to reconstruct the events of the day. Do any of you happen to know where Zoila went or who she met with that morning or the day before?"

Mae, Tom, Jane and Alice looked at each other and shrugged.

"Well, both Kenneth and Shane said they were at Zoila's the day before yesterday." Mae tilted her head toward the counter to jog their memories of the previous days conversation.

"And we know Norma and Zoila had ... umm ... words ... yesterday morning," Tom added.

"Other than that, I don't know Zoila's schedule. Did you guys get a copy of her appointment book?" Mae asked.

"Unfortunately, only the police are privy to that information," Claire answered.

"Then seems to me you ought to be out following that detective Zambuco around and seeing who he talks to. He's bound to be talking to the people in that book. Those would be his suspects," Mae said.

"Right." Claire bristled with annoyance. She didn't need Mae Biddeford telling her how to investigate a murder. "We talked to Norma right after Zambuco yesterday to try to find out his line of reasoning."

"And?" Jane's brows rose over her steaming cup of chai tea.

"Norma is being very tight-lipped," Claire said. "It's hard to say what Zambuco was thinking. But we should get going and see what he's up to today."

Claire stood and fished in her pocket for some money. Dom followed suit.

"And I guess we should talk to Ben, since he was seen racing away from the gardens yesterday morning," Dom added.

Jane pressed her lips together. "Ben? He wouldn't have been there yesterday morning."

"Why not?" Dom asked.

"He visits his mother on the mainland on Wednesdays."

"Oh, that's right." Claire glanced over at the counter, caught Sarah's eye and waved her over. "It will be easy to just verify that by asking. The kids probably made a mistake—you know how kids are."

"Can I get you guys something else?" Sarah stood at the end of the table.

"Oh, no, I was just wondering if Ben was around. I have a question for him," Claire said.

Sarah's eyes flicked toward the back room, then toward the door, then back to Claire. She shuffled her feet. "Why would you have a question for Ben?"

"I just wanted—"

But Claire didn't get to finish the sentence, because just then the door burst open and Hazel came running in, her face flushed and eyes wide.

Silence fell over the diner as everyone stopped what they were doing to stare at the elderly innkeeper, who stood in the doorway wringing her hands.

"You guys won't believe it—Norma's been arrested for the murder of Zoila Rivers!"

Chapter Fifteen

Claire ripped open the door to the Mooseamuck Island police station and stormed up to the counter. Behind it, Gail Waller looked at her with large eyes.

"Hi, Claire. Is something wr—"

"I want to see Robby right now," Claire demanded, cutting her off.

Gail pushed up from the desk and scurried down the hall, bumping into Robby who was just entering the front room.

"What's going on?" Claire frowned at her nephew. "Did you arrest Norma?"

Robby's face hardened. "Zambuco did, but she's being held here."

"On what grounds? Do you have enough evidence?"

Robby skirted around the counter to stand beside her. He put his hand on her shoulder and escorted her and Dom, who had been standing silently at her side, to the row of orange plastic chairs that sat along one wall.

Robby pushed the irate Claire into a chair and sat beside her. "He does have evidence."

"Like what?" Claire asked.

Robby's face hardened. "You know I can't discuss that with you."

"The murder weapon?" Claire persisted.

"No. We haven't found that yet. She might have tossed it in the ocean."

"Well, then I don't see how you can make a case." Claire glanced at Dom who nodded his agreement.

"Unless there was a witness?" Dom suggested.

Robby shook his head. "No. I can't say any more, but I agree with Zambuco that this is the best course of action."

"What?" Claire pushed out of her seat, flapping her arms in frustration. "How could it be best? You know Norma is no killer."

"You have to trust the justice system," Robby said.

"Well, if this is the kind of system we have on the island, I think I'll consider moving." Claire spat out the words, then crossed her arms over her chest with a sigh. "Can we at least see her?"

"They've just finished processing her. I can take you back." Robby stood and walked toward the back, with Claire and Dom following.

The Mooseamuck Island Police Station was small, occupying an area in the basement of the town hall which they shared with the public works department, so they didn't have far to go. Claire followed Robby down a short hallway that led to the two jail cells. Norma was in one, the other was empty.

Norma looked up as they entered the room, a scowl on her face.

"What do you two want?"

Claire's heart pinched. She could tell the scowl and harsh words were just a front. Or at least she thought so.

"We're here to help. We know you didn't kill Zoila," Claire said.

After a moment of silence from Norma, Dom added. "Did you?"

"Of course not."

Claire turned to Robby. "Why does she have to stay in jail? She hasn't been convicted or anything and just what, exactly, is the evidence, anyway?"

Robby sighed and ticked off the items with his fingers. "Well, she was seen fighting with the victim. She fled the island. And she won't tell us a thing. Usually, that all adds up to guilty."

Norma harrumphed, jamming her cane loudly on the floor.

"Norma, why won't you tell us about the fight and clear yourself from this bogus charge?"

"Well, I don't know if that would clear me and besides, I can't tell you. It's not for me to tell."

Robby shrugged. "If she won't help herself, I can't help her. She needs a lawyer who can get her out on bail. In the meantime, Zambuco has agreed to let her stay here instead of sending her over to the big jail on the mainland."

Claire gripped the bars of the cell with her fingers. "We'll get you a lawyer and get you out of here."

Norma simply shrugged, pulled a pencil out from behind her ear and started sketching on a napkin that sat on her lunch tray.

Claire tried one last time. "Norma, I wish you would think about at least telling me and Dom what went on between you and Zoila. We won't tell anyone, and it could give us a clue that might help us find the real killer."

Norma shook her head, her eyes never leaving the napkin. "I can't *say* what it was. Some trusts cannot be broken. Anyway, it's not so bad in here. I get three free meals a day and would probably be able to catch up on some rest if everyone would leave me alone."

Claire sighed as she watched Norma's pencil work furiously. "Can you at least tell us what was on that piece of paper she had?"

Norma looked up from her sketch. "I'm not going to tell and that's final. You need to run along now—all of you. But remember, murder cases can be like an impressionist painting—sometimes, if you are standing too close, you can't really see the whole scene."

Leave it to Norma to wave off help and then say something cryptic, Claire thought as she glanced down at the napkin before turning away. She was surprised at how quickly Norma had worked up an amazingly realistic sketch. There was a background of pine trees and scrub brush, then, nestled in a clearing, an old cabin with a tall stone chimney—Zoila's cabin.

***

"I just don't understand what is wrong with her," Claire said as they left the police station. "And I don't see how Zambuco could have arrested her ... I mean, don't they need something more solid than that flimsy evidence Robby mentioned?"

Dom nodded. "Yes, it does seem a bit premature."

"But I guess if I didn't know Norma so well, I would say the clues *did* point in her direction."

"True, but clues can also be deceiving."

Claire glanced sideways at Dom. She'd always thought he considered clues to be cut and dried. Perhaps there was another side to him that she hadn't seen before. "What do you mean?"

"Well ... I can't be sure ... but I have a theory." He preened his eyebrows. Then he shook his head. "No, I can't say anything until I can prove it."

Claire studied him. He was on to something, but she knew from experience she wouldn't be able to get a thing out of him until he was ready. She stood at her car door and replayed their talk with Norma in her head while she waited for Dom to get in the passenger side.

"What she said at the end—about the impressionist painting—do you think that was some kind of clue?" she asked Dom over the roof of the Fiat.

"I think she might have been *sketching* us a clue." Dom opened the door and slid into the passenger seat while Claire got into the driver's seat.

"You mean the hunting camp?"

Dom nodded.

"But Zoila wasn't killed there." Claire started the car but didn't put it into gear—she was too interested in hearing Dom's theory on Norma's sketch.

"We already know where she was killed, so that wouldn't have been much of a clue," Dom pointed out.

"But how could the hunting camp be a clue?"

Dom shrugged. "Maybe it started there. The argument with the killer. Or maybe there is a clue still there to be found."

Claire's brows crept up. "That could be. But how would we get in? The police must have it locked up tight."

"Maybe we need to look at it from another angle. Who do we know who was at the camp before she died?"

Claire pressed her lips together and thought. "Well,

Kenneth and Shane were both there the day before she died. They said so at the diner that morning."

"That's right." Dom remembered the sand he felt under his feet at the counter that morning after Shane left. Could that sand have come from the zen garden? He pictured his later visit when Shane had been fixing the oven, his round-toed work boots in clear view. "And Sarah and Shane acted awfully jumpy when I asked about Ben."

"You know, I hate to say it, but I've always felt like Sarah was hiding something."

"What do you mean?"

"I don't know. Something about her past," Claire hesitated. "She just kind of has an air about her like she has some kind of secret she doesn't want anyone to know."

Dom nodded, much to Claire's surprise. "I noticed that, too."

"You don't think she could have anything to do with it? I don't even think she knew Zoila."

"*She* might not have known Zoila ... but maybe Zoila knew *her*."

"Or her secret."

Chapter Sixteen

Claire and Dom knew from experience that they couldn't just ask Sarah about her secret ... especially if it had something to do with Zoila's murder. Even if it didn't, she clearly didn't want anyone to know about it, so they doubted direct questioning would yield any results.

They took a more indirect route. Claire researched her on the internet, and Dom discreetly tried to find out her whereabouts on the morning of the murder.

They agreed to spend a few hours on their tasks and meet at a small coffee shop in the cove to discuss their findings at two p.m. Which is exactly where Claire was sitting with her hand wrapped around a steaming mug of green tea when Dom walked in the door.

He nodded at Claire, then paid for a coffee which he poured from the self-serve carafes before sliding into the booth opposite her.

"How'd you make out?" he asked without preamble.

Claire shook her head. "Not good. Or maybe it was good, depending on how you look at it."

Dom raised a brow and Claire continued.

"I did a search on Sarah White, starting with Lowell Massachusetts where she claims to be from, and the only person living there with that name during that timeframe is eighty-seven years old!"

"Well, that can't be her. But maybe you got the town wrong." Dom sipped his coffee. "Or maybe she lived in a smaller town near Lowell. Sometimes people say they are from the next biggest town because others don't recognize the smaller town names."

"I thought of that. There are no Sarah Whites that fit the description in any surrounding towns."

Dom pressed his lips together. "Well, that certainly does raise suspicions. However, Sarah could not have murdered Zoila."

Claire didn't know whether to be glad or depressed about that. She liked Sarah and didn't want her to be the killer, but if it wasn't her, then who did they have left as suspects?

"Why not?"

"I checked around and she was at *Chowders* all morning. Several witnesses say she was there as early as six a.m. And since you saw Zoila alive at six, that means she was killed some time after six, so it couldn't have been Sarah who killed her."

Claire stared out the window. The cove waters across the street were dappled with sunlight. Tourists in colorful clothes walked by with shopping bags dangling from their hands. They were happy, smiling. Claire sighed and turned her attention back to her tea. She was in no mood to see happy people.

"So, Sarah has an alibi. But she also has a secret ... and it must be important, seeing as she seems to be lying about who she really is." Claire looked up at Dom. "So, if she didn't do it, maybe someone did it for her."

"Someone who cares enough about her to kill for her?" Dom asked.

Claire nodded.

"Well, I noticed Shane seems to be pretty sweet on her." Dom lowered his voice. "And I felt sand on the floor in the diner at the counter, right where he had been standing the morning of the murder."

"You think he might have been the one who left the footprint in the zen garden?"

Dom shrugged. "Maybe."

"But he seemed so surprised when he found out Zoila had been killed."

"Maybe he's a good actor. We've seen killers act surprised before."

It was true—even the most hardened killers seemed to be able to pull off an award-winning performance when it came to diverting suspicion. But Shane wasn't a hardened killer ... she'd known his family since he was a baby. Then again, they'd also seen love make people do crazy things ... including murder.

Claire didn't want to say it out loud, but Shane wasn't the only one who cared about Sarah. She knew Sarah and Ben had grown very close since Sarah came to the island. Especially after Anna got sick. Sarah had been almost like a sister to him. She'd encouraged him to take the delivery job and that had given Ben much-needed self-esteem. Claire knew Ben looked up to Sarah ... but would he kill for her?

"We need to find out Zoila's time of death and then figure out if Shane had opportunity." Claire eyed her phone, noticing there was no reception, as usual. "Maybe I can get that information from Robby."

"If he's feeling generous, maybe you can get him to tell us the exact make and size of shoe that made that footprint and if there was any distinguishing tread wear," Dom said.

"I'll try."

"There's something else strange." Dom rubbed his eyebrows. "Shane's account of when he was at Zoila's doesn't match with Kenneth's. Kenneth said he saw Shane around one o'clock, but Shane said he was there after three."

"Why would Shane lie about that?" Claire asked. "Zoila wasn't killed until the next day, so it's not like he would lie so as to not be placed at the scene of the crime."

"Not *that* crime," Dom said. "But maybe there was something else that happened at Zoila's that he didn't want to be implicated in."

"Like what?"

"I have no idea. Perhaps that will come out as we investigate further. I do know one thing, though. We need to take a trip out to Zoila's and see if there's anything out there that might yield a clue."

Claire looked down into her empty cup. "But it's probably locked up and on this case, we don't have the benefit of being able to just browse around the properties that the police have secured."

"That's unfortunate. But we can still go out and take a look around outside ... maybe even peek in the windows. One never knows what one might find. "Dom pushed himself up from his chair and looked at Claire expectantly. "You game?"

***

Claire had been out to the old hunting camp many times before in her youth, but today, it looked different. She eyed it ominously as they drove slowly up the dirt road where it sat shrouded in the darkness of the forest trees, enveloped in the stillness of death.

That's silly, she thought as she hopped out of Dom's Smart Car. It was just her imagination running wild, applying emotions to the camp knowing the owner was now dead. The camp was an inanimate object—no more menacing now than it had been before Zoila's murder.

The rustic, log exterior blended perfectly with the deep-woods setting. Darkened windows glared at Claire as they approached the wide porch that ran along the front of the house.

Dom reached out and twisted the knob on the thick, oak door. "It's locked."

"Not surprised." Claire cupped her hand over her eyes and peered through the window next to the door into the living room. Zoila had decorated it comfortably with a leather sofa facing the oversized stone fireplace. Claire wondered if the granny-square afghan draped over the back of the sofa was one of Alice's creations. An oval, braided rug lay in the center of the tidy room. Claire felt a tug of sadness as she looked, in realizing that when Zoila left the cabin on Wednesday morning, she never realized it would be for the last time.

"Do you see anything of interest?" Dom moved to the window at the end of the porch, cupping his own hands over his eyes to look in.

"Not really." Claire noticed a few stones had come loose from the side of the chimney and were lying on the hearth. "The chimney looks like it needs some repair, but didn't

Shane say that was part of what she was having redone?"

"Yep." Dom was already off the porch and circling the house. From the side, Claire could see the various add-ons that had been built over the years. The different siding and architectural styles made them obvious. They peered into windows as they went around, but nothing seemed amiss.

Behind the camp was an old toolshed. Dom lifted the latch and the door squealed open.

"At least we can get in here," Claire said as she surveyed the small shed full of gardening equipment, old tires, a snowblower and even a baby carriage that looked like it was from the early 1900s.

"I guess the Barretts left some of their stuff here after they sold the place." Dom took down a rake that had been hanging on the side of the wall and looked it over, reminding Claire that the murder weapon—which they presumed was the rake from the zen garden—was still missing.

Dom smiled ruefully as he noticed her attention to the rake. "Wrong kind."

"Just as well. It would be very strange for the murder weapon to show up here in Zoila's tool shed when she'd been murdered in the zen garden."

"True, but maybe our killer is very clever. It's the last place anyone would look."

Claire nodded, her attention drifting to a stack of old, framed pictures leaning against the side of the shed. "Looks like they even left old pictures."

Dom came to stand beside her, pointing to the smudged dust in the middle of the tops of the frames. "It looks like someone has handled these recently."

"Maybe Zoila moved them from the house for the renovations," Claire suggested.

"Kenneth said Zoila had called him over to pick up some family pictures. I wonder why he didn't take them."

Claire held up a framed photograph that looked to be about seventy years old. "I know why. Kenneth didn't get along with his father."

Dom's brow creased and he pointed to a handsome young man in the photo. "Is this his father?"

Claire nodded. "His name was Silas. He died a few years ago."

"I see the resemblance," Dom said as he studied the image of the man. Even though the picture was in black and white, he could tell the man had the same blond hair and preppy looks as Kenneth, right down to the dimple on his chin. "He seems kind of old to be Kenneth's father. Isn't Kenneth only in his forties?"

"He had Kenneth late in life. I guess he was too busy making money to take a wife. Kenneth's mother was a lot younger."

Dom was quiet while he studied the picture for a few seconds. "Who are the others?"

Claire looked at the picture again, then laughed. "You won't believe it, but this is Norma and the woman next to her is Anna Campbell."

"Ben's mother?" Dom looked at the picture. Now that Claire had pointed it out, he recognized a younger and less grumpy Norma. She stood next to a woman who was a true beauty. Silas stood on the other side of the woman, looking at her with a bemused smile on his face as if she'd just said something clever. "They look like good friends."

"I guess they were, back in the day. That was before Silas took over the family business. Norma said he changed after that and they didn't hang around together anymore, but she and Anna remained best friends."

Dom put the photo down and thumbed through the others. They were old family portraits, some in oil paint. He noticed one in an elaborate gold frame that had the paper backing torn at the top. The man immortalized by the painting had the Barrett blonde hair and dimple.

"That's Kenneth's grandfather. Jeb Barrett," Claire said.

"I see the resemblance," Dom sighed, and carefully placed the picture back with the others. "Unfortunately, there's no clue here as to why Shane ... or anyone else ... would want to kill Zoila."

"I'm not really convinced Shane had anything to do with it," Claire said as they shut the shed door and started toward the car. "As you saw, the fireplace does need repair so he did have a legitimate reason to be here."

"Well, if we want to clear Norma, we have to start eliminating the suspects and see where it leads us."

"I guess Shane *is* one of our suspects." Claire picked up her cell phone and glanced at the bars. "Still no service. I'll text Robby about the footprint and time of death and hope it goes through when we get back in range."

Dom turned the car around and started down the dirt road that served as the cabin's driveway while Claire formulated her text. Glancing in the rearview mirror at the house and then the shed, he felt his left eyebrow tingle. He patted it with his index finger, then turned his attention to the road ahead of him. "Back in the day, we would have proceeded by figuring out where each suspect was at the time of the murder so we could narrow it down."

"Yeah, and back in the day we'd have been able to haul them into the station for questioning."

"True. We might have to use a more indirect method now."

"You mean like asking around? The Mooseamuck Island grapevine knows everything that is going on around town."

"Yes, that could help." Dom glanced in his rear-view mirror to see a familiar car traveling about a half-mile behind them. "I already asked him where he was and now we just need to verify that."

"Great. Where was he?" Claire checked her phone again. One bar.

"He said he was at the Dumonts'."

"Perfect. I know Ginny very well. I'll just call her up and verify." Another bar popped up and Claire dialed Ginny's number.

"Aloha!"

Claire laughed. "Well, you're in a good mood."

"Who wouldn't be in paradise."

"Paradise?"

"Yes, didn't you know? We're on vacation in Hawaii!"

Oh." Claire's brow wrinkled. "I didn't know about that. Are you having work done on your house while you're away?"

"Shane is repointing our chimney, but not this week. We

don't want anyone there until we come back. We gave him explicit instructions." Ginny's voice took on a flat tone. "Why, was he there?"

"Oh, no. I was just wondering." Claire caught Dom's sideways glance and asked one last question. "So, you've been away all week?"

"Yep, since Saturday. We're coming back next Wednesday."

"Okay." Claire tried to sound cheerful. "Well, have a nice vacation!"

Claire's stomach sank as she hung up the phone.

"What did she say?" Dom asked.

"Shane wasn't there ... or at least he wasn't supposed to be there. The Dumonts are on vacation and Ginny said she told him to suspend work until they got back. She didn't want anyone on the property while they were away."

Dom pressed his lips together and glanced in the side view mirror before turning right toward the road that led to Crab Cove. "So he *was* lying to me. I thought so."

"But why would he lie? Do you really think he killed Zoila to protect Sarah's secret?"

"I'm not sure, but we're going to find out."

Chapter Seventeen

"Why do you keep looking in the rearview mirror?" Claire asked as they pulled into the small parking lot next to *Chowders*.

"Someone is following us."

Claire twisted around in her seat. "Who? Where?"

"Oh, he's being rather discreet about it, but I know how to spot a tail." Dom turned off the engine and turned to Claire. "I think it's Zambuco."

"Zambuco? Why would he be following *us*?"

"Maybe he's fresh out of leads and is using us for inspiration."

Claire mashed her brows together. "Fresh out of leads for what? He's already arrested Norma. What would he be investigating?"

"He needs better evidence, don't you think? I'm not even sure how he can justify keeping Norma ... unless he knows something we don't."

Claire glanced over her shoulder as she followed Dom into *Chowders*. She didn't see Zambuco, but if Dom was right, there might be hope for Norma to get released. At least she could be in the comfort of her home while Claire and Dom tracked down the real killer ... who she hoped wasn't standing inside *Chowders* looking out at them right now.

Walking through the lot, her heart grew heavy at the sight of Shane's truck.

"This is good." Dom jerked his head in the direction of the truck. "We'll be able to question both of them at the same time."

Anxiety surged through Claire as Dom opened the door.

She was glad the diner was empty of customers—she had a feeling the conversation might get heated.

Sarah was behind the counter, slicing into a golden crusted pie. Shane sat on the other side, a white mug of dark coffee in front of him. Both heads swiveled toward the door. Two sets of eyes narrowed suspiciously, alerting Claire to the fact that Sarah and Shane knew they weren't there on a social visit.

"What brings you two here?" Sarah asked guardedly.

"I'm afraid we have some hard questions to ask," Dom said.

"Like what?" Shane's hand clenched his mug.

"Now, look." Dom leaned against the counter, looking down at Shane. "It's better we ask these questions before Zambuco does. Because he's going to come to the same conclusion sooner or later and I'm sure you'd rather come clean to your friends. Maybe we can help keep Zambuco off your back."

"What are you talking about?" Sarah asked.

"We know you have a secret," Dom said. "Did Zoila find out about it and threaten to tell someone?"

Sarah's eyes widened. "What? No. And besides, it's none of your damn business."

"Now, Sarah," Claire soothed. "We aren't prying into your business. But there was a murder here and we know it wasn't Norma. It's just a matter of time before she's cleared and Zambuco comes looking for anyone with a past."

Sarah crossed her arms over her chest and glared at Claire. "Are you saying that just because I didn't grow up here on the island I'll be suspected of killing Zoila?"

"No. Not because you didn't grow up here." Claire kept her voice unemotional. "Because you're running away from something."

Shane jumped up from his seat. "Hey, now, you wait just a minute. Sarah didn't do anything!"

Sarah put her hand on his arm. Claire's heart pinched as she noticed Sarah's eyes were wet with tears. She felt like a heel.

"How do you know I'm running from something?"

Claire shrugged. "I'm a psychologist. I saw the signs."

"But I don't understand why that makes me suspicious."

"Look, I don't know what you have in your past, but if it was something you didn't want anyone to know and Zoila found out about it through her psychic abilities and then threatened to tell people ... well ..." Claire let her voice trail off.

"And that's what you think happened? That I killed her because she found out about my past?"

"No. Not you. We know you have an alibi." Dom turned to Shane. "It's you who's the suspect."

"What?" Sarah and Shane yelled in unison, causing Claire to cringe. She noticed Shane's face was beet red, his hands clenched into fists.

"We know you lied about where you were yesterday morning when Zoila was killed," Dom said. "You told me you were at the Dumonts', but Claire checked with them and they said you weren't working there this week."

Claire chewed her bottom lip. If Shane really was the killer, confronting him like this might not have been a very smart idea. On other cases, they usually had police backup, but they didn't have that now.

She was suddenly very nervous ... if he'd killed once, he might kill again to keep them quiet. But instead of rising up in anger, Shane collapsed in a sigh. Claire noticed him exchange a look with Sarah and wondered if it was true. Had Shane killed for her, and if so, would he confess now and wait quietly for them to call Zambuco?

Sarah shook her head in resignation. "First of all, my past isn't anything I'd kill over and I certainly wouldn't have anyone do my killing for me. It *is* private, though, so I'm not telling anyone, even if you do throw me in jail. And second of all, Shane couldn't have killed Zoila ... he was here all morning that day."

"He was?" Dom's brows tingled as they scrunched into a bushy 'V' in the middle of his forehead. No one had mentioned that Shane was in the restaurant when he'd asked around about Sarah's whereabouts that morning, but then again, he'd only asked about Sarah. It was easy enough to verify later as plenty of people were working that morning, so he doubted they would be lying now. "But why did you lie and say you were at the Dumonts'?"

Sarah and Shane exchanged another glance and Claire thought they *did* have something to hide—it just wasn't something about Zoila.

Shane looked at them sheepishly. "I lied because I was here that morning helping Sarah out in the back. I was covering for Ben."

"Ben?" Claire looked between Sarah and Shane in confusion. "Why would you cover for him?"

"He usually comes in early, before he goes to visit Anna, and does the salad bar," Sarah said. "But that morning, he didn't come in, so Shane helped me out."

"When you asked where I was, I didn't want to mention anything about Ben not coming in, so I just said I was at the first job that popped into my head." Shane looked at Claire ruefully. "Guess I picked the wrong one."

"I don't understand why you would cover for Ben," Dom said. "Didn't you say he called in sick?"

"That's what I *said*, but he actually didn't call in. I just told Zambuco that because I didn't want him to hassle Ben." Sarah turned pleading eyes to Claire. "You know how sensitive he is."

"Yes, of course. Zambuco would scare him silly."

"And of course he couldn't have had anything to do with Zoila's murder." Sarah wrung her hands together, looking not at all certain that what she said was true. "Because he visits his mother over on the mainland on Wednesdays after kitchen duty, so he wouldn't even have been on the island when Zoila was killed."

"Right." Claire nodded, then narrowed her eyes. "So why were the two of you lying and covering up for him, then?"

Shane glanced at Sarah, who nodded slightly.

"When people started asking questions about him, we didn't know what to do. The truth is that no one's seen him since the day before Zoila died," Shane said.

"That's right." Sarah's face twisted in anguish and her next words pinched Claire's heart. "Ben has disappeared."

Chapter Eighteen

"I hate to say it, but Ben just moved to the top of our suspect list," Dom whispered as they slid into a small table on the outdoor dining deck of the *Gull View Inn* where they'd decided to grab a bite to eat while figuring out their next course of action.

Claire's lips thinned. "I can't imagine why he would disappear. It's not like him to run off and not tell Sarah. I wonder if Norma knows where he is. His disappearance may just be a manifestation of his grief for his mother."

"Or it could be that he *is* guilty, which would explain Norma's silence. She's been covering for him all along," Dom suggested.

"I'm sure that's not it," Claire said with an air of certainty that she didn't feel. The clues were stacking up oddly and covering for Ben did explain Norma's strange reluctance to tell them about her fight with Zoila. Norma would do anything for Ben—even go to jail. But what she couldn't figure was *why* Ben would kill Zoila. "Besides, I'm sure we can prove Ben couldn't have done it through his alibi at the hospice house."

"*If* he went there before he disappeared."

Claire tapped her foot under the table. Leave it to Dom to stick to the facts instead of taking the personalities into consideration. She was about to come out with a sarcastic reply when Velma showed up at her elbow, her blue eyes alive with excitement and an order pad and pencil in her hand.

"It's lovely to see you folks." She winked at them, then bent closer to the table, which didn't really bring her much closer considering her normal posture was at almost a ninety degree angle. She lowered her voice to just above a whisper. "How is the investigation going? Are you guys trying to clear Norma?"

Claire nodded. "Have you heard anything?"

Velma looked around to make sure no one was listening, then she shook her head. "I'm afraid not. Zambuco's in the dining room and he's pretty close-mouthed about the case."

Claire sighed. Had Zambuco coincidentally stopped in for lunch, or was Dom right in thinking the detective had been following them? Either way, the last thing she needed was Zambuco wandering over and interrupting them.

"Anyway, would you like to order?" Velma asked. "We're having a special on the haddock sandwiches today, but there's no Jonah crab soup because Ben didn't bring us any crabs today like he usually does."

Claire caught Dom's eye over their menus.

"Did you say Ben brings you live crabs?" Dom asked.

"Oh yes, every other day." Velma's snow-white bun bobbed up and down on her head as she nodded, then her face creased with concern. "But he hasn't been here in three days now."

"And he gets them from the island?" Dom persisted.

"Yes, there's only one spot you can get them here, you know."

"We know."

Velma stared at them expectantly and it took Claire a few minutes to realize she was waiting for their order. Claire's mind was too busy considering the ramifications of what she'd just heard.

"I'll take the house salad with oil and vinegar." Claire handed her menu over to Velma before she changed her mind and veered off track of her healthy eating regimen.

"And I'll have the meatball sandwich." Dom handed his menu over, too.

"Be back in a jiff." Velma turned on her heel and scurried off.

"This does not look good at all." Dom patted down his eyebrows while he stared out into the ocean.

"I know, but lots of people could go to that section of the island. The crab shells in the footprint don't mean much on their own ... Oh, that reminds me." Claire dug in her pocket for her cell phone. Lifting it up, she squinted at the display, wishing she'd brought her half-moon reading glasses. "These damn things are so hard to read in the light. Oh, there's three bars. Now let me send that text to Robby. We can't make any rash conclusions until we know the shoe size."

Claire sent the text, then looked back up to find Dom still staring out at the ocean. He was clearly deep in thought. Hopefully, not about how he was going to prove Ben was the killer.

"I think you are right," he said.

"Of course I am," Claire said. "About what?"

"The footprint. Something is wrong about it."

"That's what I thin—"

Claire was interrupted by the chirping of her phone. A text from Robby was on the screen. "The shoe size is twelve ... I don't know what size Ben takes. It was too smudged to see much of the tread. Oh, and he said the time of death was eight twenty-five."

Dom nodded, but kept silent while the waitress slid their plates onto the table. He lifted the top piece of bread to inspect the meatballs, then nodded his satisfaction when he saw they were lightly covered in sauce—just the way he liked them. "We need to find out who wears a size twelve shoe. The time of death can be very helpful."

Claire nodded as she worked on spearing a piece of lettuce, tomato and cucumber on her fork. She had it raised halfway to her lips when she sensed someone at her left elbow.

"So, you two are at it again." Zambuco stood next to the table, glaring down at them.

Claire gave him her most innocent look. "At what, Detective Zambuco?"

"You know what I'm talking about." Zambuco tapped his finger on the table. "You need to stop pestering Robby about things pertaining to the case ... like shoe sizes and time of death."

"Did you say time of death?"

Claire jumped at the voice coming from her right. Mae

Biddeford sat one table over.

When had she come in?

Claire hadn't even noticed her. And now, here she was, her chair pushed back from her table and almost halfway to Claire and Dom's.

Claire glanced uneasily at Dom and Zambuco. She didn't really want the whole restaurant to be listening to the details of their investigation.

"I don't need you butting in, too. The case details are supposed to be kept inside the department." Zambuco gave Claire a pointed look and her heart pinched. She hoped she hadn't gotten Robby into trouble. She knew his confidence in doing his job as a cop was already pretty low and she didn't want to make him feel even worse.

"I'm not butting in," Mae said indignantly. "I might have information that is pertinent to the case. But if you're not interested ..."

Mae turned and scooted her chair a half-inch back toward her own table.

"What kind of information?" Zambuco bellowed.

Mae turned back around, then scooted her chair even closer than it was before. She was practically sitting at their table now. She tilted her head back and looked up at Zambuco, who towered over them.

"As you know, I bring a few jars of my jams over to the hospice house on Wednesdays as a donation." She paused, apparently waiting for them to make some sort of recognition of her generosity.

"That's so nice of you." Claire tried not to roll her eyes at Dom.

"Yes. Well, anyway, when I was signing in yesterday, I happened to notice that Norma had signed in before me. I always glance at the list ... not that I'm nosy or anything, but one can hardly help looking at the other names when one signs in."

Dom leaned forward with interest. "And what time did she sign in?"

"Eight-fifteen," Mae said to Dom, then glanced back up at Zambuco. "So, you see, depending on the time of death, Norma might have a solid alibi."

Zambuco's eyes sparked with interest. "And she hadn't signed out?"

"No, she was still there. I peeked into Anna's room and saw her," Mae said. "The two of them had their heads bent together and were discussing something. It seemed important. Anna looked a little upset, so I didn't interrupt them."

Claire felt a ripple of hope. "So, Norma couldn't possibly have killed Zoila."

Mae's brows rose, and she brushed an imaginary piece of lint from her shoulder. "Well, I wouldn't know that, because I'm not privy to police information and I don't know the time of death."

"But if she had a solid alibi, why wouldn't she just tell the police?" Dom asked. "It would be so easy to verify."

Zambuco frowned down at Mae. "Are you sure about this? She didn't mention it."

"Sure as I'm sitting here. And there was another strange thing I noticed when I was there," Mae said eagerly.

"What's that? Another person on the list with an alibi?" Zambuco asked.

"Well, it wasn't so much anyone that was on the sign-in list, it was someone who was missing from the list."

"Missing? I don't understand."

"Well, there's someone who is always on there every Wednesday. Signs in two lines above me ... and yesterday, that name wasn't there."

"Well, who is it?" Claire asked impatiently, her stomach sinking as she feared she already knew the answer.

"Ben Campbell."

Chapter Nineteen

Claire flew down the steps of the *Gull View Inn* behind Zambuco.
"I hope you're not going to do what I think you're going to do," she yelled at his back.
"I thought you'd be happy. I'm going to let Norma Hopper out," he shouted over his shoulder.
"I am happy about that. But you can't be serious about suspecting Ben Campbell."
Zambuco whirled on her, causing her to pull up short. He scowled down at her, his gray eyebrows puckering over beady, black eyes. "Why not?"
"I just know he couldn't have done it."
"Listen. I know about your psych degree. I know you're well respected in the field, but I also know that you're friends with Ben. I think your friendship is clouding your judgment, and right now I need to follow the evidence."
Claire's brow furrowed. She wondered what, exactly, Zambuco had for evidence. "What evidence?"
Zambuco held up his large hand, ticking off the items on his cigar-like fingers. "Ben was seen riding away from Zoila's in an agitated state. Norma is covering for someone, and everyone knows Ben is like a son to her. The footprint near the body had Jonah crab shells and I just found out I can't get my favorite crab soup here because Ben hasn't delivered the crabs, so I know he frequents the spot that has those crabs. Ben was seen fleeing the zen garden the morning of Zoila's murder. Ben didn't show up at the hospice center to visit his mother that morning and, according to what a little birdie told me, no one has seen him since."
Claire's stomach sank. How did Zambuco know all that?

Maybe he had been following them and questioning the same people, or maybe he was a competent detective in his own right. Either way, it didn't matter. He had a point. There was a lot of evidence against Ben.

"If that's not enough evidence to satisfy you, I don't know what to tell you." Zambuco turned and strode toward his car. "Now, if you'll excuse me, I have a new suspect to search for."

Claire slapped her arms against her sides in frustration as Zambuco slammed the car door and sped off. She felt someone beside her and turned to see Dom. "We can't let him arrest Ben."

"He probably won't be able to find him," Dom said wryly.

"What do we do now?"

"Well, if you're done with your lunch, I think we need to go find Ben and talk to him before Zambuco does. I'm not convinced he is the killer, either, and I'm not sure Zambuco will question him properly, given Ben's handicap."

Claire signed. "Great idea. You have any idea where we can find him?"

"No. But we should start where we always start. At his home."

"At Anna and Ben's place? I'm sure Sarah and Shane already looked there."

"Right, but with our trained eyes, we may be able to pick out a clue they missed."

Claire nodded. Dom was right. They had to start somewhere and it might as well be Ben's house.

***

Anna and Ben lived in a small, but meticulously cared for, home. Anna had updated the old cottage with vinyl shingles and new windows. Claire hadn't been there since Anna had been moved to the hospice facility on the mainland, but she was glad to see that Ben had kept it up. He'd even kept the plants in Anna's extensive garden trimmed.

Claire felt a pang of sadness as she looked over the

garden. She'd heard from Norma that Ben probably wouldn't be able to keep up the payments on the house once Anna died and she hated to think of how losing the only home he'd ever known so soon after losing his mother would affect him.

Then again, if Zambuco had his way, Ben had bigger problems ahead of him. Claire brushed past the smooth winterberry holly plant and remembered how Porch Cat had brought a leaf to her patio.

Had the cat been trying to tell her something?

No, that was too crazy. She was starting to grasp at straws—best to stick to the clues at hand.

A trio of colorful pansies in clay pots stood on the front steps and Dom stuck his finger into one of the pots. "This dirt is moist. Someone has been here within the last thirty hours."

Claire nodded. She knew plants in pots dried out quickly and there had been no rain.

"Maybe Ben has been here the whole time. Hiding out in his house," she suggested.

"Why would he hide in the house if he wasn't guilty of something?"

Good question. Claire considered it, then thought of an answer. "Maybe something scared him enough to make him hide."

Dom rapped loudly on the door. "Ben! Are you in there? We just want to talk."

No answer.

Claire looked in the window beside the door. She couldn't detect any movement. "Ben, it's Claire. We can help you."

No answer.

"He may have been here earlier, but I don't think he's here now," Dom said as he peered in one of the windows. "It doesn't look like he left in a hurry. Everything is in its place."

Claire looked in beside him, craning her neck to see as far to each side as she could.

"Yeah, you'd think there would be some sort of mess if he left in a hurry. I wonder where he could be." Her heart clenched at the thought of Ben out there alone somewhere. The thought of him lonely and scared made her feel even worse as she looked at the pictures of a happy Ben, his shock of blond hair swooped over his forehead, the wide smile he always seemed to wear accentuating the dimple on his chin. "Look at how happy he is in the pictures. He was like that all the time, but now ..."

Dom squinted at the pictures and made a funny sound.

"What?" Claire asked.

Dom had that nagging feeling of something important in the back of his mind but he just couldn't pull it up. In his younger days, that never would have happened ... but now that he was near seventy, he found it happening more and more. "Oh, nothing. I just had a familiar feeling is all."

"You mean like deja vu?"

"Sort of, but it's not anything that will help us find a clue."

"That's too bad, because I feel like there has to be something here that will help us figure this whole thing out. We just need to take the time to find it."

"Too bad time just ran out." Dom nodded in the direction of the road and Claire turned, her stomach swooping as she saw the Mooseamuck Island police car pull in with Robby at the wheel and Zambuco riding shotgun. Zambuco folded himself out of the passenger seat and walked over to them.

"Well, fancy meeting you two here." Zambuco looked around the yard, then frowned down at Claire. "I thought I told you to stop butting in."

"We were just looking for Ben." Claire fisted her hands on her hips.

Robby shot her a warning glance over the hood of the car and Claire relaxed a little. No sense in getting into it with Zambuco. She knew by the look on Robby's face that she was pushing her luck.

"Did you find him?" Zambuco asked.

"No."

"Yeah. I doubt he's here." Zambuco walked over to the side of the house and looked into the back yard. "I have a warrant that gives me permission to search the premises.

I'm going to start in the tool shed because breaking into the house is messy."

He jerked his head toward Robby and they all marched toward the back of the house. Robby and Zambuco snapped on white latex gloves. Claire felt her nerves prickling as they walked past Anna's prize rose bushes, then the empty space where she usually planted her vegetable garden and finally stopping at the shed with its row of tiger lilies lining the front, their tall stalks waiting for summer buds to bloom.

The shed door squealed as Robby slid it open and they all looked in. It was crammed full of gardening gear and various outdoor supplies. A snowblower sat in one corner, a giant wheelbarrow beside it.

"Let's go in, Skinner." Zambuco looked back over his shoulder at Claire and Dom. "You two stay out here. And don't touch anything."

Robby stepped in and Zambuco went in after him, tripping over the threshold and stepping on a shovel, then turning and stumbling over a pile of rakes that were leaning against the wall.

Dom watched him fumble with the rakes, amazed at how many kinds of rakes it takes to run a garden. There were old, rusty rakes, newer rakes with plastic tines, rakes with wooden handles, metal handles and even one with a fancy gold and maroon handle.

Zambuco reached in and pulled out one particular rake with a long, wooden handle and sharp metal tines at the end. He held up the tines and Dom's eyes widened as he noticed the rusty-colored stains on them—they were looking at Zoila's murder weapon.

Zambuco's face was grim as he came out of the shed, the rake held out away from his body in his glove-clad hand. "I guess we need to step up our search for Ben Campbell. He's no longer just a person of interest ... he's now a murder suspect."

Chapter Twenty

Zambuco left in a hurry, sending Claire and Dom on their way with a warning not to interfere in the search for Ben. Since neither of them had any idea where to start looking, they'd decided to split up and take a break until an idea presented itself.

Claire thought Norma might know where Ben was, but she was nowhere to be found, either.

Was Norma out looking for Ben?

Claire wanted to be looking, too, but it was late afternoon and her brain was getting foggy. The turn of events had stunned her and she needed a large cup of green tea to clear her thinking.

She stood at the sink overlooking her garden and the Atlantic Ocean beyond. The view from her spot on the hill was breathtaking, but Claire couldn't enjoy it. Ben's freedom was at stake and she just knew there was some other explanation for the rake being in his shed.

She set the teapot on the stove, grabbed some flax seed oil from the fridge, then took out a bottle of apple cider vinegar and two shot glasses from the cupboard. She poured apple cider vinegar into one glass and flax seed oil into the other.

Picking up the apple cider vinegar glass, she threw her head back and tossed the vile, caustic liquid down her throat. Coughing and sputtering, she reached for the flax seed oil to chase it with. It was noxious, but helped smooth out the acidity of the vinegar.

The healthy concoction left a nasty taste in her mouth, and Claire knew just what could fix it. Dark chocolate. Now, if she could just remember where she'd hidden it.

She rummaged through several drawers, her chest

tightening as she came up empty. It was disturbing that she couldn't remember where she'd hidden them. Forty years ago, her mind was like a steel trap. Now? Not so much. Good thing she was diligent about her health regimen. She intended to remain healthy and active well into her nineties. Hopefully, that would help her mind stay healthy and active, too.

The tea kettle whistled and she reached into the cabinet where she kept the green tea, her spirits rising as her fingers curled around a thin square of dark chocolate.

"Aha! I remember now." She unwrapped the chocolate, popped it into her mouth, put a tea bag into her mug and then poured the boiling water over it.

Relishing the silky texture of the bittersweet chocolate melting in her mouth, Claire stepped out into her garden, her hand curled around the mug of steeping tea.

She walked down the garden path toward the edge of her property, as if drawn toward the sea. From the edge, she looked down at Crab Cove.

Was Zambuco down there talking to the fishermen?

She thought it was likely—he was probably trying to find out if Ben left the island after Zoila's murder.

Which made Claire wonder ... had Ben left the island, or was he safe somewhere? He would turn to either Sarah or Norma for help. Sarah denied knowing where Ben was and Claire believed her, which left Norma.

Norma had been in jail, but what if Ben had turned to her before she'd been jailed?

Claire wandered through her garden, pinching a dead bloom here and plucking a dead leaf there, her mind whirling with questions about the case.

Why hadn't Norma told the truth? She must have known she would have an alibi at the hospice house, but she'd let herself be jailed rather than tell anyone what her and Zoila had argued about or that she'd gone to visit Anna.

Did the murder have something to do with Anna?

If Ben wasn't the killer, then how did the murder weapon get in his shed?

Claire sipped her tea and looked out over the railing, feeling like a failure. She *used* to be able to solve these cases easily but she was much older now and out of practice. Still, this case was more important than any others because it involved her friends. Her fists tightened around the railing in frustration.

Down below, she could see Dom sitting on the bench that overlooked Long Sands Beach and wondered if he felt the same way she did. Were they too old to solve cases effectively?

Claire didn't think so. Her mind still worked pretty good. Even now, it was going over the facts and sifting through the different personalities, trying to find inconsistencies that could help her solve the case.

There was one discrepancy that niggled at her.

Why would Shane lie about the time he was at Zoila's the day before her murder?

Kenneth had said he'd seen Shane there at one o'clock, but Shane was pretty specific that he wasn't there until after three.

"Meow!"

Claire looked down to see Porch Cat weaving her way through the garden, her eyes slitted against the bright sunlight.

"Hi, kitty. I don't have anything for you today." Claire made a mental note to pick up some cat treats next time she was in town.

She watched the cat rub her face against the trellis where she was growing a border of Imposter roses. This was her first year trying the pink flowers that looked like a clematis, but were actually a rose that would bloom all summer long. Several buds had formed on the plant during the last week and Claire was anxious to see them bloom.

Porch Cat sniffed at the plant, then reached out a paw and touched one of the buds as if she were trying to figure out if it was a rose or a clematis.

"Fools you, doesn't it?" Claire sipped her tea and marveled at the plant. She never ceased to be amazed by nature, which fooled you into thinking things were one way when they were actually another.

She reached down to pet the cat, who was purring at her

ankles. "In the garden, just like in life, things aren't always what they seem."

And then Claire realized what had been bothering her about Shane's lie. She ran into the house, tossed her mug into the sink, grabbed her car keys and rushed out the door.

She had to talk to Dom right away. They'd made a terrible mistake. They'd taken the evidence at face value and thought things were one way, when that really wasn't the case at all. And now, because of it, Zambuco was about to arrest the wrong person.

Chapter Twenty-One

Dom bit into the bocconotti cookie as he watched the waves lap at the beach. The confection, baked fresh this morning in the north end of Boston and delivered on the afternoon ferry, was lightly dusted in powdered sugar and bursting with strawberry jam. He barely tasted it, though. His mind was too busy trying to figure out where they'd gone wrong in solving the case.

Something didn't add up, but for the life of him, he couldn't figure out what it was. Maybe he really was losing his touch. He hadn't investigated a murder case in many years, and as much as he hated to admit it, he was getting older. But that was on the outside—on the inside, he still felt young and this case had rekindled his enthusiasm and made him feel alive for the first time since Sophia's death.

There were still so many unanswered questions.

Why would Shane lie about the time he was at Zoila's?

Who else was at the zen garden that morning? Was it the real killer who dropped the *Chowders* bag?

Why didn't Kenneth take the family pictures from Zoila's?

What was on that old paper Zoila was arguing with Norma over?

What was Norma hiding, or who was she protecting?

Was the sketch of Zoila's cabin a clue?

Dom was sure something happened the morning of Zoila's death that made it urgent for the killer to silence her, because otherwise it would have been much smarter to kill her in her remote cabin. The killer had taken a big chance doing it in the public garden.

Zoila had a paper in her hand when she'd argued with Norma that morning. It must have something to do with the paper, but what would be so important that someone would kill Zoila and Norma wouldn't say a thing about it?

And if Norma knew whatever it was that got Zoila killed, would the killer go after Norma next?

He pulled another cookie out of the bag as he continued to contemplate the case. He had to admit, the clues did seem to point to Ben.

Ben was seen rushing away from the murder scene on his bike.

The white bag from *Chowders* had been dropped in the area.

Ben had previously visited Zoila.

Norma had visited Ben's mother that morning and was now protecting someone with her silence.

Ben frequented the one spot on the island where you could find Jonah crab.

... And now Ben was missing.

But his instincts told him something about those clues were not as they seemed. Claire was adamant that Ben wasn't capable of murder and he trusted her judgment.

Dom watched a sandpiper scurrying along the water line, pecking at the sand on the very edge of the water, then scurrying back as each wave approached.

Dom watched as the bird darted forward, leaving little forked footprints in the sand, then scurried back, the wave erasing the footprints he'd just left.

Over and over, he darted forward along the shore and over and over, the waves drove him back and erased his footprints.

Dom admired his persistence ... and then Dom's eyebrows tingled electrically—he knew what had been bothering him all this time!

He jumped up from the bench. Shoving the bag of cookies in his pocket, he sprinted to his car for his cell phone. He had to contact Claire—they'd made a grave error in judgment and he hoped they could make up for it before it was too late!

***

Dom was almost to his car when Claire whipped into the parking lot, screeching to a stop beside him.

"I think I've figured part of it out—Shane wasn't the one who lied about what time he was at Zoila's, it was Kenneth!" Claire said excitedly. "I think he's trying to frame Ben."

Dom nodded. "Ben didn't do it and the footprint proves that."

"It does? But the footprint had the crab shells embedded in it."

"Precisely. Something's bothered me about that footprint all along and I just realized what it was. Zoila was killed violently, so there would have been a struggle, yet there was only one footprint there."

"So?"

"Don't you see, there would have been many footprints. The killer must have raked the sand to get rid of the footprints he made so they couldn't be used as evidence."

"And then Ben came along after and saw Zoila already dead! That's why he's disappeared ... he must have run off scared."

"We need to get in touch with Zambuco. Those crab shells in the footprint prove that Ben isn't the killer and I think the rake was planted in his shed. When Zambuco found the pile of rakes, I recognized one handle ... I didn't realize it at the time, but one of the handles matches the equipment I saw in Kenneth's barn."

"And if all that's true, my theory about Kenneth lying about the time they were at Zoila's instead of Shane being the one who lied makes sense. Kenneth knew Ben delivered lunches between noon and two, so he had to say he was there during that time frame in order to claim he'd seen Ben there. Ben never was at Zoila's that day."

"And Shane told the truth." Dom pressed his lips together, remembering the sand he'd felt under his feet at the counter that day. "The morning Zoila was killed, Kenneth came to the counter and then Shane came in after him. I felt sand under my feet when I went up and assumed it was from Shane ... but given what we know now, I think the sand might have been from Kenneth, who was standing there *before* Shane."

"So Kenneth killed Zoila?" Claire asked. "But why? And why frame Ben *and* how does Norma fit into this?"

Dom's face turned grim. "I couldn't figure that out, either, but I might have an idea as to why ... and if my theory is correct, Ben is in grave danger."

Chapter Twenty-Two

Claire desperately tried to get her cell phone to show some bars as they rushed to the point.

Where was Zambuco when they needed him?

Unfortunately, the detective was no longer following them around town. Dom and Claire were on their own.

To make matters worse, a thunderstorm was rolling in. Dark, gray clouds hung over the ocean adding a menacing feel, and the air felt alive with humid electricity. It was early dusk, but the clouds had made it darker than normal. Naturally, the lights were off in the Barrett mansion and just when Claire thought the scene couldn't get any more cliche, the sky lit up and a boom of thunder split the air just as they skidded to a stop in the circular driveway.

Fat drops of rain splattered on the car as they jumped out.

"The barn." Dom pointed toward the barn where a slice of yellow light spilled out from underneath the door and they made their way over quietly.

Claire's heart pounded as they stopped outside the door. Dom put his finger up to his lips to indicate silence and Claire rolled her eyes. After a career of consulting with the police, she knew enough to be quiet.

Voices wafted out from inside and she leaned forward to hear what they were saying while the rain drops soaked her hair and ran down her neck.

"Just write it on the paper and I won't hurt you." Claire cringed at the menacing tone in Kenneth's voice.

"But I didn't kill her." Ben's voice, trusting and innocent. Claire glanced at Dom, who was preening his eyebrows as he edged his way around the door trying to get inside.

Claire felt anger flood her chest. Kenneth was trying to

frame Ben for Zoila's murder. He'd make a good scapegoat, too—his simple nature allowed him to be easily manipulated and he wasn't equipped to defend himself.

But she still couldn't figure out one thing ... why had Kenneth killed Zoila in the first place?

"Kenny, I'm hungry." The pleading tone in Ben's voice speared Claire's heart and she bit her lip to keep quiet. She shuffled to the right, hiding behind a stack of boxes just inside the door so she could get a better look at what was going on.

Ben sat in the middle of the barn, his legs and torso tied to a metal chair. He had a pen and a piece of paper in his hand. Kenneth loomed over him, his back to Claire.

"Listen, you little jerk, just write the letter and I'll get you a pizza."

"But I didn't do it. I can't lie!"

Kenneth kicked the chair.

Ben cried out.

The lights flickered.

A deafening clap of thunder caused Claire to jump, dislodging the boxes which clattered to the floor.

Kenneth whirled around in her direction.

Claire's heart froze. She was caught.

Claire was unable to move. She realized she'd made a big mistake. She didn't have the power of an armed police team behind her like in the old days. All she had was Dom ... and he didn't even have a gun.

Too bad Kenneth *did* have one, and he was pointing it at her right now.

"You!" Kenneth sneered. "I should have taken care of you when you were here before. But I'll just have to get rid of you now. Looks like Ben might have to kill you, too."

Claire's heart started up again. Kenneth was focusing on her, which meant he hadn't spotted Dom.

Was Dom still hidden outside the door?

She didn't dare look in that direction, afraid Kenneth might catch on that someone else was there if she did. Without a gun, she didn't know how helpful Dom would be, but at least he could run for the car and drive to the police.

Cozy Mystery Collection 465

"What are you talking about, Kenny? I didn't kill Claire—she's right here." Ben turned trusting eyes on Claire and her heart pinched.

Kenneth snorted. "I might have to change your note. You killed Zoila and Claire found out and confronted you, then you had to kill her, too. The guilt was too much so you killed yourself."

"No." Ben shook his head. "I did not hurt Zoila. I saw her lying in the garden."

"It's okay, Ben," Claire soothed, partly because her heart ached for Ben and partly because she knew her best chance of escape was to keep Kenneth talking while Dom ran for help. "We know you didn't hurt Zoila. Kenneth did."

Ben scrunched up his face and turned to Kenneth. "Why?"

"Yeah. Why *did* you kill Zoila?" Claire echoed.

"You and your great detective friend, Benedetti, couldn't figure it out?"

Claire crossed her arms over her chest. "Well, we figured out it was you ..."

"Yeah. You see, I had to stop her. I couldn't give half my fortune to him." Kenneth jerked his head toward Ben.

"Half your fortune? What are you—?" Claire looked from Kenneth to Ben and then to Kenneth again. Her mouth dropped open when realization dawned on her.

She remembered Dom's feeling of deja-vu when they were at Ben's house, and now she knew what it was even if Dom hadn't recognized it himself. Ben and Kenneth bore an uncanny resemblance to each other, right down to the cleft chin which Claire knew was a genetic trait ... one that Silas Barrett also had.

Kenneth and Ben were half-brothers.

Chapter Twenty-Three

"Zoila found out you were brothers," Claire said softly.

Kenneth looked at Ben with contempt. "*Half*-brothers. Dear old Daddy couldn't be faithful."

"And Zoila was going to tell."

"That's right," Kenneth said. "Like most of the sappy islanders here, she had a soft spot for Ben and thought he should get a cut of the Barrett fortune. She had proof in Daddy's own hand that he wanted it that way, and she said she'd give me one day to tell Ben myself and or she was going to tell him. She had a meeting with Ben that morning at the zen garden, but I got there first."

"That's the paper that she and Norma were arguing about," Claire said.

"Norma?"

"Yes, they argued right before she died. That's why Zambuco arrested her."

"Arrested her?" Kenneth's face crumbled. "But that means that Norma knows..."

"That's right." Claire saw her chance and decided to take advantage of her psych skills to try to persuade Kenneth into giving up. "Norma knows and Dom knows, too, so it won't do you any good to kill me and Ben. It's better to give yourself up now and I'll help persuade the judge to go lenient on you."

Another clap of thunder, and Claire almost peed her pants as she watched Kenneth's gun wave around in his hand. His eyes had taken on a glazed look and were darting from her to Ben.

"I won't give up! No one will believe Norma, she's too crotchety. And I'll have to make sure that old washed up detective, Benedetti, meets with an accident."

Kenneth advanced toward Claire and brought his gun level with her forehead. She heard the click of the safety and she felt like a stone was lodged in her throat as she wracked her brain for something to say to persuade him to give her the gun.

She opened her mouth to speak but was silenced by another clap of thunder. The sound of a gunshot rang in her ears.

And then the lights went out.

***

Dom burst through the door just as the lights went out. He didn't know if Claire had been hit or not, but his old cop instincts kicked in and he launched himself in the direction of Kenneth without even thinking twice. As he flew through the air toward the gunman, he vaguely remembered that he didn't have a Kevlar vest on, but he wasn't concerned with his own safety. There were two people in danger in there and he had to do what he could to keep them safe.

The lights flickered on again just as Dom crashed into Kenneth, sending them both to the floor amidst the sharp report of another gunshot.

Out of the corner of his eye, he saw Claire rushing toward them. She kicked out at Kenneth, trying to dislodge the gun but to no avail.

"Let go, old man!" Kenneth yelled as he brought his knee up hard into Dom's stomach.

Dom grunted in pain, but managed to keep his grip on the hand with the gun. Claire kicked out again, this time connecting with Dom in a fatal mistake that caused him to loosen his hold.

Kenneth rolled away and sprang to his feet, waving his gun between Claire and Dom.

"Killing you two is going to be fun." Kenneth jerked the gun toward the middle of the barn where Ben was tied up. "Get over by Ben. That way, I can take care of the three of —"

"*Meow!*" A bundle of black and brown fur came flying

down from the loft, landing on Kenneth's arm with all claws extended. Kenneth waved his hand to dislodge the cat, losing his grip on the gun that landed in the corner with a clatter.

Claire ran for the gun.

Dom ran for Kenneth, plowing into him like a linebacker. They rolled around on the floor again. This time, Dom had the advantage over Kenneth, whose cat-scratched arm slowed him down.

Dom managed to get Kenneth over onto his stomach and, with his knee on his back, he jerked his arms behind him.

Claire rushed over, the gun safe in her hand.

"Ben, are you okay?" Claire asked. Dom managed to look over to see Ben smiling down at Porch Cat, who was curled in his lap licking her paws leisurely. Before Dom turned away, the cat turned her bright green eyes on him and he could have sworn she winked.

Dom shoved his knee harder into Kenneth's back.

"Not so bad for an old washed up detective, eh?" Dom's chest swelled with pride. He wasn't too old to chase bad guys after all.

Kenneth didn't have time to answer because just then, the barn door burst open and a voice yelled:

"Hands up in the air and don't move!"

***

"Robby, what are you doing here?" Claire was surprised to see her nephew standing alone in the doorway. Surprised that he'd known they were there *and* that he'd had the guts to bust in on his own after hearing the shots. She knew he'd never been in a situation this dangerous before and the look on his face alternated between pride and terror as he took in the situation.

"What's going on here?" Robby asked, his eyes darting from Claire to Ben to Kenneth and Dom on the ground.

"Kenneth kidnapped Ben ... he was the killer all along," Claire blurted out.

Robby's eyes widened. "He killed Zoila? But why?"

Claire explained how Zoila had discovered the relation between Kenneth and Ben and was going to tell everyone. "Apparently, Kenneth didn't want Ben to get any of the Barrett money."

Robby scowled down at Kenneth. "I never did like him. Is everyone okay?"

"I could use a little help with the bad guy," Dom said from his position on the floor, where he was still holding Kenneth down.

"Right. Of course." Robby hurriedly holstered his gun and took a set of handcuffs off his belt, then knelt down and snapped them on Kenneth's wrists. Dom stood up and Claire noticed his leg was oozing with sticky, red blood.

"You've been shot!" Claire pointed to Dom's leg and they all turned to look.

Dom looked down, then back up at them, a sheepish grin spreading on his face.

"That's not blood," He pulled out a bakery bag from of his pocket—the outside was stained with red goo. "It's my bocconottis. They must have gotten squished in the scuffle."

"Can you guys untie me?" Ben asked in a small voice, and Claire ran over and started loosening the ropes while Robby pulled the now docile Kenneth to his feet.

"Kenny did something bad? Are you arresting him?" Ben stood up shakily and lowered Porch Cat gently to the floor. The cat strolled over to Dom and licked a blob of jelly that was on his pants, then turned her back to him and strolled off.

"I'm afraid so," Claire said, then turned to Robby. "How did you know we were in here?"

"I knew Ben wasn't a murderer and I figured you two knew more about what was really going on than anyone else, so I took a play out of Zambuco's book and followed you."

"Well, you got here just in time." Dom glanced over at Claire. "I don't know if we could have pulled off the capture if it wasn't for you."

Robby's face turned red. "Well, it looked like you had things pretty much tied up when I got here. I didn't do much."

"Oh, that's not true," Dom said graciously. "You played a critical role. Isn't that right, Claire?"

"Yep, we were struggling ... you came in just at the right time," Claire said earnestly.

"Well ... if you guys say so." Robby straightened with obvious pride and Claire shot Dom a grateful look. Capturing Kenny would do wonders for Robby's self-esteem and who knew, maybe he'd even share clues in the future without her having to bribe him with baked goods.

"I gotta secure the prisoner in my police car and call this in." Robby nodded at them and propelled Kenneth out the door.

Ben followed quickly behind them, asking Robby if he could ride in the police car, too.

Claire and Dom trailed at a more leisurely pace. Claire noticed the rain had stopped as they stepped outside. Thunder roiled in the distance but softer now, not the loud claps they'd heard when the storm was overhead. Robby already had Kenneth in the back of the car and could be heard on the police radio.

"That's right, you can call off the search for Ben Campbell—I have him with me. But he's not the murderer. Kenneth Barrett is and I've captured him, too."

Claire heard something crackle across the radio, then Robby's voice again:

"By myself. Well, almost ... I had two civilians help ... Yes, *those* two civilians ..."

Claire and Dom exchanged raised-brow looks. Robby must have been talking to Zambuco, and Claire figured he'd guess it was her and Dom. They walked past Robby toward her car.

"We don't need to take the credit for this one, right?" Claire asked.

"Of course not. We've had plenty of credit in our day. Now, we do it just for fun." Dom reached into the bakery bag and pulled out a smooshed cookie. "You want a bocconotti?"

The squished thing oozing red goo in Dom's hand looked more like some sort of amputated body part than a cookie.

Claire didn't find it the least bit appetizing—and anyway, sugar wasn't part of her health regimen.

"No, thanks." Claire glanced back at the barn. "I'm glad you busted in like that and saved us, but that was dangerous. Why didn't you just take off in the car and go to the police station."

Dom's face was thoughtful as he chewed his cookie. He swallowed, then shrugged. "I never even considered driving away in the car. I guess my police training kicked in. This old dog still has some tricks in him."

Claire smiled. She was glad to see *she* still had some tricks in her, too. "We did pretty good working together."

Dom nodded and held his knuckles out for a fist tap. "It feels good to be useful even if we are a bit rusty."

"Yeah, I'm glad we still have our skills. Too bad we won't get a chance to use them again any time soon."

Dom's face fell with disappointment. "Why not?"

"Until this week, there hadn't been a murder on Mooseamuck Island in over a hundred years. What are the odds another one will happen any time soon?"

Dom glanced up at the clearing sky, then smoothed his bushy eyebrows. He thought for a few seconds, then looked back at Claire with twinkling eyes.

"It's hard to say, but with no murders in the past hundred years, perhaps Mooseamuck Island is due for a few more."

Chapter Twenty-Four

"And Dom burst in and saved everyone?" Mae asked, looking at Dom with a level of admiration that made him extremely uncomfortable.

"Oh, no, I just tried to subdue Kenneth until Robby got there. Robby's the one who saved us," Dom replied graciously. He was happy to give Robby the credit and fend off Mae's unwanted attention, especially since he noticed Tom Landry frowning at the way Mae was looking at him.

"Well, I didn't really do anything …" Robby stammered.

"Oh, yes, you did," Claire cut in. "You figured out who the real killer was and that something was going on at the point. Why, if you hadn't come in when you did, there's no telling what might have happened."

"What about Zambuco?" Jane craned her neck, looking around the diner. "Did he just take off into the wild blue yonder?"

Robby nodded. "He took Kenneth back to the jail on the mainland."

"Well, you showed him us islanders don't need any help from the mainland police," Tom said.

"I don't know about that." Robby lowered his voice. "He did put me in for a commendation, but I don't think we've seen the last of him."

Robby blushed as Sarah put a mug of coffee down in front of him. "That's on the house, Officer Skinner."

Sarah shot Claire and Dom a knowing look as she walked away. They'd never figured out what her secret was, but had promised they wouldn't let on they knew she had one. Claire thought that was just as well. It had nothing to do with Zoila's murder and Sarah deserved her privacy.

Besides, she'd probably come to Moosamuck Island to get away from whatever it was that was such a secret, and it was no one's business but Sarah's. Claire watched Sarah and Shane exchange special smiles as Sarah made her way back behind the counter and her heart lifted. She hoped whatever had plagued Sarah in her previous life was well behind her now.

"I still don't understand why you didn't say something, Norma." Jane turned to Norma, who sat at the end of the table, her floppy hat casting a shadow onto her plate of Maine blueberry pancakes

"Well, you wouldn't," Norma said gruffly. "You young people don't understand things like loyalty. I gave Anna my word all those years ago, and I ain't be going breaking it now."

"Even though you ended up in jail?" Lucy asked.

Norma snorted. "Jail doesn't scare me. The food's actually pretty good, you know. But if I'd known Kenneth would kidnap Ben, I might have said something. When I got out of jail, I knew Ben was missing and I looked everywhere for him. I just thought he was hiding. It never occurred to me Kenneth might try to kill him."

"So Anna never wanted Ben to get any money from Silas?" Mae asked. "Seems like she would have wanted that for him. I mean, the Barrett's have a bundle."

Norma's eyes took on a faraway look. "Anna's judgment was clouded when it came to Silas Barrett. He was a good guy when we were young. He and Anna were head over heels. But when his father died and he took over the Barrett family fortune, he changed into a hard, angry man. He would hardly give us the time of day, anymore. I guess he thought we were beneath him.

"Anna had one indiscretion with him after that and the result was Ben. But she never told Silas Ben was his son. I'm not sure how Silas found out, but Anna didn't want anything to do with him and she didn't want Ben soiled by his money. She was afraid Ben would end up a spoiled brat, like Kenneth."

"Will Ben get all of it now?" Mae asked.

"With Kenneth in jail, he'll be in charge of the estate. I

hired some smarty pants financial folks from the mainland to help him," Norma said. "At least he won't hurt for money, which should actually give Anna some comfort. And being the same sweet old Ben, he's putting a lot of money into Kenneth's defense. He said that Kenneth is his family now and family does what it can to help out family."

"So it looks like Anna's worries over money changing Ben were for nothing." Claire sipped her red rooibos tea. "I just hope Kenneth appreciates what Ben is doing and treats him like a real brother."

"Just how did you figure out they *were* brothers?" Tom asked.

"It took a while for my old noggin to process the clues," Dom said. "But then they all came together. In the end, it was really one thing that stood out. Zoila had called Kenneth out to the cabin to give him some old family photos and paintings she'd discovered in the cabin. But Kenneth didn't take them. When Claire and I went out to investigate the cabin, we found them in the shed. The paper backing of one of them was split and it didn't dawn on me until later that people used to hide important documents behind pictures like that. I guess Silas must have had something documenting Ben's parentage and Zoila stumbled across it when she was handling the picture."

"That's right," Norma mumbled around a mouthful of pancake. "I guess old Silas had some sort of proof and a codicil to his will. I'm not sure why he had it hidden in the picture, but my guess is he was waiting for the right time to drop the bomb on Kenneth. Or maybe he wasn't even sure *if* he wanted to make it public at all. If you remember, he died suddenly and I guess he never got a chance to show it to anyone."

"And Zoila thought it should be made public ... or was she blackmailing Kenneth?" Mae asked slyly.

"Oh, no. She thought Ben should get his share. In fact, she tried to get me to help her persuade Kenneth to tell Ben himself." Norma looked at Claire. "That's what you saw us arguing about that morning."

"In the jail when you were sketching Zoilas cabin, were

you trying to give us a clue?" Dom asked.

"Maybe." Norma looked at Dom with a twinkle in her eye. "I figured you'd be too dense to catch on, though."

"But we *did* catch on. Sort of. We did go to the cabin, which led to Dom figuring it out," Claire said. "Well that and a few other clues."

"Oh, what were they?" Jane asked.

"One thing that really stuck with me was that we thought Shane had lied about the time he visited Zoila the day before the murder. We couldn't figure out why," Claire replied. "And then we realized that wasn't the case at all. It was *Kenneth* who had lied."

Jane's brow creased. "Why would he do that?"

"He wanted to place Ben at Zoila's that day so we'd think they had some kind of argument. He knew Ben only delivered food between noon and two, so he had to lie and say he was there during that time."

"He sure did a lot of planning to frame Ben," Tom said.

"He did," Dom agreed. "He planted the murder weapon in Ben's shed, too. Except he made another mistake there. He'd taken the zen garden rake home and hidden it among the tools in his barn right after he killed Zoila. He figured no one would notice it there and he could keep it until an opportune moment presented itself to plant it at Ben's place. Except when the time came, he didn't know which one was the rake from the zen garden. So he took all the rakes to Ben's. Claire and I were there when Zambuco pulled the murder weapon from Ben's shed. I saw the rake with the Barrett family colors in the pile and I knew something was off, but not exactly what that *something* was."

"But he wasn't going to just frame Ben for the murder," Claire added. "He was going to have Ben write up a fake confession saying he killed Zoila because she 'saw' something he didn't like in her vision, and then he planned to kill him and make it look like Ben had killed himself because he couldn't live with the guilt."

"That would solve both his problems. Once Anna died no one would be around to tell that Ben was Silas's son and even if someone did find out years later, Ben wouldn't be around to stake a claim on any of the Barrett money," Jane said.

"Yep. Kenneth had already burned the paper that Zoila found."

"But didn't Kenneth realize that Norma would have told the truth if anything happened to Ben?" Tom asked.

"He actually didn't know that Norma knew about it," Dom replied. "He was too busy implementing his plan and abducting Ben to pay attention to what was going on in town, so he had no idea Norma and Zoila had argued or even that Norma had been arrested."

"That's right,' Claire chimed in. "Zoila had asked Ben to meet her at the zen garden that morning. She'd already given Kenneth the ultimatum to tell Ben himself. She made the mistake of telling Kenneth where and when she was meeting Ben, and Kenneth got there first and killed her. Ben came along after and found her dead. He left his footprint in the sand and dropped the take-out bag from *Chowders* that Banes found in the woods as he ran away. He said he'd been taking a donut to Zoila."

"Meanwhile, Kenneth came into the diner to gather information," Dom continued. "Then he waited until he knew Ben was at home alone, brought the rake over and kidnapped Ben."

"Well, you guys certainly are brave, risking a run-in with a killer,' Mae twittered.

Dom waved his hand dismissively. "We have special training."

Claire pushed up from the table as the others kept talking. She needed some quiet time and there was a bench outside the restaurant that overlooked the cove, which was the perfect place for quiet reflection.

She curled her hand around her tea mug and sat on the bench, watching the boats sway on their moorings and listening to the seagulls' call. The smell of salt air and fried food made her lips curl in a smile. Investigating the murder had been fun, but she was glad things had quieted down.

"*Meow.*"

Claire looked down to see Porch Cat meandering through

the colorful impatiens that were planted alongside the front of the restaurant.

"Hey, kitty." Claire held out her hand and the cat came over. Claire noticed she was carrying something in her mouth.

"What do you have there?"

Porch Cat sat in front of Claire and gazed up at her. Claire noticed that in the sunlight, the cat's green eyes were loaded with gold flecks which sparkled in the sunlight.

Porch Cat flicked her tail, then bent over and spit something out on the ground.

Claire looked down to see that it was a plump, juicy blackberry, which was odd since blackberries didn't come into season for another month. She remembered how Porch Cat had spit out the smooth winterberry holly leaf from Anna's rare plant on her patio and wondered if the cat had been trying to tell her something.

Maybe she'd been trying to lead her to Anna's. And if so, was this blackberry a clue? But a clue to what? Zoila's murder had already been solved.

Claire felt a mixture of trepidation and excitement as she remembered Dom's words about Mooseamuck Island being 'due' for a few more murders. Maybe the cat was trying to tell her another murder lay just around the corner.

That's silly, Claire thought as she watched the cat disappear under the leaves of a lush rhododendron. Porch Cat was just your average Maine Coon ... she didn't have any powers of premonition and stray cats didn't go around dropping clues at your feet.

Claire settled back on the bench and took another sip of tea as she eyed the empty space where Porch Cat had been a few seconds ago. Zoila's murder investigation had taken a lot of energy and she needed to rest up and replenish her strength.

She made a mental note to beef up her health regimen. She wanted to be sure she was in top condition with lots of energy to spare ... just in case another murder investigation happened to come her way.

***

Join Leighann's mailing list and get in on the early bird specials to get her latest books at the lowest price:
http://www.leighanndobbs.com/newsletter

DEAD & BURIED

Chapter One

Morgan Blackmoore slipped out the kitchen door of the seaside mansion she shared with her sisters in the sleepy town of Noquitt, Maine. Stretching her arms over her head she closed her eyes, and took a deep breath, relishing the sting of the salty sea air and the warmth of the early morning sun on her face.

She turned east toward the Atlantic Ocean where the sun was just coming up. Her cat, Belladonna, rustled in the leaves at her feet and a group of seagulls made a cacophony of sound to her right. There seemed to be more gulls than usual this morning. Morgan opened her eyes, turning toward the sound.

Her heart skipped a beat when she saw the flock of gulls circling. There were *way* too many birds. Something must have attracted them and Morgan had a feeling it wasn't anything good.

She picked her way through her herb garden toward the edge of the cliff, Belladonna trotting along at her side, while the seagulls circled and flapped noisily above. Her stomach felt like she'd swallowed a lead ball, and her mind conjured up a scene from the old Hitchcock classic, *The Birds*, as she approached the point of land where the channel leading to the cove on the right of her house met with the ocean on the left.

Belladonna sprinted ahead of her and poked her head over the side of the cliff, then looked up at Morgan with her ice-blue eyes.

"Mew."

"What is it?" Morgan craned her neck over the side, but whatever was attracting the seagulls was hidden behind an outcropping of rock about seven feet down.

She sighed, rubbed her palms on her faded jeans and put one foot tentatively on the slope of the cliff. Unlike the ocean side of the cliff, which was a straight drop, the point was more gradual with outcroppings of rock that she could navigate on the way down.

She balanced herself by grabbing onto a rock while her foot grappled for placement. Her heart jerked wildly as she dislodged some small stones, creating a mini rockslide. Holding her breath, she watched the rocks plunge almost one hundred feet into the turbulent ocean below. If she fell, it would mean a painful and certain death.

"Meow!"

Morgan looked up at the white cat who was staring down at her. "Yeah, easy for you to say. How come you're not down here with your perfect balance and nine lives?"

Belladonna just blinked at her lazily from above, then trotted off.

"Okay, fine. I get it. I'm on my own." Morgan grabbed onto a tree that was growing sideways on the slope and inched over to the outcropping, her free arm grabbing onto the rock and pulling herself along until she was far enough to peer over.

She sucked in a breath, a jolt of electricity piercing her heart when her eyes found the object of the seagulls' attention.

Lying on the rocks was a man, his legs and neck bent at impossible angles. His dead eyes stared straight through her. His right arm was twisted underneath him. His left was visible and Morgan noticed an unusual black mark on the palm.

She jerked back, then whirled around and scrambled back up the slope, kicking loose stones that pinged against the rocks below in her wake. Pushing herself up onto the grass, she turned to run in the direction of her house at full speed. But instead of moving forward, she smacked straight into her biggest enemy.

Sheriff Overton.

* * *

"Leaving the scene of the crime?"

Overton glared down at her, his large belly bulging over the belt of his brown pants. Sweat trickled down his forehead under the brim of his hat.

Morgan pushed herself away from him and looked back in the direction of the cliff.

"What are you talking about? I saw the seagulls and went down to see why they were gathered there. It is, after all, my property."

Overton narrowed his eyes at her, the toothpick jutting out of the side of his mouth wiggled back and forth as his teeth ground on it. "Or you could have been down there covering something up."

Morgan's eyebrows knit together as she turned back to face him. She spread her hands. "What would I be covering up? And how did *you* get here before I even called the police?"

"Gordy Wright saw the body on his way out to pull his lobster traps this morning. He called it in."

Morgan looked at the channel that led to Perkins Cove where most of the fishermen docked their boats. Her house sat at the very end of the channel—the point where it emptied out into the ocean so, naturally, the boats had to sail by her house to get out. Gordy always went out at sunrise and would certainly have noticed the gulls and body on the cliff.

"It's awfully suspicious in my book that a body shows up in your yard after the whole Littlefield incident," Overton said.

Morgan crossed her arms over her chest, struggling to stay calm. "You know I had nothing to do with that."

Earlier in the summer, Overton had accused Morgan of killing the town shrew, Prudence Littlefield. It had taken some clever detective work on the part of her and her sisters to find the real killer and clear Morgan's name. Even so, it seemed Overton had it in for them and Morgan could think of no good reason why.

Which was why she had to tread carefully with this dead body on the cliff. If Overton could find a way to pin it on her or one of her sisters, she was sure he would.

A noise over by the house captured her attention and she glanced over to see her sister, Fiona, hurrying toward them, her long red curls flying behind her as she walked.

"What's going on?"

"There's a body on the cliff." Morgan nodded her chin toward the point.

Fiona gasped, her eyes growing wide. "A body? Who?"

"I don't know. I saw the seagulls and went over to investigate. Never saw him before."

Overton snorted. "We'll see about that. I doubt you girls are as innocent as you want me to believe."

Fiona took a step closer to him, pulling herself up as tall as she could. "Now you see here, Overton. You can't go around accusing us of everything that happens in this town—"

"Sheriff? Where's the body."

Several members of their small town police force had come up behind them and the girls turned in their direction.

"Over here." Overton started toward the cliff then turned back toward Morgan and Fiona. "I have a sneaky suspicion there's more to this than meets the eye and I bet the two of you are right in the middle of it."

He glanced back at the officers who had continued on and were halfway to the cliff's edge. Removing the toothpick from his mouth, he jabbed it in Morgan's direction.

"You might want to call your fancy lawyer, because if I find evidence you had anything to do with this, I'm going to make sure you feel the full force of the law. This time you won't get away so easy."

Morgan watched him shove the toothpick back in his mouth and lumber off toward the cliff. She half hoped he would trip and fall right over then caught herself, realizing that would be a terrible fate, even for him.

The two girls watched him while he approached the cliff's edge when, out of nowhere, Belladonna streaked in front of him causing him to stumble and almost pitch over the side.

"Damn cat! Thing should be shot." He glared after the

cat who had disappeared into the bushes.

Morgan and Fiona had to clamp their hands over their mouths to keep from laughing out loud as they walked back toward the house.

* * *

Morgan opened the kitchen door and Belladonna appeared from nowhere, scooting inside ahead of them.

Fiona reached down to pet the cat. "Good girl, you want a treat?"

Belladonna walked over to her bowl and sat in front of it licking her paw, as if she were ambivalent about the treat, while Fiona got a can of tuna from the cupboard.

"I see Overton is still as big a jerk as ever," Fiona said.

"Yep. He worries me. There's no telling what he might do." Morgan peered out the back door window toward the cliff, where she could see the police department turning out in full force.

"What's going on out there?"

Morgan's sister, Celeste, stood in the doorway, her concerned gaze directed at the corner of the yard where the police were now swarming.

"There's a body on the cliff," Fiona said as she flipped open the tuna can then bent to scoop the fish into Belladonna's dish.

"Excuse me?" Celeste ruffled her short blonde hair, still wet from showering, as she walked over to the window.

"Yeah, it was weird. I saw a bunch of seagulls over by the cliff and went over to investigate and there was a guy lying on the rocks. Dead." Morgan felt a shiver go up her spine. It had been only four years since her mother had taken her own life near that same spot. This one was too close for comfort.

"Why would a dead body be in our yard?" Celeste turned her wide, ice-blue eyes on Morgan.

"That's a good question. What *would* someone be doing on the cliff?" Morgan's eyebrows creased in the middle.

"And why would someone kill him there?" Fiona asked. "Or did he die from falling off the cliff?"

Morgan pursed her lips together. "You know, I'm not exactly sure. He wasn't far down so I don't see how he could have died from a fall, but in the dark I guess he might have tripped and hit his head or something. I didn't really look at him that close."

"Maybe they killed him somewhere else and dumped him there," Celeste said as she opened the double wide refrigerator and took out some spinach.

"But why?"

"I don't know," Fiona said, "I'll ask Jake later today what he knows."

"Yeah, I'm surprised he's not here." Morgan glanced out the window looking for the handsome former detective and newest member of the Noquitt Police department. Jake Cooper had proved to be an invaluable ally when Morgan had been accused of murdering Prudence Littlefield.

Morgan smiled at the way Fiona's ice-blue eyes got all dreamy when she said Jake's name. Jake and Fiona had gotten close during the Littlefield investigation and now they were practically inseparable. Morgan tried to push down the pang of sadness she felt for herself.

Would she ever be able to find love like that again?

She'd had that kind of love once with her high school sweetheart, Luke Hunter. They'd dated into their early twenties. But Luke had decided he wanted to join the military and had broken it off with her. She hadn't seen him in over a decade and hadn't found anyone else that sparked her interest either.

Morgan remembered several weeks earlier when she'd *thought* she'd seen Luke downtown. But it hadn't been him ... just someone who looked like him. Still, it had raised all those old feelings, of love and betrayal. She should be over him by now. But ...

"... Morgan?" Celeste interrupted her thoughts.

"Sorry, what?"

"Did you say it was a man? What did the guy look like?" Celeste stood in front of the juicer, a cupful of spinach and some green sprouted stuff in her hand.

Morgan's heart clenched as she thought back to the body

on the cliff. "He was a big guy, blonde and muscular. Rough looking. One thing was strange though."

Celeste raised a blonde eyebrow. "What was that?"

"He had a black mark on his hand. Like a big circle. It just struck me as odd."

Celeste stood looking at Morgan, chewing her bottom lip, her brows creased with worry.

"Celeste, is something wrong?" Fiona asked.

"It's just that I had a dream about something similar." Celeste shrugged and turned back to the juicer. "Just a coincidence, I'm sure."

Morgan watched her sister, a strange feeling of foreboding starting to spread in her stomach.

"Meow."

Belladonna flopped down over by the back stairs that led to the attic, which was once servants' quarters and now housed several generations of Blackmoore family cast offs, and proceeded to clean her snow white fur.

"I guess Belladonna agrees." Morgan opened the cupboard, sifting through the herbal tea bags for chamomile. She could use something to soothe her nerves.

"Do you think we should call Delphine?" Fiona asked, referring to the lawyer who had been instrumental in shielding the girls from the threats of Overton earlier that summer.

"I think Overton was just trying to scare us. I mean, he doesn't have anything to tie us to the body, since we didn't kill him." Morgan plunked her tea cup into the microwave. "We don't even know if he actually was murdered."

"Yeah, I guess you're right." Fiona nodded. "Hey, where's Jolene?"

Celeste rolled her eyes. "Still sleeping."

Jolene, Morgan's youngest sister, had only been fourteen when their mother jumped to her death. The three older sisters had tried to raise her as best they could. She'd been a handful, but was recently starting to come around. Still, like most teens, she loved sleeping in.

"Celeste, will you let her know what's going on out there?" Fiona nodded toward the cliff. "I don't want her to wake up and panic when she sees the Noquitt Police

Department in the back yard."

"Sure, I don't go into the yoga studio until noon." Celeste ran her greens through the juicer producing a cup full of thick green goo.

"I guess we better go open the shop." Fiona turned to Morgan, car keys in her hand. "There's nothing for us to do anyway. I'll call Jake later and find out what Overton's game plan is, and if we should be worried."

Morgan shrugged. "I guess you're right."

She grabbed her tea and headed for the door, the feeling of foreboding growing stronger—whatever Overton's game plan was, Morgan was pretty sure she wasn't going to like it.

Chapter Two

Morgan felt her spirits lift as Fiona pulled her truck up to their shop, *Sticks and Stones*. The old cottage that had been in the family for generations, sat at one of the highest points in their town of Noquitt, Maine. It was quaint with antique weathered cedar clapboards, crisp white trim and an abundance of flowers.

Set back in the woods, the shop was just slightly off the beaten path, but not so out of the way that it discouraged customers. In fact, the wooded location helped add to the mystique of the herbs and crystals the girls sold.

Morgan finished the last of her tea then hopped out of the truck, eager to get inside and start the day's work. She always felt content in the little cottage and she needed a little bit of contentment after the morning's events.

"We need to cut some of these roses." Fiona pointed to a thick red rose bush to the right of the porch steps which was loaded with a carpet of blooms.

"I'll do that later." Morgan bent over to smell a rose. She loved having vases full of fresh cut flowers from their garden in the shop and cutting off the blooms would keep the plant flowering all summer.

As she straightened, she felt a prickle at the back of her neck. She spun around, her stomach sinking.

Was someone watching her?

Narrowing her eyes, she scanned the woods around the shop but didn't see anything.

"What's the matter?" Fiona was standing on the porch, her hand poised in front of the electric keypad that disarmed the alarm.

"Oh nothing." Morgan shrugged. "I guess I'm just jittery from finding that body."

"No doubt."

Fiona punched in the code and went inside. Morgan followed her in, taking one last backward glance out into the woods before she turned the sign to "open" and closed the door.

Inside, the earthy smell of old wood and herbs soothed her senses. Fiona went straight to her workbench where an array of jewelers tools lay surrounding her latest piece—a moonstone and peridot necklace commissioned by one of their regular customers.

Morgan turned to the left where tall wooden racks with small cubby holes housed a variety of herbs. She picked out some chamomile, loaded it into a tea infuser, and heated some water on her small gas burner.

On the other side of the shop, Fiona let out a sigh. "I can't stop wondering *why* someone would turn up dead on our cliff. I mean, what was he doing there in the first place?"

"That's a good question. I don't think he got there by boat. It's too treacherous to land anywhere near there. He must have walked in." Morgan felt a chill run up her spine thinking of a random stranger walking around in their yard while they slept.

"Well, maybe we'll get some answers once we find out who the guy was and why he was killed. Until then, there's not much we can do except work."

Fiona turned her attention back to the necklace. Morgan looked at the stack of orders she had for herbal mixtures. Picking one from the top she gathered various herbs from her stock, placing small amounts into a stone mortar for grinding.

The girls worked in silence and time passed slowly, measured by the ticking of the grandfather clock in the back of the store.

Morgan was almost in a trance, grinding together a mixture of ginger, black horehound, raspberry leaf and mint for a seasickness remedy when the bell over the shop door announced a customer.

"Hello girls!" Amelia Budding, one of their elderly regulars, shuffled into the shop, her magenta polyester shirt and shorts somehow made her four foot frame seem even smaller.

"Hey, Amelia." Fiona put down the moonstone cabochon she was working with and stood up. "What can we do for you?"

"Oh I'm looking for some black onyx, you know, to protect myself in case evil descends on the town." Amelia shuffled toward Fiona's antique oak jewelry display case, which she was barely tall enough to look down into.

Morgan and Fiona exchanged raised eyebrow looks over her head.

"Evil?" Morgan ventured.

"Well, I heard about the trouble out at your place."

"And you think some evil menace is involved?" Fiona bent down on the other side of the case and removed a black bracelet.

"Well, I heard tell it might have something to do with pirates ... and you know how nasty they can be."

"Pirates? I thought they died out two hundred years ago?" Morgan narrowed her eyes at Amelia. *Surely the woman couldn't be serious?*

Amelia shrugged and looked across the room at Morgan over the tops of her eyeglasses. "Believe what you want. If you're great-grandma were alive she'd have some tales to tell you."

The girls exchanged another look. Morgan was three years older than Fiona and only had the vaguest of memories of their great-grandmother. She wasn't even sure if they were real memories or just from pictures and stories she'd been told. She didn't remember anything about pirates in those stories.

Fiona laid the black bracelet on a purple velvet cushion. "This one is all black onyx with a sterling silver clasp." She unhooked the bracelet, laying it over her wrist to demonstrate how it would look.

"And black onyx will protect me, right?"

"That's one of its powers. It will also make you stronger and alleviate worry," Fiona said then raised her head to look at Morgan. "And it can also help you let go of past relationships and move on with your life."

Morgan ignored the pointed look from her sister. Since Fiona had gotten involved with Jake, she'd been on a mission to get Morgan to forget about Luke and find someone new. It's not like Morgan didn't *want* to. She glanced over at the jewelry case warily. Maybe she *should* consider wearing some black onyx.

"It's perfect." Amelia unsnapped her purse and dug out an overstuffed wallet, squinting into it as she retrieved some bills.

Fiona rang up the sale and they watched Amelia shuffle toward the door. Just as she reached for the handle, she turned back dramatically, pointing her bespectacled gaze at Fiona and then Morgan.

"You girls be careful now. I think dangerous times are upon us," she said, then opened the door and shuffled out.

"Is she for real?" Morgan squinted at the door then looked at Fiona.

"Pirates? Seriously? I don't think so." Fiona laughed. "She's almost one hundred years old for crying out loud. She's probably senile."

Morgan laughed. "Yeah, she's probably just inventing danger to make her life more interesting. After all, what else is there to do when you get to be in your nineties?"

"Right. I'm sure there's a logical explanation for the body on the cliff that has nothing to do with pirates or some evil menace that's going to descend on the town."

"Of course, that would be ridiculous," Morgan agreed. But, as she turned back to her work, she had to wonder—if it was so ridiculous, why did she have that nagging feeling of doom in the pit of her stomach.

Chapter Three

Luke stared at Morgan through his high powered binoculars. She was even more beautiful than he remembered.

He was glad to see she still had that long ebony hair he'd found so appealing. His pulse quickened as he remembered the silky feel of it in his hands. And even though he couldn't see them, his heart clenched remembering her ice-blue eyes that could make him melt with a single look.

He put the binoculars down with a sigh. He was better off not remembering. He'd chosen the military over her. It really wasn't a decision he had much control over—it was more of a calling he couldn't ignore ... to do his part for the country.

He didn't think it was fair to expect her to wait for him. What if he got maimed or killed in action? He'd loved her too much to put her through that, so he'd broken things off. It had nearly killed him to do it, but he felt she deserved a chance to find someone who could be there for her. His gut churned as he wondered if she'd found that someone.

Seeing her after all these years stirred up feelings that he hadn't had in a long time. Feelings that he thought were dead and buried ... feelings that he had no time for now.

Luke used his Special Forces training to shut off his thoughts. It wouldn't do him any good to start pining over something he couldn't have.

True, he was no longer in the Special Forces. Now he had a different job. A more dangerous job. That was why he had to push aside his longing to see Morgan. He'd do everything he could to protect her while he insured the success of the job he had come here for, but he had to do that all from afar.

He was afraid of what might happen if he let himself talk to Morgan. Afraid of his feelings, and also of what he might tell her. Morgan always had a way of getting him to spill his guts and he knew he wouldn't be able to lie to her.

He picked up his binoculars and scanned the forest while pushing all thoughts of Morgan from his mind. The sooner he forgot about their past relationship, the better. He'd have to take care to keep his distance. Her safety and the success of his mission depended on it.

No matter how much he wanted to talk to her, Morgan Blackmoore was off limits—he couldn't take any chances on her discovering the secret of why he was really back in town.

Chapter Four

"What do you mean you can't find anything on him? Can't you trace him by his fingerprints or dental records or something?" Morgan looked across the table at Jake as she took a sip from her beer bottle.

"Only if they have records on file. This guy apparently didn't. And he had no ID on him so ..." Jake bent down to scratch Belladonna who had flopped down adoringly at his feet.

"Surely, you guys must have other ways of identifying a body?" Fiona asked.

"Well, the Noquitt P.D. isn't exactly on the cutting edge of technology and Overton seems to be dragging his feet with this one." Jake creased his brow. "For some strange reason, he's not really putting a big effort into figuring out who this guy is."

Morgan glanced across their yard at the crisp, blue Atlantic Ocean, her eyes falling on the section of cliff still marred by yellow police tape. She wondered why Overton wouldn't be pulling out all the stops to find the identity of the man who died there. She could think of only one reason—he knew something they didn't.

"Anyway, he's keeping me as far from the case as he possibly can." Jake's words pulled Morgan's attention back to the patio table on the edge of their backyard where she sat with Jake and her sisters. Even though Jake and Fiona had tried to keep their relationship a secret from the sheriff, this was a small town and everyone knew everyone else's business. Morgan figured Overton probably had it in for Jake now, too.

She looked at the beer bottle in front of her, condensation running down the sides created a puddle on the table. The evening sun was low in the sky and the day had cooled slightly, but it was still hot and humid—a typical Maine summer night.

She took a deep breath of salty ocean air mingled with the smell of fried clams and drained the rest of her beer. Grabbing another one from the cooler, she picked nervously at the edge of the label.

"Was he murdered?" Morgan asked.

Jake shrugged. "All I could find out was that he was killed by a blow to the head. He might have fallen and cracked his head on the rock, but he would have had to have fallen pretty hard for it to be fatal."

"Is Overton going to try to blame us somehow?" Celeste asked from the edge of the patio where she had been watering the colorful flowers they had set in large pots and containers.

Jake ran his hands through his short cropped hair. "I think he'd like to, but without knowing who the guy is, he can't come up with a plausible motive. Although I did hear him mention that you all had means and opportunity."

"Well, that's crazy. It doesn't have anything to do with us!" Fiona's blue eyes sparked with anger.

"I'm not so sure," Morgan said handing Fiona a beer. "I mean, I know none of us killed him, but I'm not so sure his being on our cliff had nothing to do with us. I have a funny feeling about this."

Celeste joined them at the table. "Oh, that's right—Nana wanted me to tell you that you should trust your feelings, Morgan."

Everyone's head swiveled in Celeste's direction, even Jolene who'd had her head buried in her smartphone the whole time they'd been sitting there.

"What?" A tingle ran up Morgan's spine and she narrowed her eyes at her sister.

Celeste shrugged. "When I meditate, sometimes she comes and talks to me. It's nothing unusual."

"Sounds pretty unusual to me, Nana's been dead for ten years." Jolene lifted her sunglasses to stare at Celeste.

Fiona and Jake stared at her as if she'd announced she could walk on water, but Morgan noticed that didn't seem to faze Celeste at all.

Celeste had always been spiritually minded and Morgan knew she took her yoga and meditation seriously. But she'd never heard Celeste mention anything about talking to dead people before. Morgan didn't know what to think. She wasn't sure she actually believed in any of that stuff, but Celeste had never been one to act all "woo woo". Anyway, she had more important things to worry about right now.

"And what about that black hand thing?" Celeste was saying, "I feel like that might be some kind of clue, don't you, Morgan?"

Morgan wrinkled her brow. The black mark was odd. She had no idea what it meant, but it was the only thing they had to go on at this point.

"Black hand thing?" Jolene shifted her gaze between Morgan and Celeste.

"Yeah, the victim had a round black mark on his hand. Kind of like a tattoo."

Jolene raised her eyebrows and picked up her smartphone. "Maybe we can find something on the internet about that."

Morgan leaned back in her chair. They'd discovered a few months ago that Jolene was something of a whiz with computers when she'd uncovered some vital information that led them to find the real killer of Prudence Littlefield and clear Morgan's name. Morgan's chest swelled with pride, especially since they had been worried that Jolene might not find any positive direction in life given some of her shenanigans in high school.

She'd matured a lot since she had graduated and was even taking a computer forensics class during the summer. Maybe she'd have a career in law enforcement? God knows Morgan could use her help given the trouble Overton seemed hell bent on causing them.

Jolene's laughter pulled her out of her thoughts. "Did you find something?"

"Not hardly. The only thing I can find is that pirates use a black mark to indicate doom or death. If a pirate is marked with it, his days are numbered." Jolene looked up at Morgan, a smirk on her face. "Isn't that ridiculous?"

Morgan's heart jerked in her chest and she looked up at Fiona who was staring back at her wide-eyed. Amelia Budding's warning about pirates and evil echoed in her head.

Jolene's brow creased. "What? That's silly, right? There's no such thing as pirates anymore."

Morgan was about to answer when Belladonna leapt up on the table, let out a screech and then ran off into the bushes on the side of the house. Everyone jumped back, their chairs scraping on the patio, beers spilling on the table.

Morgan blotted beer from the crotch of her jeans, staring in the direction of the disappearing cat.

An icy tingle crept up her spine at the cat's unlikely timing. It was almost as if she had reacted to the discussion of pirates. Morgan laughed at herself. That was ridiculous, Belladonna didn't have uncanny powers and the days of pirates died out long ago.

But at this point she couldn't afford to ignore any clues no matter how silly they seemed. And since she didn't have much else to go on, it might be worth her while to learn a little bit more about pirates. Luckily she knew exactly the right person to help her.

Chapter Five

The day was heating up to be a scorcher, Morgan thought, as she and Celeste walked down Maine Street toward *Reed Pawn and Antiques*. The pawn shop was located in the city, about twenty miles from their small town, and Morgan didn't come to the city too often.

They'd taken her car because Celeste's was loaded with yoga mats and various pieces of odd looking exercise equipment, including her latest obsession—kettle bells. Morgan had forgotten how busy and crowded it could be and how hard it would be to find a parking spot.

"I'm glad we parked a few blocks away, the morning is gorgeous, and it's not too hot yet." Celeste echoed her thoughts.

"Yeah, I can use the exercise after those beers last night." Morgan looked down at her slim hips and stomach. *Were they getting bigger, or was it just her imagination?* Maybe she should cut back on the beer and ice cream.

The girls stopped in front of the upscale pawn shop, owned by their childhood friend Cal Reed. Cal was a history buff and antique expert—if anyone could tell them about pirates, it was him.

Celeste held the door open and a blast of cold air hit Morgan as soon as she stepped over the threshold.

"Brrr ... It's freezing in here." Morgan rubbed her bare shoulders wishing she'd brought a sweater.

"Well, if it isn't my favorite girls!" Cal stood behind the glass display case, a genuine smile highlighted the dimples on his handsome face.

Just seeing Cal always cheered Morgan up. They'd been friends since they were kids and he was a frequent visitor to the Blackmoore house. He was practically like a brother to them, which probably explained why he'd never dated any of them. Cal was considered one of the most charming, handsome and eligible bachelors in the county, and literally had women swooning at his feet.

He was well known for being a playboy, but he was also a really nice guy and Morgan was glad he hadn't ruined the special friendship he had with the Blackmoore girls by getting romantically involved with any of them. Cal's romances never lasted very long.

"What brings you guys here?" He asked, coming out from behind the case to envelop them both in a big hug.

"We need a history lesson," Celeste said.

Cal raised an eyebrow and looked from Celeste to Morgan. "About what?"

"Pirates," Morgan offered.

"Pirates?" Cal cocked an eyebrow at Morgan. "What's going on?"

"Well, you heard about the guy on our cliff, right?" Celeste ventured.

"What? No. I just got back from Barbados." Cal stared at her, concern clouding his deep blue eyes. "What guy?"

Morgan sighed. "A guy ended up dead on the cliff in our backyard. I discovered him yesterday morning."

"How did he die?" Cal alternated his gaze between Morgan and Celeste. "What was he doing on the cliff?"

"That's what we're trying to figure out," Celeste said.

"And you have no idea who he is?"

"Nope and Overton can't seem to figure it out either."

Cal snorted. "I'm not surprised. Overton's an idiot. It's a miracle he can find his way to the police station every morning. No wonder you guys have to investigate it on your own." He rubbed his chin then narrowed his eyes at Morgan. "But how do pirates figure into it?"

"The only clue we have is that the guy had a large black circle on his hand. Jolene looked it up and it's supposed to be some kind of pirate sign of doom or something." Morgan laughed. "I know it's silly. There's no such thing as pirates anymore, but we figure it was worth talking about. Maybe it will tie in to something useful ... and we always like to have an excuse to come and talk to you."

"Aww, you guys know you don't need an excuse to see me. But the pirate angle might not be as farfetched as you think." Cal leaned back against the display case.

"Really?" Morgan's brow creased, her stomach fluttering.

"Well, there *are* modern day pirates, but I don't think that would tie into your dead guy. Modern pirates hijack cargo ships and steal the goods or hold them for ransom. But they don't do that around here." Cal walked over to one of the bookshelves that lined the store and pulled out a thick leather bound book, then leafed through it. "The black mark really is a pirate warning. I believe it's mostly fictional though. It was used to mark a pirate for death—a warning of sorts."

"Well, the guy on the cliff sure did end up dead," Celeste said looking over Cal's shoulder at the page of the book he was holding open.

"I still don't get what that has to do with us," Morgan said.

"It might not have anything to do with you, but it could be that the guy thought your cliff was a likely place for pirates to have buried their treasure."

Morgan laughed. "What? They only did that in the Caribbean. There's no pirate treasure around here."

Cal shook his head. "Legend has it many pirates buried treasure all over the Maine coast. The most Famous is Capt. William Kidd, but there were others. In fact, a cache of gold and silver Spanish coins were dug up just over in Biddeford, in the 1930s that many believe was buried there by pirates."

Morgan felt her eyes grow wider. "Seriously? But, why our cliff?"

Cal shrugged. "Who knows? I do know there are people who make a living out of trying to find this type of treasure. Maybe someone's research led them to your location."

Morgan looked at Celeste. "Boy, finding a chest full of pirate treasure would sure solve all our money problems."

Morgan and Fiona made a modest living with *Sticks and Stones* and Celeste did fairly well with her yoga studio, but it was barely enough to put food on the table and pay the taxes on their property—which for a waterfront mansion was a small fortune. The house had been built generations ago so, luckily, they had no mortgage. Otherwise they wouldn't be able to afford to keep the house.

Celeste laughed. "Yeah, I'm sure there's a bunch of pirate treasure just buried all over our yard and no one found it in the three hundred some odd years people have been living there."

"So who are these people that search for treasure. Do you mean like that guy who has the boat that looks for old shipwrecks?" Morgan rubbed her forehead. *What was that guy's name?* She snapped her fingers. "Ballard."

"Sort of. Except these guys aren't nearly as nice. Ballard is legit. The guys I am talking about do it under the radar. They want to steal the treasure and keep all of it, without paying taxes or giving any to the rightful owners it was originally stolen from. And they'll do whatever they have to do to keep from getting caught." Cal's blue eyes drilled into Morgan's. "They are very dangerous people."

Morgan felt her stomach clench. "But he's dead now, so we probably don't have to worry, right?"

Cal shook his head. "I wish. But they usually travel in groups. There are probably others and if that guy thought your property had treasure, then the others might too."

Morgan and Celeste exchanged worried glances.

"When was your house built?" Cal asked.

Morgan wrinkled her brow and looked at Celeste uncertainly. "I don't know, sometime in the early 1700s I think. At least that's when the first part was built and then they added to it over the years."

"Did your family own the land before that? There were pirates back in that time ... maybe ..."

"You don't really think there would be pirate treasure there do you?"

"You never know." Cal shrugged. "What did you say your ancestor that build the house did for a living?"

"He was a merchant," Celeste said then her eyes went wide. "A sailing merchant."

Cal raised his eyebrows. "Didn't you guys find some old journals of his in your attic?"

"We found old journals, but we're not sure what year they are from," Celeste said. "They did look very old, but I don't know if they could be 300 years old."

"Well, maybe it's worth going up there and taking a look. Who knows? You might find an old treasure map or something." Cal winked at Morgan.

"A treasure map would be great." Morgan laughed, "but even if he was there looking for treasure, which I highly doubt, how did he end up dead?"

"Well, you said he had that black mark on his hand. Legend has it that when a pirate woke up with that mark on his hand, he'd better watch out because it meant he was marked for death. And that's exactly what happened to him." Cal wiggled his eyebrows at Morgan and Celeste. "So you see, it makes perfect sense."

"Pfft." Morgan waved her hand in the air. "I'm sure there's a logical explanation for all of it. There has to be, because believing a pirate ended up dead on our cliff because of some old curse is just too crazy for anyone to believe ... even me."

Chapter Six

"All this pirate stuff is nonsense, don't you think?" Morgan asked as they left the pawn shop and headed down the sidewalk.

"It is rather fanciful, but anything is possible, Morgan."

Morgan sighed. Leave it to Celeste to believe in something like pirates and curses.

"Hey, you wanna stop in at *Riley's* for lunch?" Morgan glanced at her watch. "Fi isn't expecting me back at *Sticks and Stones* until noon and all this pirate talk made me hungry."

"Sure. I love their veggie burgers."

They took a right down the side street that was a shortcut to *Riley's*—one of the city's most popular burger places. The route wasn't the most scenic and would take them through an undesirable section of town, but it cut a half mile out of the walk so it was a good trade off.

An uneasy feeling came over Morgan as they walked—like a heavy feeling of doom deep in the pit of her stomach. *Probably all this pirate talk has me unsettled*. She tried pushing the feeling away, but it insisted on staying like an unwanted houseguest that won't leave no matter how many hints you give them.

"... dying to read more of that journal," Celeste was saying.

"What?" Morgan asked, the strange feeling deepening as they turned down an out of the way street that housed a few abandoned buildings.

"I was saying, ever since we discovered that journal in the attic, I've been dying to get back up there and try to figure out what it says." Celeste stopped in her tracks her face a mask of concern. "Is something wrong?"

"No." Morgan shook her head. "This street just kind of gives me the creeps."

Morgan's thoughts drifted to the journal they had found in the attic as the girls walked a little faster down the street. None of them ever went in the attic. Ever. Their mother had told them it was off limits when they were little girls and the threat had carried over into adulthood. None of them wanted to go in there—the place creeped Morgan out and she was sure her sisters felt the same way.

But when Morgan had been arrested for Prudence Littlefield's murder, earlier that summer, Fiona had been forced to go up there in the hopes she could find something of value to hire a lawyer. After all, the place was loaded with several generations of Blackmoore family "stuff" so there was bound to be something of value.

And that's when they'd found the journal. An old, handwritten leather bound book, tucked in a bookshelf. Celeste had tried to make sense of it, but the writing was old and faded. They hadn't been back up there since.

Morgan's thoughts were interrupted by a prickly sensation running through her body. Like a current of electricity that started deep in the pit of her stomach and put her senses on edge. It was like her usual "gut feeling" times twenty.

Morgan's attention was drawn to a narrow alley that opened up onto the street about ten feet ahead of them. She could feel the hairs on the back of her neck stand up and she had an overwhelming urge to run back in the direction they had come from. She glanced down the street in either direction. It was empty. No one would run to their rescue or hear them scream.

This is silly. She tried to push her feelings away, but they wouldn't budge.

Just as they approached the alley, Celeste's message from her grandmother echoed in her mind. *Trust your feelings.*

Morgan reacted without thinking. She pulled Celeste back just as a man lunged out from the alley. Her quick reaction caused him to just miss grabbing Celeste!

In a second Celeste crouched down and kicked her foot

up, connecting with the guys jaw and sending him staggering backwards but not before a second man made a grab for her.

Morgan watched, amazed, as Celeste's elbow shot out into the man's face. She heard a crunch and saw a spray of blood. The man fell back into the alley holding his nose.

The first guy had recovered quickly and made a grab for Morgan while Celeste was giving the second guy a bloody nose. Morgan kicked out, connecting with his crotch and the man went down in a heap.

A noise in the alley across the street caught Morgan's attention. She saw men running toward them. The two men they'd been dealing with were rolling on the ground and she didn't feel like taking on anymore so she grabbed Celeste.

"Run!"

They ran back the way they had come, toward their car. Morgan glanced back over her shoulder and saw the men coming out of the alley weren't running for them, they went straight after the men that had attacked them. That didn't stop her from running though—her gut told her to get the hell out of there and, from now on, she was going to trust her feelings.

It wasn't until they were safely locked inside the car that Morgan realized one of the men who had come running out of the alley across from them looked an awful lot like Luke Hunter.

* * *

Morgan gasped for breath as her white knuckled fists clutched the steering wheel.

"Are you okay?" Celeste maneuvered her arm to inspect her elbow for damage. Morgan noticed her sister didn't seem nearly as out of breath as she was. Maybe she should take up yoga and kettle bells?

"Yeah. What was that all about?" Morgan twisted in her seat to look down the street. It looked like a normal sunny day in the city. People were window shopping casually. No one was coming after them. It was hard to believe they had just been attacked.

"Apparently those guys were meaning to grab us. For what, I don't know." Celeste shuddered visibly in her seat.

Morgan narrowed her eyes at her sister. "Where'd you learn to fight like that?"

"Oh, I take Karate and self-defense." Celeste turned concerned eyes on Morgan. "You might want to think about taking a class or two yourself, although you do have a mean crotch kick."

The girls giggled. Then Celeste turned serious.

"What made you grab me like that—at that very second?" Morgan saw Celeste's brow furrow.

"I trusted my feelings."

Celeste smiled. "So you did listen ... and it's a good thing too, because if you hadn't pulled me back when you did, this whole incident might have had a different ending."

"Speaking of endings, did you see those guys that came running from the other alley?"

Celeste nodded.

"At first I thought they were after us, but I think they were trying to help us. Or at least they were going after the guys that tried to grab us."

Celeste turned to look out the back window. "Maybe we should go back and thank them?"

"I don't know. It's strange but one of those guys looked just like Luke Hunter." Morgan felt her stomach clench. *Could Luke be back in town?*

Celeste swiveled around to face Morgan. "Luke? What would he be doing here? Besides, wouldn't he contact you if he was back in town?"

Morgan's heart tightened in her chest. "I don't know. We broke up almost ten years ago, so he certainly doesn't have to tell me where he goes. Besides he's probably married with kids by now."

"I thought he was still in the military?"

Morgan shrugged. "Yeah, it was probably just someone who looked like him."

"Didn't you see someone you thought looked like him a couple of weeks ago?" Celeste raised a brow at Morgan. "I think maybe you need to start dating again."

Morgan laughed as she started up the car. "Yeah, you can say that again."

"Do you think we should tell the cops?"

Morgan bit her lower lip. Given her experiences with Overton, she didn't have much confidence in the police. "Nah. We're not hurt and I'm sure those thugs are gone by now. What would the police do?"

"Yeah, I guess there's not much they can do. Do you think this has something to do with the guy on the cliff?"

Morgan's stomach churned. *Did it?* "No. How could it? I mean we're not even near home. That was probably just a couple of thugs who were waiting around to mug the next person that walked down the street."

"Yeah, probably." Celeste looked in the side view mirror uncertainly.

"But, let's not tell Fiona or Jolene. I don't want them to get all worried."

"Okay," Celeste agreed.

Morgan eased out of the parking spot, glancing nervously behind her one last time.

Did she really believe it was just a random mugging?

Her logical brain told her it was, but her gut was telling her something else entirely. And, if her gut instincts were right, she'd have to find out who the dead guy was, and what he wanted, quickly ... before something worse happened.

* * *

Morgan sipped a steaming cup of chamomile and valerian tea to calm her nerves as she sat at her worktable at *Sticks and Stones* and filled Fiona in on the meeting with Cal.

"Do you really think he was after some sort of treasure?" Fiona looked at Morgan with wide blue eyes.

"No. Don't you think if our family had a treasure we'd know about it?"

"Maybe it was buried there before any Blackmoores got here. You did say that pirates were rumored to bury treasure all up and down the coast, right?"

"Yeah, but that's reaching pretty far to think treasure could be on our land."

"Well, if it is, I want *us* to find it, not some treasure hunters."

Morgan laughed. "Me too. But even if that *was* why he was there, it doesn't explain why he ended up dead."

"True. Well, maybe it was just one of those things and we'll never hear anything about it again."

"I wish," Morgan said looking out the front window of *Sticks and Stones* where she could see Sheriff Overton's car pulling up to the shop. She watched him get out, hitch up his pants and stomp to the door which he yanked open, then stood in the opening silhouetted in the sunlight.

"Good afternoon, Sheriff. Come on in," Morgan said with feigned cheerfulness.

Overton glared in her direction, stepped inside and shut the door.

"What brings *you* here?" Fiona stood up from her workbench and narrowed her eyes at Overton.

"I have some questions for you girls. You can answer them here or I can take you down to the station."

Morgan shot Fiona a warning glance and shrugged. "We can answer them here."

Overton looked disappointed. He switched the toothpick from the right side of his mouth to the left and leaned back on his heels.

"Alrighty, then." He pulled a notebook and pencil out of his pocket and licked the tip of the pencil causing Fiona to make a face. "How long did you know the deceased?"

"Huh? You mean the man I found on the cliff?" Morgan's brows mashed together. "We didn't know him at all."

Overton looked at her from under his shaggy eyebrows. "Really? You expect me to believe that?"

"It's the truth." Morgan struggled to remain calm. She knew Overton was looking for them to overreact. He was probably trying to incite them, hoping they'd do something crazy so he could arrest them. She refused to play his game.

"Well, now how could a big man like that walk all the

way past your house and out onto the cliff without anyone noticing?"

Morgan's stomach clenched. She'd been wondering the same thing. "He must have snuck out there in the middle of the night."

Overton cocked an eyebrow at her. "Now why would someone do that?"

"We have no idea. Are you accusing us of something?" Fiona cut in from across the room.

Overton smirked at her. "Not yet. But I know you girls are involved somehow."

Morgan drew in a deep breath. "Really Sheriff, we're not involved in every crime that happens in this town."

Overton turned to Morgan, the toothpick wiggling back and forth as he talked. "With your track record and the fact the deceased was found on your property, I'm sure it's only a matter of time before I'm able to charge you with something."

Morgan walked over to the door and held it open, gesturing for Overton to leave.

"I doubt that. You won't find anything relating us to that guy's murder because *we didn't have anything to do with it*." She punctuated the last words by leaning forward, almost in his face.

Morgan felt a wave of triumph when Overton started to leave, but the triumph was soon replaced with a twinge of worry when she saw the satisfied smirk on his face.

He turned just inside the doorway and his words caused Morgan's stomach to twist into a knot.

"Oh really? Then why did we find a copy of the *Ocean's Revenge* ship's manifest from 1722 showing Isaiah Blackmoore as the captain in his pocket?"

Chapter Seven

Celeste sat cross legged on the floor of the Library. She always meditated in this room—it was her favorite. She loved the dusty smell of antique furniture and old leather books and the way the sun spilled in through the nine foot tall windows highlighting rich colored slices of the antique Persian rugs.

She didn't know if it was the hand carved oak bookcases or the centuries old leather couches and chairs or the gigantic marble fireplace, but somehow, the room felt both awe inspiring and cozy at the same time.

The room also seemed spiritual somehow. Maybe because of all the old books and furniture that were once read and used by ancestors long dead, or maybe because it was so quiet—especially now when no one else was home.

She settled herself in a patch of sun and closed her eyes, breathing slowly in through her nose and out through her mouth. Slowly in ... and slowly out.

She cleared all thoughts from her mind. Every time a conscious thought tried to invade she dismissed it, promising her conscious mind she would deal with it later. Slowly, she counted backwards, clearing her mind of any thoughts that tugged at it, waiting for her subconscious to take over.

She could feel herself drift off ... still conscious, but not really. It was almost as if she could go to some other land inside her mind. She was getting better at entering this special land the more she meditated. It was coming to her faster and faster. And now she was even hearing the voices.

At first she could only hear a few whispered words from her spirit guide, Andrew. But that gradually progressed to full conversations and the past few times she'd meditated she'd also talked to her grandmother. At first it had freaked her out a little, but now she was starting to look forward to her meditations and these little visits from the other side.

"Well, don't you think you should be up in the attic looking for that book?"

Celeste jumped at her grandmother's voice. She'd heard it before, of course, but this time instead of being inside her head, it sounded like it was right in the room beside her.

Celeste focused on thinking up a response in her head.

I'm not sure. My sisters don't seem too keen on going up there.

"Nonsense, why not? There's lots of neat family stuff up there. And, of course, the journals."

Mom always told us to stay away, is it okay with her?

"How would I know?"

Isn't she there with you?

"No."

Celeste felt her brows knit together. Her mother had died four years ago, if she wasn't "over there" with Nana, then where was she? She found herself wishing she could see her grandmother and not just hear her disembodied voice in her thoughts.

"Well, why don't you just open your eyes if you want to see me?"

Celeste's heart skipped a beat. *See her?*

She tentatively cracked open one eyelid. She didn't see her Nana. She did see Belladonna, though. The cat was over by the window swatting at the haze that drifted in from the late afternoon sun. No, wait, it was more of a mist ... and the mist was bending down to pet the cat.

Celeste opened her other eye and watched open-mouthed as the cat rolled over on her back, the mist taking the shape of a human, bending over, its arm extended toward the cat and rubbing her belly.

The mist stood up and turned to her. "See dear, you can see me *and* hear me."

Celeste squinted. The figure was fuzzy, but she could just

make out some of her grandmother's features. Her eyeglasses, and her hair in a bun on top of her head. She was even wearing an apron that Celeste remembered from her childhood, or at least that she'd seen Nana wearing in pictures.

Celeste stared at the apparition, speechless.

"What's a matter, cat got your tongue?" Nana laughed and Belladonna let out a meow.

Celeste wondered if she'd fallen asleep and was dreaming.

The misty figure looked at its watch. "Well, I've gotta run, but I wanted to put a bee in your bonnet about the attic. There's important stuff up there you girls are going to need."

"Okay," Celeste stammered.

"Well, then, ta-ta." Nana bent to scratch Belladonna behind the ears and then vanished in a misty swirl.

Celeste sat still for a few minutes, her heart pounding against her ribs. *Did that really just happen?*

Belladonna came over and rubbed herself against Celeste's legs. She scratched the cat's head in return.

"Mew." Belladonna flopped down on her side and aimed her ice-blue eyes at Celeste then flicked them up towards the ceiling ... where the attic was.

She heard the front door open and glanced at the green onyx art deco clock on the mantel. It was five thirty, which meant it must be Morgan and Fiona coming home.

Celeste took a deep breath and stood up on shaky legs. All indications pointed toward the attic and if that's where the powers that be wanted her to go, then who was she to argue?

She just hoped she would have as easy a time convincing her sisters of that as her grandmother'd had convincing her.

***

Morgan shut the front door and proceeded down the hall toward the kitchen, her heart skittering when she saw a pale and shaken Celeste coming out of the library.

"What's the matter? You look like you've seen a ghost?" Morgan wrinkled her brow in concern as she studied her sister's face.

"Oh." Celeste ran her fingers through her perky blonde hair. "Sorry, I was napping and I'm still half asleep, I guess."

Morgan put her arm around Celeste's shoulders and led her into the kitchen. "Come on. We'll make some supper and tell you all about our visit from Overton."

"Sheriff Overton? Oh no. Is he going to arrest one of us or something?"

"I'm sure he'd like to but, fortunately, he doesn't have any evidence. He did, however, let it slip that he found something very interesting on the dead guy."

The girls stepped into the spacious black and white tiled kitchen. The kitchen itself had been built during one of the many home renovations in the 1800s and still had the original dark wood cabinets which were offset by white marble counter tops. The stainless steel appliances were a newer addition to the kitchen as was the large island in the center.

The smell of shrimp, garlic and fresh herbs hit Morgan's nose, causing her mouth to water. Fiona turned from the stove and looked at them as they each took a seat at the island.

"So, what's this interesting thing that Overton told you about?" Celeste reminded Morgan.

"You won't believe it." Morgan felt her heart speed up with a flitter of excitement despite the logical part of her brain telling her this all had nothing to do with pirate treasure. "Overton said the guy had a copy of some sort of ship's manifest that one of our relatives was the captain of in his pocket!"

"What?" Celeste's eyes widened as she divided her attention between Morgan and Fiona.

"Yep," Fiona said, swirling the shrimp in the pan "Jake's going to see if he can snag a copy of it and bring it over for us to look at."

"So what does that mean, the guy really was looking for treasure?" Celeste asked.

"Maybe." Morgan got up and grabbed a large bowl of salad from the fridge, placing it on the island. "That doesn't mean there really *is* treasure, though."

"It will be kind of cool to see what sorts of things were on the ship of our great-great-great-great-great-great-grandfather though." Fiona poured the shrimp concoction over a bowl of pasta, tossed it together and set it on the island next to the salad.

"Are you sure that's enough 'greats'?" Morgan asked, grabbing plates from the cupboard.

Fiona laughed, waving her hand in the air. "Well, who knows how many, I know there's a lot. The guy lived over three hundred years ago."

Morgan filled her plate and sat at the island beside her sisters. She had a forkful of food halfway to her mouth when a knock sounded on the front door.

Fiona jumped up. "That must be Jake."

"I'm sure it is. He has an uncanny way of showing up just when the food is ready to eat," Morgan said good-naturedly. The truth was she adored Jake as did all the sisters.

Fiona ran off to open the door and Morgan used the opportunity to dig into her supper. She was almost done by the time Fiona ushered Jake into the kitchen.

"Did you get a copy?" Morgan asked, handing a plate to Jake.

"Yeah, I got one of the other cops to sneak me one. Overton is keeping me far away from the case. Putting me on crap jobs like traffic detail." Jake made a face as he dug in his pocket and pulled out a folded piece of paper.

He opened it and spread it on the island. The three girls bent their heads over the paper to examine it.

"This is pretty cool," Celeste said. "The *Ocean's Revenge* ... I never heard of it but I like the name. Kind of sinister for a merchant ship though, don't you think?"

Morgan looked at the paper. The copy was blurry, the writing faint. She could see the original manifest itself had rough edges and many folds and creases. At the top was the date, ship's name and captain's name—Isaiah Blackmoore—below that columns with lists of items and numbers.

She ran her finger down the left column and read off the items. "Pottery, cowhide, turtle shell, cacao ... who knew they shipped this stuff around the world back then?"

"And who would care about recovering it now?" Celeste asked.

"Maybe not that stuff, but look at the bottom," Jake said between mouthfuls of shrimp.

Morgan skipped down to the bottom of the page and her heart jerked in her chest. "Gold and silver coins, copper ingots, silver bars ..." she looked up at her sisters. "Now *that's* worth recovering."

Fiona raised her brows. "For sure. But that was the stuff on his ship. It's not like he brought it home and buried it in the yard. He had to deliver that stuff to where ever it was supposed to go, didn't he?"

Morgan nodded. "And we don't even know if this is really an authentic ship's manifest."

"But it does give us a lead as to why the guy was on our cliff," Celeste said.

Morgan pursed her lips. "True, but not why he was killed."

"Do we even need to know that? I say it can't hurt to do a little treasure hunting ourselves. I mean, that guy certainly went to a lot of trouble to get killed on our cliff, maybe there is something to this whole buried treasure thing?" Fiona tore a piece of bread from the loaf on the table and used it to sop up what was left on her plate.

Jake looked up at them. "You might *have* to figure out why he was killed ... or at least who killed him. Overton is all fired up about the manifest linking the dead guy to your family. I eavesdropped on one of his conversations and he was talking about getting a search warrant."

Morgan's stomach clenched. Someone had planted evidence in their yard to try to frame her for Prudence Littlefield's murder earlier in the summer and she suspected it was Overton.

"If he gets a search warrant, who knows what kind of evidence he might plant. We can't let that happen."

Jake nodded. "You guys need to be careful, though. If

that guy got killed looking for the treasure, it might be dangerous for *you* to look for it, not to mention how dangerous it would be to try to track down his killer."

Morgan's heart skipped a beat and she glanced over at Celeste, the memory of the guys who tried to grab them earlier that morning fresh in her head.

Celeste tapped her finger to her lips. "Either someone thinks this supposed treasure is worth killing over, or someone had a beef with this guy and just happened to kill him in our yard."

"Either way, I think we need to find out more about these treasure hunters. Maybe we can get Jolene to do some research online," Morgan said.

"I think we need to find out more about the *Ocean's Revenge*. If we can get a clue as to why this guy was interested in the ship we might uncover a motive for someone wanting to kill him," Celeste offered.

"And a motive could lead us to the killer," Jake added. "But be forewarned, you might find out your relative wasn't the honorable merchant you have been lead to believe."

The girls exchanged a look. *Was it possible their relative was some sort of pirate?*

"I think I know one way we can find out," Celeste said, glancing up at the ceiling toward the attic.

Morgan's stomach fluttered nervously as she followed Celeste's gaze. She never liked going up in the attic, but Celeste was right. If there were secrets to be uncovered about their ancestors, the attic was the place to find them.

Chapter Eight

"I say there's no time like the present," Fiona said, as she loaded the last of the dinner dishes into the dishwasher.

"To go in the attic?" Celeste asked.

"Why are you going in the attic?" Jolene appeared in the pantry doorway.

"Oh, there you are," Fiona said. "We just finished eating, are you hungry?"

"No, I ate at the restaurant."

Recently graduated from high school, Jolene had a summer job at *Barnacle Bill's*, a local restaurant, until she figured out what she wanted to do with her life. The side benefit was that she was fed well and often surprised them with some great take out.

"What's this about going in the attic?" She persisted.

Fiona glanced at Morgan. The two oldest sisters were used to sheltering Jolene from anything unpleasant, but Morgan figured Jolene was all grown up now and, if they wanted her to act like an adult, they should treat her like one. She nodded her head.

"We've got some more information on the dead guy Morgan found," Fiona said, then filled Jolene in about the pirate treasure hunters and the ship's manifest.

"We were hoping you could do some research online about these treasure hunter guys," Morgan added.

"Of course, whatever you guys need, just ask."

Celeste stood up, and started over toward the back stairs that led to the attic. "I'm heading up ... who's coming?"

"Meoooow!" Belladonna streaked by her and ran up the stairs in a flash of white causing everyone in the room to laugh.

"Well, I guess one of us is excited," Morgan said as she

followed behind Celeste.

The stairs, originally built for servants to travel from their quarters to the other floors without using the main staircase, were narrow. They ascended in single file amidst the groaning and creaking of the centuries old wood.

At each floor, the stairway opened up into a hallway for access—they went up four flights, each one seeming ten degrees warmer than the last.

By the time they got to the top, Morgan was breathing heavy. She bent over and put her hands on her knees. Sweat drenched her tee-shirt.

"Sheesh Celeste, you must be in good shape—you aren't winded at all," she said sucking in a deep breath and flapping the bottom of her shirt to let some air in.

Celeste smiled at her and Morgan smiled back despite the butterflies that were swarming in her stomach. The attic always made her feel this way. All that old stuff piled up with God knows what hiding behind it creeped her out.

Morgan looked around. It was dark out and the lighting in the attic wasn't that great—which made it even creepier. She suddenly had an image of them in old fashioned dresses, carrying torches and lanterns to light the way. She was glad they didn't have to resort to use torches ... even though the image seemed quite real for a split second.

"Where was the book? Do you remember?"

Jake, Fiona and Jolene had caught up to them and the five of them stood in the doorway squinting into the attic. The space was immense, taking up the whole fourth floor and consisted of a main room with alcoves and other rooms beyond it. The stairs dumped them out into the main room which ran the width of the house and was just about as long as it was wide.

"It looks different up here now. Because there's not as much light, I suppose." Fiona stood on her tiptoes and swiveled her head around. "I think it was in that direction ... over by the window."

They picked their way through the various piles toward the window. The attic was crammed full of old furniture, trunks, rugs and boxes. Morgan could tell they were on the right path as she recognized some of the boxes they had opened on their trip up there earlier in the summer.

"That's it!" Celeste pointed to a bookcase near one of the dormer windows. Morgan wasn't surprised to find Belladonna sleeping right on top of it. The cat opened one eye lazily then closed it again.

Celeste carefully took the thick leather bound book out of the shelf and set it on a nearby table. She opened the cover, gently lifting the first page. Morgan held her breath, afraid the old paper might disintegrate into dust with each touch.

They gathered behind Celeste, peeking over her shoulder as she turned the yellowed pages.

"That looks like gibberish," Fiona said.

Morgan leaned closer, her brows creasing together, and tried to make sense of the writing. It had clearly been done with some sort of quill or fountain pen. The ink had faded almost to nothing and there were swirly flourishes and splotches that made it hard to make out the words.

"Can you understand any of this? The words are so strange."

"Well, they did have different words and spellings back then ... but this seems like the words don't go together." Celeste leaned even closer.

"I think it might be some sort of code," Jolene said.

Everyone turned to her. "Code?"

"Yeah, you know like a secret message where you use code words and then have a key that tells you what the words mean."

Morgan felt her stomach sink. "Well, how the heck are we going to figure that out?"

"Maybe the key is around here somewhere." Fiona started poking in the bookcase. "Would it be a paper, or something else?"

"There could be a piece of paper that tells you how to decode it, but it's probably a code that he knew by heart, I doubt you would find anything here that's going to help you break the code," Jolene said.

Morgan felt her shoulder slump. "So we'll never know what it says?"

"There's some well-known codes that have been used for

ages. You know, like replacing the letters of the alphabet with a number and so on. There were many ways people used to encode writing. We should find out some of the most common methods and see if they work on this book," Jake offered.

"I bet Cal will know about that," Celeste said, then looked at her watch. "It's too late to call him and I don't want to take the book anywhere—it's too fragile. Someone get me a paper and pen and I'll copy some of it down, then hook up with him tomorrow and see if he recognizes any of it."

Jolene scampered off and Morgan turned her attention to the rest of the room. It was filled with castoffs from previous generations. Family heirlooms ... or junk? She wasn't sure which.

Over on the bookcase, Belladonna stretched lazily then jumped off and brushed past Morgan with a flick of her tail and a quick look over her shoulder. Morgan followed her. The cat weaved her way through the maze and Morgan trailed along, mesmerized by her ancestor's belongings that she passed along the way. A beautiful oak bureau with a marble top, a full length mirror with baroque gilt frame, an old playpen—Morgan wondered if it had been hers—and dozens of boxes and trunks.

Belladonna stopped at a small box and started sniffing. Morgan crouched down beside her and studied it. It was shaped like a miniature dome top trunk, about a foot long and four inches tall. It looked ancient.

Belladonna scratched at it and Morgan picked it up. It looked to be made from some sort of shiny hard, mottled substance. *Turtle shell?* Morgan felt a familiar tingle in her gut as she remembered the manifest from the *Ocean's Revenge*.

"Morgan? Where are you?"

Celeste's voice startled her and she looked around, noticing Jake and her sisters were rather far away on the other side of the attic. *Had she really strayed that far?*

"Oh, there you are. We're done here so we're heading back down. Are you going to stay up here alone?"

Morgan's heart jerked in her chest. *No way was she*

staying up here alone.

"I'm coming," she said, then put the box back where she had found it and hurried to catch up to the rest of them.

Chapter Nine

"It's a gorgeous day today," Morgan said as she opened one of the back windows at *Sticks and Stones*. She poked her head out the window and inhaled the sharp, salty ocean air. The cottage was up on a cliff and set quite a ways in from the ocean, but she could still smell it as well as see the brilliant patch of blue sparkling through the trees.

"That it is." Fiona joined her at the window, her vanilla latte in hand. The woods behind the cottage were filled with old, thick trees and they watched the birds flitter between the branches, their chirps echoing through the forest. One tree, in particular was Morgan's favorite because someone had carved a heart with an "X" and two sets of initials in it generations ago—so long ago that the carving was now twenty feet high off the ground.

"Did you sleep good last night? I was up all night with nightmares about the attic." Fiona broke into her thoughts.

"Oh, I thought all that thrashing had something to do with Jake being in your room." Morgan teased her sister whose cheeks turned bright red. "But, to answer your question, I did sleep very well, surprisingly enough."

"Yeah, all this pirate stuff is a little disturbing," Fiona said as she headed back to her work table. "I mean what if the dead guy on the cliff isn't just some unrelated incident and more things are going to happen?"

Morgan thought back to the attack on her and Celeste the day before, but said nothing. *What good would it do to get Fiona more worried?*

"Well hopefully Jolene will be able to find something on those guys that hunt for treasure and that will give us a lead on the dead guy so we can put this all behind us," Morgan said, slipping in behind her work table.

"Yeah, Jake said he was getting off early today and he was going to get together with Jo and see what they could come up with. Hopefully they'll have some answers by the time we get home tonight."

Morgan nodded her agreement. The sooner they got to the bottom of this, the better—that tingly feeling of being watched was getting to her. She was starting to feel like she was just waiting for the next attack, which made her all nervous and jumpy.

The bell on the shop door tingled and Anastasia LePage floated inside, her aqua and lime green caftan fluttering around her like a cloud.

"Girls, I need your help!"

Morgan raised her brow at the elderly, somewhat eccentric woman. One of their regular customers, Anastasia's quirky personality and repeat business had quickly made her one of Morgan's favorites.

"What do you need Anastasia?"

"Oh, I desperately need something for the gout. My big toe is all swollen and the pain is excruciating!"

She shoved her foot out from underneath her dress to illustrate. Morgan caught a glimpse of aqua rhinestone sandals and blue nail polish. Her toe did look a tad swollen.

"Oh, that looks painful," Morgan said. "Devils claw is good for gout. I think I have some in stock, would you like me to get you some?"

"Oh please dear, a big bag if you will."

Morgan turned to rummage through her shelves then said over her shoulder "Oh, and eat lots of tart cherries, and drink cherry juice ... they'll help reduce the uric acid that causes gout."

"I'll have extra cherries in my cocktails, then." Anastasia winked at her.

"Labradorite can help with gout, too." Fiona held up an aqua and gray stone that glowed iridescent when the light hit it. "Wrap it in a bandage and put it right on the joint or use it in a foot bath. It can also help you have prophetic dreams if you sleep with it under your pillow."

Anastasia crossed over to Fiona and reached out for the gem. "It's so pretty. And I sure could use some dreams. If I can sleep at all that is—the lights from those damn boats were shining in my windows all night last night."

"Boats?" Fiona and Morgan asked at the same time.

"Yes, out near the entrance to Perkins Cove. On the ocean side of you girls' house. My cottage faces there and the lights glared right into my window. Woke me about two in the morning. Back and forth, back and forth ... it went on for hours."

Morgan and Fiona exchanged a look. None of the boats went out at that time of night and they certainly didn't go back and forth in the mouth of the cove like Anastasia was describing. *Could the boats have something to do with everything that was going on?*

"I can give you some chamomile and valerian for sleeping if you want," Morgan offered.

"Oh, that would be lovely, I hope those boats aren't back again tonight."

"How many nights has this happened?"

"Just last night as far as I remember. Or if they were there previously it didn't wake me up. I'll take this lovely stone too." Anastasia handed the labradorite back to Fiona and the girls packaged up her purchases and sent her on her way.

Morgan looked at Fiona as soon as the door shut. "We have to find out more about those boats."

"Do you think it could have something to do with the dead guy?"

"Well it's certainly unusual. Have you ever heard of boats out at that time of night like that?"

"Nope, never. No lobsterman I know would be out in the dark."

"Right, I think I'll look into it after work. It could turn out to be the lead we've been waiting for."

Chapter Ten

Morgan decided to stop down at Perkins Cove as soon as she got home to see if she could find out anything about the boats. If they had moored in the cove, the fishermen were sure to know about it.

Perkins Cove was a cluster of weathered buildings set on a finger of land that had the ocean on one side and an inlet on the other. Once old fisherman's shacks, they had been turned into quaint shops that sold everything from sweatshirts to jewelry to clam rolls. The shopping area was shaped in a horseshoe. The cove itself was on one side of the horseshoe and dotted with boats making a postcard perfect scene. There was a cluster of shops in the middle of the "U" and more shops on the other side which backed up to the Atlantic Ocean. A white, wooden self-serve drawbridge spanned across the narrowest part of the cove and tourists delighted in walking across it in the hopes a tall boat would come in and they could raise the bridge by pressing the button on one side.

The shopping area was small with about fourteen shops, but tourists loved it. The street, which was barely wide enough for one car, was usually packed with window shoppers. The Blackmoore house was just beyond the top of the horseshoe at the very peak of land that separated the cove from the ocean. Rather than try to find a parking spot, Morgan walked the short one eighth mile from her house.

The summer activity in the Cove always picked up her spirits. Happy tourists, kids eating ice cream, shoppers buying souvenirs and the smell of fried clams and seaweed made her smile as she made her way past the shops to the small parking lot reserved for fishermen that docked their boats in the Cove.

A couple of fishermen were gathered around the carcass of a giant tuna. Morgan joined them.

"Hi Brian, is that your catch?" Morgan asked a tall dark haired man, one of her high school classmates.

"Yep." Brian grinned with good reason, a tuna that size made for a nice pay day.

"Hey Morgan, heard you had some trouble over at yer' place." This from Josiah Littlefield, an old weathered lobsterman Morgan had known since she was a little girl.

"Yeah, the guy on the cliff? Any of you know anything about him?" Morgan glanced around the group, but they all shook their heads.

"Have there been any new boats docking in the cove the past few nights?" She ventured.

More head shaking.

"Have you guys heard anything about any boats trolling the waters on the ocean side near the cove?" she raised her eyebrows at them.

"Are 'ya thinkin' that has somethin' to do with the body you found?" Josiah asked.

"Yeah, one of my customers at *Sticks and Stones* said she saw boats going back and forth near the mouth of the cove last night in the middle of the night. Who would do that?"

"No one here would." Brian looked around the group. "That's kind of crazy."

"I know, I was wondering if they moored the boats in the cove ... whoever they are."

Morgan, Brian and Josiah turned to look at the boats stacked up in their moorings.

"Nope, nothin' but the usual boats in there," Josiah said.

"And you haven't heard about any strange boat activity?"

"Nope."

Morgan took a deep breath and blew it out. "Okay, well if you hear anything let me know. The police haven't been able to identify the deceased and it could be important."

"Sure'n we will."

Morgan turned back toward home, her stomach sinking. If the boats weren't moored in Perkins cove, then where were they?

* * *

Morgan trudged back to the house barely noticing the sights and smells of the cove. She was so occupied with her thoughts of how she could find out more about the boats that she almost didn't notice a movement to the left by the stand of trees that lined the cliff. Almost.

She jerked her head in that direction. *Was someone over there?* She stopped and squinted into the trees for a minute, but didn't see anyone. Continuing up the driveway, she chastised herself for being so jittery. It wasn't like her to get all jumpy over nothing.

Inside Fiona, Jake and Jolene were gathered around Jolene's laptop in the informal living room, one of the smaller rooms in the twenty four room home. This room was Morgan's favorite. She found the gray and blue decor to be soothing and the view of the Atlantic Ocean from the large bay window stunning. The giant starfish, seashells and rustic painted furnishings with overstuffed cushions made it comfy and homey.

Fiona looked up at her as she entered the room. "Did they know anything about the boats?"

Morgan shook her head.

"What boats?" Jolene asked.

"One of our customers said she saw boats trolling around out there in the middle of the night." Morgan tilted her chin toward the ocean.

"Trolling around? What do you mean?"

"She said they were going back and forth in a pattern around 2 a.m. The lights woke her up," Fiona said.

"I think I might know why," Jake cut in and everyone looked in his direction.

"Jolene and I did a lot of research this afternoon and one of the things that treasure hunters can do to look for sunken treasure is to ping the bottom with sonar or boat-towed marine metal detectors. If those boats were going back and forth in a pattern, then that could have been what they were doing."

"And if it's the treasure stealers, then that would explain

why they were doing it at two in the morning—they didn't want anyone to know," Jolene added.

Morgan glanced out the window at the Atlantic. *Had there been a sunken treasure just a stone's throw from their house all this time?*

"What else did you guys find out?" Morgan asked.

"Well, there really isn't much online about these treasure pirates. They're sort of an underground group. Well, actually, there are several groups. They get leads on where there might be some treasure and they try to go and steal it. They are very secretive because they don't want anyone to know what they are after, or even to know they have it once they get it." Jolene looked up at Morgan, her ice-blue eyes turning serious. "They're very dangerous people, so you better be careful if you plan to mess with them."

Morgan felt the funny feeling in the pit of her stomach intensify. "Well, it appears they think we have some treasure around here, so I don't see we have much choice."

"Yeah. If only we knew where it was—we could sure use the money ourselves. And if we found it first that might solve our problems with the treasure stealers *and* the tax office."

"I think we might be able to help with that," Celeste said from where she stood in the doorway with Cal.

"What do you mean?" Morgan raised an eyebrow in their direction.

"I showed Cal the code from the journal and he says it's something called a book cipher," Celeste said.

"Basically, the words in the journal indicate the chapter, verse and word in a second book. You use the second book, which is called the key, to decode what the journal says," Cal added.

"So we need the second book to decode it? How do we know which book it is?"

Cal ran his fingers through his hair. "Well, it would have to be a book that was as old as, or older than the journal. We need to look at the journal and see if it has a date, then try out any other books we can find that were published near that date. It's really a long shot that you'll have the key book here."

Morgan felt a spark of enthusiasm. Judging by the contents of the attic, her ancestors never threw *anything* away. There were a lot of books up there and she had a gut feeling the key book they needed was among them ... and she was learning her gut feelings were usually right.

"Well, let's get a move on," she said heading for the stairs. "That journal could lead us to the treasure, and if there's a treasure out there from the *Ocean's Revenge* then it belongs to us. I don't know about you guys, but I'm not going to sit around doing nothing while some treasure stealing pirates take it right from under our noses!"

* * *

Morgan sprinted up the stairs to the attic, the others close behind. They headed straight for the bookshelf where the journal was. No one was surprised to find Belladonna lying on top of it, watching them lazily.

"Let's see if this thing has a date," Celeste said taking the journal gently from the shelf.

Cal cringed when she opened it and leafed through the brittle pages. "You should think about wearing gloves when you handle that, the oils from your fingers could damage it."

"Oh." Celeste looked down at her fingers. "I didn't think about that."

"Lucky for you there's a pair right here." Fiona picked a pair of white lace gloves from a pile of antique clothing and handed them to Celeste.

"Jeez, these are tiny," she said, stuffing her hands into the gloves.

Morgan got busy at the bookcase, pulling out anything that looked as ancient as the journal. Belladonna jumped off the shelf, twirled herself around Celeste's feet then meandered off toward the back of the room.

"This one looks pretty old." Morgan picked up a leather bound book that was falling apart at the spine and glanced at Celeste. She noticed her sister's fingers were poised over the book and she was looking toward the window, almost in a trance.

"Celeste?" Celeste nodded her head, but not at Morgan.

"Earth to Celeste," Fiona said from her position crouched on the other side of the bookcase.

"What? Oh. Sorry." She turned the pages in the book then pointed. "Here's the date, August 10, 1722."

"The same year as that ship's manifest." Morgan's heart beat a little faster.

Celeste turned ice-blue eyes on Morgan. "Yes, but the key book isn't in this bookshelf. It's back there." She pointed toward the back of the room in the direction Belladonna had headed.

"Huh? How do you know that?" Jolene furrowed her brow at Celeste.

"Oh no. Not Nana again?" Fiona asked.

Celeste just smiled. "Let's just look back there, okay?"

Morgan shrugged and started toward the back.

"What's this about your Nana?" Cal asked.

"We'll fill you in later," Morgan said over her shoulder.

They stopped at a stack of books. She was half expecting Belladonna to be there, pointing at the book with her tail or something, but the cat was nowhere to be seen.

She looked through the stack. The top ones were canvas bound, the books toward the bottom of the stack had leather spines. She carefully moved the books off the top and handed the leather ones out to Fiona, Jolene, Jake and Cal. She took the last one for herself and Celeste bent over her shoulder.

"This one's dated 1795. Too new." Cal put the book down gently on the pile.

"This one is too," Jake said.

"This one is 1717." Jolene held up a book. The binding was cracked and dusty, the pages thick and rough.

Cal took the book. "It's a poetry book. Perfect for a cipher key."

"Do you think that's the key?"

"It could be. We might as well try it, right?"

Morgan felt a tingle run through her veins. Finding a treasure would be cool, but would that help her find the killer?

She glanced out the attic window at the ocean. It had

grown dark and the sea was black, the full moon's light sparkled on the caps of the waves. There were no boats out there. Yet.

"You guys go ahead and work on deciphering the book," Morgan said. "I'm going to keep a watch and see if those boats show up again. Maybe I can get a name or registration number. We still need to get a handle on the killer, and I have a funny feeling the closer we get to finding a treasure—if there even is one—the more dangerous it could be for us."

Morgan caught the look from Celeste. She was almost certain the attack the other day wasn't a random mugging and from the look her sister was giving her, she felt the same way.

"And everyone please be careful." Morgan looked around.

These were the people she loved most in the world. Her heart ached at the thought of anything happening to one of them. "If the treasure pirates Jolene told us about are the ones who killed the guy on the cliff, and they're after pirate treasure on our land, then I'm pretty sure they won't think twice about killing one of us to get it."

Chapter Eleven

Morgan jerked awake in the dark, her heart pounding against her ribs.

Was that a noise or a bad dream?

She glanced out the window of the turret room toward the Atlantic. No boats were out there. Looking at her watch, she saw it was 1:45.

And then she heard it again.

It came from the ground floor, smashing glass and loud voices. She was up from her seat in an instant and running downstairs.

She skidded into the living room at the same time as Fiona and Jake. It was pitch black and Morgan could only see shadowy figures. There was a fight going on, but she couldn't make out exactly who was fighting.

Someone grabbed her arm and she reached behind her, grabbing a thick crystal vase she knew was on the sideboard. She swung it toward her assailant and was rewarded when they let go of her uttering a string of curse words.

The moonlight filtered in through the smashed side window and her eyes strained to adjust to the dark.

She could see men in dark clothing, some with ski masks. Surprisingly, it seemed like they were fighting each other.

How many people were in here?

She glanced around in time to see Celeste's blonde hair—one of the masked men was reaching for her!

"Celeste! Look out!" Morgan bolted across the room and launched herself at Celeste's assailant.

He went down in a heap on the floor, Morgan on top of him. She kicked at him as he tried to grab her. Out of the corner of her eye, she saw someone push over the china cabinet with a resounding crash. Broken glass and china spilled out all over the floor. Belladonna ran hissing from the room.

Someone grabbed her by the waist and pulled her back. She squirmed around, clawing at him, trying to get in a good position to inflict some damage but he was too strong.

Her heart raced as she kicked back, but her efforts only resounded in a muffled grunt and a tighter hold on her.

"Hey, I'm not going to hurt you ... I'm here to help you."

Morgan froze in mid kick. She recognized that voice. Spinning around, she yanked off the mask.

Her heart jerked wildly in her chest when her eyes confirmed what her ears had already told her. The man holding her was her high school sweetheart, the man who had left her a decade ago—Luke Hunter.

She pushed away from him, hauled her arm back and slapped him across the face as hard as she could.

* * *

Luke's hand flew up to his cheek. She still had a mean slap. He wasn't sure what stung more—his cheek or his heart. It wasn't exactly the greeting he'd been hoping for. He could hardly blame her, though. Showing up like this after all these years. She was sure to be mad at him.

"What are *you* doing here?" Morgan backed away from him and he stood where he was even though he ached to go after her.

"Like I said ... I'm here to help you."

"What are you talking about, you broke into my house!" Morgan spread her arms to indicate the chaotic room. The lights had come on and Luke could see smashed glass, broken windows and five of his men dressed all in black wrestling two other men into handcuffs.

"We didn't break in." Luke nodded toward the two men being forced into the cuffs. "They did. We just followed them in so we could capture them."

The Blackmoore sisters huddled against the opposite

wall staring at him with wide eyes.

"Luke Hunter?" Fiona's eyes darted from Luke to Morgan.

Luke spread his hands. "In the flesh."

"But what are you doing here? I thought you were in Afghanistan or something."

"I was. My tour ended and now I'm back. Well, for a little while." He glanced over at Morgan who was shooting daggers at him from her eyes.

"Luke is Morgan's ... umm ... he grew up here." Fiona turned to explain to a man who was standing with a protective arm around her. Luke wondered who he was but figured it wasn't the time for him to ask questions. He couldn't help but smile when he noticed there was no man with a protective arm around Morgan.

"So, what is he doing in your house in the middle of the night?" The man stepped forward.

"Yeah, what *are* you doing here?" Morgan stood with her hands on her hips looking ridiculously cute in pink pajamas with French poodles on them.

"And who are these other guys?" The blonde who Luke recognized as Celeste said. She had only been a teenager when he'd left and she'd grown into a beautiful woman. Not as beautiful as Morgan, though.

Luke rubbed his hands through his day old stubble. Morgan used to like that stubble. He found himself wondering if she still felt anything for him—then immediately pushed those thoughts aside. He was only in Noquitt to do a job and then his work would take him somewhere else, possibly to the other side of the world. This job didn't leave any room for relationships and he wished he hadn't had to let Morgan know he was here. He wished he'd never gotten this close to her—to touch her. But he had to in order to stop the guys that had broken in. And now that he had ...

He let out a long breath, wondering how to explain just why he was there. He decided the simplest way was the best.

He nodded toward the handcuffed men who were being dragged out. "Those men are after something they think you have, and my job is to stop them."

"What? So you're like some sort of secret police force?" Morgan's brow was all scrunched up.

"Sort of. Have you guys noticed anything strange going on?"

"Hell 'ya," a voice said from the other side of the room.

Luke's eyes widened when he realized the petite brunette must be Jolene. She'd only been around nine years old the last time he saw her, but she had those ice-blue eyes ... the same as Morgan and all the Blackmoore sisters.

"First a dead guy shows up on the cliff. Then we start hearing stories about pirates and next thing you know we're getting broken into." She spread her arms to indicate the mess around them and Luke noticed she was bleeding.

"You're bleeding!" Fiona rushed over to the girl's side and took her arm, looking at the wound below the elbow.

Jolene looked down at her arm. "Ahh, that's not so bad."

"I'll get a bandage and some stuff to clean it off." Fiona rushed out of the room.

"Anyway, what exactly do *you* have to do with any of this?" Morgan stared him down.

"My company tracks down people that steal treasure and stops them."

"Your company? What kind of company is that? And just how do you find out where to track these people down?" The man that had been with Fiona narrowed his eyes at Luke and Luke figured he'd better make friends fast.

He put his hand out toward the guy. "I'm sorry, we haven't been introduced. I'm Luke Hunter."

The man reluctantly took his hand. "Jake Cooper."

Luke nodded. "Nice to meet you."

Jake's handshake was firm and the guy definitely had some muscles. He looked like he could take care of himself which was good. Luke might need his help protecting the Blackmoore girls if the shit hit the fan like he thought it was going to.

Fiona came back with some cotton swabs, alcohol, bandages and a big orange rock. Luke raised an eyebrow at the rock, but kept silent.

"Jake works on the Noquitt police force," Fiona said over

her shoulder as she cleaned Jolene's arm and applied the bandage.

Luke raised his brows. "Oh? How do you like that?"

"It's okay."

Luke could tell by the look on Jake's face that he didn't like it much at all. Which was good, because Luke had a feeling Sheriff Overton wasn't to be trusted. And if Jake didn't get along with Overton that probably meant Jake *could* be trusted.

Everyone was silent for a moment, watching Fiona wrap Jolene's arm. It was a deep, nasty gash.

Fiona put the rock on the wound and wrapped gauze around it.

"Keep the stone wrapped close to it until we can get some herbs and medicines from the pharmacy. It should help you heal," Fiona said then, noticing everyone was looking at her with raised brows, she shrugged and added, "it's carnelian which is good for healing wounds. At least it can't hurt."

Everyone's attention was drawn toward the window where the men in black outfits were now nailing a large sheet of plywood in place.

"We'll get that glass replaced for you tomorrow ... and clean up this mess," Luke said. "You guys might want to think about getting an alarm system."

"Can we move into the kitchen?" Fiona asked, "I could use some coffee. And, since Luke still hasn't fully explained himself, I think we're going to be up for a while."

The group moved into the kitchen. Luke noticed that Morgan kept her distance from him. He leaned against the counter while the others took positions standing and sitting around the island.

Fiona grabbed some mugs from the cabinet and popped a K-cup in the coffee maker.

"So Luke, you were saying ..." Celeste gestured for him to continue the explanation he'd started in the other room.

"Yes, tell us more about your company," Jake said. By the way Jake was studying him Luke knew it wasn't going to be easy to earn the other man's trust.

"The men that broke in here aren't nice people. They belong to a group of treasure hunters that scour the world for long lost treasure, and take it by any means they can. They're kind of like modern day pirates," Luke said. "The people that invest in my company pay me to get rid of them."

"We read up about them online. But why are they here?"

"They figure out where to go by digging into old documents and archives. As far as we can tell, they got a lead that there is treasure from an old ship here somewhere."

"Does this tie into the dead guy on the cliff?" Morgan asked.

"There are two groups of treasure hunters here in town. Rivals. One of the groups killed a member from the other group as a warning to back off."

Celeste's face brightened. "Well that's good to know, we can just tell Overton and he'll stop bothering us."

"Bothering you? About the murder?" Luke narrowed his eyes at Celeste.

"Yes, he seems to want to pin every murder in town on Morgan."

"*Every* murder?"

Morgan waved her hand. "I don't think Luke needs to know about all that."

Luke raised his brows at her.

"It's old news," she said. "But he did threaten us about the guy on the cliff. So tell us how to find these pirate guys and Jake can let him know they did the killing, and then Overton will leave us alone ... at least about that, anyway."

"It might not be that simple. These guys hide out. It's not like they have an address or anything. They're practically invisible." Luke took a chance and said to Jake, "I'm not so sure Overton can be trusted to do the right thing. What do you think?"

Jake nodded, his stance relaxing a bit. "I agree. What makes you say that, though?"

"Just a feeling." Luke stared at Jake and he felt like he'd moved up a notch on the trust scale.

"Okay, so now that you have those guys." Jolene nodded

toward the living room, "no one will be bothering us, right?"

"I wish it was that easy. Unfortunately, there are more where they came from."

"Sheesh, how many of these guys are there?" Fiona handed Luke a coffee.

"Quite a few. But I have quite a few guys too, and we're going keep a close eye on them ... and on you, to make sure nothing more happens."

Morgan snorted. "I don't think you need to keep an eye on us, we're perfectly capable of taking care of ourselves ... unless you're after the treasure too?"

Luke's heart clenched at the look of mistrust she gave him. "These guys are very dangerous and the fact that the two groups are in a fight for this treasure makes them even more so. You *do* need our help whether you want to admit it or not ... and we're not after the treasure, we get paid very well by the people that hire us."

"I still don't understand what your job is or why we should trust you," Morgan said. "Where did you take those men, anyway? To Overton?"

"No, not to Overton. We have ways of dealing with them that you don't need to know about. Just be glad there's two less that will be bothering you. And my job is to wipe out these scum—let's just say the people that pay me have a vested interest in getting rid of their kind and leave it at that."

He saw Morgan bite her bottom lip and knew he had his job cut out for him, getting her to trust him again.

"Now, the more you guys can tell me about this supposed treasure, the better I can help you."

Jolene looked up from her coffee mug. "The dead guy had a copy of a ship's manifest in his pocket from the ancestor that originally built this house. We tried to decipher one of his journals—"

"We're not sure the journals have anything to do with it," Morgan interrupted.

Luke raised an eyebrow. He knew they weren't telling him everything, but he hadn't expected them to right off the bat. "Well the more I know, the easier it will be for me to anticipate what the treasure hunters will do and the faster I'll be able to get rid of them."

He noticed Fiona, Jolene and Celeste flick their eyes over at Morgan and she shook her head.

"We'll let you know if we come up with something." She looked at the clock. "But now it's late. And I'd appreciate it if you, and your men, get out of my house."

Luke put his coffee mug down on the counter and nodded at Morgan.

"We'll get out of your house, but we'll still be watching. Those guys *will* make another attempt, probably not tonight but soon." He paused, his heart skipping a beat as he looked directly into her ice-blue eyes. "I know you know more than you're letting on and I understand why you don't want to open up to me. But I think you're just going to have to trust me on this one ... your lives may depend on it."

Then he turned and walked off toward the front door.

* * *

Morgan's pulse raced as she stared at Luke Hunter's retreating back. *Trust him?* She didn't think so.

He had a hell of a nerve showing up like this ... after all these years and not one letter or phone call.

"We should listen to what he says," Celeste said quietly.

Morgan ground her teeth together. "And just *why* would we do that? He's a stranger to us now. I see no reason to trust him."

"But Morgan, Luke grew up here. You knew him better than any of us ... don't you think he's telling the truth."

"*Knew* him ... as in used to ... I don't know him anymore. We have no idea where he's been for the past 10 years or what he's been up to. I wouldn't trust him any more than I'd trust a perfect stranger." Morgan felt her cheeks flush with anger.

"Well, he did bail us out tonight," Jolene offered. "Who knows what those men would have done if Luke and his guys weren't here."

Morgan shifted in her seat and looked across the hall

into the living room. A chill crept up her spine thinking about the two men who broke in. What *were* they going to do? And what would have happened if Luke and his men weren't here?

"It's a mess in there," she said. "The china cabinet and everything in it is ruined. Nana's probably rolling over in her grave with all her good china smashed on the floor like that."

"No she's not," Celeste offered.

Everyone turned to stare at her.

Celeste shrugged. "Well, she's not. She doesn't care about that stuff anymore ... and she approves of Luke."

Morgan narrowed her eyes at Celeste. She wasn't sure what she thought about Celeste talking to their dead grandmother. She decided to change the subject.

"Did you guys have any luck deciphering the book?"

Celeste's face brightened. "We didn't get it all figured out, but we made good progress. The poetry book seems to be the key, but the journal ... well, there's just so much of it and it's mostly just a recording of the days events—weather, rough seas and so on."

"Oh, I was hoping there would be some sort of treasure clue." Jolene's face fell into a frown.

"I think that's too much to expect. All this talk of treasure and pirates is kind of silly. Most people don't have treasure buried in their yard," Morgan pointed out.

"Well, most people don't have an ancestor that sailed the seas in a ship either," Fiona said.

"Cal suggested we look at the book from a different angle. Try to find text that isn't in the format of the daily journal. There could be a clue." Celeste looked at Morgan. "Those men didn't break in here for nothing. I think you might have to admit there might be something to all this treasure stuff."

Morgan sighed. "Well I guess it won't hurt to look at the book some more. It's late and I'm tired. I'm heading off to bed and I suggest you all do the same."

Everyone murmured their agreement and the group headed for the main stair way together. Morgan's stomach clenched when they passed the living room. She turned to her sisters and Jake.

"I'm really glad none of us were badly hurt tonight."

"Me too," Fiona added then glanced at Morgan out of the corner of her eye. "But I agree with Luke. This isn't the end of our troubles with these treasure hunters. Maybe we should think about getting him on board with what we're doing?"

Morgan sighed. "Maybe. Let's see how it goes. I still don't see why we *need* him. And I wouldn't trust him as far as I could throw him."

"Yeah, we should think it over carefully," Celeste said as they made their way up the stairs. "And don't forget to trust your gut feeling, Morgan."

Morgan thought about that. Lately it had turned out to be smart— life saving even—to trust her gut feeling. But right now, her guts were all roiled up. The truth was she didn't know how she felt.

Seeing Luke again had caused a variety of emotions. She was mad, for sure, but she also couldn't help but notice how he seemed to have gotten even more handsome in the past ten years. She couldn't deny the way her stomach flip-flopped when she'd pulled off that mask or the way her senses had reveled in his familiar earthy clean smell.

She reached her bedroom door, said goodnight and tried to push all thoughts of Luke from her mind.

She didn't want ... or need ... him to help them and she'd be *damned* if she'd let him screw with her feelings again. The further away he stayed the better. She'd done just fine these past ten years without him and she sure as heck didn't need him now.

Chapter Twelve

The next morning Morgan stumbled into the kitchen, heading straight for the coffee maker. She needed something stronger than her usual cup of herbal tea.

Fiona was already sitting at the island, sipping from a steaming mug, her red hair pulled back neatly in a ponytail at the nape of her neck.

"The strong stuff is in the left drawer." Fiona pointed to one of the kitchen drawers and Morgan grunted her thanks.

She put the K-cup in the coffee maker. The thirty seconds it took to produce the strong brew seemed like an eternity and she drummed her fingers on the counter hoping to speed it up. Finally, the mug was full and she took it over to the island.

Closing her eyes, she inhaled the pungent aroma then took a sip.

"Ahh ... that's better," she said as the caffeine started to do its job.

"Well, it's not vanilla latte, but it does the trick," Fiona said. "Still, I want to stop at the coffee shop on the way to work and get my regular."

Morgan nodded. Fiona couldn't function without a latte of some sort in her bloodstream and she'd settled on vanilla as her favorite of late.

"Speaking of the shop, remind me to bring home some arnica and aloe vera to put on that cut Jolene got last night," Morgan said.

"I don't think you need to bother," Jolene said from the doorway.

Morgan's eye's widened when she saw Jolene's arm. She had unwrapped the bandage to reveal a long scar underneath—the wound had almost completely healed.

"But that's impossible," Morgan heard herself say as she and Fiona got up to inspect the wound.

"Well, it should be," Jolene said. "But apparently, it's not."

"How did that happen?" Morgan asked as Fiona pulled the carnelian stone from the middle of the gauze wrappings.

"Is that glowing?" Morgan squinted at the stone which appeared to be glowing bright orange from the inside. Fiona and Jolene bent closer.

"No, I think it's just the sunlight reflecting from the window." Jolene nodded toward the large kitchen window where the morning sun shone through.

Morgan ran her fingers across the scar. "This is amazing."

"There's a lot of strange things going on around us," Fiona added.

Morgan agreed—cuts that heal themselves, gut feelings that proved to be accurate, pirates, buried treasure, a cat that seemed to know what they were talking about and relatives that talked to Celeste from beyond the grave sure were strange.

"That's true." Celeste appeared in the doorway with Luke. "A lot of things that shouldn't be happening are. Maybe we should just accept it and go with the flow."

Morgan felt heat rise in her body at the sight of Luke. Anger ... or something else?

"What are *you* doing here?" she demanded.

Luke pointed in the direction of the living room. "The window, remember?"

"Oh, right." Morgan looked toward the living room. "Hopefully that won't take long."

"About an hour. There's a real mess in there. Should we just pick everything up and toss it, or do you want to save it?"

Morgan's brow furrowed and she turned to ask her sisters, only to find they had snuck out of the room. "I don't know. Let me look."

They walked to the living room together, Morgan took

care not to get too close to Luke—as if he had some disease she could catch.

Her heart clenched when she looked at the mess. The oak china cabinet lay on its front, the rounded glass doors shattered. She knew getting replacement glass would be expensive, but that was nothing compared to the antique china and crystal—family heirlooms that now lay in pieces on the floor. Those were priceless.

Battling the tears that stung the backs of her eyes, she squatted down and picked through the shards. There was nothing worth saving.

"I guess we should throw it out. The china cabinet we'll have repaired but everything else is broken." She ran her fingers through the pile, jerking her hand back when she felt the sharp sting of a shard of glass.

"Ouch!" She looked at her finger as it turned bright red.

Luke was next to her in an instant, grabbing her hand before she could react. "You cut yourself. Let me see."

Their eyes met and the past ten years melted away. Morgan's heart fluttered like a frightened bird. Then she remembered how hurt she'd been when Luke had chosen the military over her.

She wrenched her hand away.

"It's nothing," she said standing up and going back to the kitchen, feeling annoyed when she noticed Luke was following her.

She ran her finger under water then turned to face him. "Is there something else?"

"I was hoping you would have changed your mind about trusting me." Luke's green eyes stared into hers.

"And why would I do that?"

"We're both after the same thing. If we keep the lines of communication open it will be easier for both of us."

Morgan snorted. "Communication? I hope you're better at it now than you have been for the past ten years."

Luke ran his hands through his short cropped hair while Morgan wrapped her finger in a paper towel.

"Morgan, I'm sorry about all that. I couldn't stay here and lead a cushy life while others were fighting for our country. I wanted to talk to you ... to write, or call but I figured it was better for you if I didn't."

Morgan ripped her gaze from the pleading look in his eyes. She never could resist that look and he knew it. He was probably using it on purpose now to get her to tell him about the treasure.

"Well, I didn't need you to decide what was best for me then, and I certainly don't need you to do it now." She started toward the stairs, turning to look at him over her shoulder as she left the room. "I trust you can show yourself out."

Then, before the tears that were threatening could fall, she ran up to her room.

Chapter Thirteen

Morgan breathed a sigh of relief when they pulled into the driveway after work. The day had been torturous. She was overtired and couldn't concentrate on anything. She'd had to toss out several herbal mixtures because she'd made them wrong. And the worst part was unwanted thoughts about Luke kept forming in her mind no matter how hard she tried to stop them.

When Celeste called to announce that she and Cal had found something in the journal, it was just the excuse Morgan and Fiona needed to close up early for the day.

As she walked up the porch steps into the house, Morgan felt a tingle in the back of her neck that was starting to become all too familiar. She whirled around, but no one was there. *Was Luke watching her ... or the bad guys?*

Inside, Jolene, Cal and Celeste were huddled over a piece of paper on the kitchen island.

"I hope you guys can help us decipher this poem—it's a haiku," Celeste said.

Morgan and Fiona crossed over to the island and Celeste slid the paper around so they could read it.

Those seeking the map
Find joy in the turtle's dome
And under the rhomb

Morgan's brows mashed together. "Huh? What's this mean?"

"That's what we're trying to figure out," Jolene said.

"Turtle? What turtle?" Fiona asked.

"And what the hell is a rhomb?" Morgan added.

"Who knows?" Jolene shrugged as she tapped something

into her smart phone. "Oh, here, it says it's another word for rhombus ... you know, the geometric figure."

Morgan raised her brows. "This poem doesn't even make any sense. Could it be another code of some sort?"

"It could," Cal said. "Don't forget it was written long ago—and probably meant for someone who would understand the hidden meaning."

"The important thing is it seems to verify there is some sort of map." Celeste pointed to the first line of the poem.

"Or was," Morgan said.

"Right. Now if we only knew what it meant by turtle dome we might be on to something." Jolene settled back into her chair with a sigh.

Morgan felt something niggle at the back of her brain. Turtle. Dome. *Why did that seem familiar?*

Morgan snapped her fingers. "I've got it!"

She ran for the stairs to the attic with everyone following. At the top she surveyed the space, trying to remember where she had seen the little trunk.

"Mew."

She should have known Belladonna would be up here and she followed the sound.

"What is it?" Fiona's slightly out of breath voice came from behind her.

"I saw a domed box when I was up here before and I think it was made of tortoise. That could be the *turtle's dome* mentioned in the poem."

The cat led them to an alcove and Morgan's heart clenched when she saw the box. She reached down and picked it up, holding it in front of her for the others to see.

Cal reached out and she handed it to him.

"This is really old," Cal said. "It definitely could be from the era of the poem."

His words sent a chill up Morgan's spine. *Could there really be a treasure map inside?*

"What are you waiting for? Open it up," Jolene said, leaning over Cal's shoulder to look at the box.

Cal held it out to Morgan. "Go ahead."

Morgan took the box in her hand, thinking how delicate it looked. A ripple of excitement surged through her like an electric current as she held the box. She grabbed the top and pulled.

Her heart sunk like a stone.

"It won't open." She tried to pull harder, but the box was sealed tight.

"It's probably locked." Cal pointed to the tiny keyhole on the front.

Morgan's excitement deflated. "What are the odds of finding the key in this?" She spread her hands to indicate the vast space.

"Let me see." Jolene held out her hand and Morgan placed the box in it.

Jolene squinted at the lock, turned the box this way and that then rummaged in an open trunk that was sitting on the floor. She pulled out an antique hairpin which was about eight inches long and had a large pearl on the end. She stuck the pin end into the keyhole, wiggled it around and the box popped open.

Morgan's heart dropped when she looked inside. It was empty.

"Hey, where'd you learn to do that?" Fiona furrowed her brow at Jolene.

"Oh, I've been looking into some private investigator stuff online ... just a little trick I picked up." Jolene shrugged.

"Figures, it's empty," Morgan said. "I guess it was silly to think an old treasure map would still be in here after all these years."

"It's a nice box though." Celeste took the box from Jolene.

"Very nice ... and very valuable," Cal said.

Morgan shrugged. "I guess we should put it back."

"Wait," Cal said. "A lot of times, these old boxes had false bottoms."

Morgan peered over Celeste's shoulder into the box.

"It doesn't look like it has a false bottom," she said, bending down to look at the box from underneath.

She held out her hand and Celeste put the box in it. The inside bottom was an indigo blue velvety material—worn and faded over the years. She could barely make out the pattern, oddly shaped diamonds in gold.

A jolt of electricity shot through her heart as she remembered the last line of the poem "*and under the rhomb*". She jerked her head in Jolene's direction. "What shape is a rhombus?"

Jolene made a face. "I think it's like a diamond with equal sides or something. Why?"

Morgan didn't answer. She was too busy ripping out the velvet lining. Her stomach flip-flopped when she saw the aged parchment underneath. Gently, she reached into the box and pulled it out.

Celeste, Fiona and Jolene gasped as she held it up by the corner.

"It's the map!"

"Careful, that looks awfully brittle," Cal said. "Let's bring it over to this bureau.

He indicated a large Eastlake style bureau a few feet away and Morgan carried it over and spread it out on the marble top.

The dry parchment was tattered on the edges, the ink faded, but there was enough for them to make out a small map and some writing. The map depicted a point of land with water on three sides. Arrows pointed toward a large tree and the writing gave further directions.

"That looks like our land." Fiona looked out the window.

"Yes!" Jolene pointed excitedly. "Here's the Atlantic on this side and the channel leading to the cove on the other ... there's no big tree there though."

"Maybe there was a tree three hundred years ago," Celeste offered.

"We need to copy this so that we don't damage the original," Cal said.

"Right," Morgan agreed, looking around for a paper and pencil.

"There's a paper and pencil over by the bookcase, where I copied some of the journal," Celeste said and Cal started off in that direction.

"Do you really think this is our yard?" Fiona asked.

"Sure looks like it." Jolene's eyes sparkled as she studied the map.

"There could be buried treasure right out there." Celeste pointed out the window.

Morgan looked out to where Celeste was pointing, a familiar tingle forming in her lower belly. Even though her logical brain kept telling her the thought of pirate treasure being buried in her yard was ridiculous, her gut instincts were telling her something big was about to happen.

Chapter Fourteen

The sun was about to set by the time Celeste had copied the map. They stood in the side yard, huddled around the copy, shovels at the ready. The wind from the ocean licked at the edges of the paper, threatening to tear it from Cal's hand.

"It says start at the tree. Anyone know where the tree was?" Cal asked.

Morgan didn't remember any tree, so she tried to figure it out by looking at the map.

"Meow." Belladonna sat off to the left, her tail twitching in the grass.

"From looking at the map, it looks like the tree was right about where Belladonna is." Morgan was getting used to the cat showing up in the exact right spot and at the right time.

"Okay, it looks like it says thirty paces east." Cal walked over to Belladonna's spot, then turned east and took thirty steps. Everyone ran over to stand beside him.

"Then ten steps toward the point. What's that mean?" Celeste asked.

"I assume the point of the cliff." Cal took the ten steps.

"Now three quarter turn as the sun rises."

"Does that mean toward the east? That's where the sun rises," Jolene said.

"I guess so. Let's try that." Morgan watched Cal turn then take a few more steps indicated by the directions on the map. After a few more turns and paces he stopped.

"Well, if I followed the directions correctly, this is the spot." Cal pointed to an area of grass right in front of him.

The five of them looked at each other uncertainly.

Should they start digging?

Jolene broke the ice by plunging her shovel into the grass and the rest followed suit.

Morgan jabbed her shovel into the rocky ground. It wasn't as easy as she thought it was going to be and she had to jump on the edge of the blade in order to get it to sink in. She removed a small shovel full of dirt and placed it aside.

"How deep do you think this thing is buried?"

Cal shrugged. "Who knows? Probably not too deep, I mean it's not like whoever buried it in 1722 had machinery. They would have had to dig by hand. Just like we are."

Morgan wiped a bead of sweat from her forehead with the back of her hand. "Well I hope he went easy with the digging, this could take a long time."

"That's why I called in a favor from a friend," Jolene said as her cellphone chimed. She looked at the display, then jogged toward the front of the house.

Morgan raised an eyebrow at Fiona who shrugged and continued digging. Morgan's enthusiasm waned as she looked in the hole.

"I don't see any sign of treasure," she said.

"We're not that far down ye—"

Fiona's words were cut off by the sound of an engine coming from the side of the house and Morgan turned to see Jolene directing a small Bobcat bulldozer toward them. She gladly set her shovel aside and waved them over.

"This is the favor you called in?"

"Yep," Jolene said. "It pays to have friends that owe you. This is Randy." Jolene went through the round of introductions between her sisters, Cal and the Bobcat operator.

They stood back while Randy operated the machine, expertly digging just a little bit at a time so as not to damage whatever might be in there.

Out of the corner of her eye, Morgan could see Belladonna about fifteen feet away, watching them, her tail flicking animatedly. She tried to focus on the digging, but her attention was drawn more and more toward the cat who was now digging furiously.

Morgan walked over and squatted next to her. "What are you doing Belladonna?"

"Meow!" The cat glanced over at her, then resumed her frenzied digging.

Morgan reached out to pet her, but the cat moved away, looked at her reproachfully, and attacked the hole from another angle.

Morgan noticed she'd dug about six inches down. Peering into the hole, her heart lurched when she saw a sliver of light reflecting off something.

What was that?

She reached into the hole and Belladonna sat back on her haunches, proceeding to clean the dirt from her front paws. Morgan's fingers closed on something cool and smooth, about the size of a quarter. She pulled it out.

Adrenalin shot through her body as she held it up to the light. The fading sun glinted off the small round object like it was gold. Morgan's heartbeat quickened when she realized it probably *was* gold.

But what was it?

She laid it flat in her palm to take a better look. It looked like it could be some sort of coin, but the edges were unevenly cut. There was writing and images on it, but they were well worn. One side had what looked like a cross in the middle, the other a grid which reminded her of tic tac toe.

"Hey guys ..." She rose to her feet holding the coin out for them to see.

Cal's eyes grew wide. He came over and held his hand out for the coin.

"Where did you get this?"

"In the hole Belladonna was digging." Morgan gestured toward the hole and Cal looked down at it, then back at the coin.

"This is an 8 Escudo—a gold Spanish coin. It dates to the early 1700s. This thing is worth about ten grand."

Morgan looked at the Bobcat, then down at the little hole that had produced the coin.

"Do you think we could be digging in the wrong spot?"

"I don't know ... we're digging where the map said." Cal rubbed his chin. "Unless the map was in some sort of code, like instead of going right we should have gone left."

He whistled toward the other group and they stopped and turned to look at him.

"Hey, bring that thing over here. Morgan found something." He held up the coin and everyone came over to admire it.

"I found it in this hole. We should dig it out, just in case there is more."

"What made you decide to dig over here?" Fiona asked.

"I didn't. It was Belladonna." Morgan nodded toward the cat who was now laying on the top granite step at the kitchen door.

Fiona raised an eyebrow and Belladonna stared at them, flicking her tail.

The Bobcat started up and Cal directed the operator to dig slowly, only a little bit at a time.

Morgan and her sisters stared anxiously into the hole, waiting. For what, she had no idea, but she had a feeling she'd know it when she saw it.

It didn't take long. She heard a metallic scrape and saw something silver flash in the hole. Cal must have heard it too because he held up his hand.

"Hold up!"

The Bobcat shovel stopped in midair. Cal bent down and reached into the hole, lifting out a silver box. It was beautiful with a flowery carved, repousse design and gold details on the corners. Beautiful, but small, Morgan thought. Cal passed it around, handing it to Celeste, who admired it for a minute then handed it to Jolene.

How much treasure could that thing possibly hold?

She was about to reach for the box when a voice cut through the air behind her and stopped her cold.

"Hold it right there!"

Chapter Fifteen

Morgan's heart froze as she turned toward the sound of the voice—Sheriff Overton.

He ambled over to them, the ever present toothpick sticking out of the side of his mouth, a satisfied smirk plastered on his face.

"Do you have a permit to dig here?" He gestured toward the two holes.

"Permit? Why would we need that? It's our property." Morgan stood with her hands on her hips. She could see Jolene with the box sneaking away, off to the side behind Overton and tried her best to draw his attention away from her.

"Town ordinance. A permit is required for all machined digging." He nodded toward the Bobcat.

Morgan flicked her eyes toward Fiona who shrugged. *Was he telling the truth?* Morgan wished she'd paid more attention to the town laws.

Overton walked over to the hole and looked in. "What are you digging for? Or are you digging a hole to hide your next dead body?"

Morgan's shoulders stiffened and she fought the desire to slap the smirk off his face.

"We're testing out soil conditions for a special herb garden," Morgan lied, sending a warning glance to the others.

Overton furrowed his brow. "Is that so?"

Morgan nodded. "Yep, we're going to plant some herbs that need deep, sandy soil, so we were digging around to find the best spot."

"Yeah, you know how hard it is to grow plants without the right conditions," Fiona added amidst nods from everyone else.

Overton walked over to the other hole and peered in, then turned and narrowed his eyes at Morgan. He took a pad of paper out of his pocket.

"I'll have to write you up. That's a five hundred dollar fine." Overton smiled.

Morgan's heart plummeted. They barely had enough to pay the taxes on the house and now this?

"But we're only digging a couple of little holes. We're filling them in right away," she protested.

"Don't matter." He wiggled the toothpick back and forth as he wrote.

Morgan's cheeks grew warm with anger but she held herself back from doing something she might regret later. At least Overton hadn't seen the coin or the box. Her gut feeling told her it was better to just take the ticket and get him out of there as soon as possible then to instigate something that might cause him to linger.

"This needs to be paid in ten days or I might have to exercise my right to put out a warrant on you." Overton stared at Morgan as he ripped the paper from the pad. "And put you in jail ... where you belong."

Morgan stared Overton down as she took the paper. "Is that all?"

"I think I have cause to look around some."

Morgan's stomach lurched as he started over by the house. She knew he was looking for any little thing he could find to use as an excuse to get some sort of warrant to look inside.

"Sheriff! Dispatch just called in, there's an accident over on Route 1," one of the uniformed cops yelled from the side of the house.

Overton grunted then spun around and ambled off, turning only long enough to shoot Morgan a warning glance.

"Don't forget to pay that promptly."

Morgan's shoulders relaxed as he rounded the side of the house.

"What was that all about? I've never had that happen before," Randy asked.

"Don't ask," Morgan said. "Overton doesn't like us and he'll use any excuse to hassle us."

The boy shrugged. "It's getting pretty dark—I assume you guys are done with the Bobcat, right?"

"Yes, we got what we were looking for. Thanks so much for helping us."

"Umm ... You won't say anything about what we dug up, will you?" Celeste added.

"Mum's the word. Jolene already swore me to secrecy." He gave a "scouts honor" sign, started up the Bobcat and headed toward the front.

"Speaking of Jolene, where did she run off to with that box?" Fiona asked.

"I don't know. But I have a feeling it's a good thing Overton didn't see that fancy box or the coin. The less he knows about what's going on here, the better."

* * *

Cal grabbed a shovel. "I'll fill these holes back in, you guys go inside."

Fiona and Celeste headed toward the kitchen door on the side, but Morgan went toward the front—she wanted to make sure Overton was really gone. Her mind started to wander to the box they had pulled from the hole.

What was in it?

She couldn't help but think it seemed pretty small to contain much of a treasure. She glanced back. *Maybe there was more buried deeper in the hole?*

She hesitated between going forward to the front or back to look deeper into the hole. The front door won. She wanted to see what was in the box and they could always dig it out more, later. She stepped forward before looking where she was going and ran smack into—

Luke Hunter.

"What the—"

"Whoa. You should watch where you're going."

Luke smiled at her causing her heart to skitter around in her ribcage. He had put his arm on her waist to keep her from toppling over and she noticed he hadn't bothered to remove it. It felt familiar, exciting and annoying all at the same time.

"You scared the crap out of me. You shouldn't sneak up on people like that." She took a step backward and Luke dropped his hand to his side.

"Sorry. I saw the ruckus and wanted to know what was going on." Luke thrust his chin toward the holes.

Morgan bit her bottom lip.

Should she tell him?

She didn't want to. Probably because she was still hurt about the way he left ten years ago. She felt like he'd betrayed her then and didn't see what would stop him from doing it now. Then again, he *had* saved them the other night and he was too smart to accept the lame gardening excuse she'd given to Overton.

"We found a map in the attic. A treasure map," she said.

Luke raised his eyebrows. "And did you find a treasure in one of those holes?"

Morgan shrugged. "Not really. We found a coin and a small box."

Luke cursed under his breath making Morgan's stomach clench.

"What?" She narrowed her eyes, was he mad they found something or mad that it was so small?

"I'm sure those treasure hunters are watching you from somewhere." Luke glanced out into the Atlantic Ocean. "They probably saw that you dug something up and now they will be coming after you for it."

"Well, they already broke into our house once. I figured they'd be coming back." Morgan looked out at the wooded area, then past it to the ocean. *Was there a boat out there beyond her scope of vision with high powered binoculars trained on her house?*

Luke grabbed her upper arms, forcing her to look back at him. She noticed his green eyes were hard and cold.

"Morgan, this is serious. These guys are killers." She saw his eyes soften. He reached out and brushed a lock of hair away from her forehead, causing a riot of emotions to run through her.

"I couldn't stand it if anything happened to you—you

have to come clean with me and tell me everything you know. *And* let me know what you plan to do next."

She let out a sigh. "I don't know what was in the box and I'm not sure what we'll do next. I guess it depends on what's in the box."

"And what about Overton, what did he want?"

"To hassle us, as usual. I told you before how he has it in for us ... and I have no idea why."

"Yeah, I don't trust him. What about this Jake guy that was with Fiona? Can you trust him or is he in close with Overton?"

Morgan thought back to how Jake had risked his own job and gone against Overton to help prove she was innocent in the Littlefield murder. She'd trust him with her life.

"Jake is totally trustworthy. He doesn't like Overton either. In fact, Overton is doing everything he can to keep Jake away from the case of the dead guy on the cliff."

Luke nodded. "Okay. Good. We need all the people on our side we can get."

Morgan shuffled her feet. She felt awkward and unsure of herself. Part of her wanted to bolt into the house and the other part of her wanted to stand here with Luke all night.

She gave herself a mental head slap. *What was she thinking?*

"We cleaned up the mess in your living room and we're getting the glass replaced in the china cabinet. Sorry about your grandma's china, I remember how much you loved it."

Morgan's heart softened another notch toward him. *He remembered how much she loved that china.*

A variety of words tried to battle their way from her brain to her mouth, but she only managed to get one out. "Thanks."

"Okay, well if you find out anything else, or see anyone or anything suspicious call me right away." He reached into his pocket and pulled out a black business card with nothing but a phone number on it in silver. Morgan turned the card over, the back was blank.

"That's my private cell number. Call me no matter what

time of day or night."

Morgan's stomach did a somersault as he turned to go and she stared at his back, unable to move. After a few steps he turned to face her again.

"In the meantime, my men and I will be keeping a close eye on you ... and your sisters."

Then he turned and trotted off toward the woods.

* * *

She almost called after him.

Then she remembered that she had no idea where he'd been or what he'd been doing for the past ten years. For all she knew, he was the head of these treasure hunting pirates and was just trying to worm the information out of her.

Still, for a few minutes, it had seemed like old times. Like the Luke she'd once loved. She'd have to be careful. She couldn't let herself get hurt by him again.

Stuffing his business card in her back pocket, she ran up the porch steps into the house, pausing only for a second to glance over in the direction that Luke had disappeared in.

Was he watching her now?

The thought made her feel safe ... and a little creeped out at the same time.

She turned back and opened the front door, heading in the direction of the kitchen where she could hear everyone talking.

"Can you guys believe this? What a jerk." She slapped the citation Overton had given her on the counter.

"I know. He really hates you guys," Cal said.

"Good thing we dug up this coin, looks like we're going to need some extra money." Celeste held up the escudo and turned to Cal. "Are you sure this is real?"

"Of course. I *am* an expert you know." He raised his eyebrows at Celeste.

Celeste laughed. "I know, sorry."

"I can lend you guys some money if you need it to pay that right away. I'm sure I can find a buyer for the coin."

He pointed at the citation.

Morgan looked at her sisters. "Should we sell the coin? I'm not sure what to do but I know the money would sure come in handy."

"Fine by me. Hopefully there will be plenty more inside this box." Jolene held up the little box they had taken from the hole and shook it carefully.

"I don't hear anything rattling around inside." Morgan's brow creased as she looked at the box. "Did you open it?"

"We were waiting for you." Fiona looked at Morgan out of the corner of her eye. "What were you doing out there with Luke?"

Morgan felt her cheeks grow warm. "What? He wanted to know what was going on. That's all."

"Oh?"

Morgan turned to the cupboard on the pretense of getting a coffee mug.

"He saw us digging and was wondering what we were up to. Anyone want tea?"

"What did you tell him?" Celeste asked.

Morgan shrugged as she rummaged for a tea bag. "I kind of had to tell him we dug up the box there, but I didn't tell him much else."

"Why not? He bailed us out last night." Celeste tapped her finger on her lips. "Come to think of it, that was probably him that chased off those muggers."

"What muggers?" Cal wrinkled his brows at Celeste.

"Yeah, what muggers?" Fiona and Jolene said at the same time.

"Oops." Celeste shrugged. "Well, there's really no sense in keeping it from everyone. I think we all know that we're in danger here with the break in last night and all."

"I guess you're right," Morgan said. "Celeste and I got jumped the other day when we went to see Cal."

"What? Why didn't you say something?" Cal's eyes clouded over with concern.

"Well, we got away. Celeste kicked the crap out of the guys and we ran off. Then some other guys came out of nowhere and I guess they took care of the attackers."

"Hey I wonder if those other guys were Luke's guys?"

Celeste said.

Morgan remembered how she had thought she'd seen Luke that day. "I think it might have been, now that I remember, I thought one of them looked like Luke."

"And you still don't trust him?" Fiona raised an eyebrow at her.

"You don't trust Luke?" Cal turned to Morgan.

"Well, it's not that I don't trust him. It's just that we don't know anything about him anymore."

Cal shrugged. "Jeez, Morgan. We've known Luke since we were kids and he was always a good guy. A few years in the military probably hasn't changed that. Are you sure you aren't letting your emotions get in the way of your better judgment?"

Morgan bristled. "I just think we need to be really careful."

"I know you're still hurt about the way he left, but I think he was doing what he thought was best for you," Cal said.

"Yeah, he seems like he really *is* on our side," Fiona added.

"Well, we'll see. I know we can trust each other and anything else ... well." Morgan shrugged, looking at the little box that Jolene had set on the breakfast bar island in front of her.

"Forget about Luke. Let's open this thing up and see what's inside.

* * *

Jolene pushed the box toward Morgan. "Go ahead."

Morgan stared at it. It wasn't very big, not much bigger than a couple of decks of cards.

"It doesn't look like it could hold much of a treasure." Fiona sounded disappointed.

"You can say that again. I was wondering if there might be more in the holes," Morgan said. "I mean a tiny box like this hardly seems worth all the trouble we've had with these pirate guys and everything."

"Are you going to open it and find out, or what?" Jolene's fingers drummed on the counter.

Morgan looked at the front. This one didn't have a lock like the last one, it had a button. Morgan pressed it and the lid flew open. Her stomach dropped—the box was empty except for a brittle piece of paper.

Fiona, Jolene, Cal and Celeste bent their heads over the box to look inside.

"That's it?" Jolene scrunched up her face.

"Maybe this one has a false bottom too?" Fiona crouched down so that the bottom of the box was eye level.

Morgan carefully picked out the piece of paper and laid it on the island in front of her. The faded swirly writing was similar to that in the journal.

You'll find the key you seek beneath the tree we vowed our love.

"Oh geez, another cryptic clue. What the heck does that mean?" Jolene blew out a breath strong enough to cause her wavy bangs to puff out.

"I don't know. What tree do you think it means?" Fiona asked.

"Who knows? That tree could be long gone by now—the note was written almost three hundred years ago," Morgan pointed out.

Fiona picked up the box, inspecting it from all angles. "I don't think there's any hidden compartment in this one. Geez, what a letdown."

"Yeah, I knew all this pirate stuff was silly," Morgan added.

"Well, I guess it gives us something to think about," Cal said. "In the meantime, I'm going to setup camp in the spare bedroom."

"What?" Morgan scrunched her eyebrows at him. "Are you being stalked by one of your girlfriends and need to hide out here?"

Everyone giggled. Cal was known for being a ladies man but he often had a couple of girls going at the same time which sometimes got dangerous for him.

"No, Miss smarty pants. I'm staying here until you guys are out of danger. I don't want to leave you guys alone to get attacked again."

"And Jake is staying too. In fact, he should be here any minute," Fiona added.

Morgan pursed her lips. Normally she would argue. As the oldest Blackmoore, she felt like she could take care of her sisters by herself, but her common sense prevailed. They'd already been attacked and broken into. Having two strong guys here couldn't hurt.

"Okay. Thanks." She smiled at Cal.

"Come on, I'll help you pick out a room." Celeste stood up. The house had twelve bedrooms. Some were closed off, but they still had quite a few guest rooms for Cal to choose from.

Morgan suppressed a yawn. "Yeah, I'm pretty tired. I think I'll go upstairs and read or something. Maybe I'll get an inspiration about what "*the tree we vowed our love*" means."

"Let's hope so," Fiona said. "I don't want to be looking over my shoulder for pirates for much longer."

Morgan nodded. "Or worrying about finding dead guys on the cliff."

Chapter Sixteen

Morgan was surprised that she'd slept so well the night before. She hated to admit it, but knowing that Cal and Jake were in the house and Luke had an army of men watching them made her feel secure.

Too bad she hadn't come up with any ideas about what the writing on the paper meant.

"I think today is going to be a good day," Fiona said as she opened the door to *Sticks and Stones*.

"Well, no one tried to break in and no dead bodies appeared on the cliff, so it's already shaping up to be pretty good in my eyes," Morgan replied as she turned the sign on the door to "Open".

"I have something for you." Fiona rummaged in her jewelry case, coming up with a pendant on a chain. The stone was a rich honey brown, shaded from dark to light.

Morgan held her hand out and the gemstone sparked as one sister handed it to another.

"It's tiger's eye." Fiona said. "It will help protect you."

Morgan narrowed her eyes at the stone. A week ago she might have scoffed at the idea of a rock protecting her against anything, but after seeing Jolene's wound heal so quickly and the odd things that had been happening, she didn't know what to think anymore. She fastened the necklace around her neck as she looked out the back window of the shop.

"Hopefully I won't need to be protected."

Fiona shrugged. "Better safe, than sorry."

Morgan pursed her lips as she looked into the forest behind the shop. The birds hopped between branches, squirrels scurried around on the ground. Out of the corner of her eye she saw something white streak by.

Was that who she thought it was?

She opened the window and poked her head out.

"What are you doing?" Fiona asked.

"You won't believe who I thought I just saw."

"In the woods? Who would be there? Oh wait ... you don't mean?"

"Yep, it's her."

Morgan stared at Belladonna who sat at the bottom of the ancient oak tree, staring back at her. This wasn't the first time the cat had shown up here and Morgan had no idea how she even knew the way. Granted, it was only about a mile from their house, but Morgan's stomach clenched at the thought of the cat running around in traffic.

Fiona came to the window. "I don't know what gets into her."

"Who knows?" Morgan shrugged. "I guess we should bring her inside. At least we can make sure she gets a ride home with us and isn't out wandering the streets."

Morgan went out through the back door of the cottage. Belladonna had started digging under the tree and scooted away from Morgan when she tried to pick her up.

"Belladonna, come."

The cat ignored her.

"Want a treat?"

Belladonna dug even faster.

"You know cats don't fall for that stuff." Fiona said. "What is she digging for?"

"I have no idea. Probably a mouse or something."

"Mew!" The cat glanced back at them then returned to digging.

"Well, it's an old tree ..."

Morgan didn't hear the rest of the sentence. She was busy looking up at the initials carved in the tree. Her heart jerked as if someone had zapped it with electricity.

You'll find the key you seek beneath the tree we vowed our love.

"This is it!" Morgan's mind whirled. *Did they have any*

shovels here?

"Huh?" Fiona frowned at her.

"This is the tree from the clue in the box. Look at the initials." She pointed upwards and Fiona bent her head back.

"IB and MB. Do you think that's Isaiah Blackmoore?"

Morgan nodded. "Yep. This land has been in our family for generations. In fact, I think we owned all of it around here at one time." Morgan grabbed a hoe and trowel they used for putting flowers in the front garden from the side of the cottage.

"Here you use the hoe to loosen stuff up. I'll dig with the trowel." Morgan handed the hoe to Fiona.

Belladonna sat back and watched the sister's dig. They fell into a rhythm, Fiona churning up the dirt and Morgan digging around after her.

Morgan was just starting to wonder if they should close the shop when her trowel scraped against metal.

"I've got something!"

She reached into the hole, her stomach flipping as her fingers slid over cold metal. She brushed away the dirt to reveal gleaming silver.

"What is it?" Fiona had squatted beside her.

"I think it's a box." Morgan wiggled the corner and it slid out of the dirt.

She held it up, feeling slightly disappointed. The box was small—smaller than the last one. It fit in the palm of her hand and was only about an inch high. The finish looked like a match to the last box, finely detailed silver in a flower pattern.

"That's kind of small. What's in it?" Fiona asked.

Morgan looked at the front. It had a push clasp, similar to the other box. She felt a stab of disappointment. The box was too small for any real treasure.

She pressed the clasp and the box popped open as if the hinges were just oiled yesterday. Morgan stared at the contents.

An old skeleton key sat gleaming on a blue velvet lining.

"A key?" Fiona asked.

"I wonder what it goes to?"

"I hope it's something good, this treasure hunt is getting tedious."

Morgan nodded. Maybe her ancestor had a warped sense of humor and all these clues led to nothing ... or maybe the treasure had been taken years ago. But if it was, why would the treasure hunters be so keen to find it? They must have something pretty solid to think the treasure was still around.

Morgan felt the hairs on the back her neck stand up, her heart lurched. In her excitement of figuring out the clue, she'd forgotten that the treasure hunters could be watching.

"We better get inside," she said glancing around. "They could be watching us and we don't want them to know we dug up another clue."

"Right," Fiona said as they quickly shoved the dirt back into place, then scurried in the back door, leaving the trowel and hoe leaning against the cottage. Belladonna squeaked through in between their feet and found a sunny spot to curl up and sleep in.

The girls stood in the center of the shop looking at the shiny key that lay flat in the palm of Morgan's hand.

"I wonder what it goes to?" Morgan asked.

"I hope it's something good, this treasure hunt is getting tedious."

"The logical place to look would be—"

Morgan was interrupted by the sound of the door being jerked open. The girls swiveled their heads toward the door and Morgan's stomach dropped when she saw a giant of a man standing inside the door way.

"I'll take that," The giant said as he turned the shop sign to "Closed" and slammed the door shut.

Morgan closed her hand and took a step backwards as the man lunged for the key. Her heart pounded as he advanced on them, backing the girls further into the shop.

"Hand it over and I won't have to hurt 'ya." His harsh, angry voice sent chills up Morgan's spine.

"No," she said.

His eyebrows shot up and his face turned red, then he lurched forward grabbing for her arm.

Some of Celeste's quick moves must have worn off on her because Morgan shot her elbow out at the exact right moment and it connected with his nose making a sickening crunching sound.

Blood spurted out of the giant's nose and his hands flew up to cover it. He bent forward at the waist, stumbled and stepped on Belladonna's tail.

Belladonna screeched and flew through the air, landing on his back with her claws fully extended.

He let out a wail, flailing with one hand toward his back as he straightened up. Morgan saw Belladonna slide down his back, leaving a trail of claw marks. He spun around, reaching for the cat.

"Damn cat!"

Belladonna flew up to the top of the bookcase and sat there hissing and spitting at him. Out of the corner of her eye, Morgan could see Fiona grappling behind her, her hands flailing around the display where she kept her geodes. Her right hand found the largest one which was about twice the size of a candlepin bowling ball.

The giant turned his attention back toward the girls. His face was twisted in anger as he closed the distance between them quicker than seemed humanly possible.

His arm shot out toward Morgan. Her heart lurched in her chest as his large hand wrapped around her throat and squeezed. She tried to struggle, but that only made it worse, her vision started to fade. Pin pricks of stars floated in front of her eyes as she watched Fiona smash the geode right into the giant's face.

He went down with a crash and lay still on the floor.

Morgan sucked in a deep breath.

"Are you okay?" Fiona stared at her.

"Yeah." Her voice sounded raspy and her fingers flew to her throat which felt raw.

"We better tie him up in case he wakes up before I can call Luke," Morgan said, thankful she had put Luke's card in her pocket this morning before work.

Fiona ripped open a drawer and pulled out some twine. "I hope he's not dead." She looked at him uncertainly.

Morgan bent over the still body. Belladonna hopped onto

his stomach and sat there.

"He's breathing. He's not dead." Morgan held her hand out for the twine. She had no idea how to tie someone up to restrain them but she'd have to do her best.

"Help me flip him over, then we can tie his arms behind him."

The girls got on one side and pried him over on to his back. Morgan caught a glimpse of Fiona's wrist as they pushed him over and her heartbeat quickened. The stones on Fiona's bracelet were glowing.

"Look at your bracelet!"

Fiona looked down. "What the heck? It's never done that before."

The girls were staring down at the bracelet when the door to their shop jerked open a second time.

Chapter Seventeen

Morgan's heart jolted and she ripped her gaze away from the bracelet, bracing herself for another fight.

"Luke!"

"What happened? Are you okay?"

Luke was at her side in a second, his green eyes clouded with concern.

"I'm fine," she said, her voice still a little raspy. Then she motioned toward the giant on the floor. 'This guy must be one of those treasure hunters."

"Your throat—it's all red. Did he hurt you?" Luke put his hand tenderly on her neck to inspect it. Morgan's pulse quickened, a warm glow spreading throughout her body.

Her hand flew up to her throat on instinct. "He tried to strangle me, but I'm okay."

Luke stared at her for a few seconds more, and then narrowed his eyes at the guy on the floor.

"What did he want?"

Morgan caught Fiona's glance and knew her sister was right. It was time to tell Luke everything.

"Remember the box we dug up yesterday?" Morgan asked as Luke opened the door, making hand motions apparently to someone outside.

"Yes." He glanced at her while he held the door open for three guys who got busy tying up the giant.

"It only had a piece of paper in it, but that paper was a clue," Fiona added.

"A clue that led us to the giant tree out back. We dug around and found this." Morgan opened her fist to show him the key.

"What does it go to?" Luke asked.

"We don't know." Morgan flipped the key over. "We've

been going on some sort of treasure hunt. First we found a passage in this old journal we had in the attic. That led us to an old box that had a map in it. We followed the map and dug the holes yesterday, which had another box where the clue was to dig under the tree here."

Luke raised his eyebrows at her. "And the dead pirate in your yard. What do you know about him?"

"Nothing," Morgan said. "Well, except that Overton said he was found with a manifest from a ship called the *Ocean's Revenge* that was supposedly captained by some relative of ours. That's why we went to look in the journal in the attic in the first place."

Luke nodded. "Is there anything else I should know?"

Morgan shook her head.

"Well, there is one thing ... maybe two," Fiona interjected. "Morgan and Celeste were attacked the other day."

"Yeah, I saw that. Celeste has a mean karate kick."

"So, you *were* there," Morgan said.

"Yep, we've been here watching things for a while." Luke stepped aside to let the men drag the giant outside. "What was the other thing?"

"Oh, I think Fiona is talking about the boats, right?" Morgan cocked an eyebrow at her sister.

"Yep. A customer said she saw boats going back and forth in the water around the entrance to the cove at two in the morning," Fiona explained.

Luke frowned. "Have you seen the boats? How many nights did they do this?"

"We haven't seen them." Morgan looked at Fiona. "I think it was only one night, right?"

Fiona nodded. "As far as I know."

Luke rubbed his chin. "They were probably trolling for sunken treasure."

"That's what Jake said!"

Luke nodded. "Sometimes pirates would sink their ships on purpose in an out of the way place so no one else would get the treasure. They would come back and retrieve it later. The treasure hunters were looking for a sunken ship ... but if they haven't come back that probably means they didn't find any evidence of one."

"So then why are they still bugging us?" Fiona asked.

"They didn't find any evidence *in the water*. But they sure do think there is something in this area, so now they are going to focus on the land."

Morgan shuddered. "So we just have to find it first then, right?"

"It's not really that simple. And you guys shouldn't be digging around without talking to me. In addition to sinking their ships, pirates were well known for booby-trapping the places they buried their treasure—to protect it from thieves. Whoever came digging around to steal it would meet with an untimely and unpleasant end. You guys need to be careful that you don't get caught in a booby trap when you are digging."

Morgan's eyes went wide and she ventured a look out to the tree in back.

Luke read her mind. "That's right, you could have been hurt ... or killed ... today or last night. The treasure hunters aren't your only worry here."

Luke paused and his green eyes turned serious as he looked at Fiona, then back at Morgan.

"Now that they know you are getting closer to the treasure, they'll probably step up their efforts. We've reduced their numbers, but I think there are still a few of them out there and they'll stop at nothing. I know you guys like to take care of yourselves but I'd like to have some of my guys in the house with you," Luke said.

"We have Cal and Jake staying over." Morgan stuck out her chin, stubbornly.

Luke nodded. "So far nothing too bad has happened—we diffused the situation with the break in and you and Celeste were able to outwit the attackers the other day. But you might not always be so lucky." He narrowed his eyes at Morgan. "By the way, how did you know to pull Celeste back from that alley just at the right moment?"

Morgan felt her stomach clench. *Should she tell him the truth about the strange things that were happening?* Her gut instincts told her "yes".

"I just had a gut feeling, and Celeste said that Nana told

her to tell me to trust my gut feelings. It worked out pretty good in that case."

"Your Nana? Isn't she dead?" Luke switched his gaze from Morgan to Fiona.

"Yes," Fiona said. "Apparently Celeste has been talking to dead people. You know how she was always kind of spiritual what with all her meditation and stuff. I guess she connected with '*the other side*'."

Luke looked down at Morgan and shook his head. "Carnelian stones that heal wounds, dead people giving you guys advice, and gut feelings that save you from getting abducted ... I guess it's going to be a challenge for me to get reacquainted with the Blackmoore girls."

Luke took Morgan's hand and her heart fluttered as he pulled her to him. "I have some things to take care of, but I'm coming to your house tonight. By the way things are heating up, I think I need to keep you girls under very close surveillance. And I'm not taking no for an answer."

Then he kissed her cheek, turned on his heel and left.

Morgan's heart took off like a thoroughbred at the starting gate. She felt that familiar pull in her lower belly. She had to admit, the thought of Luke keeping them under close surveillance wasn't really all that unpleasant.

But then she felt a warning tingle in her gut. After all the hurt he had caused her ten years ago, she couldn't let herself fall for Luke Hunter all over again. Could she?

Chapter Eighteen

"We need to get home and into the attic to look for the box that key opens." Fiona picked up the geode that still lay on the floor and returned it to its place on the shelf.

"Right." Morgan stood staring at the door Luke had just disappeared through, wondering what his kiss on the cheek meant. It was really just a peck. But was it a friendly peck or something more?

"Earth to Morgan." Fiona was standing at the door, Belladonna under one arm.

"Oh, sorry." Morgan followed her out the door and the three of them climbed into Fiona's old truck.

"We should call Celeste and Jolene and tell them what we found ... and about the attack," Fiona said as she pulled out onto the main road.

Morgan pulled out her cell phone and made the calls.

"They're both home and so is Cal. Looks like we'll have plenty of help." Belladonna had curled up in Morgan's lap and she stroked her silky fur with one hand as she looked at the key with the other.

"I have no idea what this would go to. A trunk or another box?"

Fiona glanced over as she turned onto the road leading to Perkins cove. "I don't know. I mean what are the odds that whatever it opens is even in the attic?"

Morgan nodded. "But we really don't have any place else to try."

They made the rest of the short drive in silence and Celeste, Jolene and Cal were standing at the door when they pulled into their driveway.

Celeste and Jolene ran over and hugged them.

"I can't believe you guys got attacked!" Jolene said. "Are

you all right?"

"Yes. Turns out we can take pretty good care of ourselves," Morgan said.

"But I'm still thankful Luke was there to pick up the pieces." Fiona winked at Morgan and she felt her cheeks grow warm.

"Let's see this key." Cal held out his hand and Morgan put the key in it.

"Oh yeah, this is an oldie." He held the long skeleton key up to the light, squinted at it then handed it back to Morgan.

"Jeez Cal, I hope we aren't keeping you from going to work. You don't have to watch over us day and night," Fiona said as they started up the main stairway.

"It's okay," he answered. "I have plenty of people to keep the shop running and I could use a little break. Plus I'll take any excuse to get back up into your attic and get my hands on all those antiques."

The girls laughed and Celeste swatted at him as they emerged into the attic.

Morgan stood at the top of the stairs and looked around.

"I have no idea where to start." She looked tentatively at Belladonna. She felt a little silly thinking the cat could show her the way, but Belladonna had led them to many important finds in the past.

This time, though, the cat simply curled up by the window, gave Morgan a blank stare and started cleaning herself.

"Follow your intuition, Morgan," Celeste said. "I mean really dig deep and see if you get a feeling for where we should look."

Morgan took a deep breath and closed her eyes. She tried to focus on her feelings. *Was there a specific part of the attic that stood out?* She felt herself drawn toward an area in the very back and started moving toward it.

She stopped in front of a door and looked back at Cal and her sisters. "I think it's in here."

Her pulse kicked into high gear as she pushed the door open, the hinges squealing in the silent attic. Inside was a small room, probably ten feet by eight. It looked like it had once been one of the servants' rooms but now it held boxes stacked almost from floor to ceiling, along with haphazard piles of ... stuff.

Cal walked over to one corner and started rummaging in a pile.

"These are really old," he said holding up a silver creamer and sugar.

"And look at this thing." Jolene pointed to long sword that stood against the wall.

Fiona had started looking through one of the trunks and Celeste rifled a pile of linens.

Morgan was busy sorting through a box of what looked like old pewter cups when she heard Fiona gasp.

She jerked her head in Fiona's direction. Her sister was sitting on the floor staring into a box.

"What is it?" Morgan shuffled over to see what was so interesting.

Fiona pulled what looked like a pile of burlap out of the box and laid it on the floor. Morgan's stomach flittered with butterflies as she watched her sister slowly open the flaps.

An array of gemstones and crystals lay inside. Morgan marveled at how they sparkled in the light and then her stomach squeezed when she realized the ones closest to Fiona were actually glowing.

"They're beautiful," Morgan said watching as Fiona reached for a brown stone in the corner. Morgan recognized it as tiger's eye—the same stone in the pendant Fiona had given her. Her hand flew up to the pendant and closed around it. It felt warm and she drew in a sharp breath when she saw the stone on the burlap glow as Fiona's hand touched it.

"What's that?" Celeste joined them.

"Old crystals." Fiona dropped the tiger's eye and looked up at them. "Well, all crystals are old, but these look like they have been here for centuries."

"They probably have, judging by the age of the other stuff in this room," Cal said.

"Looks like one of our ancestors was into crystals and gemstones, just like you," Jolene added.

"Yeah, I guess so." Fiona folded the burlap flaps back over the crystals and Morgan noticed the faint outline of printing on the material.

"Wait. What's that?" She pointed to the letters.

Fiona squinted down at it. "Looks like initials. MB. Guess I'll have to research who that was. Do you guys mind if I take these?"

No one minded. Fiona wrapped the crystals back up and the group got busy rummaging through the items. Morgan was just starting to feel like the whole exercise had been for nothing when she heard a sharp intake of breath from the other side of the room.

"Hey guys, I think I found something."

Jolene was crouched down in the corner, boxes pushed out of the way on either side of her. Morgan rushed over and looked down, her heart lurching up into her throat when she saw what had caused Jolene to call out.

There, on the floor in front of them was a box very similar to the other boxes they had found. Like the others, this one was silver, with gold on the corners and an ornate carved flower design. But it was much bigger—about a one and a half feet long and six inches wide. Morgan reached down and picked it up, her pulse picking up speed as she held it.

"Wowser. That's one nice box," Cal said.

"Does the key fit it?" Celeste asked.

Morgan found a table off to the side and put the box on top, then took the key out of her pocket.

She held her breath as she lined the key up with the hole in the lock. She inserted and turned. *Click*.

The top flew open. Inside was a long piece of leather, rolled up tight, the outside was dry and cracked with age.

"Be careful with that," Cal warned. "Old Leather can be very brittle."

She lifted the leather out and placed it on the table, then unrolled it very slowly. Her heart beat faster and faster as the images and writing inside were revealed.

It was a treasure map.

Chapter Nineteen

By the time they brought the map down to the informal living room, Jake had come home from work and joined them. They spread it out flat on the coffee table. Morgan inhaled the smell of old leather as she bent over to study the lines of the map which had been crudely burned into it.

"This looks like our yard, but it's shaped different," Jolene said.

"The geography of this area was changed about a hundred years ago, when the area started becoming attractive to tourists," Cal replied.

"Yeah, I remember reading about how the channel to the cove was made deeper and the cove itself much wider. Then on the other side, some land was filled in near Oarweed Cove where it abuts our land." Celeste pointed to the different parts of the map as she talked.

"So, our land as it sits now is here ... and here?" Morgan drew a circle with her finger to indicate where she thought the land was.

"I think so," Cal said.

"So part of this isn't even our land."

"You're right ... but the important part looks like it is." Cal pointed to the big X in the middle of the map where the supposed treasure was.

Morgan squinted at the map, it did look like the treasure was buried somewhere near the point of land at the edge of their property. Near where the body had been found.

She glanced outside. Plenty of daylight left. "We should start digg—"

The knock on the door interrupted her and she raised an eyebrow at the group.

"Anyone expecting company?"

Nobody was.

"We should hide this, just in case." She gestured to the map and Celeste and Jolene got busy rolling it up and finding a hiding spot. Morgan and Fiona went to answer the door that the insistent visitor was now pounding on.

"Hold your horses ... I'm coming." She ripped the door open and her heart froze when she saw who was standing there.

Sheriff Overton.

And he wasn't alone, he had several uniformed policemen with him and they looked like they were there for backup. But why would he need backup?

"Well 'bout time. I hope you aren't trying to hide any evidence because it's too late," Overton said with a smug smile on his face.

"What are you talking about?" Morgan stood feet apart, fists on her hips. She didn't invite Overton in, but he opened the screen door and stepped in anyway. The commotion had caused everyone else to gather in the hall.

"Oh good, I see you're all here. That will make it easy to arrest the killer."

Morgan's heart clenched. *What was he talking about?*

Fiona narrowed her eyes at the Sheriff. "No one invited you in, so you can turn around and leave."

"Oh, I don't think so. See, I got this little piece of paper here that says I got probable cause to bring the killer in for questioning."

The toothpick switched from one side of his mouth to the other as he pulled some papers from his front pocket and shoved them in Fiona's face.

Morgan felt her anger rising. "I already told you, I had nothing to do with killing that guy."

Overton looked at her and nodded. "Yep and, much to my surprise, you were telling the truth."

Morgan scrunched her face at him.

"It's not you I'm here to arrest ... It's her." Overton pointed past Morgan's shoulder.

Her heart squeezed as she turned to follow the direction of his finger. It was pointing straight at Celeste.

"What!" Cal boomed, putting a protective arm around Celeste. "You can't just come in here and arrest people with no evidence."

"Oh, I have evidence." Overton smiled his Cheshire cat smile. "Found the murder weapon right in little Blondie's car."

"What are you talking about?" Morgan shot a glance at Celeste who looked as baffled as she was.

"Yep. The coroner got back to us this morning. The victim's head was bashed in with a round object ... oh about this big." Overton cupped his hands to illustrate a circumference of about six or seven inches.

Morgan narrowed her eyes. "And you found one in Celeste's car?"

"Yep. Just happened to notice it when we were here last night." He turned to one of the uniforms behind him. "Show her."

Morgan's eyes widened as the gangly kid held up a large plastic bag with one of Celeste's kettle bells inside.

"That handle makes 'em perfect for getting a good swing for bashing someone's head in, wouldn't you say?" Overton raised his eyebrows at Morgan.

"Those are for exercising!" Morgan louvered her eyes between Overton and Celeste. This had to be some sort of mistake or one of Overton's tricks.

"Let me see that." Jake pushed forward and grabbed at the paper Overton had shown to Fiona.

He glanced over it then looked at the kettle bell. "Is there forensic evidence on that?"

"We haven't run it through the lab yet but I'm sure it will prove to be the weapon." Overton stepped over toward Jake, taking the toothpick out of his mouth. "You better keep your nose out of this. In fact I think I'll put you on administrative leave until this case is over."

Jake opened his mouth to protest but Overton put his hand up to stop him.

"I should have you fired for consorting with known criminals," he said, jerking his chin toward Morgan and Celeste.

He turned to the uniforms behind him. "Now cuff her

and take her away."

Cal stepped in front of Celeste. "Now wait just a minute!"

The uniforms froze and looked back at Overton uncertainly.

"Better step aside, Reed, or I'll have you brought in for obstruction of justice."

Celeste pushed in front of Cal, holding her wrists out together in front of her. "It's okay. I'll go with them and you guys can come and post bail. I'm not worried since I didn't kill anyone."

Morgan was impressed with her sister's calm demeanor.

It took everything she had to step aside while they cuffed Celeste and brought her out to the car, but she knew it was the best thing to do. As soon as they were gone, she'd be on the phone to the lawyer and working to get Celeste out of jail. There was nothing she could do right now to stop it, though, so she let them take her.

"We'll be down right behind you," she said to Celeste as they led her by.

Celeste nodded. "No hurry."

Morgan stood in the doorway, her fists clenched and the map all but forgotten as she watched them shove Celeste into the back of the police car and drive away.

She'd never felt so helpless in all her life.

* * *

"We have to get her out right away. I don't want her spending one night in there." Morgan turned to face the group, her mind whirling.

"I'll get on the phone to Delphine," Fiona said. Delphine Jones was the sharp witted lawyer they had used when Morgan had been accused of murder earlier in the summer. She'd done a fantastic job and Morgan couldn't think of anyone better to help Celeste.

"I'll put a call into some of my friends at the station." Jake whipped out his cell phone.

"We'll need money for a retainer," Morgan said.

"Don't worry about that," Cal replied. "I'll give you whatever you need for the lawyer."

"We're not taking your money."

"Consider it a loan, then. What you have in the attic is worth plenty of money ... you can sell some of it later if you want, but for now I have cash at the ready and we don't want to hold up getting Celeste out."

Morgan nodded. He was right.

"Delphine's going to meet us down there," Fiona said as she headed out the door.

Morgan, Cal and Jolene followed. Jake stayed behind. His presence at the station wouldn't help things after the run in he'd just had with Overton.

Delphine Jones was already in the police station parking lot when they pulled up in Cal's pearl white Lincoln Navigator. She was on her cell phone, pacing back and forth in front of her car, arms gesturing wildly. Her hot pink jacket and pink, white and orange broom skirt fluttered in the breeze behind her.

She hung up when they pulled up next to her.

"Okay, give me the quick version." She tapped her nails on the hood of the Lincoln as Morgan told her how Celeste's kettle bells were the suspected murder weapon for the dead body on the cliff.

"Was there any evidence on the weapon?"

"Overton said they hadn't run them through the lab yet."

Delphine narrowed her eyes in the direction of the police station.

"Jerk." She spat the word out like it was sour yogurt.

Morgan knew from their previous dealings that there was no love lost between Delphine and the Sheriff. She didn't know why but Overton seemed afraid of the feisty lawyer and Morgan knew that worked to their advantage.

"Can you get her out?" Fiona asked.

"Sure. Well, I might need a judge, especially if Overton is playing games with the murder weapon and delaying the testing. But I'll do my damn best to get her out tonight." They started off toward the police station entrance. "I'll go straight in to Overton and see if I can get him to release her and you guys can go down for a visit."

A blast of cool air hit Morgan as the entered the lobby and her stomach clenched remembering when *she* had been arrested. Delphine headed off to see Overton and Fiona demanded that they be allowed to visit Celeste.

Someone came out and led them down to the cells. Morgan's nerves grew more tense with each step. They filed past four empty cells, Celeste was in the last one—the same one Morgan had been in.

Morgan peered into the cell, her heart pounding wondering what kind of condition her sister was in.

Celeste sat on the bed, cross legged. Her eyes closed, breathing steady. She opened one eye then the other as a smile lit her face.

"Oh hi guys. You didn't have to come so fast," she said as if they had dropped in for a leisurely Sunday afternoon visit.

"Celeste, are you okay? Did they hurt you?" Cal's face was lined with concern. Morgan narrowed her eyes at him, they were all concerned about Celeste but Cal seemed overly so. *What was up with that?*

"Oh I'm fine." She waved her hand. "It's not that bad here. The bed is comfortable and it's a great place to meditate ... very quiet and lots of emotional energy."

"We brought Delphine and she's going to get you out," Fiona said.

Celeste got up from the bed and came over to edge of the cell, looking out at them through the bars.

"I think I might be staying here tonight, but I don't want you guys to worry. I didn't kill that guy so I won't be here long. You need to focus on taking care of the guys that are after us ... I have it on good authority it's only going to get worse."

"What? You're not going to have to stay here," Jolene said.

"I'm afraid she is." Delphine came rushing toward them. "I need a judge to let her out and they've all gone home but I promise I'll get her out first thing in the morning."

Morgan felt like she'd been punched in the gut. "Seriously? But she didn't do anything."

"I know, sometimes the wheels of justice move backwards." Delphine patted Morgan's arm.

"It's okay, guys, really. Go—take care of things at home.

Brandon's bringing me a lobster dinner and I'll be quite comfortable here." Celeste waved them off and Morgan saw Cal and her sisters reluctantly turn toward the door. Their tense faces echoing Morgan's worries.

They filed past Celeste, hugging her through the bars and saying good-bye. Delphine was already halfway down the hall when Morgan got her turn. Celeste grabbed her arm and held her back.

"Make sure you study that map. I don't know why you need to, but you do." Celeste's ice-blue eyes drilled into her own and Morgan felt an electrical current surge through her veins.

She nodded and Celeste let go of her arm. "Now get out of here ... I'll see you tomorrow. Oh and Nana says be nice to your guest."

Morgan frowned at her. *Guest?* She was still wondering what Celeste meant when she climbed into Cal's car in the parking lot.

Chapter Twenty

She didn't have to wonder for long.

Luke was waiting on the front porch when they got home. Sitting in the white wicker settee drinking a beer next to Jake, who was in one of the rockers. Making himself right at home.

Cal ran over and the two of them got re-acquainted with the usual back slapping and hand shaking. They'd been friends before Luke left and, as far as Morgan knew, hadn't seen each other since.

Morgan's stomach flip-flopped as she approached the porch. Probably from all the excitement with Celeste, she reasoned. Surely it had nothing to do with how good Luke looked sitting on *her* porch drinking one of *her* beers.

"How did it go? Where's Celeste?" Jake stood from his rocking chair, greeting Fiona with a peck on the cheek.

"Delphine couldn't get her out until tomorrow." Morgan felt her chest squeeze as she said it and she realized she was surprisingly close to tears.

Cal paced the porch. "Is there nothing we can do?"

"Short of going down with a nail file in a cake and breaking her out, I don't think so," Jake said. "She'll be okay. Is there anyone else in there?"

"The other cells were empty," Jolene replied.

"She'll be fine, we don't get too many criminals in there so she'll probably be alone ... I guess I should say *they* don't since I'm officially on leave." Jake pressed his lips together. "Besides, my contact at the station assured me they'd treat her like a queen. Probably be like a vacation for her."

"Yeah, she did say someone named Brandon was bringing her lobster." Cal frowned.

Jake nodded. "That's Brandon Burchard. He'll take good care of her."

Morgan noticed Cal's frown deepen.

"Well, I don't know about the rest of you, but I could use a drink." Fiona reached for the door handle and everyone lined up behind her. Except Luke.

"Does someone want to fill me in on what's going on?" He frowned over his beer.

"Morgan will." Fiona shot over her shoulder as she went inside.

Morgan glanced at the door, then at Luke, her stomach flopping around like a fish out of water. They were alone on the porch.

Why did that make her so nervous?

Luke reached over and grabbed her hand, pulling her to the settee beside him.

"What's wrong, you look upset." He brushed a lock of hair behind her ear sending her pulse skittering like a frightened rabbit.

"Celeste got arrested for murder." Her voice cracked on the last word and the tears she felt sting her eyes earlier, threatened to spill out. It made her feel vulnerable. She hated feeling that way. She noticed that Luke had pulled her down close to him and she slid away to the other side of the settee. At least she could think better over there.

"Jake filled me in a little. He didn't tell me too much though. Probably didn't know how much he should tell me ... I guess he doesn't trust me fully." Luke turned his sea green eyes on her. "Do you?"

Morgan's breath caught in her throat. *Did she?*

"Well, you *have* helped us out of a few spots now. But you've been gone for so long. I don't feel like I know you anymore." She picked at the wicker arm of the settee, avoiding his gaze.

"I'm the same person I always was. Just a little better traveled."

Morgan looked at him and realized he had slid a little closer to her. She pressed herself into the corner.

"Well, you'll excuse me if I'm not brimming over with trust. You disappeared out of my life ten years ago and I haven't heard a word from you since." Morgan tried to ignore the flutter in her stomach and act nonchalant, as if that was old news that barely affected her now.

He sighed and took a pull on his beer. Staring out at the ocean, he rubbed his dark short cropped hair which made it stick out as if he just got up. Out of bed. Morgan tried to push the memories of other times, when she'd seen his hair like that, out of her mind.

He put this beer down and turned to face her, his arm up on the back of the settee. She suddenly became very interested in studying her hands which were clasped in her lap.

"I didn't want to just walk out of your life. But I had to do what was right for you. It wasn't fair for me to expect you to wait for me." He put his thumb under her chin and gently turned her face toward him. "I thought about you every day."

Her heart squeezed in her chest. *Did he really?* She realized he'd slid over even closer to her. Suddenly, he was leaning toward her. She could smell the spicy scent of his after shave and feel the heat radiating from his body.

She flattened her palm on his chest to push him away, except she didn't push very hard. Beneath his thin shirt, she could feel hard muscle and the steady beat of his heart. She wondered if it was beating as fast as hers as she watched his lips get closer.

Before she knew what was happening, her eyes were drifting shut and his lips were brushing against hers. Tenderly at first, then pressing harder. She sighed and relaxed into his kiss.

"Meow!"

Belladonna jumped up onto Luke's lap and they jerked apart like two teenagers caught necking behind the rectory.

"Hey, this looks just like the cat you used to have." Luke reached down to pet the cat who had curled up in his lap and was staring up at him adoringly.

"It is."

Luke wrinkled his brow at her. "It's the same cat? She must be ancient by now."

Morgan bit her lip as she thought about that. How old *was* Belladonna? She'd had her since she was a kid, which would make the cat in her late teens.

How long did cats live, anyway?

Her stomach clenched thinking her cat might be nearing old age. She'd never thought much about it, but Belladonna had always been around—she didn't know what she'd do without her.

Morgan realized her earliest memories included the cat. That's impossible, she thought. It must have been a different cat. Her mother always doted on the cat and probably got another one that looked just like her when the first one passed.

Her thoughts were interrupted by the cat thwacking her arm with her tail as Luke petted her. She'd never heard Belladonna purr so loud.

"So anyway, tell me about the key, did you find the lock it fits in?"

Morgan took a deep breath and told him about the search in the attic and the leather map.

"In fact, we were trying to figure it out when Overton came to the door and arrested Celeste."

"Can I see the map?"

"Sure, it's right inside."

Luke dislodged Belladonna from his lap and she grunted out a discontented "mew" as the two of them went inside.

"The map's in the informal living room. You remember where that is?"

Luke smiled that disarming smile he had and Morgan's stomach turned inside out.

Why did he have to be so damn handsome?

He started walking toward the room and she couldn't help but check him out. He'd always been tall and well built, but she could see that he'd put on some weight in the past ten years. And judging by what she'd felt through his tee-shirt, it was pure muscle.

Thinking of that reminded her of their brief kiss and she felt her cheeks heat up. She pushed away any of *those* type of thoughts about Luke before the heat could spread to other parts of her body.

It was just as well the cat had interrupted their kiss. She couldn't deny she was still attracted to Luke, but he'd be gone after this was all over and where would that leave her?

In the living room, the map had been spread out on the table again and everyone was discussing the various instructions so intently they barely noticed Luke and Morgan.

Jake glanced over. "Hey Luke, what do you make of this? It says two steps as the crow flies. What does that mean?"

Luke rubbed the stubble on his chin. "Usually it means straight ahead without having to go around an obstacle."

"That's strange, there's no obstacle there." Jake pointed to a spot on the map then looked out the window.

"Well, sometimes they wrote up trick maps, or put the instructions in backwards or in code," Luke said. "In case the map fell into the wrong hands."

"I guess that explains why we dug the hole in the wrong place last time," Morgan said.

"That's right! I thought we had followed it wrong, but what really happened is that it was written backwards." Jolene pointed out the window to where they had dug up the box. "See how we were digging over there, but the box was found on the opposite side of the yard."

"So, do you think this map could be written backwards or in some sort of code?" Fiona raised a brow at Luke.

"It could be." He stared down at the map. "It's impossible to tell but the thing is you need to be really careful in case the treasure is booby trapped."

"Oh, that's right." Cal looked up at them, wide eyed. "I had forgotten that pirates routinely did that. We could blow ourselves up."

"Not only that, but now that the pirates know you have the key and are getting close, I'm sure they are going to step up their efforts to try to get the treasure from you."

Morgan's heart squeezed. Luke was right, the danger was getting worse and there was no sign of it letting up. She knew she had to do something to stop it. She just wasn't sure exactly what.

"I'm not sure I like the way things are heading—we need

to be proactive instead of waiting for them to attack us," Fiona echoed Morgan's thoughts.

"What prompted Overton to arrest Celeste?" Luke asked.

"He was poking around in her car and saw something the same shape as the murder weapon," Fiona replied

"And what was that?"

"Kettle bells."

"Huh?" Luke cocked an eyebrow at her.

"They're like weights for exercising, but they have a handle and a round ball on the bottom. You kind of swing them around." Jolene made swinging motions with her arms.

Luke ruffled his hair and looked out the window. After a few seconds he turned back to the group

"Are they about this big?" He cupped his hands making about a seven inch circle.

"Yes!"

He nodded then did more staring out the window.

"Okay, I think I have an idea that might help us get the treasure hunters off your back *and* give Overton the real murder weapon, which will clear Celeste and put the real killer in jail." He looked around the group, staring each of them directly in the eye in turn.

"But I'm going to need one of you to act as a decoy."

Chapter Twenty One

Morgan felt bats flapping around in her stomach as everyone stared at Luke in silence.

A decoy? That sounded dangerous.

"I'll do it," she blurted out.

Luke narrowed his eyes at her. "Morgan it could be dangerous."

Duh.

"No, it should be me," Jake volunteered.

"Or me," Cal added.

Luke sighed. "It has to be one of the girls. Otherwise *I'd* do it. The treasure hunters won't bite if it's a guy. They'll be expecting it to be one of the Blackmoore sisters and ... well ... they won't be as intimidated by a woman."

"Well, that settles it, then. I'll be the decoy. I'm not letting Fiona or Jolene do it." Morgan's mind was made up.

Luke raised his hands in a gesture of defeat. "I guess you're right. I don't like it, but there's no other way."

"So what do I do?"

"I need you to lure the treasure hunters out into the open. I haven't been able to get the ones we captured to talk and I can't figure out where the rest of them are hiding. I think they are on those boats you guys saw, but they could be docking them anywhere and they're probably moving them around all the time."

"I'm not sure I like the sounds of this." Fiona narrowed her eyes at Luke.

"Me either," he said. "But they know you guys are getting close and I think they realize they won't have many more chances. They'll probably send most of their guys considering what's happened the last two times. All I need is for Morgan to pretend like she has some sort of a lead and that will get them swarming."

"What do you mean?" Jake asked.

"We know they are watching because they were on Morgan and Fiona pretty quick today when they dug up the key. So, I'm thinking that Morgan can act like she's onto the treasure or has another clue and start digging. I figure if we do it at *Sticks and Stones* we won't lead them to the real treasure here." Luke turned to look at Morgan. "And if Morgan is alone, she'll make an easy target."

Morgan's stomach clenched but she straightened her back. She wasn't one to back down from a challenge. "Okay. Let's go."

"Well, hold on. I need to put my men in place. We'll be watching you every second, of course, and I'm also going to have you wear a wire so we can hear you and rush in as soon as possible. That will be the safest way. I could never forgive myself if anything happened to you."

Morgan's heart melted at the tender look in Luke's eyes.

"So we'll do it tomorrow," He said then turned to the rest of the group, "if everyone agrees."

"Only if you're sure Morgan won't get hurt." Jolene's blue eye's challenged Luke.

"I won't let anything happen to her."

Jolene nodded. "Okay by me, then."

"I guess we don't have much of a choice," Fiona said. "The sooner we can get this all over with the better."

"Agreed," Jake said and Cal nodded.

"Okay then, I better get things going," Luke said. "I'm going to leave through the side door over by the Cove, I can use the cover of the hedges in case the bad guys are watching ... we don't want to tip them off that we've been planning anything."

"I'll show you out." Morgan heard herself say then convinced herself that it wasn't that she wanted to be alone with him—it was the polite thing to do.

They crossed the hallway and went through the kitchen to the butler's pantry that led to the side door.

The small area on this side of the house had been one of Morgan's favorite places since childhood. It was like a secret garden. A rounded trellis covered in pink roses framed the door, colorful flowers sprouted up on either side and two honeysuckle bushes sent a sweet perfume through the air.

The shrubs, about ten feet away, enclosed the area in a private cocoon and a wrought iron bench with a stuffed canvas cushion tucked away under a large oak tree made a perfect place for reading.

Morgan stood on the top step and Luke a step down, his eyes level with hers.

"Are you sure you're okay doing this?" Luke's had caught her by the wrist and her heart skipped a beat.

"Yeah, of course. We need to do *something*, right?" She shrugged.

Luke looked thoughtful for a few seconds and Morgan felt a warm summer breeze flirt with her cheek. It was dusk, that magical moment when the daylight fades and the moonlight takes over. She could smell the flowery perfume of the honeysuckle and hear the summer peepers cheeping away.

How many other nights had she and Luke spent listening to peepers in the dusk?

She could feel the heat where his hand encircled her wrist and was suddenly intensely aware of him. She saw indecision in his eyes and then they turned dark with desire. His hand left her wrist and he wrapped it in her hair as he pulled her toward him.

She didn't resist.

Even though she knew she should.

Instead she met his lips eagerly, her arms snaking around his neck, her body pressing closer to his.

His lips were warm and tasted sweetly salty. They were familiar, but different somehow. She briefly wondered how many other women had tasted those lips in the past ten years as Luke's arm encircled her waist pulling her in even closer.

The feel of his hands on her body sent tiny frissons of pleasure shooting through her, reawakening the passion that had lain dormant all these years.

***

Luke curled his hand around Morgan's soft, silky hair as she responded to his kisses, heating his veins with passion. He let his hand fall to her slim waist, her hips and then down her backside.

He pulled her hard against him and her moan of pleasure almost brought him to the brink of no return.

He shouldn't be kissing her like this, but he couldn't help it. In the past ten years he hadn't met anyone else that could even come close to matching his feelings for Morgan.

He was beginning to question why he ever left here in the first place, and, in the back of his mind, was already coming up with a plan for sticking around after this was all over.

But first, he had to do whatever he could to make sure Morgan was safe tomorrow and that was going to take a lot of thinking and planning. Which meant he better stop kissing her ... while he could still think.

Reluctantly, he pulled away.

Looking at her in the twilight, his heart flipped in his chest at how beautiful she was. Her raven colored hair shone in the moonlight. He brushed a silky strand away from her face and gazed into her half closed ice-blue eyes. Desire burned in his veins as his thumb traced the line of her bottom lip, all pouty and swollen from their kiss.

He fought off the urge to pull her close and kiss her again. He knew this time he wouldn't be able to stop, so he stepped away, plunging his hands into the pockets of his cargo pants.

"You don't have to do this, you know ... the decoy thing tomorrow, I mean. I can figure out another way to get rid of the treasure hunters."

He hoped she'd change her mind and decide not to, but he knew she wouldn't. He would have called the whole thing off but he also knew how stubborn she could be and figured she'd do something crazy on her own—especially if it helped prove Celeste wasn't the killer. It was better to follow through with his plan so he could keep an eye on her.

Luke saw her dreamy half closed eyes snap wide open and her back stiffen. "No, I want to do it. I'm not afraid of some old pirates. Don't even think about trying to talk me out of it."

Luke took his hands out of his pockets, spreading them wide. "I wouldn't dream of it. But I want to make sure you're comfortable with doing this ... and I also want to make sure you don't get hurt."

He reached out, running his fingers lightly down her arm. He could see suspicion lurking behind her narrowed eyes.

Better quit while you're ahead.

He backed away, his heart squeezing tighter with each step. He suddenly felt like a schoolboy after his first kiss, not knowing the right thing to say. He cleared his throat, taking another backwards step.

"I'll be here first thing tomorrow then ... to let you know the exact plan."

Morgan nodded. "Okay."

Then he turned his heart pounding as he disappeared through the shrubs. The job he had ahead of him was probably the most important one he'd ever had. He had to make sure the plan was perfect ... his whole future depended on it.

* * *

Morgan stared at Luke's retreating back and kicked herself for falling under his spell so easily. Her fingers flew to her lips that were still burning from his kiss.

He'd sure kissed her like he meant it, but what Morgan couldn't figure out was why? The past ten years had made it perfectly clear that he didn't have room for her in his life and she certainly had no intention of being just a passing dalliance.

Her hand closed around the cold metal of the doorknob. Better to get on with the task at hand than to stand there wondering. The sooner all this pirate stuff was over with, the sooner Luke Hunter would be gone from her life—

hopefully this time for good.

But right now she had something more important to do.

She slipped inside to the butler's pantry and made her way to the informal living room. She was glad to find it empty—she didn't want to answer any embarrassing questions about her and Luke tonight.

The map was still laid out on the table. She sat down on the couch to study it. Celeste's parting words echoed in her head and she was learning that it was smart to follow Celeste's advice.

Staring down at the lines in the map, she realized something wasn't quite right. The map was a series of markers with lines leading from one to the next and some sparse instructions. Presumably you would follow the lines and find the treasure at the end.

But, something about the lines wasn't right—she could feel it in her gut. Morgan closed her eyes and pictured the map in her mind. It seemed to float, almost three dimensionally as if the map was drawn for terrain that was at different elevations instead of a straight line on flat ground.

A sudden sound in front of her made her heart lurched. Her eyes flew open, her body tensing.

She relaxed when she saw it was only Belladonna. The cat had hopped up on the table and sat on the map, her tail swishing over the corner of it, blue eyes staring intently at Morgan.

Morgan remembered how the cat threw herself at Luke earlier.

"Traitor."

Belladonna simply blinked at Morgan, licked her paw, washed her ear a couple of times then continued staring.

Morgan returned her attention to the map, studying it as she was instructed. Belladonna sat patiently on the table and Morgan couldn't help but wonder if the cat knew something she didn't.

Morgan could feel her eyes growing heavy. It had been a long day and an even longer one was in store tomorrow. Her chest constricted at the thought of being a decoy, but she *had* to do it—her family was being threatened and if she could make it go away then it was worth the risk.

She wandered into the kitchen and made a cup of chamomile tea to help her sleep.

Where was everyone?

A quick glance at the clock told her it was late—they were probably in bed. And that's exactly where she should be, trying to get a good night's sleep. She'd need her wits about her tomorrow to deal with the bad guys ... and Luke Hunter.

Chapter Twenty Two

Morgan was up early the next day, anxiety seeping into her every pore, making her jumpy and jittery. She hadn't slept well, but figured coffee was a bad idea so she padded down to the kitchen in her bare feet, black tank top and favorite pair of faded jeans for some tea.

Fiona, Cal, Jake and Jolene were quietly sitting at the kitchen island staring into steaming mugs of coffee.

"I guess I'm not the only one up early," Morgan said as she hunted in the cabinet for her favorite mug.

"Yeah who can sleep with Celeste in jail and you acting as some sort of decoy?" Fiona raised a sleepy eyebrow.

Morgan shrugged. "I'm sure I'll be fine, and Delphine will get Celeste out today."

"Yeah, we're going to meet her in a little bit," Cal said looking at his watch.

Morgan's heart thumped. They were all going off to get Celeste out of jail and she'd be going off to get captured by pirates.

"Morgan will be perfectly safe and under our watchful eye with these gadgets," Luke said from the kitchen doorway as if reading her mind.

Everyone swiveled in his direction. He was dressed in a black tee-shirt that somehow managed to show off every muscle in his chest and arms along with black cargo pants and big steel toed boots, also in black.

Morgan's heart thumped even harder. "How did you get in here?"

"Oh, sorry, I snuck in. Didn't want to come to the front door in case anyone was watching." Luke shrugged. "I wasn't kidding when I said you guys should get an alarm system."

Morgan narrowed her eyes at him, taking in the three small items he was holding in his hand.

"What are those?"

"These are your lifeline. This will allow us to see everything going on around you." He held up what looked like a barrette in his right hand.

"And these will let us hear everything." He held up a pair of earrings in his left.

Jolene went over to inspect the items. "These are pretty cool. Unobtrusive. Do they really work?"

"Like a charm. You wanna try them out?"

"I'd love to. Actually I was hoping I could kind of tag along and see how the whole process works."

Luke frowned at her.

"I'm taking some private investigator courses and a computer forensics course. It would be really helpful for me to see some real life stuff." Morgan noticed that she was giving Luke that wide-eyed look she always gave Morgan whenever she wanted to talk her into something. Apparently it worked on Luke too.

Luke pursed his lips. "Okay, but don't be alarmed by my men—they can be kind of gruff. And don't get in the way."

"I won't. I've seen gruff guys before." Jolene winked at him.

Morgan realized there was a whole bunch she didn't know about her little sister.

Luke crossed the room and leaned against the counter next to Morgan who focused on sipping her tea while trying not to notice how good he smelled ... or looked.

"Okay, so here's how we're going to do this. We'll set Morgan up with the camera and audio. I have several guys in strategic locations and we can monitor her on these." He reached into his cargo pants and pulled out a small tablet.

"That looks like an iPad." Jolene craned her neck to check out the device.

"It's very similar but specialized for surveillance work."

"Cool."

"I'll also be watching Morgan directly with high powered binoculars as will a couple of my associates. We should be able to see and hear everything and rush in as soon as the other guys try to grab her."

Morgan took a deep breath, setting down her mug. "Well, it all sounds very simple and easy. When do we get started?"

Luke looked at his watch. "What time do you usually open the shop?"

"Around eight."

"You should go there like normal. Open the shop and then walk around out back in the woods like you are looking for something. Maybe it would be a good idea to take a piece of paper, like you are following a map. Bring a shovel like you did the other day and start digging." Luke shrugged. "Then just let things happen."

"We better run." Fiona got up from her chair and hugged Morgan. "Good luck."

Morgan's heart squeezed and her stomach felt heavy with dread. She shook off the brief thought that this could be the last time she talked to her sisters.

"Thanks. Say hi to Celeste for me."

Cal and Jake hugged Morgan, then slapped Luke on the back and filed out.

Luke looked at Jolene. "You can come with me. But you need to change into all black so you'll be less noticeable."

Jolene's eye lit up and she jumped off her chair.

"I have just the outfit." She raced out of the room leaving Morgan and Luke alone.

Morgan feigned interest in her mug of tea, her heart racing like an overwound toy.

Luke moved closer to her, holding the earrings and barrette. "Let me help you get these on."

"I can do it." She grabbed the items, accidentally brushing his hand with hers, sending sparks running up her arm.

Her hands were shaking as she stabbed the earrings at the holes in her ears.

Luke leaned back, hands crossed over his chest with an amused look on his face as she rammed the barrette into her hair.

"It's crooked," he said, reaching over to straighten it. He

let his hand linger, then ran his fingers down the length of her hair all the while moving closer and looking at her with those damn sea green eyes.

He leaned in. Was he going to kiss her? Did she want him to?

Morgan's heart jerked in her chest, either from the task ahead of her or the closeness of Luke. She didn't know which. But either way, kissing him wasn't on her agenda this morning.

She backed away, ignoring the look of disappointment and confusion in his eyes.

"Let's get this over with." She grabbed her purse and headed for the door.

* * *

Morgan's pulse raced as she punched in the security code at *Sticks and Stones*. The hairs on the back of her neck prickled. She knew Luke and his men were watching ... but who else was?

Inside the shop seemed unusually quiet. Every creak and groan of the old floorboards set Morgan's heart skittering. She wasn't used to being alone in the shop and she felt a heavy weight in the pit of her stomach wishing Fiona was there with her.

She puffed her cheeks and blew out a long breath of air.

Better get to it.

Digging in her purse, she pulled out a piece of paper that would serve as her fake map and made her way to the back door. The trowel she used the day before was still leaning against the cottage and she grabbed it then headed off into the woods.

Morgan's heart raced as she wound her way through the trees, pretending like she was following instructions on the map. She clutched at the pendant Fiona had given her the day before. It felt warm, pulsating with energy.

Holding the paper in front of her, she walked east a few paces, then turned and walked north. The woods that always seemed so friendly and inviting took on a dark and foreboding air. Every noise set her nerves on edge.

A movement to her left set her heart jerking wildly. She whipped her head around and sighed when she realized it was only a squirrel scurrying up a tree.

She stopped at a giant pine that looked like it had been there for centuries. Squatting down, she placed the map on the ground next to her and cleared away the leaves and pine needles before shoving the trowel into the dirt.

Her heart was beating so loudly she wondered if Luke could hear it in the audio. Surely he could hear her raspy breath and see her shaky hands as she dug.

She tried to push away the heavy feeling of doom that was growing in the pit of her stomach. The bad guys would come then Luke would rush in and capture them and it would all be over. At least that was what was supposed to happen. But why did she *feel* like there wasn't going to be a happy ending?

A movement to her right caught her attention.

Another squirrel?

Then a movement behind her caused her to jerk her head in that direction. Her heart exploded in her chest when she saw them rushing at her from all directions. She bolted up and tried to run but strong, hairy arms grabbed her.

Morgan struggled, kicking out, trying to wriggle out of his grasp. Her eyes darted around frantically.

Where was Luke?

Her nose twitched as it was struck by a cloyingly sweet smell. She saw a red bandana rushing up to her face. She tried to jerk her head away, but the hairy paw held it in place as the bandana covered her nose and mouth.

Morgan's eyes bulged, her lungs gasped for fresh air.

Her struggles grew weaker.

And then, everything went black.

* * *

Luke jabbed at the buttons on the tablet in frustration.

Why wasn't this thing working?

He'd seen Morgan go into the shop, but once she was inside, the video feed had turned to static. He couldn't hear the audio either, but that was probably because she wasn't saying anything.

"Is something wrong?" Jolene peered over his shoulder.

"This feed isn't working right." Luke turned the display on the tablet toward her.

Jolene looked at it then glanced through the shrubs toward *Sticks and Stones*.

"Electromagnetic interference," she said.

"What?" Luke wrinkled his brow at her.

"There's something weird going on at Sticks and Stones. I'm not sure if it's the building or the land but every time I go there I feel a surge of energy. My hair gets all staticy and stands on end. It's weird." Jolene turned to face him. "If there was some strange energy field there, would that interfere with your device?"

Luke pursed his lips together. An electromagnetic energy field? It seemed rather farfetched, but then some of the other things going on around the Blackmoore sisters were pretty farfetched so why should this be any different?

"I suppose it could."

Luke tapped on his headset to communicate with the rest of the team. "Does anyone have a good display?"

He got five negative responses.

"So no one can see or hear what's going on?"

More negative responses.

"Anyone have a visual with binocs?"

"I think she's still inside. I'm looking at the back door," a voice replied in his ear.

Luke grabbed his binoculars and trained them on the cottage. They were situated about one eighth mile away, on a ridge behind some shrubs facing the south end.

He didn't see anyone.

He jabbed at his tablet again, his stomach clenching when neither the visual or sound worked. If he couldn't see or hear Morgan, then she could be in real danger.

"There she is," a voice in his ear announced and Luke picked up the binoculars again. This time, he could see Morgan come out the back door of the shop with a piece of paper in hand. He watched her grab a trowel and head off to the east.

Beside him, Jolene raised her binoculars, pointing them

in the same direction as his.

He scanned the woods, looking for movement.

No one else was near.

He turned the binoculars back on Morgan just in time to see her turn and disappear behind a tree.

"Shit," Jolene muttered beside him.

The thick tree trunk blocked their line of vision. Morgan must have been traveling straight north because Luke couldn't see her at all.

He glanced down at the tablet, his heart thudding against his ribcage. It was mostly static, but he could see flashes of video now.

The woods looked clear.

Another flash of video and the angle changed, as if Morgan was bending down. In the next flash, he saw the trowel move toward the dirt.

Luke alternated between the binoculars and the tablet, his muscles tense, heart racing.

And then he saw an explosion of activity from several places in the woods. His heart lurched in his chest as he saw the men were dangerously close to Morgan. He dropped the tablet and binoculars and burst out of his hiding spot, heading straight for the woods as he gave the command on his headset.

"Go! Go! They've got her!"

As he ran toward the woods, his heart sank to his stomach. The static on the video had caused them to miss the bad guys' arrival and had given them an advantage. He hadn't planned on letting them get anywhere near Morgan, and now it looked like they'd gotten very close.

He burst into high gear, his legs pumping faster than they ever had.

He didn't know if the GPS tracker on his devices would work with all the static interference and he had to get to Morgan before they took her anywhere, otherwise he might not be able to track her.

He just hoped he wasn't already too late.

Chapter Twenty Three

Morgan slowly drifted out of the darkness to consciousness. Her back pressed against something hard and damp. Her nostrils stung with the sharpness of the salty sea air. She opened her eyes for a second then had to squeeze them shut to fight a wave of nausea.

Where was she?

Through half opened eyes she saw that it was dark, wherever she was, but she could see a light a few feet away. Some sort of lantern. She opened her eyes all the way. Above her was solid black, no stars or moon.

She was inside somewhere ... no, not inside—*underground*.

She rolled to a sitting position, thankful the nausea seemed to be disappearing. Her pulse quickened as she looked around. She was in some sort of cave. The walls were rock and the floor hard, compacted dirt. It was damp and smelled of the sea—was she below sea level?

The room, if you could call it that, was big with a few empty crates in the middle and a large iron door that was set into a stone opening on one end. She could see a tunnel and flickering light through the open bars. Her heart stuttered when she saw iron chains bolted unto large metal plaques in the stone wall in various places around the room.

Was she in an old pirates' dungeon?

She heard voices coming from the direction of the iron door and her blood turned cold.

Was it the men who captured her?

What did they want with her?

She could hear them laughing and her nerves zinged with anxiety as the voices drew closer.

"Oh, I see you're awake." A large man with an unruly red beard unlocked the padlock on the door and came into the room along with another dark haired man.

Morgan backed up as they approached her. Red beard stopped about a foot from her. He smelled like he hadn't bathed in a month and she could see crumbs in his beard. Her stomach turned over and she tried not to gag.

"What do you want?" She tried to make her voice sound strong and powerful, but it came out in more of a squeak.

The two men looked at each other and laughed.

"We want to know where the treasure is," dark hair said stepping a little closer.

"I don't know where it is." Morgan touched her earrings, wondering if Luke could hear what was going on. *Do these things work in caves?* She tilted her head to the side so the barrette faced the two men, just in case.

"Sure you do. You found the map by now, didn't you? The real map I mean, not that fake one you had when we nabbed you."

Morgan's heart squeezed and she thought about the leather map. She hesitated too long before answering which set off more laughter. Then red beard got right in her face and his eyes weren't laughing or smiling—they were hard and cold. Her blood froze in her veins.

"No more games now. You're going to show us what's on the map or that young sister of yours is going to have a very bad day."

Morgan's heart clenched. "What do you mean? Have you done something to her?"

Black hair laughed. "Not yet, but if you don't give us what we want, she'll wish she was never born."

Red beard looked at black hair out of the corner of his eye. "Yeah and she's just your type isn't she?"

The two men laughed lewdly and Morgan remembered Celeste's warning to memorize the map. Could this be why? Was she *supposed* to tell them where the treasure was?

"If I tell you what's on the map, how do I know you still won't hurt my sister?"

"You don't, but you also don't have any choice, so you

might as well spill or we'll let you watch us hurt all of your sisters before we do the same to you."

Morgan's heart dropped in her chest. She didn't have much of a choice and drawing them a map would buy her time and hopefully in that time Luke would be able to find her and dispense with the bad guys.

"Okay, I'll draw it for you."

Red beard produced paper and a pencil and Morgan used one of the boxes as a surface for the drawing. She contemplated drawing the map wrong, but her gut feeling told her to go with what was exactly on the leather map as she had memorized it.

When she was done, she handed him the paper. "Are you going to let me go now?"

The two men laughed.

"Do you think we're stupid? We're going to check this out and then ... *maybe* we'll let you go," he said then glanced down at the paper. "Unless you tried to trick us with a fake map. Then we'll come back and make you wish you hadn't."

Morgan shivered at his words, rubbing her upper arms as the men turned to leave. She watched them slam the iron door shut and lock it then listened to their retreating footsteps echo off the walls.

As soon as they were out of earshot, she ran over to the door. She pushed. She pulled. It wouldn't budge. She looked down at the lock, remembering how Jolene had popped the lock on the box with a hairpin in the attic. It wasn't the same kind of lock but she took the barrette out of her hair and tried anyway. The only thing she succeeded in doing was mangling the barrette.

Morgan pressed her back against the wall, her stomach sinking like a lead ball. She was trapped. She slid down the wall, to a sitting position and put her face in her hands.

"Mew."

What was that?

Morgan jerked her head up and looked toward the iron door. Nothing was there.

"Meeew." More insistent this time, but the cave like walls acted as an echo chamber and she couldn't tell where it was coming from.

"Meeeooooow."

That sounded just like Belladonna.

Morgan stood up, swiveling her head from side to side. She walked to the far end of the room, the one that was furthest away from the lantern. Her eyes adjusted to the darkness and she saw the cat sitting near one of the chains that hung from the wall.

"Where did you come from?" Morgan bent down to pet her. She must have snuck in through the bars of the door when Morgan had her head in her hands.

Did that mean Luke was coming?

The cat weaved her way around Morgan's ankles, then headed over toward the wall.

"Meow."

Morgan looked over. The cat was in front of a giant iron plaque that held in one of the chains that came out of the wall.

Then suddenly, she was gone!

Then back again.

Belladonna was going in and out of a big hole in the wall just behind the plaque!

Morgan rushed over and poked her head in. It looked like there was some kind of passageway or tunnel behind there. Too bad the opening was only big enough for her head.

If she could just move the plaque a little more ...

She pushed, but it didn't budge.

Belladonna poked her head out of the opening. "Meeeooow!"

"Okay, okay. I'm trying."

Morgan braced herself against the floor and pushed on the plaque with her feet.

It moved an inch.

She pushed harder.

Another inch.

She pulled back her leg and kicked out with all her might and the plaque slid about six inches. Just enough to fit her body through.

Belladonna poked her head out again, then turned

around and flicked her tail as if for Morgan to follow.

Morgan took one backwards glance at the room then wriggled through the hole into the tiny tunnel on the other side.

* * *

The smell of rotting seaweed and dead fish made her want to vomit. Morgan had to crawl on her hands and knees as the tunnel wasn't big enough to stand in. The bottom was slimy and she shuddered to think what that slime was. Every so often her fingers would touch something squishy and her stomach churned wondering what icky creatures lived there.

It was dark in the tunnel. She could barely see Belladonna's white tail, like a flag, waving in front of her. As she crawled along behind it, she realized she had no idea where she was.

Underground somewhere, but where?

And how *far* underground?

The smell of the ocean was strong, so she figured she must be on the coast, but that could be a dozen places near where she was captured. She realized she had no idea how long she was unconscious—they could have taken her anywhere.

It seemed like she was going uphill—hopefully toward the surface. She'd had about enough of the damp underground.

The passage got increasingly larger until she could almost stand up. Her hands and knees were bruised and bleeding from crawling so she stood as best she could. She still had to bend over a little, but walking upright was much faster.

After a minute or two, she noticed it was getting brighter in the tunnel as if there was an opening not too far ahead. At least she hoped that's what it was. She picked up the pace.

Suddenly Belladonna stopped short in front of her. Morgan felt the floor beneath her shake. She heard a strange rumbling sound.

Belladonna looked back at her then started forward at a trot.

Morgan did the same, her heart beating wildly against her chest as she noticed small rocks becoming dislodged from the sides and top of the passage.

Bang!

The explosion rocked the passage. Morgan watched in horror as the walls and ceiling seemed to cave in before her eyes.

Her heart seized as she looked in front of her just in time to see a large rock hit Belladonna. The cat fell, then sprang up again but Morgan could see more rocks heading toward her.

Without thinking, she threw herself on top of Belladonna to shield the small cat from the onslaught of rocks. Two seconds later, the entire tunnel collapsed burying them both.

* * *

So this is what it's like to be buried alive.

The stones and dirt lay heavy on Morgan, pressing the air out of her lungs as she waited to die. She could hear voices and wondered if they were spirits welcoming her to 'the other side'. Maybe her mother and grandmother would be there. She wondered if she'd come back as a ghost and start talking to Celeste.

The voices were getting louder, the air in her lungs getting smaller.

Was the pile on top of her getting lighter, or was that her spirit departing?

She could hear rocks scraping, then she felt someone tugging at her arms.

"I've got her!"

Was that Luke?

Morgan tried to open her eyes as she felt the pile being cleared away on top of her. Strong arms tried to turn her over. Someone brushed the hair away from her face.

"Morgan, can you hear me?"

She nodded then slitted her eyes open. Luke's face was

hovering above her, his eyes clouded with concern. He reached down and tenderly touched her face.

"Let's get you out of here," he said scraping at the rest of the rocks.

Morgan's heart lurched when she remembered Belladonna. The cat was right underneath her, but she didn't feel her moving.

Her heart dropped. *Was Belladonna dead?*

Tears stung her eyes as she wriggled free from the debris, looking underneath where she had been for a sign of the cat but there was none.

Luke pulled her the rest of the way out and took her in his arms, kissing her face, her lips, her forehead. Jolene was hugging her from behind. But Morgan was still thinking about the cat.

"Wait." Morgan pushed away from them and they looked at her with alarm.

"Belladonna is still in there, she may be hurt." Morgan practically sobbed out the words.

"What are you talking about?" Jolene raised an eyebrow at her. "She's sitting right here."

Morgan looked over to where Jolene was pointing. Belladonna sat on the grass next to the rubble-filled hole Morgan had just come out of, her fur white as snow, no sign of injury, calmly licking her paw as if it was just another regular day.

Morgan felt a surge of relief run through her body as Belladonna looked up at her with big ice-blue eyes.

And then, she could have sworn, the darn cat winked at her.

Epilogue

Two days later, Morgan settled into the most comfortable chair in the informal living room, a cup of tea in her hand and Belladonna in her lap. Somehow she'd only sustained minor cuts when the tunnel caved in on her and those were bandaged along with some small carnelian stones Fiona had shoved in under the gauze.

"How did you figure out what the *real* murder weapon was?" Fiona looked at Luke who hovered around Morgan making sure her tea cup was full and her bandages were secure.

"That was easy. When I heard the description of the kettle bells, I knew that it matched the size and shape of old cannon balls. And what better thing for a pirate treasure hunter to use to bash in a rivals skull than an old cannon ball?" He spread his hands. "Then once we found the bad guys' boats, it was easy to get on board and find the actual cannon ball that did it. We figure the treasure hunters from one group must have killed him on their boat and put him on the cliff as a warning to the members of the other group."

"I'm just glad you could turn all that over to Overton and get Celeste cleared," Cal said.

"And put the group of pirates that didn't blow themselves up in jail so we won't have to worry about them anymore," Jolene added.

"Well, Overton didn't seem very happy about the evidence. He seemed rather disappointed, but he couldn't argue with it. The two rival groups kind of helped us since they were getting in the way of each other's efforts. Thankfully they have both now been neutralized," Luke said.

"Too bad it took blowing up half our yard to do it." Celeste jerked her chin toward the window and Morgan felt her stomach clench as she looked outside.

The yard was about twenty feet shorter now. A giant half-moon shaped crater had been blown out of the cliff facing the Atlantic during the explosion which had caused the tunnel on the other end of the yard, that Morgan had been in, to cave in. Luckily she'd been near the surface. Otherwise she might not be sitting here today. She shivered and scratched Belladonna behind the ears.

The cat had saved her.

"That old treasure was booby-trapped just like you said it might be." Morgan looked up at Luke. "I guess I got lucky that I was far enough away. I'm still not sure exactly how you found me, though."

"You can thank Jolene for that," Luke said. "The tracking devices didn't work because of some strange interference at *Sticks and Stones* so I didn't see the treasure hunters sneak in. I tried to run over there when they grabbed you, but I wasn't fast enough. Jolene was the one who figured out to watch the road and then we knew which direction they took you in."

Morgan looked at Jolene, her heart swelling with pride. "Thanks."

Jolene laughed. "Well, I guess those private investigator classes are paying off."

"And then Jake was smart enough to take a dinghy out from the cove and he noticed the tunnel in the cliff. It's just above the low tide mark so it's underwater most of the time ... or well it was until it got blown up. They must have been planning to grab you right at low tide to get you in there the whole time."

Morgan's stomach churned remembering the dank ocean smell inside the tunnel. No wonder the smell was so strong.

"Then the GPS in the barrette started working and we were practically on top of you when the explosion happened." Luke looked out the window. "There must be a warren of caves and passages out there if they brought you in on the side of the cliff and you came out down by the end of your driveway."

Morgan remembered the room she had been in with the iron door. There was a passage leading to it, presumably the one from the cliff, and then the tunnel that she crawled out of. She hadn't seen any sign of other passages but it was certainly possible.

She was just glad she was out of there, safe and sound with her family.

"It sounds like you guys did some awesome teamwork to find me. I'm really overwhelmed and grateful," she said, tears pricking the backs of her eyes. "It was scary down there."

"We did work pretty good together," Jake said, "which helped me make an important decision."

Morgan's eyes widened. "Oh, really?"

"Yes. I'm quitting the police force and going into private investigation. Jolene is going to work with me."

"Oh, that's wonderful!" Morgan was genuinely pleased. "Are you sure you won't miss Overton too much?"

Everyone laughed.

"Not in the least." Jake winked at Morgan. "Although I am sorry I won't be there to keep you girls company when you get arrested."

Morgan widened her eyes in mock consternation and Celeste swatted at Jake playfully.

"Well, that works out good for me then," Luke said.

"And why is that?" Jake narrowed his eyes at him.

"Well ..." Luke looked hesitantly at Morgan and her stomach flip flopped. *What was he up to?*

"I might have to hire you because I'm going to be needing some extra help ... since I'm going to be spending less time traveling and more time right here in Noquitt." Morgan's heart thumped loudly against her ribcage as he put his hand over hers.

"Well, I'm glad everyone is safe and the pirates won't be bothering us anymore. I was kind of hoping we could recover the treasure, but now I guess it's been blown to smithereens." Fiona gazed out the window.

"You have plenty of treasure right up in your attic. Just these boxes alone are worth a lot of money." Cal gestured to the silver box in the table in front of Morgan that had contained the map.

Morgan picked it up. It *was* a beautiful box—Cal had verified it was solid sterling silver with 20k gold edging. Worth a lot just for the metal content alone, but the design and age of the box made the value skyrocket.

She opened it up—the inside was lined in blue velvet and was just as beautiful as the outside. Belladonna sat up in her lap and sniffed the edge.

"Even Belladonna likes it," Morgan said as the cat pushed her head further into the box.

"Meow." Belladonna poked her paw into the box pushing at the lining, then with a swipe of her claw she ripped the lining from the side of the box.

"Belladonna!" Morgan jerked the box away from the cat. Something that had been hidden inside the lining caught her attention.

She gingerly pulled the small piece of paper out.

"What's that?" Celeste asked.

"Looks like a note." Morgan unfolded the aging paper to reveal old fashioned writing on the inside.

The sea is my love,
The Ocean's Revenge lies below my love.

Jolene peered over her shoulder. "What's that mean?"

Morgan put the note on the coffee table. "I'm not sure. The *Ocean's Revenge* was the ship that Isaiah Blackmoore captained."

"Does that mean the ship is below the sea? Like sunken?" Fiona cocked an eyebrow at the note.

"No," Luke said gazing out the window at the Atlantic. "I saw the sonar readings on the treasure hunter's ship and there's no sunken treasure out there."

Morgan frowned at the note. "Maybe it *was* out there once and has since been recovered. I mean the note *was* written three hundred years ago."

"Yeah, you're probably right," Fiona said. "Anyway, I don't know about the rest of you, but I've had enough of pirates and treasure hunts to last me a lifetime—maybe some things are better off staying dead and buried."

"Hear, hear," Celeste said raising her juice glass for a toast.

Morgan clinked her tea mug against the coffee, tea and juice glasses of everyone else. She'd had enough of pirates and treasure too. Besides, with three hundred years of family members and treasure hunters searching for it, the treasure was probably long gone.

Morgan settled back into her chair ignoring the niggling of doubt that was tugging at her gut.

She had everything she needed right in this room ... her sisters, her good friends Jake and Cal, Belladonna—and Luke.

And, since it looked like Luke was going to be sticking around for a while, she had a feeling that she wasn't going to be very interested in spending her time digging around for buried treasure ... no matter what her gut feeling was telling her.

**

Sign up for Leighann Dobbs' newsletter
and be the first to know about new releases.
Early birds get them for the lowest possible price!
http://www.leighanndobbs.com/newsletter

More Books By Leighann Dobbs:

Mooseamuck Island Cozy Mystery Series

A Zen For Murder
A Crabby Killer

* * *

Mystic Notch Cat Cozy Mystery Series

Ghostly Paws
A Spirited Tail
A Mew To A Kill
Paws and Effect

* * *

Blackmoore Sisters Cozy Mystery Series

Dead Wrong
Dead & Buried
Dead Tide
Buried Secrets
Deadly Intentions
A Grave Mistake

* * *

Lexy Baker Cozy Mystery Series

Lexy Baker Cozy Mystery Series Boxed Set
Vol 1 (Books 1-4)

Or buy the books separately:

Killer Cupcakes
Dying For Danish
Murder, Money and Marzipan
3 Bodies and a Biscotti
Brownies, Bodies & Bad Guys
Bake, Battle & Roll
Wedded Blintz
Scones, Skulls & Scams
Ice Cream Murder
Mummified Meringues
Brutal Brulee (Novella)

ABOUT THE AUTHOR

USA Today Bestselling author Leighann Dobbs has had a passion for reading since she was old enough to hold a book, but she didn't put pen to paper until much later in life. After a twenty-year career as a software engineer with a few side trips into selling antiques and making jewelry, she realized you can't make a living reading books, so she tried her hand at writing them and discovered she had a passion for that, too! She lives in New Hampshire with her husband, Bruce, their trusty Chihuahua mix, Mojo, and beautiful rescue cat, Kitty.

Find out about her latest books and how to get discounts on them by signing up at:
http://www.leighanndobbs.com/newsletter

If you want to receive a text message alert on your cell phone for new releases, text **COZYMYSTERY** to **88202** (sorry, this only works for US cell phones!)

Connect with Leighann on Facebook:
http://facebook.com/leighanndobbsbooks

Made in the USA
Coppell, TX
29 July 2025

52492630R00351